"A TENSE
OCCULT
THRILLER"
—*Publishers Weekly*

Francine Covington was the first to know the tragic
secret. Then, seven years later, Kate Rawlins felt the
relentless fear—the eyes gleaming from the shadows
—the townspeople warning her to leave, then, strangely, urging her to stay. And then in 1906 there was
Sarah Covington, then Addie Ryland, and finally in
1976, lovelorn Jeanine Stewart. Each fell in love—
souls swooning softly to a powerful embrace. Later,
when it was too late, they learned a secret as old as
time, as deep as love . . . the secret of a mortal feud
unavenged, a raging legacy of undying love!

Other Avon books by
Florence Hurd

ROMMANY   28340 $1.75

FLORENCE HURD

LEGACY

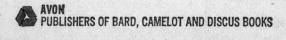

AVON
PUBLISHERS OF BARD, CAMELOT AND DISCUS BOOKS

LEGACY is an original publication of Avon Books. This work has never before appeared in book form.

AVON BOOKS
A division of
The Hearst Corporation
959 Eighth Avenue
New York, New York 10019

First Avon Printing, July, 1977

Printed in the U.S.A.

To Susanne Jo

Part I

GILMAN CLAYBORNE
(1864)

Chapter 1

ALL that afternoon I rode through the dark and somber forest. I traveled alone, a solitary figure in the gloom, the brooding silence broken only by the echo of the mare's hoofbeats and a fitful wind soughing in the treetops. Once I heard the tinkle of a stream as it purled its way down from the heights, but the cheerful little sound was soon swallowed up by the stillness.

As the day wore on, a mist began to rise from the bottoms, a gray-white fog trailing like smoke under the close-set pines. A bird suddenly pierced the silence with a shrill cry, and I buttoned my coat against the gathering chill.

I was going home—and the thought laid a cold hand on my heart.

The letter had come by way of Washington and Harpers Ferry, a month-old, tattered missive brought up to Winchester on the supply wagon. How the wagonmaster, a tobacco-chewing, red-faced oldster for whom I had once done a small favor, managed to locate me was a mystery, for the smoke of battle had scarcely cleared and our men were still scattered over the field helping to gather up the dead and wounded.

But find me he did, striding across the churned, scorched ground to where I and a comrade were lifting a lad with a ball in his leg to a stretcher.

"Word from home, looks like," the wagonmaster said.

"Thank you, Charlie."

It was from Francine. I stuffed the letter in my pocket under two pairs of curious eyes. "Can't read it here," I mumbled. But I was impatient, and the lad cried out when I jarred the stretcher, trying to hurry our task along.

Once we had the boy settled I slipped out of the hospital tent and around to the side, where I could be alone. My hand shook as I held the smudged envelope, staring at the fine, spidery scrawl: *Gilman Clayborne, Army of the Potomac, Sixth Corps.* It seemed that I could smell the faint fragrance of rosewater, and in my mind I saw her eyes, blue as gentians, and the soft rosebud mouth, the lips slightly parted. I saw the swell of her bosom and the slender waist, and the arms, white and rounded, arms that could twine so lovingly about a man's neck.

Oh, God! How I missed that girl!

The letter was short. "Dear Gilman," it read. "I hope this finds you well. Papa would be displeased with me if he knew I was writing, but I thought I ought to. Your father is very poorly—they say he's dying. Come home if you can. God knows I long for you and love you and pray for you every day of my life. Love, Francine."

I stared at the words for a long time. *I long for you and I love you,* Francine had written, but—Pa dying? Asa Clayborne?

A wounded soldier from inside the tent groaned miserably. Voices murmured, metal clinked and scraped.

I read the letter again. There must be some mistake. Francine had got it all wrong. Why, the last time I'd seen Pa he looked as robust as ever, only a streak of white in his cowlick to show he was putting on age. A bull of a man, thickset, strong. He could cut down the tallest tree, lift a wagon, or lick the six of us—all six of his sons—if he had a mind to, and hardly draw a deep breath. Never sick a day in his life, *never* that I could remember. How could he be dying?

I folded the letter and returned it to my pocket. It had taken courage for Francine to send that letter. Shy by nature, timid, she wouldn't have dared write unless something had really happened to Pa. An accident, maybe—cut timber falling at the wrong angle, an injured bear charging out of the brush, a gun misfiring . . .

I began to sweat. What if he were dead, even now as I sat there with the letter in my pocket, dead and buried in the churchyard next to Ma and baby Chris? I couldn't imagine the Claybornes without Pa. God knows I had seen plenty of dying in these last few months, but Pa. . . .

I had to get home. I had to see and talk to him. I had to ask him once more, "Pa, do you understand why I did what I did?"

When I first told him of my decision, he had said, "Yes, son, if that's what you believe." Yes, son. A Virginian going over to the Yankees. Yes, son. But how did he *feel*?

It was hard to tell with Pa. When Virginia seceded from the Union in April of '61 and our neighbors began to whoop and holler, Pa snorted. " 'Preserve slavery.' Why—there ain't a slave to be found on the whole damned mountain," he had said. "Never was, far as I know. And furthermore, folks here never paid the least mind to what were goin' on in Richmond. Beats me why they should care now."

Still, independent cuss that he was, I think he resented the government in Washington telling folks what to do. He was a staunch states' righter.

I saw it differently. I truly believed—as I did now, else I wouldn't have put up with the muck, the bloodshed and terror—that the country, the Union, had to stay together, that our great-grandfathers had fought for a good cause, that the Constitution was worth keeping. . . .

I remember saying those things to a bunch of idlers hanging around the mill door one afternoon, and how they all howled me down. Preacher Davidson hooted the loudest. "That's what comes of your paw givin' you all that fancy schoolin'."

Even that bit the mule-headed preacher got wrong. It wasn't Pa but Ma who insisted I go over to Novotno for more learning when I'd finished the few grades they taught in our own schoolhouse. "Folks whose britches are too big for 'em," Davidson sneered. And everyone jabbered their agreement.

Fact is, the town was jealous of the Claybornes. After Ma died (I was fourteen when she caught the fever) they expected old Asa to go to pieces because he doted so on his Mary. But he didn't. He took out all his anger and grief in work and made that farm of ours the most prosperous on the mountain. Single-handed, he got a road put in so he could haul his corn, potatoes, apples, and sheep down to Front Royal and get higher prices for them. And when Eli Covington bought the old flour mill and converted it to lumber, Pa was the first to cut timber. He did right well, and they hated him for it. Even after they began to copy Pa's ways and make good, too, they kept their distance. A cool howdy, a smile or a handshake, maybe, but no real friendship.

After I said my piece at the mill door, the old bitter hate returned twofold. "Turncoat Gilman," they called me. And, "Ain't it just like a Clayborne?"

And now Pa was dying.

I hurried off in search of my lieutenant. I found him sitting under the flap of the mess tent. He had been a professor at a college in New York State, but I never met a man cooler under fire, nor one with a fancier set of cuss words. A fair man. Every inch for the Union—like me.

I told him I wanted leave to go home, and why.

He didn't answer right away, but lit a cigar and, taking a short puff, blew the smoke out and squinted his eyes up at me.

"You haven't had a leave?"

"No, sir, not since I joined."

"Where's your home, Clayborne?"

"Stone Mill Hollow, sir."

He frowned and took another puff. "And where might that be?"

"In the Blue Ridge, sir."

A long silence as he gazed thoughtfully at the tip of his cigar. "May I ask why you came over to us?"

I told him.

"Haven't changed your mind?"

"No, sir."

His jaw was blue with a day's growth of beard. "Not thinking of deserting?"

"No—no, sir."

"All right, Clayborne, you did well. We all did, come to think of it. 'A smashing victory!' as the old man says. For a little fellow that Phil Sheridan packs a lot of temper. By damn! I can afford to be generous. Two weeks. But," waving his cigar at me, "mind you, not a day more."

"Thank you, sir." Two weeks was a week more than I had expected.

Since most of the Shenandoah Valley was still held by the Rebs and I had more sense than to make myself a target, I changed out of uniform into the baggy trousers and moth-eaten coat I had bought from the wagonmaster for two plugs of tobacco. My uniform and canteen were bundled into a borrowed blanket which I strapped to my back as a pack. My gun and cartridge box I left in Simmons's care, a comrade who had fought by my side for the past six months.

Two hours after I'd received Francine's letter I rode out of camp with the wagonmaster. We parted at the crossroads, he to go on to Harpers Ferry and I to Stone Mill Hollow. That night I slept under a haystack in a stubbled field on the far side of Kernstown. What with the chill nip in the September air and my own troubled thoughts, I caught but a few winks in brief nightmare snatches. The predawn crow of a rooster and the barking of a dog finally roused me out of a dream in which my father became General Sheridan riding a charging bull through our apple orchard. Stretching the kinks from my neck and shoulders, I reached into my coat pocket and brought out a loaf of bread. I bit off a chunk and chewed on it, stale and dusty dry, washing it down with a pull from a bottle of corn whiskey I had bartered from Simmons.

Then I began to walk swiftly across the field.

My plan was to buy a horse, using my accumulated army pay, most of which I hadn't had call to spend so far. Horseback was the most direct, the quickest way to get home. But I had not anticipated the skill and thoroughness with which Lee's army had foraged this rich "breadbasket" area. The only creature I could find for sale was a scrofulous jackass, lame in one leg. The farmer, a man made wise and wary by a war which had swept up and down the valley in successive tides, wanted one hundred dollars for the animal. When I said no, he said seventy-five, and that was his final figure, all the while sucking on a corncob pipe and eyeing me suspiciously.

I said no again, thank you kindly. He said, "How come an ablebodied man like you ain't in uniform?" And his eyes lingered for a moment on my boots, the one part of my uniform I hadn't changed. But they were old, cracked and worn.

"I'm on a secret mission for Early," I said, the first thing that came into my head. And not the smartest, I realized at once. If it was so secret, why would I be telling him?

But he didn't seem to notice. "Fifty," he said, "fifty dollars."

"Cheap enough, but I'm looking for a horse." I smiled at him again and, turning, forced myself to walk slowly down the long dusty lane, his dog nipping at my heels, feeling his glinting gimlet eyes on my back. I had learned my lesson. If I wanted a horse, I daren't ask to buy one—I had to steal it.

I avoided Cedar Creek proper, crossing the stream about two miles below the town. Though the creek had shrunk considerably from its banks, it got too deep to wade all the way, and so with my boots (which I had tied around my neck) bobbing under my chin, I swam the last few yards. Clambering out, I sat down and dried my feet on a tuft of grass. I was pulling on my boots when suddenly a voice behind me said,

"Lookit here!"

I twisted my head around. There were five of them, all wearing gray Confederate caps. Lee's army.

"Howdy," I said, giving them my best Virginia drawl.

They were pitifully young, still boys, carrying rifles and looking more ragged than the Grays I had seen in battle. New recruits. Bad. New, untried recruits were too zealous, too fired up with romantic, daredevil notions, their fingers itchy on the trigger.

Only one of them, a blond lad with a thin bristle of hair under a narrow nose, was in fairly respectable uniform—a lieutenant, from the bars on his coat. He said, "Who are you?"

"Gilmore Clayborne," I answered, seeing no reason to hide my name.

"How is it you are not in uniform?" he wanted to know, just as the farmer had.

"I'm looking to enlist," I said, changing my story from the one I had given the farmer. "At Cedar Creek, Lieutenant." Smile, I told myself—not too cocky, not too friendly, just a pleasant smile. But, God, how my heart was hammering!

"Took you a long time," the blond lieutenant said.

Conscious of my hollow, sleepless eyes and the grizzly stubble of unshaven cheeks, I knew I looked every year of my twenty-six.

"I've had a sick pappy," I said, stretching the drawl. "And I was needed at home. But now he's gone—there's nothing to hold me."

"Where you from?" the bumptious little devil demanded in a voice blown up with authority.

"The Blue Ridge," I said, waving my arm vaguely in the direction of the hills.

He studied me for a few aching moments, eyes like the farmer's lingering on my muddied Union boots, and then shifting to the rolled blanket on my back. The concealed uniform seemed to press like a red-hot iron into my spine. "You're headin' in the wrong direction," he said at last.

"I am?"—raising my eyebrows. "But I reckoned—" scratching my head—"which way, then?" I gave him a sheepish grin.

"We're goin' into Cedar Creek," the young lieutenant said, and my heart sank. "You come along with us."

He fingered the hilt of his sword, and the Gray behind him shifted his rifle. Five against one—and me with nothing but bare hands.

"Sure," I said. "That's fine. Good company."

They led me along a path upstream—I chittering like an idiot about how I hoped the war wouldn't be over before I joined up, while my mind darted this way and that, wondering how I could give them the slip.

We crossed a bridge, and ahead, squatting astride the paved road, was the main district of the town. Full of Rebs. I could see myself marched in by this self-appointed committee, signing up in their damned, doomed army, sent out to fight my comrades, dying for the wrong cause.

And Pa up there in Stone Mill Hollow probably breathing his last.

But when we got to the first cross street the blond lieutenant said, "Down that road," pointing, "half a mile, first turn to your right, you'll find the recruiting tent."

"Thank you." And because I was so relieved, added a fatuous "Sir."

I walked very slowly. After a few minutes I took a quick look back, and when I saw that the little band had disappeared, I cut across the road, slipped behind a house, slid down the creek bank, and, finding a footlog a half mile upstream, crossed over.

Luck was with me, for at noon I came upon a mare who had broken loose from her hobble and was grazing in a meadow out of sight of human habitation. She did not object when I swung myself up on her bare back and pointed her toward the hills.

We rode for an anxious hour. Several times I thought I heard the sound of horses in pursuit, and once I passed a man driving a plow across a distant field who stopped to stare at me.

When the forest closed around us at last, I breathed easier, slowly guiding the mare along a faint track up the mountain. But as the shadows began to thicken, my feeling of ease slowly faded. The brooding limestone rock, the dark, canopied oaks and alders, the hollow, soughing silence filled me with a strange sense of foreboding. I couldn't shake the notion that the forest was haunted, that ghostlike gray-clad men were hiding behind every bush, every stone, every clump of vines.

Before long the clip-clop of the mare's shod feet in the silence acted as a drug, and it seemed, in my half-dazed, exhausted state, that I heard the rat-a-tat-tat of musketry again and smelled the acrid smoke of war. Memories fused, and the trees about me became the same as those in the Wilderness, that infamous forest where I fought in the worst, the most vicious battle of them all. Once again I held the heated rifle in my hand, felt its kick; once again my eyes burned in their sockets as I groped through the thick, appalling smoke where neither friend nor foe could be seen, only the vague moving shapes of men and guns and beasts. I felt the stunning weight of sound trapped under the trees, shells exploding, guns, cries and shouts, the rumble of wheels—noise hammering, pressing on the ears, pressing on the skull, on the brain—and no end to it. No end.

Once again, God help me, I saw the woods catch fire, the flames licking and crackling, adding smoke to gunsmoke, turning that whole bloody Wilderness into one boiling, stinking caldron of hell. And through it all came the shrieks and screams of the wounded roasting to death.

Two days, two nights—and then the word came, "Move out. South." South? So we—those of us who could—fell into a ragged line and marched.

Who won? Some said the North, some the South. *Strategy* was a word much bandied about.

Now, as I rode the twisting, tortuous path up the mountain, fording leaf-choked creeks, coaxing the flank-sweated mare on, the faces of the dead came to haunt me. For the first time since I had left the farm, I asked myself: Is it worth it?

Then I thought of Eli Covington, Francine's father, his

forced, cheerful smile, Eli with his handsome brown curly head cocked to the surest wind—whatever, whichever way it blew. And I thought of Preacher Davidson and his slitted, bright blue eyes, the Rylands, the Perrys, the Loefflers, the Bradleys, and how they always hated us, hated us because I had said the world outside the narrow Hollow mattered. The Union. No—I hadn't changed my mind. No—I wasn't sorry I'd enlisted.

Damn them all!

I was fond of my brothers, but Pa and Francine were the ones I cared most about. I had sworn them both to secrecy when I went away, though by now everyone in town must have guessed what had happened. *Gilman Clayborne gone over to the Yankees. That's a Clayborne for you.*

Yet who had better claim to roots in Stone Mill Hollow than the Claybornes? (Certainly not the Covingtons, who were Johnny-come-latelies—or Preacher Davidson, who had been born in Oakton Hollow and could scarcely write his name.) There had been Claybornes in Stone Hill since my great-great-grandfather, a Scotch-Irish Ulsterman, had emigrated, coming up the mountains by way of Pennsylvania and Maryland, looking for cheap land.

All he had to his name was packed on a single horse and a small mule—his young wife and baby, bedding, a few pots and pans, and a rusty old musket. From the stories Grandpa told, two families had first settled the Hollow—the Bradleys and Claybornes. In a few years more came, Ulstermen mostly, bringing with them the Scotsman's penchant for brewing his own whiskey and for feuding, for taking revenge whenever and wherever the need arose, a dangerous mix which wiped out two families, the McAllisters and Kerrs, by the turn of the century. But new people kept drifting in, Germans and Scotch-Irish, not many, just enough to make Stone Mill a larger settlement than its sister hollows hidden in the pockets of the Blue Ridge.

I don't know exactly how or why the Claybornes had their first falling out with the rest of the community. I have a hunch it could have been when Pa, instead of marrying a local girl, went down the mountain to Front Royal and got himself a bride. Ma was not what most people would call a beauty—too stout for fashion—but she had the purest, sweetest smile and the gentlest ways. They said she gave herself airs. In a pig's eye! Was keeping a clean house, dressing neatly, seeing the children had schooling putting on airs? She wanted me to read for the law, bless her heart. I think I would have done well at it, too. I liked studying, debating points of view with people. But after she died, Pa was so struck down with grief I thought I'd best quit school and stay at home helping him with his farm.

A low-hanging branch slapped me smartly in the face, bringing me back to the present. While my mind had been meandering, night had fallen, and under the trees it had become dark as pitch. Dismounting, I tethered the horse, and using my pack for a pillow, I stretched out on a bed of pine needles. How many nights since I'd slept through? It seemed every muscle and bone in my body ached with weariness. Yet now, for some reason, my eyes remained open, wide and staring.

An owl suddenly hooted, and my skin jumped. His cry echoed and reechoed eerily through the black forest. I remembered my grandpa telling me that it was hard to know whether the hooting owl in the dead of night was really an owl or the ghost of Cherokee Sam. Sam, according to legend, had been an Indian whose wife and children were murdered by a band of whiskey-soaked mountaineers. Although he was long dead, it was said that Sam continued to hunt out his enemies at night, falling upon unsuspecting travelers and strangling them with a moccasin lace. Myself, I disbelieved in "hants and boogers." Granny tales, Pa called them. He was a scoffer, too. But I do think there is something to hate and revenge lingering on, poisoning the atmosphere. And there is no denying that the woods at night, with a chill, damp mist rising from the bottoms, the strange mutterings and little twitterings, make the eyes start and the heart beat a little faster.

An hour after sunrise I reached the Loeffler farm. Old Man Loeffler and his son were gathering squash in a field as I rode past. I could see them from a distance, shading their eyes against the sun to stare, but I slouched my cap low over my forehead, pretending not to notice.

Five minutes later I was urging the mare down the last bit of road—and there it was, the house white, square, solid, and the chestnut shading the front porch. It seemed strangely deserted. No smoke rose from the chimney, the curtains were pulled to at the windows, not even the dogs ran out to greet me. The boys had probably finished their barn chores and had all gone to the orchard to gather the early apples. Maybe, I thought, with a rising surge of hope, Pa is with them.

Dismounting, I led the mare around back to the trough. The pump squeaked as I worked it. I put my head under the cool, splashing water, then turned my mouth up and drank. Sweet, deep well water, none better anywhere.

I wiped my face on my sleeve and looked over at the barn. It was awfully quiet—too quiet. Suddenly I had the cold feeling that someone was watching me.

Slowly I turned. There, framed in the doorway, was a gray-clad Confederate. I couldn't see his face on account of the light in my eyes, but I saw the rifle, all right, the sun glinting on its long barrel as it came up to aim directly at me.

Chapter 2

NEITHER of us moved. Frozen like two pointing hounds, we stared at one another—he with the rifle aimed at my heart, I with my arm still raised to my face.

Rebs! No wonder it had been so quiet. They had marched my brothers and Pa off and taken over the house.

Behind me the horse lapped noisily.

"So it's you." A familiar voice. The sun's rays burned my eyes. "Come home, have you?"

Shocked, I dropped my arm. "Phil!"

My brother lowered the rifle and gave me a crooked grin. "Surprised?" he asked.

"Damned right! What you doing in that getup?"

"I'm a Confederate soldier," he said, adding with pride, "a Southerner."

"Since when?" And I laughed. Phil was the middle one—only seventeen—a baby. But with that gray, overlarge coat draped across his shoulders he looked older than I remembered.

"You quit the Yankee army?" he asked, leaning his rifle against the wall.

"Who told you I was in the Yankee army?"

"Guessed." He stepped down into the yard.

"I came to see Pa. How is he?"

Phil looked away for a few moments before answering. "He's low, Gil, terrible low." His face without the smile looked drawn. "We don't rightly know what ails him. He says he has stomach pains, and there's a knot big as my fist there, a growth. He wouldn't let any of us write."

"Francine did."

"Thought she might. She came by here to see Pa last week. Wondering if any of us had heard from you." He shook his head. "Never thought I'd see him this way."

14

I went past him to the door. "Take care of my horse, will you, Phil?"

I walked in through the kitchen, where the remains of breakfast were still on the long trestle table. A fly buzzed over a pot of sourwood honey, and there was the strong smell of fried pork. Crossing the small parlor to the big bedroom, I peeked in at the door. Pa was lying in bed, his large, hairy fists clenching the covers. His eyes, sunk deep in his head, were closed; his face the color of pudding. It shocked me. How could a man change so in a year's time?

He must have felt my presence, for his eyes fluttered open. For a moment they rested on me, glazed and unseeing. Then, as they focused, a slow, painful smile twisted his mouth. "Gilman . . . !"

I came in and hung over him at the foot of the bed, too overcome to trust my voice, too afraid to do more than nod.

"Well, ain't you a sight for sore eyes. Come 'round and have you a seat."

I sat on the edge of the bed. "Francine wrote that you were ailing. And I had a leave coming. . . ." I tried to sound hearty, but I didn't fool him. Pa knew me too well.

"Don't go a-frettin' over me. I'll be up in a day or two. It's somethin' I et disagreed with me."

"Have you had a doctor?"

"Doctor . . . !" he snorted. There were none in Stone Mill, but a doctor could be fetched from Novotno. "I wouldn't have one of them bone-setters if I was dying."

Dying. I wished he hadn't used that word. I stared at the bedpost above his head.

" 'Nuff about me," he said. "What have y'been up to?"

I told him about our fight at Winchester, about the Sixth Corps.

"So y'gave Jubal Early his," he said. "Thought nothin' could stop the old grizzly."

"For a while it looked like nothing would," I said. "Somehow we got our orders mixed, and we came up to the line late. Before we had time to get into position, Early and his gray-clads were on us with that damned Rebel yell and their guns chattering away. Bad—it was bad. That thick, greasy smoke and men falling all around." I shook my head with the memory.

"Well—then?" Pa asked. "What happened to keep you from takin' to your heels?"

"Sheridan. He came out of nowhere, riding at a pelting gallop, cussing and shouting, whipping us back into line. Held us there until reinforcements came up—and the rest you know."

He sighed and closed his eyes.

"Pa," I said, "you aren't mad at me for joining, are you?"

His eyes flew open. "Hell, no! I said I didn't mind. Y'did what y'had to. A man ain't a man unless he does what he has to." He blinked as a spasm of pain crossed his face. "But you shouldn't have come home, Gil. There's a company of Rebs quartered in town. Under some lootenant called Beau Hodges."

"Here, at Stone Mill?"

He nodded.

"And Phil's with them?"

"You saw Phil? Well, the durned fool. He got himself conscripted. Been in the army a month and got a shell in his right arm."

"His right arm? I didn't notice."

"Didn't lose it, but might as well have. The thing's useless as a tit on a boar."

I thought of the way Phil had worn his jacket, loose about his shoulders. An arm . . .

"Where did it happen?" I asked, my mouth suddenly gone dry.

"Tennessee," Pa said.

The unspoken question hung in the air. "I wasn't there," I said, answering it.

And Pa smiled, a little color coming into his face. "It'll be over, someday soon. Family, kin is stronger than any war." He touched my hand in the same old gentle, hairy-fisted way he'd touched me when I was a small boy and needed comfort. "Still, you shouldna come. And now that you seen me, get yourself back to Winchester as soon as you can."

I laughed. "I'm not afraid. I'll keep out of the Rebs' way. Who else would be my enemy? Preacher Davidson? The Rylands?"

"You allus was stubborn." He sighed and closed his eyes again. The groove between his brows had become deeply etched. He looked old and gaunt.

"The lieutenant gave me two weeks," I said, "and I mean to stay. There's Francine. I can't leave without seeing her."

"Francine . . ." His eyes flickered. "Her pa's been doin' good business with Lee's army."

"I expect he is." I wondered if there was something else he wanted to tell me, but he kept his eyes shut and said nothing.

He didn't come to supper that night. "Tomorrow," he told me when I brought him his meal. "Tomorrow, for breakfast."

We sat at the trestle table, all six of us. I was the oldest. Lonnie, two years younger than me, had married the Bradley girl, Tess, while I had been away. She was visiting kin on the other side of Stone Mill that night. Then there was red-haired Patrick, twenty, Phil, and the two younger ones, twins, Timmy and Harley. Four fair (including me), taking after Ma; two dark, favoring Pa.

"Pass the biscuits," Lonnie said, drawing his thick brows together in a frown. Lonnie always did take his food seriously.

"Don't go and eat 'em all." Timmy said, and Harley laughed. "Eatin' his own biscuits and likin' 'em."

Lonnie ignored them, buttering his biscuit with a lavish hand.

Except for Pa being in the other room, it was as though I had never gone away. Same food—hard biscuits, fried chicken, lump gravy—same conversation, same pointless fooling. But it gave me a feeling of comfort. Some things ought never to change.

"Still wearing your uniform?" I asked Phil. I noticed he ate with his left hand, but I didn't say anything. Phil was a touchy sort. The last thing he would welcome was sympathy.

"I sorta like it," he said. "I wasn't crazy to go, but once I did, well, I think the South is in the right."

Lonnie, spooning gravy on a chicken leg, said, "I s'pose the North feels the same."

"It isn't the North," I said, breaking my vow not to talk politics. "It's the Union."

"Some Union," Phil sneered. "They're hating bastards at heart. They want to destroy the South." A faint flush had come to his downy cheeks.

I took a long pull from the milk jug and then set it carefully down. "Do you think I hate you, Phil?"

The blaze went out of his eyes. " 'Course not."

Lonnie, his mouth full of chicken, said, "Well, then, that's settled, pass the mustard pickles."

And everybody laughed.

"Talking about hate," Patrick said, waving his fork, "you don't have to go no further than Stone Mill to get plenty of that. Preacher Davidson sure laid it down on the Claybornes last Sunday."

"He did?" I asked, grabbing the last biscuit a moment before Lonnie's fingers reached for it. "What did the old fire-brand say?"

"Said we was a bunch of traitors. Ought to be strung up. Exceptin' Phil. All of us."

"He named the Claybornes, did he?"

"Sure did."

"Why do you go to his blasted church, then?" I said, annoyed.

"We didn't. Old Man Dinwiddie told us when he came by to get his milk."

Old Man Dinwiddie lived in a log cabin down Burnham Road. Too crippled to work his patch of land, he relied on the charity of neighbors for food. At our house he was welcome to all the milk and eggs he could use.

Patrick said, "We stopped going to church after we had the accident."

I stared at him. "What accident?"

"Well," said Patrick, swallowing. "It was on a Sunday about a month after you'd gone away. We all been to church, went in the wagon. When the meeting was over, we started on home, and just about a mile out—you know the grade down Burnham?—well, right halfway down a wheel broke off and—and the wagon went over." He swallowed again, and the others stared into their plates. "No one was hurt," Patrick said. "Sure scared the hell out of us, though. Pa thinks someone loosened the wheel while we was inside the church."

"Damn them!" I muttered, heat rising to my face. "Damn them!"

"Could have been anybody done it," Patrick said, "but the preacher. He was making his sermon, so it couldn't have been him."

"Damn them!"

Lonnie said, "Any more of that gravy?"

And Patrick, "No use getting mad, Gil. Whoever it was ain't tried anything since."

Lonnie said, "I'll finish up them 'taters if you don't mind."

"Pa's stepped on too many feet," Patrick said.

"Whose?" I asked angrily. "Pa's stepped on no one. It's the other way 'round."

No one spoke again until Lonnie brought the coffeepot from the stove and Phil, holding his cup up, said, "Saw Francine yesterday. She come by the mill. Saw her talking to one of Lee's men." He cast a sidelong glance at me.

"So? I suppose she can talk to whoever she has a mind to."

"She was smiling at him," Phil goaded, and I felt my gut tighten. " 'Course, it don't mean anything. Pretty girl like that can't help smiling."

I stared hard at him. "You looking for a fight? 'Cause if you are . . ." And then I suddenly remembered his withered arm. " 'Cause if you are," I smiled weakly, "you can fight by yourself. I'm all done." I pushed away from the table and got to my feet.

"How long you gonna stay?" Phil asked.

"Couple of days, maybe."

At eight o'clock, after I spruced up as best I could, changing from my mud-caked clothes into my wrinkled uniform, I slipped out of the house and walked across the lower field. I went through the orchard, following the shortcut to the Covington house, a path worn by my own feet in the years I'd been courting Francine.

Though we all thought of the Covingtons as latecomers to Stone Mill, this was not strictly true. Covingtons had resided in the Hollow for years, before Eli's father had locked up his house and gone to live in Charlottesville. There he opened a tavern—The White Goose, I think he called it—and prospered. When he died, Eli sold the tavern at a good profit and came back up to Stone Mill with a new wife. The Covingtons had never been much for farming. Trade was more in their line, and Eli, looking around for a place to make his money grow, thought a sawmill was just what Stone Mill needed. So he bought the old flour mill from Tom Clarke and had it reconverted to timber. He did well—well enough to rebuild the Covington house from the ground up. It was the grandest house in Stone Mill, with a wide veranda (no porches for *them*), a large parlor, a dining room, and four bedrooms upstairs. Yet, in spite of his money and elegant house, Eli never seemed sure of himself, fidgety, always with that damned clown's smile on his face.

I remembered the night before I went away, when Francine, trembling in my arms, promised to keep my secret. "Oh, I do love you, Gilman," she had said. "But if Papa knew you were going, he'd make me break our engagement."

I smiled down at her. "Your papa will think I'm the best husband you could find, once the Union wins." Eli liked to be on the winning side, to be with the popular crowd, a good-fellow-well-met, not really the kind of father-in-law I liked or could even respect. But I wasn't marrying him, I was marrying Francine.

I had fallen in love with Francine one morning in church. She was fourteen and I twenty, an age when many of my friends were contemplating marriage. I had thought of girls —of women—a great deal, but no one in particular until I turned my head in church that Easter morning and Francine smiled timidly at me from under a lavender bonnet. From that moment on, I had eyes for no other girl.

Her mother said she was too young for walking out, so I'd linger after church meeting to have a few words with her. She had an older brother, Judd, a dark, brooding fellow, and a younger sister, Bertha, who some said was "tetched" in the head. They all came to church together, and they all left together, so I never really got to be with Francine alone.

One day just after Francine's fifteenth birthday, I asked Eli right off if I could keep company with his daughter. Eli hedged and hemmed and hawed, giving me that quick, nervous smile of his. "Well . . . now, Gilman . . ."

I knew I had him in a bind—the Claybornes being unpopular on the one hand, and Asa Clayborne, my father, his best customer on the other. His business sense finally won out—and Francine and I became sweethearts. I wanted to marry her right away, but again her mother put her foot down. "Too young," she said. "Francine is way too young." But I knew it was me, not Francine's age, that bothered Margaret Covington. A Charlottesville girl, Margaret thought all mountain folk "lumps." One winter she sent Francine to relatives in Charlottesville, "to finish her education," she said, but I knew it was because Mrs. Covington hoped Francine would find a more likely beau. She didn't. She loved me. Later she told me that none of the boys she had met in her cousin's house could begin to measure up.

We got engaged. I bought her a diamond ring, not a big, flashy one, but she was right proud of it.

And then Virginia seceded.

It shook me. I hadn't finished my education, but I was a reader and I wasn't ignorant. I knew my history, knew what travail this country had gone through to be born, and it seemed sheer, dumb muleheadedness to break it up now. Over slavery. Never mind the moral point, the ugliness of one man owning another, never mind that slavery was the most inefficient way to farm; it was hacking a nation apart that upset me.

We had no newspaper in Stone Mill, but they published a weekly in Novotno and I'd go over there as often as I could to get the latest word. I read every single line—Bull Run, Sharpsburg, Fredericksburg—and though I couldn't help but feel proud of the way the Southern boys in gray fought, I couldn't bring any sympathy to their cause. "The North," one editorial said, "can wave the Constitution at us, but conveniently forget its provision for states' rights." Biased, slanted, of course.

I thought and thought about the war for a long time, and when I finally decided to join the Yankees, Francine was the first person I told.

She took it hard. "How can you do this to me?" she sobbed.

I said, "I'll be back, I swear I'll be back. And we'll be married."

And I kissed that sweet mouth. I kissed her cheeks and the little hollow in her throat, and she clung to me. "Promise me, Gilman. . . ."

A year, three months, two weeks, five days—a long time since I had held her close.

I hurried along the path through the orchard, and when I came to the creek, crossed on the footlog. Though it was dark and the log was slippery, my feet knew the pattern, every wrinkle and knob, so well. The water gurgled and chuckled and gossiped beneath me as it ran along down to do its work at the mill proper. *He's come back,* it sang, *he's come back.*

I scrambled up the bank and opened the back gate. The vines and chokeberries grew thick and wild on either side of the fence, and as I climbed the path I saw with surprise that the swing under the oak was gone. It had been a child's swing, but Francine and I had used it many times, she sitting in my lap, laughing as I swung us higher and higher into the leafy branches.

A child's game, child's play. So long ago. How sad that it had to end.

Lights were still on in the parlor and a second-story window—Brother Judd's bedroom if I remembered correctly. So he was home, I thought. Judd had signed up with the Confederates at the very start of the war. His mother's influence, no doubt. She had great pretensions. Claimed she was a relative of Fairfax, the Englishman who once owned half of Virginia.

I waited in the garden for the lights to go out. The War Between the States. My experience in it, especially these last few days, had made me wary.

The katydids chorused, hoarse and rasping, while the frogs from the bottoms made a croaking din of their own. The sickle moon, lopsided and a little swollen, rode among the swaying treetops. I leaned against the gum tree, looking up at the house, and though I was never much of a smoker, I longed for a cigar.

Suddenly the parlor went dark, and a few minutes later lights shone in all the upstairs windows. I waited impatiently, counting my heartbeats as seconds. Fifteen minutes? A half hour? Still, I waited. After an eternity the bedroom lights were extinguished one by one. When I thought the Covington house was fast asleep, I picked up a pebble and aimed it at Francine's window. It plunked softly against the pane, an old, familiar sound. How many times in the past had I done the same?

Again I waited. Clouds had formed overhead, and the moon drifted slowly in and out like a lamp carried through a ghost-haunted house. I watched the stars overhead winking and blinking.

And then she was there—in a white, trailing wrapper, her long blond hair tied back with a ribbon, running toward me, her arms outstretched. I grabbed her like a drowning man grabs a lifeline, raining kisses on her sweet-smelling hair, her cheeks, her throat, and at last her mouth, a mouth that was honey and fire to me. It was not until the madness passed and I had released her that I felt her wet cheeks, her tears.

"What is it, darling?"

She shook her head and could not speak for weeping. But whether she sobbed from happiness or from fear, I did not know.

"Come," I said, putting my arm around her slender waist, guiding her down the path which led to the creek. "Don't be afraid, darling, don't cry."

A tremor went through her body, and I drew her closer. "Don't be afraid," I murmured in her hair.

We sat on the wooden bench under the white alder, its trunk and branches like bleached bones in the moonlight. At our feet the creek tinkled and laughed over the stones.

"Aren't you glad to see me, darling?" I asked.

"Oh, yes, Gilman, yes"—her voice muffled, her face resting on my chest.

I wiped the tears from her eyes and kissed the tip of her nose.

"I'm sorry now I wrote you," she said. "Made you come all that way. . . ."

"Hush, now. You did right. I would have been unhappy if anything—if anything happened to Pa and I hadn't had a chance to see him."

"How is Asa?"

"Not good, but he thinks he'll get better. I hope so." I took her hand in mine, a cold little hand.

"You oughtn't to have come," she said.

"Why? Because of the Rebs in town?"

She started. "You saw them?"

"No, Pa told me. Funny they should be here at Stone Mill. I wonder why they came?"

"I don't know," she said in a small voice. "I don't know."

"Phil said he saw you talking to an officer," I teased.

Her face seemed to blanch in the moonlight. "Just hello and a fine day. I had to be polite. He's a friend of Judd's."

My head jerked toward the house. "Did he know I might be coming back?"

"Oh, no, no. I'd never tell." She began to tremble again. "I'd never tell a living soul—I swear."

I held her close.

"Gilman," she said, "let's run away, darling, just you and

me. Now. We could take one of the horses and go down the mountain. . . ."

"In your wrapper?" I laughed.

"Please don't mock me, Gilman. My wrapper don't matter. Let's leave it . . . all of it, this place and the ugly war."

"The ugly war is everywhere," I said.

"Not out West . . . we could go out West—to California."

"I'd be a deserter. And besides, I have very little money."

"They don't look for deserters. And I could sell my ring—until you bought me another. . . ."

Francine, so impractical. "The ring wouldn't get us very far, sweetheart."

"Oh—we'll find a way. Please, Gilman." And she flung her slender arms about my neck, kissing me wildly, almost hysterically.

"Francine . . . !" Never, never had she acted so passionately. Her mouth silenced mine. My arms tightened, pressing her to me. I felt her warm skin through the cloth, the beating of her heart, her smallness and fragility, and a sudden vision of her naked body beneath the wrapper flashed through my mind—small, white, coral-tipped breasts, the curve of smooth hips and slender thighs. . . .

"No, sweetheart." Pushing her away, and at the same time the part of me denied for so long, now excited, aroused, wanting her, saying, You can take her, you fool.

"I've misbehaved," she said, lowering her head. "But, Gilman," and her eyes flashed in the darkness, "I don't care. . . ."

"You will, you will care, and you'll hate me, you'll hate yourself." I lifted her cold hand and kissed her fingers one by one. She nestled her head on my shoulder and sighed. Leaning back, I looked up through the trees and suddenly saw a strange light in the sky where there had been none before. It was a dusty orange, like the afterglow of sunset. But the sun had gone down hours earlier.

I was on my feet.

"What is it?" Francine's terrified voice whispered.

"Fire—a fire—somewhere . . . It's out on Burnham. . . . My God, it's our house!"

And I was stumbling down toward the creek.

"Gilman . . . !" she screamed. "Gilman . . . !"

She caught me by the coat at the creek's edge. "Gilman . . . !"

"You don't seem to understand, Francine. It's our house —on fire! And Pa bedridden."

"Don't go!" She clung to me. "You mustn't go."

"Are you crazy, girl? The house is on *fire!*"

I turned and splashed through the stream, with Francine still holding to my coattails.

"You mustn't go," she sobbed. "You mustn't. They'll find you. . . ."

"I have to, sweetheart." I gave her one last hurried kiss and began to run down the path, and as I fled, a gray shadow ran beside me.

And then I knew.

The awful truth exploded in my head like a mine. *Francine writing that letter, Francine weeping, Francine trembling, "Let's leave it . . . this place and the ugly war."*

Suddenly the gray shadow became four, eight hands shooting out to grab me. And in that terrible moment between shadow and substance my whole world fell apart.

Part II

KATE RAWLINS
(1871)

Chapter 3

I was born and raised in Hickory Cove, only five miles distant, as the crow flies, from Stone Mill Hollow, but I was sixteen before I ever laid eyes upon it. Sixteen—ignorant and unlettered—when I first put my foot through the Covington garden gate.

Afterward, I was to wish to God I never had.

Not that my life in Hickory Cove had been an easy one, or happy, or even content. *Content*—that was one of the many new words I came to learn. But in Hickory Cove we just took what we got from day to day and never asked, "Am I content? Am I happy?"

By Stone Mill standards we lived like beggars, though we didn't know that, either. How could we, when each of us had no more, no less than his neighbor? Tucked away in our little hollow, surrounded by dark, brooding mountains, having to grow nearly every bite we ate, we were slow to notice that nature yielded less and less each season. The soil, Tyson McAlpin would say, was mean. A century of farming, one hundred years of rain eating the earth away, and nothing put back into it. Half the corn and cabbage and potatoes we planted in our patch never came up, and the other half usually fell prey to worms and blight.

The cabin I lived in had been built of logs chinked with clay by the first Rawlins a long while before my time. When Pa was alive, he'd cover the outside wall with oak slabs during the cold months to keep out the driving rain and the snow. But Clem, my step-pa, never troubled with it, and so our winters were wet and miserable. Inside, there was but one room, one glazed paper window tacked over with an old cured bear pelt, a puncheon floor, and a smoky fireplace. We had a large bed covered with a cornhusk mattress, and in it Clem and my mother slept with the three youngest children. I had a pallet by the fireplace, and the two oldest boys slept in

29

the loft under the roof where we stored the apples and cabbages. Two chairs and a small, rough pine table made up the rest of the furniture. Ma cooked over the fireplace.

Pa died when I was a little girl. I must have been five—or six, maybe. Soon after, Ma took up with Clem McAlpin. They weren't married for a whole year—not until a traveling preacher came by. Sometimes two, three years would go by before we saw a man of God; then he'd marry a bunch of folks and speak for the dead, too.

At Hickory Cove we were all McAlpins or Rawlinses, twelve families scattered along the creek bottom in amongst the woods. The men did the hunting, whatever they could find in the way of coon, rabbit, or bear; the game, too, getting scarcer and scarcer. The women and young children tended the gardens. Springtime for planting, summer for hoeing, fall for harvest. It was hard, backbreaking work. Some days we'd go out in the morning and work until the sun was high, then eat some cold pone with a little honey on it and go back to work again. We had so many mouths to feed.

Clem was too lazy to make his own corn whiskey, though he fancied his liquor. Not that he was a drinking man—not like Rufus Rawlins, who had to have his dram soon as he stirred in the morning—but when Clem did drink, he went wild. We all knew the signs—the thick talk, the red-rimmed eyes, the whiskey belch—and we'd keep out of his way. If we weren't fast enough or he found us, he'd beat us with a birch stick until we were black and blue. I still carry a scar over my right hip, and I swear he lamed Harry. Except when he was drunk, Clem ignored us. When the boys got old enough to carry a gun, he'd take them out hunting, but even then he never showed any liking for them. He wasn't much of a talker. Neither was Ma. I remember her first years with Clem she was pert and sweet. But by the time she'd had two babies and lost a third, she'd turned old and sour and had taken to drinking corn on the sly. Clem thought it wasn't fitting for a woman to drink, and when he'd catch her at it, he'd thrash her until she screamed.

I bore the fighting, the whiskey-drinking, the cold, wet winters, and the whippings because I didn't know any different and because I had someone to lean on, Tyson McAlpin, my cousin. (We were all related one way or the other.)

Tyson and me grew up together. There was something warm and reaching between us; we could fit into each other's skin. Tyson always seemed to have just the right word to ease a hurt, always knew when to tease and when not to. Times I recall as children when we'd go berrying, and Tyson would make it a game. "Let's see who can fill their bucket first," he'd holler, pretending to jump into a patch of thorny vines. And then he'd laugh. Tyson laughed a lot, something none of us did much at home.

I liked his ma, Carrie McAlpin, too—a huge woman with large, bony hands and feet so big she had to cut out the pair of shoes her husband, William, once brought her after he'd worked a spell log-splitting in the valley. Carrie didn't seem bowed down like my own ma for all the small children pulling at her skirts. She had the cheeriest smile, baked the fluffiest biscuits, kept the neatest house in the Cove. William, along with those fotched-on shoes, had also brought Carrie a church magazine, and she'd cut out the pictures and hung them on the walls—Jesus with a halo, plump-cheeked angels, and a fierce old man with a long white beard and a stick in his hand, Moses, Carrie said. Carrie knew more about religion than all of us put together.

One morning—I must have been thirteen—I was out in the corn patch trying to hoist a big boulder that had rolled down during the night, when Tyson came along and gave me a hand. He rolled that rock over so easily; and, watching him, I suddenly got a funny feeling inside as if I'd been struck a hard blow under the heart. Love, they call it. I knew then and there I wanted to be with Tyson all my life. I loved him, not like a child, but like a grown woman. But I was too shy to tell him, too shy to tell anyone, even Carrie McAlpin, who was so good to me. I thought, Well, Tyson can't help but feel the same soon as I fill out in the right places.

Three years passed, and spring greened the trees once more in the Cove. My dress—the only one I owned, a hand-me-down from Ma made of flour-sack bleachings—had long since been let out at the sides and hem, and a person with eyes in their head could see I was no longer a child. Except Tyson didn't. Patience, I thought. It will come with time.

But the days went by, and more days, and still more, and Tyson went on acting toward me just as he always had, teasing or friendly whatever his mood or mine. I might as well have been a boy.

And then, Lord help me, I saw him talking to Lizzie Rawlins one afternoon, she flashing those pansy-blue eyes of hers at him, and he bending over to catch her every word. "Talking" in the Cove was the same as courting. Lizzie and Tyson. Wouldn't that sting you? She'd been going off into the bushes with boys since she was twelve, and already had a baby, a little girl by Rigby McAlpin. We didn't think bad on Lizzie because she'd had a married man's child. (I wasn't to learn how bad Lizzie had sinned until I came to Stone Mill.) But what made her hateful to me was the way she'd stole Tyson from behind my back.

Still, fool that I was, I went on hoping until one morning there wasn't any reason to hope anymore. I had skipped over to the McAlpins' to borrow a little sorghum, and Allie, Tyson's sister, happened to be the only one at home.

"Tyson's taking up with Lizzie," she said. "He's going to marry her when the preacher comes around next time."

"Marry her?" I was shook down to my toes. "But he can't. . . ."

"And why not?" said Allie, spiteful-like. "He's a grown man, and if he has a mind to . . ."

But I didn't wait to hear more. I ran home without the sorghum and hid in the woods behind the house. I cried harder than I had ever cried, even when Clem had whipped me, cried as though I'd never stop.

But I finally did. And wiping my nose, I got to my feet and went into the house. They'd all left except Clem. He was sitting by the fire fingering a jar. The minute I saw that jar, I backed up.

But Clem said, "I ain't drunk. Just nursin' it. Your ma has gone off without fixin' somethin' to eat. Get me some breakfast."

There was leftover mush in a kettle, and I patty-caked it and fried it over the fire. As I was watching it, I felt Clem's hand on my shoulder.

"Yore gettin' to be a right purty girl," he said, blowing his whiskey breath on the back of my neck. My blood turned cold. "Right purty. C'mon here, I ain't all that hungry." And his hand went down the front of my dress, and he grabbed me there, swinging me around.

I had the pan in my hand, and I hit him a clout to the side of the head. He roared like a mountain cat, but he let go and I ran. I ran out of the cabin and up the creek bed, ran, sobbing, as fast as my legs would carry me.

When I was sure Clem wasn't following, I stopped to catch

my breath. The sun, high over the trees, made slanting rays through the branches, like the sun coming in high-roofed church windows in Carrie's pictures. The wind shook the leaves, a soft wind smelling of spruce pine. So quiet and peaceful. Brushing the hair from my eyes, I sat down and put my chin on my knees. I sat so still a squirrel ran down from a laurel and commenced to hunt for nuts in the leaves. But my mind was thinking all the time. Soon it would be noon, and Ma and the little ones would be coming into the house for dinner. She might even ask Clem, "Where's Kate?" But I couldn't go home. Home was red-eyed Clem, and Ma with her scrubbed-out face and her mouth turned down, and my half-brothers and sisters whining and fighting.

And Tyson going to marry Lizzie.

That was the worst of it. Suddenly I hated him. Hated everybody. I couldn't stay a minute longer in Hickory Cove. I'd die if I did. I'd throw myself in the creek.

But what could I do? Where could I go?

I had heard Tyson speak of Stone Mill Hollow. He'd been there twice with his pa, and he thought it wondrous strange. Big houses, he'd said. Nothing like our cabins. And horses drawing people in fancy closed wagons. Carriages, they called them. "Lots of work for the asking," he'd told me.

I'd go to Stone Mill Hollow, then. I'd get work cooking or hoeing or gathering firewood. I wasn't afraid to bend my back as long as I had a little pone and fatback to ease my hunger and a place to lay my head at night. Anything was better than the Cove, and Tyson and Lizzie so close, sharing the same bed.

I got to my feet, and the squirrel scampered away. I began to follow the creek bed, dried up now in September, the only way out of the Cove. Stone Mill Hollow, it was to be. Simple as that. No packing, for what did I have to pack? No good-byes, for who was there to say good-bye to?

I had never been further than the mouth of the Cove, and when I came to it, I paused. Beyond was the wilderness, the trees dark and shadowy, and the lonesome wind sighing, and for a moment I lost my courage. But the moment passed, and I hurried on without looking back. The creek bed was strewn with rocks and pebbles and fallen leaves and, in places, choked with sassafras. Sometimes I felt the damp under my bare feet where the water hadn't dried up completely. I had no idea how far Stone Mill would be, but I hoped to reach it by nightfall. Like all of us at the Cove, I was scared of getting caught on the mountain after the sun went down.

I had been walking an hour, maybe two, when my stomach commenced to growl with hunger. I kept a sharp eye and soon espied a strawberry bush—"hearts-a-bustin'-with-love," as Carrie called it. *Love*, I thought bitterly, plucking the glossy fruit and stuffing one after another into my mouth. They were sharp and sweet to the taste. Like love. I put several in my pocket and went on, coming to a little spring bubbling up from the creek bed. Cupping my hands, I drank of the crystal, cold water. Then, wiping my mouth, I looked up through the trees. The sky seemed paler. Surely, I thought, I should be coming to the end of the woods soon? But the forest went on and on, the creek bed running with a thin stream of water now.

I did not tarry, but hurried along, following the creek bed until I came to a place where it turkey-tailed out into numerous little forks. I chose the biggest and likeliest of the forks and kept on walking. When I looked up at the sky again, the sun was going behind the mountain in a blaze of gold and purple. Soon a white mist began to rise, growing thicker and thicker. Afraid that I might wander away from the creek, I climbed a tree in the last light and there decided to spend the night.

I was mountain-born, mountain-bred, and I could be brave when I had to. But night—the dark—brought out the "hants," and never, even later, after I got schooled, did I lose my fear of them.

That night was the longest, the most terrible of my life. Tired though I was, I couldn't sleep. Every sound, every snapping twig, every murmur, every rustle made me start and look about me with bulging eyes. I thought of all the fearsome stories I had heard since I was old enough to understand. I thought of Cherokee Sam, and the yellow dog who skimmed along in the air, the man who had been murdered by drowning for a sack of gold, a walking, dripping corpse, the flesh rotting from his blue gums. I thought of Skilly and the Devil dancing with his seven wives to the tune of a fiddle, and of the ghostly man who walked the night hunting ghostly possum, his dog trotting at his heels. The dead come back; sooner or later, they all come back.

The wind wept in the trees, and the white mist crept along the ground, rising, rising upward, touching my face with cold, wet fingers. I threw my arms around the tree trunk and closed my eyes. Dear Lord, I prayed, dear Lord. Boogers and hants. I thought of the night someone came knocking at the window and Ma said, "Don't let him in." But Clem laughed, and he went to the door and threw it wide. And a great rush of wind came in the door, and a little light hurrying over the threshold, running up the walls and over the ceiling. It was my pa risen from the dead, though Ma said she couldn't see how, since she'd put a big boulder on top of his grave.

At the first peep of day I shinnied down from my perch, my legs so stiff and sore I could barely stand. I had nothing to eat—the last of the strawberry fruit was gone—but I wasted no time in search of food. Another night like the last and I would go plumb out of my mind.

The creek bed wound and twisted, still going down, and soon a little stream came pouring into it and I was walking knee-deep in water. Other little streams joined it, and the water got muddier and swifter.

Suddenly I slipped on a mossy rock and fell before I could catch onto something. The creek came rushing over me, dragging me along, throwing me against one sharp rock, then another. I gasped like a hooked fish and swallowed a mouthful of water. I coughed and sputtered, gulping down more. I screamed, and the water came rushing into my lungs. I coughed; I screamed again.

And then I was falling, tumbling over and over, down, down, with this awful roar in my ears. More water, churning and frothing, rushing up my nose. Scared? Lordy, but I was scared! I didn't know how to swim. At Hickory Cove we were taught to fear deep water, and we stayed away from the creek when it was in flood. All I could do, between swallows, was to thrash my arms blindly. I hit another rock and went under, and just when I thought I was finished, my feet touched rough bottom. Catching hold of a hanging branch, I pulled myself out onto the steep clay bank and lay there for a long time shivering and shaking like a wet dog.

Thin wisps of mist hung in patches over the creek falls, and there was a touch of frost in the air. If I don't move, I thought, I'll freeze. I staggered to my feet, wrung out my dress as best I could, and went on. A kind of path meandered along the bank, and I took it, walking fast to keep my teeth from chattering. My elbow bled from where I had hit it, and there wasn't a spot on my body that didn't ache. My stomach gnawed and growled with hunger. I thought of the fire at home and how Ma would be stirring. I could almost smell the frying fatback. It tempted me, it really did, but I went on.

I walked and walked, and it began to feel as if I had been trudging along for years. The mist had long disappeared, and the sun glinted here and there on the creek. When I sat down to rest, I looked across the creek and saw a chimney rising above the trees, a chimney and part of a gray roof.

A footlog spanned the water, and I inched my way across carefully, ever so carefully, not wanting another ducking. When I got to the other side, I went through a wooden gate, its hinges screeching. I couldn't see the chimney or the house now, the trees and vines grew so thick. But there was a little stone path, and I followed it, coming out at last into a garden.

A woman was bending over, cutting some yellow flowers. "Miss . . . ," I said, my voice hoarse with cold and shyness, "Miss . . . ?"

The woman straightened and turned. She stared at me, her face white as milk beneath the black bonnet she wore.

"Francine . . . !" she cried. "Francine!"

And she crumpled to the ground in a heap.

Chapter 4

IT was very quiet in the garden. A bee hummed, skimming over the bed of yellow flowers, going 'round and 'round in a circle. I hadn't moved. I just stood there, my eye on the fallen woman. She wore a long black dress with a wide, puffed-out skirt all ribboned and bowed. On her feet were high-button shoes and white stockings. I had never seen such beautiful clothes. She lay very still, her arms flung out, one hand curled around a yellow flower. I wondered if she were dead.

Granny Maud had fallen down dead like that one winter. She had come over to take back the wash kettle she had lent Ma, and before she could get across the room, she had slipped to the floor and never moved again.

"Miss . . . ?" I whispered, wetting my lips. "Miss . . . ?" I couldn't tell whether she was old or young because of the bonnet. "Miss . . . ?"

I saw a man coming along the path, and I stepped back into the shadows under a large gum tree. I wanted to run because I was afraid he might say I had harmed the woman, but I had never seen a man dressed in such wonderful clothes—soft brown britches and a snowy-white shirt with a ruffle up the front.

The man gasped, "Mama . . . !" and he got down on his knees. He loosened her bonnet and began to rub her hands. He had dark hair and black brows that drew together over his nose in a frown.

"Astoria . . . !" he called over his shoulder. "Bertha . . . ?" But no one came.

He lifted the woman in his arms, and her bonnet fell off. She had gray in her dark hair.

"Oh, Judd . . . ," I heard her whisper.

"It's all right, Mama," he said, putting her down in a

green-striped chair near the yellow flower bed. "I'll get your salts."

"I don't need them," she said. "I saw Francine." And when he turned away, she grabbed him by the arm. "I saw her, I tell you."

"Mama," he said in a cold, hard voice, "Francine is dead."

I didn't know Francine. The name was strange to me, but a chill ran up my spine.

"It was *she*," the woman said. And then she happened to look my way and screamed.

I picked up my heels and ran, ran back down the stone path. But the man was swifter, and he caught me. He shook me so hard my teeth rattled and I began to cry.

"What are you doing?" the woman said. She had left her chair to follow. "What are you doing to Francine?"

"It isn't Francine," he said. "It's one of those Cove children. Can't you see?"

"Oh . . . !" The woman put her hand to her mouth.

I tried to twist free, but the man held me tighter.

"The poor child," the woman said. "She's all wet and dirty. Judd, you must bring her up to the house."

"But, Mama . . ."

"Surely it is a small thing to ask?" Then, turning to me, "You mustn't cry, child. We shan't harm you." Her voice was kind, but she kept her distance. I could tell she didn't want to touch me.

The man, Judd, said, "Come along, then," but his voice was gentler now.

"No." I shook his hand free. "I'm on my way to Stone Mill Hollow."

"This *is* Stone Mill," the man said. "Aren't you hungry? You certainly look it. Come into the house and have a bite to eat."

I could see no harm in that. I let him take my arm, and we followed the woman up the path to the house. Tyson had been right. The house was so big we could have put four, five of our cabins inside. And it was painted a clean white, the windows trimmed in dark green—more windows than I could count. We went up the steps and across a wide porch—white, too. The door had a fan of glass over it. The man opened the door, and the woman went in, beckoning to me. I stepped into a dark room smelling of beeswax.

"Perhaps you'd like to wash up," the woman said.

If I had suddenly been put down into another world, I couldn't have been more bewildered. Never in my life had I seen carpets, wallpaper, stuffed furniture, great, heavy, claw-legged chairs and tables—and mirrors. Never. And never had I been asked if I wanted to wash up.

"I'd rather have that bite to eat," I said.

The man, Judd, had disappeared.

The woman chewed her lip. She had faded blue eyes, and she spoke in a soft, tired voice. "I think you'd enjoy your food more if you had a bath. And your dress is all torn. I'll have Astoria fix you a hot bath. Your meal will taste so much better."

I could see I wasn't going to get anything to eat unless I bent to her whim. And my stomach shrinking more and more, clear up to my backbone.

"If you say so, miss."

"Mrs. Covington." And she smiled. "Astoria . . . !" she called. "Astoria . . . !"

A woman wearing a white pinafore over a gray dress came out from behind a door. Her face was black as coal. I had never seen a black woman before, and I was certain now that I had blundered into the Devil's house. But I remembered the tale of Skilly going through a whole evening with the Devil and his seven wives, unafraid and none the worse for wear. So I marched upstairs with the woman called Astoria, keeping a wary eye on her. Poor Astoria. I never guessed until later how much my coming distressed her, how much she hated and feared the Covington house.

She sat me down in a dim room with a big, fancy washtub setting in the middle, and said I was to wait. Then she went out and closed the door. It was so quiet I could hear the beating of my heart. I could run away now, I thought. But I was too hungry and too tuckered out to move.

A tree tap-tapped at the window, throwing moving sun shadows on the floor. I stared at the dappled shadows, my eyes getting heavier and heavier, when a sound made me turn. A girl was standing inside the door, a young girl somewhere about my age. She was dressed wonderfully, too, her long, dark plaits falling over a blue gown. But her eyes were queer—they didn't seem to match—one looking my way, one the other.

"Who are you?" she said.

"Kate," I answered, looking into the one eye.

"Kate who?"

"Kate—Kate Rawlins."

"Hmmmm." She came closer. The eye glittered like an ember in the dark, and my skin got prickly all over. "Where you from?"

"Hickory Cove."

She wrinkled her nose. "Never heard of it. Your hair's yellow, like Francine's."

Astoria came into the room carrying two large cans. I sat on the edge of my chair and watched as she poured steaming water into the tub. "Will y'all take your clothes off, miss?" she asked politely. She did not look at the girl.

I slipped out of my dress. "Why—you're all black and blue!" the girl said.

"I got drawn over a waterfall," I said.

The girl laughed, and suddenly I laughed, too. "My name is Bertha," she said. "Bertha Covington." And she gave me a little smile. Well, I thought, she can't be too bad, even if she is part of the Devil's household.

Astoria handed me into the tub, and I had my first bath (it shames me to think of it—my first bath at sixteen!). Afterward, she dried me and helped me into a clean shift and petticoat ("What's this? And that?") and a beautiful soft dress of pale green.

"Francine's," Bertha explained. She sat on a chair talking all during my bath, talking and talking about things that mystified me.

But Astoria never said a word, never gave Bertha a glance. The black woman's hands moved quickly as she brushed and combed my hair, but they were cold hands, cold like her face and her eyes.

She tied my hair back with a green ribbon. I had never seen myself in a proper mirror—only in the side of a shiny pan or in the creek on a still day. Now as I gazed at myself I could hardly recognize the stranger I saw. "Why, I'm pretty," I said in wonder, and a faint smile trembled at the corner of my mouth.

But Bertha tossed her head. "Pretty!" she said with scorn.

Mrs. Covington, herself, had fixed my food in the kitchen, a room as strange to me as the others had been. Bertha, watching, laughed because I did not know what to do with a knife and fork, laughed because I ate so greedily. Except for the biscuits, the preserves, and an egg, nothing set before me had the least familiar taste.

"How could anyone alive be so ignorant?" Bertha said.

"Don't you dare mock a guest," Mrs. Covington said, "just because she hasn't had your advantages."

"She eats like an animal," Bertha said in disgust.

My face flamed, and I hung my head.

"Leave the room, Bertha," her mother said quietly.

Bertha stared at Mrs. Covington out of that one good eye.

"I said, leave the room or apologize."

Bertha got up, flicking her braids over her shoulder. Suddenly she stuck her tongue out at her mother, then whirled and went through the door.

"I apologize for Bertha," Mrs. Covington said. And I wondered why she hadn't given Bertha a good clout, as my own ma would have done. "Help yourself to the ham."

But I had lost my appetite.

I drank more coffee, though, while Mrs. Covington kept staring at me.

"Why is it you came to Stone Mill Hollow?" she said at last.

"To look for work," I answered. "I can hoe and split kindling and scrub up a good wash and. . . ."

"Did you run away?"

"No," I said, shaking my head, telling what I felt was the truth. "No. Ain't no one to miss me at home."

" 'Isn't,' " she said. " 'Isn't' is the correct word instead of 'ain't.' "

"Isn't . . . isn't no one at home. I'm sixteen, a grown woman."

She sighed. "Yes, and so like Francine." She stared at me again. "You're welcome to stay here as long as you like."

I looked down at the table. It had a linen cover, white with flowers done in pink thread. Mrs. Covington had been kind to me—the dress and the food—but I didn't know if I wanted to stay.

"The black woman," I said, lowering my voice, "is she . . . is she the Devil's wife?"

Mrs. Covington said, "What?" surprised-like, and when I repeated my question, her mouth twitched. "My dear," she said, "my dear. Of course not. She is a Negro. Haven't you ever seen a Negro?"

"No."

"No, *ma'am*," she corrected. "Astoria is a servant. She's been with my family in Charlottesville for years and years. Why, I've known her most of my life. And as for the Devil, you mustn't speak of it. The Devil only shows himself to those who are evil."

"Oh." Ignorant, I thought. No wonder Bertha thinks I'm ignorant.

"You don't have to decide right away," Mrs. Covington said. "Perhaps you'd like to rest up?"

"I did sleep poorly last night."

"Come along, then."

We went upstairs again. The room was so white it hurt my eyes—white everywhere, the thin stuff hanging over the bed and windows, the walls, the cover on the floor, the furniture.

"This was Francine's room," Mrs. Covington said.

I had never felt a bed so soft. It had a sweet smell like balsam boughs, and, curling up in a ball, I thought, It must be a dream.

I opened my eyes, and, seeing a dark shadow bending over me, thought it was Clem. But when I sat up, the shadow turned into the tree outside with the moon shining through the leaves. I had slept the day through. I got out of bed, and going to the door, cracked it open. Voices, downstairs. A man and the woman—Mrs. Covington. Softly I crept down the stairs and stopped to listen behind a half-opened door.

"I don't know," the man said, "if having this girl is a good thing for you, Margaret."

"But, Eli—can't you see? She's Heaven-sent, Heaven-sent."

"Dr. Caldwell said you ought to put all that—those memories—behind."

"The old fool," she said. "*He* can talk. What does he know —*how* can he know the torment I've suffered? The shadow I live under." Her voice broke, and there was a small sob.

"There, now, Margaret, I didn't mean it. Here, here, now, don't cry," he wheedled. "Of course she may stay if that's your wish."

A door squeaked behind me, and, jumping around, I saw Bertha. She had a light in her hand, a candle, and the flame gave her face long, ugly shadows. "Have you been listening?" she whispered.

"Yes . . . I . . ."

"What did they say? Are they talking about me?"

And before I could answer, Mrs. Covington called, "Bertha? Bertha, is that you?"

"No, it's a ghost," she said and pushed me into the room, laughing a high-pitched laugh.

Mrs. Covington half rose from her chair by the fire, her face a deathly white, and I felt sure she'd faint again. But the man standing next to the fire grasped her arm, his own face white as a sheet. He blinked his eyes at me, then, seeing Bertha, said crossly, "Bertha! You must not tease your mother."

Mrs. Covington sank back into the chair. "My handkerchief, Eli. I believe I've dropped my handkerchief."

He picked up a small bit of white cloth, and she fanned her cheeks with it. "This is Kate, Eli. Kate Rawlins."

Eli smiled and bowed. He had curly hair the color of honey peppered with salt, and stout pink cheeks.

"Welcome, Kate," he said, and smiled broadly.

Mrs. Covington fanned herself. "You're to stay as long as you like. And you're to have Francine's room."

"Thank you kindly . . . ma'am. I can earn my keep."

"Earn your keep?" Eli's eyebrows went up. "Guests in the Covington house never have to earn their keep."

"No," said Mrs. Covington. "Not a guest, Eli. Kate *isn't* a guest." And her pale fish eyes turned on me. "You're one of the family. I want you to consider yourself part of the family."

Bertha said, "Well . . . ," letting out her breath.

"Wouldn't you like to have a sister again?" her mother asked.

"I don't rightly know," she said, cocking her head to one side, looking me over.

"Of course you would," said Eli, rubbing his hands together. "And now, I wonder if Astoria has supper ready."

We ate at a round table by candlelight—Judd, Bertha, Eli and Margaret Covington, and me. Judd hardly opened his mouth, but the others, like Bertha had done earlier, chatted about things and people strange to me. I kept watching from behind my lashes to see what they did with all those knives and forks. Astoria brought platters of food from the kitchen, and instead of plunking them down on the table as we would at home, she held them out so folks could help themselves. I could feel Margaret and Bertha Covington's eyes on me when it came to my turn, but I pretended not to notice, taking special care not to slop the gravy.

It was when Astoria was passing the apple pie around that Bertha said in a loud voice, "I saw a white rooster out back just as the sun was going down."

"A white rooster?" Eli said. "Why, you know very well we have no chickens or fowl of any kind."

"Perhaps it belongs to a neighbor," Margaret Covington said, cutting daintily into her pie.

"What neighbor?" Eli said.

I took up my fork. "Hit's bad luck to hear a rooster crow at night."

" '*It*,' " said Margaret Covington. " 'It,' my dear, not 'hit.' "

"It," I said carefully. "Minnie's ma died the morning after she heard one."

Astoria's hand shook as she set a plate in front of me.

Bertha, looking straight at Astoria, said, "Did she? White roosters are used by witches when they do their black magic, aren't they, Astoria?"

Judd, scowling, said, "Why don't you stop teasing Astoria?"

"Why don't you mind your own business?" Bertha said, and Eli, rubbing his hands together and smiling nervously, said, "Now, children, no fighting at the table."

"It *was* a white rooster," Bertha said.

Margaret Covington's hand fluttered to her brow. "I feel a headache coming on."

Bertha said, "It had its throat cut." She ran one finger across her neck and grinned.

Astoria dropped a plate, turned, and ran from the room.

"You'll be the death of that woman yet," said Judd between his teeth.

Later we sat in the room Mrs. Covington called the parlor. Pretty, soft lights shone from glass holders set on smooth, round tables. A fire burned in the white fireplace.

"We shall have to get shoes for Kate," Mrs. Covington was saying. "Francine's were too small."

Shoes. I thought of Carrie McAlpin and her big feet poking out the front of her fotched-on shoes, and felt a pang across my heart.

"Would you like shoes?" Bertha asked me.

"I don't mind"—tucking my bare feet under my gown.

"Well . . . ," said Eli, yawning, "another day, another dollar. I think it's bedtime."

Margaret Covington put her knitting away and got to her feet. "Coming, girls?"

"You all go on," Bertha said. "Kate and I will stay a while longer and get acquainted."

Margaret gave us a smile and, taking Eli's arm, left the room.

"Well, what do you think?" Bertha asked.

I looked at her.

"Think about *us*," she said. "The Covington family."

"Mmmmm. You don't holler and cuss. Does your pa drink corn?"

"Corn?"

"Corn whiskey."

"No, he's a teetotaler." I didn't ask what that meant. "But I think Judd takes a nip now and then."

She twisted a plait of hair about her fingers as she stared into the fire. I felt the dark night outside crowding against the window.

"Who's Francine?" I finally asked.

"What? Francine? Haven't you guessed? No, I suppose not. Here." She gòt up and fetched a lamp. "Look," she said, holding the lamp up over the fireplace.

A picture stared down at me, a picture of a girl with yellow hair and blue eyes wearing a pale-green gown, and it was like looking into the mirror all over again.

"She was my sister," Bertha said. "And she died."

"How?"

"Just died," she said. "I don't know how." And her eye, gleaming from the shadows like a hant's, sent a cold shiver up my spine.

Chapter 5

IN the morning Mrs. Covington measured my feet with a string. "For shoes," she said, scribbling a note. A boy was fetched to carry the note to the store.

"Don't linger, Artie," she told him—a tadpole of a fellow, no bigger than our Harry at home. "And here's a penny for a candy stick."

Artie returned some hours later, the shoes slung around his skinny neck by their laces. "Sure took your time," said Bertha, who had been waiting at the door.

The shoes were of shiny black leather with buttons up the side, much prettier than Carrie's, but too small. Mrs. Covington got a slipperslide, and she pushed and I pushed until we squeezed them on.

"How do they feel?" Mrs. Covington asked.

"Right good," I lied. The toes pinched so I wanted to scream. "If we cut the fronts out, they might fit better. "

Mrs. Covington pressed her thumb down on my toes. "We can get another pair. Longer. Bertha, have Astoria fetch Artie again."

Bertha chewed on a braid, watching us struggle to remove the shoes. "Why don't we go down to the store ourselves?" she asked. "Instead of sending Artie to and fro."

"Well—I don't know," her mother said. "It isn't proper for ladies to be buying shoes in public."

"Mama—the best ladies in Charlottesville do all the time."

She thought for a moment. "Very well. I suppose if they do in Charlottesville, we can in Stone Mill. Ask Judd to harness the gig, please."

Years later I was to look back on the town of Stone Mill Hollow and see that it was nothing more than a small mountain village thrown up in higgledy-piggledy fashion around a broad place on a country road. But when I first laid eyes on it, riding down its main and only street in a gig with Mrs. Covington and Bertha, the strange sights made my head spin. So many people! All those large houses! And the cobbled sidewalk, the closed carriages!

Bertha said, "And there's the smith"—sparks flying and the ring of metal—"the school"— a building fashioned of logs—"the mill"—whirring and whining.

Bertha went on pointing and talking, and my head kept going from side to side.

"And here, now, is Mr. Bradley's." We had stopped before a square, high building with dusty windows.

Bertha jumped down and tied the horse to a post.

I was wearing an old pair of Bertha's boots, and they clumped as we crossed a narrow porch where rattlesnake skins and beaver pelts dangled from the beams. Inside, a vast room was crowded with tables (counters, Bertha called them) piled high with britches, shirts, hats, bolts of pretty cloth, and all manner of things I could not begin to name. Hung from hooks on the ceiling were boots, harness, plow handles, and buckets. Never had I seen anything like it.

A man with a pencil stuck over his ear came through a latticed door. "Why, good morning, Mrs. Covington. Such a pleasure to see you. You're looking mighty well." He gave Bertha a twitchy smile.

Mrs. Covington, in her soft, sad voice, said, "Thank you, Mr. Bradley."

"Did the shoes suit?"

"As a matter of fact, they were a bit too short." Mrs. Covington took my arm and drew me to her side. "I want you to meet a new member of our family."

His eyes popped. "Oh—oh!" And he swallowed. "I didn't know you had kin visiting."

"She's not kin," Mrs. Covington said. "She's Kate Rawlins, and the shoes are for her. Let's see what you have."

"Yes—yes, mmmm. Shoes." He tapped his lip, then went behind the counter. He slid open a bin full of footwear—brown, black, white, buttoned and slippered, hightops and low—enough shoes to fit all of Hickory Cove and then some.

"Let's see," he said, pulling out another pair of shiny black shoes.

"Something in white," Mrs. Covington said grandly.

"Mmmm." He looked at the bin and frowned. "None here

that would suit, but I think I have just what you want in back. If you'll excuse me a moment."

He disappeared between two rows of heavy barrels.

Bertha leaned against the counter.

"Straighten up," her mother said.

Bertha turned her back and inspected a large glass jar. "Peppermint sticks," she said, and helped herself.

"Here you are," the storekeeper said, handing Mrs. Covington a pair of white shoes. He glanced at Bertha. She sucked on her candy, fixing him with her good eye. His face got all red, and he looked away.

Mrs. Covington untied the shoes and turned them over in her hand. "They look as if they might do. Bertha . . ."

Bertha unrolled the string bag she had brought along, and Mrs. Covington dropped the shoes inside.

"If you please, Mr. Bradley, you might add several pair of hose," Mrs. Covington said. "And while I'm here, I believe I'll have a look at the muslin."

"Dry goods is on yonder table," Mr. Bradley said. "Take your time. I'll get the hose." He opened another bin.

Bertha said, "Mr. Bradley, I do believe you have a customer, a lady over near the hats. She's been smiling and beckoning these past few minutes."

Mr. Bradley peered into the dimness. "I don't see anyone."

"Don't you?" Bertha asked in wonderment.

I looked, but all I saw was a table covered with hats.

"She's holding a pink poke bonnet in her hand," Bertha said. "A fat lady with bright red curls."

The storekeeper's eyes goggled, just as they had when he first looked at me, and his hands gripped the edges of the counter so hard the whites of his knuckles showed. "I don't see anyone," he repeated in a hoarse whisper.

Bertha nodded out toward the hats. "Why, I do declare, she's coming over to talk to us."

Again I peered into the shadows. Behind me I heard a whine of hinges, and when I turned, Mr. Bradley had disappeared.

Bertha laughed, a high, crazy laugh.

A minute later Mrs. Covington returned with a bolt of sprigged muslin under her arm. "Where has Mr. Bradley gone?"

"He took sick," said Bertha, crunching on the last of the peppermint stick. "Sudden-like."

Her mother eyed her suspiciously. "Did you say anything you shouldn't have?"

"Only that he had a customer."

"There are *no* customers except us," Mrs. Covington said in a low voice. "Maybe you and Kate ought to go out and wait in the gig while I settle up with Mr. Bradley."

When we had seated ourselves in the gig, I said, "There wasn't anyone, was there?"

" 'Course not. I just like to needle Mr. Bradley. The fat lady I described was once his wife."

"Once?"

"She died. Keeled over with stomach trouble. But *I* know he poisoned her."

"How . . . how do you know?"

"I dreamt it. I saw it all in a dream, true as I'm sitting here. He sneaked arsenic into her coffee. That's why Mr. Bradley's afraid of me. Afraid I'll tell."

I watched a small cone of dust and dead leaves whirl crazily across the wooden porch. "Skilly had dreams and visions," I said.

"Skilly? Who's Skilly?"

"She was a woman lived over the mountain. She danced with the Devil and his wives."

"Hmmm—that's a *tale*," Bertha snorted. "Mine's for real."

The second pair of shoes were hardly better than the first. To feet accustomed since birth to wiggle at pleasure, an iron box fitted over instep and toes could not have been crueler. But I wore them to please Mrs. Covington, a stubborn, picayunish woman for all her sad and gentle ways. She had given me Francine's clothes—gowns and shawls and coats, pretty things such as my wildest thoughts could not have imagined. But when I asked her what had ailed her daughter before she died, she pretended she hadn't heard.

Eli Covington owned a sawmill about a half mile from the house. He went to "business" every morning dressed in his fancy clothes and a big, cheery smile. Judd followed him an hour or so later. I don't think Judd liked sawmilling much, but Bertha said he *had* to, since he was the only son. "But your pa could give the mill to you," I said.

"No, I'm a girl. Would your pa give you his rifle?"

" 'Course not," I said, shocked.

"Well, it's the same thing."

Every day I had something new to puzzle over—chamber pots and outhouses, crinolines and corsets, knitting needles and hatpins, hooks and eyes, earbobs and scissors.

"Ignorant," Bertha would tease. Sometimes when no one was looking she pinched me, and then she would say, "Sorry."

"Haven't you heard we had a war?" she asked one afternoon.

"You mean," I said after a moment, "the one against King George?"

She laughed. "No, silly. The War Between the States. The North against the South, a *big* war, three years ago. Didn't you know?"

"It"—I had already begun to be careful about saying "it" instead of "hit"—"it must have been a long ways from here."

"Not a long ways. They were fighting down in the Shenandoah Valley, and on a quiet day we could hear the cannon. The Grays against the Blues. My brother was in the war. Cold Creek, Vicksburg . . ." She looked over at Judd, who was sitting by the fireplace smoking a cigar, but he didn't seem to notice us. "Here . . ." She took a large book from a glass-fronted cupboard and opened it to a colored drawing—a map. "Look here."

"I can't read," I said.

She whooped, "Ignorant! I don't think I'll speak to you, you're so ignorant."

Judd lifted his head and said sternly, "Behave yourself, Bertha! Apologize to Kate."

Bertha thumbed her nose at him and flounced off.

Judd said, "Impertinent child."

There was a small, awkward silence. "*Were* you in the war?" I asked shyly.

He nodded. "I'm afraid I was."

"Were you a Blue or a Gray?"

"I fought for Virginia," he said. "My mother thought I ought to defend the South's honor."

"Did you?" I asked.

A small smile stole across his face. "I tried. We all tried —a gallant, glorious, if somewhat foolhardy dream. Brave men, but the slaughter, the terrible slaughter . . ."

And then, maybe because he had said more than he

meant to, he took a watch out of his pocket and frowned at it. "I must be getting back to the mill."

That evening I overheard Mrs. Covington arguing with Astoria. I hadn't yet learned the word *eavesdropping*, hadn't yet learned that "mannerly people" considered it beneath them, so when I heard loud voices in the kitchen, I stood outside the door and listened without a twinge of guilt.

"You *can't* leave," Mrs. Covington said. "I won't allow it."

"The slaves has been freed, Mrs. Covington," Astoria said.

"I shan't be able to manage if you go."

"I'm sorry, ma'am."

"You're acting selfishly, you know."

A small silence. A heavy sigh. "I has to go," Astoria said.

"Why? Tell me the real reason."

"I can't."

"Is it Bertha?"

Another sigh.

"I'll speak to her," Mrs. Covington said. "I'll speak to her very sternly."

"There's nothin' you can say," Astoria said patiently. "She . . . she can't help it if . . ."

"I'll have Eli speak to her."

"Won't make no difference."

"Astoria, you've been with the family so many years. . . ." Mrs. Covington's voice broke. "What shall I do if you go? I'm surrounded by people who—who don't care. I know you're homesick. Don't you think *I* am?" There was the sound of weeping.

After a few moments Astoria said, "I'll stay. Please don't cry, Mrs. Covington. I'll stay. The Lord will see us through this. The Lord will see us through."

I lingered, still listening, but neither Astoria nor Mrs. Covington said what the Lord was supposed to see them through.

The only part that made any sense to me was Astoria being homesick. I understood that. Two weeks, a long, long, fourteen days since I'd been away from Hickory Cove, and I like to died, I missed it so much. I missed it in the cool mornings, thinking of how the apples would be ripe now, hanging from their crooked boughs in the old orchards, missed it in the afternoons when the sun lay warm upon the window, thinking that the children would soon be gathering hickory nuts. I forgot about all the ugliness, Ma not caring, Clem drinking and grabbing me, forgot the whining and the crying and the cussing.

My shoes pinched, and I thought of walking free, the feel of the yellow dust between my toes or the soft grass wet with dew. I ate roast beef and potato pudding and thought of hoecake and fatback, and my belly ached for a mess of green beans. I used the chamber pot and the outhouse, and I thought of the woods, the whole wide woods and how much sweeter they smelled. I hooked eyes and unbuttoned buttons, and I thought of the plain dress I had worn, just over my head and a drawstring at the neck.

Wind and balsam and runted laurel and huckleberries. And ice freezing the creek in wintertime. No need to be any place at any time (even the hoeing and planting could be left if you had a mind to), no need to eat unless you were hungry. No one to say, "You're ignorant." All the ugliness was skimmed over in my memory, and only the good things remained.

But one thing I hadn't forgotten—Tyson. I hadn't forgotten how he'd taken up with Lizzie, and that thought made everything—Stone Mill Hollow, Bertha, the Covington house, my pinching shoes—bearable.

If Bertha was unkind, Eli and Mrs. Covington tried in every way to make up for it. I suppose they fussed over me because I reminded them of Francine. But they would never talk about her. Never. Her picture smiled down from over the fireplace—rosy lips parted as if she were talking. When I was by myself, I would stare at the picture and wonder what Francine was saying. It was almost as if she were trying to tell me something.

What?

The days were empty. I tried to help with work around the house, bringing in wood for the fireplace, hoeing weeds in the garden, scrubbing the front steps. The hours were so long, and I wasn't used to sitting idle. But Mrs. Covington would not have it.

"We must see to a tutor," she said. "You will learn to read, Kate, and to write. Books are such a comfort."

I never saw her reading a book. Judd read, but none of the others did. I wondered why Mrs. Covington thought it would be a comfort to me. Strange woman. They were all strange.

One afternoon I was snipping away at the last of the yellow flowers (chrysanthemums, Mrs. Covington called them) when I heard someone say, "Kate!"

I turned, dropping the flowers. My mouth flew open. Was I having a vision like Skilly or Bertha?

"Hit's me, Tyson," he said.

"No—no." I shook my head. "Hit couldn't be. Hit just can't be!"

He laughed. "Hit's me."

I wanted to throw my arms around his neck and kiss and kiss him, but I was too shy. Besides, somebody from the house might be watching.

"You ran away," he accused.

"Maybe. How did y'know I was here?"

"Been askin' 'round. Why, Kate? Why?"

Tears filled my eyes. "Because you was goin' to marry Lizzie."

"Marry Lizzie? You must be plumb out of yore mind. Y'know there ain't never been anyone but you."

I closed my eyes. Had I suddenly died and gone to heaven?

"You ain't goin' down with somethin'?" Tyson asked anxiously.

"No. Hit's just . . . just I can't believe hit. I reckoned you and Lizzie . . ."

"Why don't you stop 'bout Lizzie. I want you. I want you to come back to Hickory Cove and be my wife."

"Your wife?" I couldn't say any more for the lump in my throat.

"We mought have to live with Ma for a spell," Tyson said.

"I . . . I like Carrie." I stood twisting my apron. Tyson didn't speak. At last, I said, "Tyson . . . Tyson, do you love me?"

"Now, ain't that a damn-fool question? Would I ask you to marry me if I didn't?"

"No," I said, looking at him. I had to smile—his face was so flushed up. "But I can't go this minute. I can't run off without a word to Mrs. Covington. She's been so good to me. She took me in, and Eli and Judd. . . ."

"Eli and Judd? Are them the people up at the house—the ones that own the mill?"

"Yes." I heard a twig snap and, looking over Tyson's shoulder, saw the bushes sway. Bertha listening?

"Come out, Bertha," I said, "and meet Tyson."

But no one came. Tyson went over to the bushes and pushed them aside with his hands. "There's nobody here," he said. "Hit must have been the wind. Now . . . what was I sayin'? Oh, yes. I heard them two talkin'—Eli and Judd—awhile back when I was lookin' for you. Somethin' funny . . ." He scratched at his head. "But I disremember. No matter. You say your good-byes, and I'll see if I can get a preacher to marry us."

"Oh—Tyson . . . !" I would return to Hickory Cove already married. And if Clem—but he wouldn't, because Tyson would be there to reckon with.

"I'll be back soon as I can," Tyson said. "This evening before dark."

Mrs. Covington took on just as she had with Astoria when I told her I was leaving. "But you can't," she said. "What shall we do without you?"

"The same as you did before," I said, not meaning to be hardhearted, but I couldn't understand why she needed me. Astoria worked for her keep—I did nothing.

"But we've grown so fond of you," she said.

"I thank you for that, but there's my people in Hickory Cove." They never had been "fond" of me, but I honestly didn't feel Margaret Covington was all that "fond" of me, either. "And I want to marry Tyson."

"Marry Tyson," she said, "and have a baby every nine months."

"I'll have my number like my ma did," I said.

She pressed her pale lips together. "Perhaps Eli can change your mind."

"I was fixin' to leave soon."

"You can't go without talking to Eli. I'll send Artie to fetch him."

We sat in the parlor while we waited. "Is it Bertha?" she asked me.

"No, hit ain't . . . it isn't Bertha."

Eli came and talked to me for a long time, smiling his smile, telling me I had so many more "advantages" living in Stone Mill, that I was such a pretty girl I'd be sure to meet another young man who could give me "my heart's desire."

I didn't want another young man. My heart's desire was Tyson.

When they saw they couldn't persuade me, Eli said, "If that's what you want, then I suppose there's nothing we can do. But you must always look upon us as friends."

They had thrown away the dress I had come in, but Mrs. Covington said I could keep the one I had on. And the shoes. She gave me a bundle of old dresses—castoffs she had been meaning to send to the missionary people in Charlottesville.

I thanked her, thanked Eli, even Bertha. (Judd was not there.) I said good-bye and went out to sit in the green-striped chair, holding the bundle on my lap while I waited for Tyson.

The hours passed. The sun sank behind the trees, and the air grew chill. Tyson was late. The preacher had probably gone somewhere to marry or to baptize, or to speak for the dead. Preachers were busy people.

I took off my shoes and hose and eased my bare feet, rolling little cool pebbles under my toes. My soles were still hard, and I wouldn't miss the shoes, wouldn't miss them a bit.

Time passed.

I got up and went to the front gate. A gray cat jumped down from the fence, and I edged out of its way so it wouldn't bring bad luck. I looked down the empty road where the maple trees had turned scarlet. I walked back through the garden carrying my shoes and my bundle and went on down to the gate at the creek. The talking water and the wind sighing up yonder in the big oak tree made me so sad I wanted to cry. But I ought to be happy, I thought. Tyson will be coming soon, and we are to be married.

I sat down again in the green-striped chair. Presently a star came out—high, in the pale night sky.

"Kate . . . !" Mrs. Covington called, coming along the path. "Kate, come in and have a bite of supper."

"I'm not hungry," I said.

"Are you sure your man is coming to fetch you?"

"Yes, I'm sure." Why would Tyson say he was if he wasn't?

"Come up and sit on the veranda, then, it's getting awfully cold."

"I ... I'm just fine here."

It got dark. I moved to the porch steps, sitting there, my eyes big and round, my ears sharpened to the sound of a step. No one came. Mrs. Covington talked to me, and Eli, too, but I wouldn't budge.

I waited all night, and when the first light of morning came, I knew that Tyson had changed his mind. Maybe he'd decided he did love Lizzie after all. I waited another hour, then I got up, stiff and chilled with the night's dew, and walked slowly up the stairs into the house.

Chapter 6

MRS. Covington said I wasn't to fret because Tyson had jilted me. "It's the best thing that could have happened to you," she said. "You'll see."

"I don't want to talk about . . . it." Easy for her to say, "You'll see," when she didn't have my heart to carry around. The past is done and finished, she said. Put Tyson and Hickory Cove out of your mind.

She wanted to make a "lady" of me. I didn't know what a "lady" was, but I said all right. It didn't matter. So they sent me to school in Stone Mill. The schoolhouse reminded me of home, especially the stick-and-clay chimney. But on the inside it was as different from home as a place could be. It had a potbellied stove in the middle and tables and chairs in rows on either side. Along one wall there were books; along another, pegs hung with coats and caps. And from behind the schoolmarm's desk a faded picture of a man with white hair and pale eyes (George Washington) looked down on us.

The first day was sheer misery. I was the oldest (though not the biggest), and the others laughed whenever I spoke. "Can't understand a word," someone snickered. I didn't know as much as the "least one," a little mite of seven, the Ryland boy. He could pick out words in the reader, while I couldn't tell which end of the book was which. If it weren't for Mrs. Jennison, the schoolmarm, I'd never have gone back the second day. But she told the children to mind their manners or she'd forget *hers* and whack them. I liked that—and when she smiled at me, I felt I had a friend.

I was slow to learn at the beginning. The hardest part was having to sit in one place and pay attention, something we never had call to do in Hickory Cove. But Mrs. Jennison kept encouraging me, and pretty soon I got the hang of my letters, and from then on, it was easier.

Mrs. Jennison was a widow lady from Front Royal. I

never saw her in anything but the same black dress, plain except for a crocheted collar held together by a coral pin at the throat. Winter and spring, always the same gown.

I can close my eyes now and see her standing tall and straight, a small woman, a pencil poking from the skinned-back bun at the nape of her neck, greeting us with a tired smile. "Good day, children. Shall we rise and sing the National Anthem?" She led us, her voice rising above our jangling, piping ones, sweet and clear, her face losing for a moment its weariness.

She held the reins over twelve, sometimes fourteen or fifteen children in that room, from the seven-year-old Loeffler boy to the storekeeper's fourteen-year-old Donald, big for his age and not too bright. For all the schoolmarm's small-ness and sweet voice, she could thrash a body if she had to. When Donald slyly kicked over the stove (a favorite trick of the big boys) she caught him at it and whacked him so thoroughly none of the others dared try it again.

I believe my days at the schoolhouse were the happiest of all. I felt easier there than at the Covingtons', closer to Mrs. Jennison than anyone. She was kind, did not laugh or call me ignorant, patiently teaching me after-hours what I had missed. In return I would help her tidy up, fetching wood for the stove and sweeping the schoolroom floor. "Kate Rawlins," she would say, "you are my right hand."

Certain things stick like burrs to my memory: the red felt-bound slate I carried, the smell of black ink, and the feel of the steel pen between my fingers. I can tell you word for word the story of the *Meddlesome Mother*—and *Which,* all about a very poor, very large family that I found fascinating. I can recall how proud I felt writing my first letter, a note to Mrs. Jennison asking her to have supper with the Covingtons —and only one correction in the spelling, thanks to *Noah Webster's Elementary Spelling Book.* And there was the *Home Geography* and *Alexander H. Stephens History.* Some folks say those books were sketchy and badly written, but for me they opened a fairy-tale world, places I never dreamed existed across and far over the ridge of the mountains.

I remained two years at the schoolhouse. What with Mrs. Covington and Mrs. Jennison both correcting my grammar, I soon left off the "hits" and the "ain'ts," and though I never lost my country accent completely, I spoke well enough to hold my own with other folk in Stone Mill.

On the day Mrs. Covington said I was too old for school, Mrs. Jennison suggested I go on to get more learning in Novotno, but Margaret Covington didn't see any sense to it. "Too much education spoils a young woman," she said, forgetting that she had once told me a book would be a comfort. "Kate ought to be thinking of making her social debut."

What she meant by "social debut," I never knew. The Covingtons didn't mingle much with the rest of the town, except in a business way, and that was Eli's doing down at the sawmill. We hardly ever had company to supper and hardly ever went to anyone else's house. It was all very puzzling, since I knew Eli liked having people around him. But except for attending church on Sundays and driving to Mr. Bradley's store on Friday afternoons, we seldom stepped beyond the garden gate. And after Mrs. Jennison retired, leaving Stone Mill to live with a sister in Roanoke, I had no one to talk to but the Covingtons.

"Look on us as family," Margaret Covington often said to me. But though I spoke in their tongue and aped their manners and dressed in their clothes, I felt no kinship. Mrs. Covington would always be Mrs. Covington to me, Eli would be Eli, not "papa," as he wished me to call him. Bertha was strange, and Judd removed, like a shadow, silent and brooding. It wasn't that I didn't *want to* "fit in" or that I kept pining for Hickory Cove—there was just this wall between us, I on one side, the Covingtons on the other.

Once I tried to ask Mrs. Covington about her dead daughter. Her face screwed up like a monkey's. "I can't . . . you mustn't . . . ," she wept. Eli pretended not to hear my question, making some joke about a man who had come to see him at the sawmill. And Bertha would only say, "She was sick and she died."

No one in the family, as far as I knew, ever visited Francine's grave, wherever she might be buried. But I did not think that too strange. We did not hold with cemetery-visiting in Hickory Cove, either. Once a body was funeralized we tried to forget it. Not that we were coldhearted or afraid of dying; we simply shied away from the buried, for everyone knew the dead became hants.

Why should I have been so curious about Francine, then? Time and again I asked myself that question. Maybe it was because she looked like me, or maybe it was because of the

Covingtons' mysterious silence. I don't rightly know.

Francine was a hant—I firmly believed that—but a hant with no harm in her. Sometimes at night I felt if I reached out she would be there. "Francine," I would whisper, and the leaves on the tree outside would shiver. It was only later that her haunting began to worry me—later, when I found it scary to sleep in her bed or to call her name.

I think Astoria felt Francine's presence, too. She did not like to "do" my room, and I, glad to find some way to pass the time, relieved her of the chore. I promised not to tell Mrs. Covington (who firmly believed "ladies" should not do a servant's work). But if I thought this little secret between Astoria and me would bring us together, I was wrong. Grown old and thin—overnight, it seemed—Astoria kept her distance, moving like dark water through the house, silent and un- noticed.

Only once did I hear her speak directly to Bertha, aside from her usual "Yes" or "No, miss." Bertha had been nag- ging at her mother over a stray cat she wanted to keep, though she already had three. Mrs. Covington got upset—the way she always did when things didn't run smoothly—and, saying she couldn't stand to hear more about it, went up- stairs. Astoria, who had quietly been dusting in the parlor around us, suddenly said, "Bertha, why don't you leave your mama alone? Don't you know this house is cursed?"

Instead of giving Astoria some of her sass, Bertha got white in the face and left the room.

"Astoria," I said, "why did you say that? What do you mean, this house is cursed?"

But she wouldn't tell me.

One morning three years after I had come to the Coving- tons', we got up to find Astoria gone. Sometime during the night she had packed her few belongings and left the little shack next to the stables she had called home for so many years. Nothing had been said, Mrs. Covington claimed. And since Astoria couldn't write, there was no note. "After all I've done for that darkie," Mrs. Covington wept. "And she promised me she wouldn't go."

Bertha said, "Maybe she heard a white rooster crowing in the night," and laughed.

Mrs. Covington wanted Eli to fetch Astoria back from Charlottesville, where she was sure the black woman had gone. But Eli said Astoria was a free soul. "We'll hire some-one else."

The someone else turned out to be a cousin of Preacher Davidson's, Janie, age seventeen, a big, towheaded girl with buck teeth, just come in from Oakton Hollow. Margaret Covington said she had two left hands. "I'm not young enough to go training someone from scratch," she told Eli.

"My dear Margaret, no one else will come," he said. "Stone Mill folks don't like to work in other people's homes."

"You mean *our* home."

"Now—don't take on, sweetheart. I'll speak to Mrs. Preacher and see what she can do."

The preacher's wife's name was Min, but everyone called her Mrs. Preacher. She was a small woman with a nose like a bird beak and a voice like a rusty hinge. She took Janie under her wing for a week, working side by side with the girl, teaching her how to cook and clean and wash. She never got Janie to wear shoes, though, nor would the girl stay beyond dark. Wintertimes when night fell early, she'd set our supper out and leave before sunset. Margaret Covington would weep and scold and threaten to find someone else, but Janie refused to be coaxed. Barefoot and afraid of the dark she remained.

Aside from these two peculiarities—as Mrs. Covington called them—Janie did well—that is, until she fell in love with the Ryland boy, Zeb.

Old Man Ryland and his three sons ran the smithy. Zeb was the middle one, a handsome, brown-headed lad with a moustache curling and twirling under his nose. Janie had seen him at church one Sunday, and our lives weren't the same after that. It was Zeb this and Zeb that, and do you think he'll notice should I wear a red ribbon? Or maybe the blue? She even went as far as to buy herself a pair of shoes, though she wore them only to church. Poor Janie. Love finished fuddling what brains God had given her. She put sugar in the soup and salted the spread-apple pie. She hot-ironed the men's shirts to a scorch and spilled embers on the parlor rug. "Why don't you have him call on you some Sunday afternoon?" Eli asked, hoping, I suppose, this might calm Janie a bit.

The idea didn't set too well with Margaret Covington, but she said Janie could have the kitchen to receive Zeb.

Bertha and I, standing behind the lace curtains in the parlor, watched him come down the garden walk. He wore his Sunday clothes, the coat too short at the wrists, the britches too short at the ankles. "Hand-me-downs," Bertha whispered. In one hand he carried a small paper sack. "Horehound candy," Bertha said. "Cheapest kind." His face was shiny with sweat as he disappeared around the back.

"How come *we* never have callers?" Bertha asked.

A small pain nudged my heart. Tyson was the only caller I ever wanted, and now I didn't care. "Who would you like?"

"Someone like him"—nodding her head in the direction of the kitchen—"but dressed in proper gentleman's clothes."

"He *is* handsome," I allowed.

I went upstairs to fetch my sewing basket (Bertha, Mrs. Covington, and me were making a quilt for Mrs. Covington's missionary friends in Charlottesville), and when I came down, I saw Bertha in the hall with her ear to the kitchen door.

"Oh . . . !" she said, jumping away. "I wondered if they were misbehaving."

She was in love with Zeb Ryland herself. I could tell by the way her eyes glittered as she watched Zeb walk away through the garden with Janie on his arm.

The next Sunday, Bertha said to Janie, "Why don't you fix your beau some China tea? I bet he never tasted such brew before, and I'm sure Mama won't mind."

"Thank you kindly, Bertha," Janie said.

From what Janie told me later, it was the China tea that suddenly cooled Zeb toward her, for when he came the next Sunday, instead of going 'round to the kitchen door, he marched boldly up the front steps. Bertha was there at the door wearing her best gown, her hair fixed in curls. "Come in and sit awhile," she said to Zeb. "I've been expecting you."

Margaret Covington was not very happy with Zeb calling on her daughter. But I heard Eli say, "under the circumstances, she'll be lucky to get anyone."

Zeb knocked at the front door three Sundays in a row, and on the fourth, Preacher Davidson came instead. He and the Covingtons talked in the parlor while Bertha and I listened at the closed door. Janie was with child, the preacher said, and Zeb was the father. As Janie's cousin he, the preacher, was duty bound to see that a wedding took place. "There ain't goin' to be a briarpatch child in my family!" he shouted.

So, the following week Preacher Davidson married Zeb and Janie in the church. We all went, even Bertha, her eyes glittering from beneath a veiled hat. Seven months later Janie's baby was born, a stout boy, but Janie herself caught mother's fever and died.

"Zeb would have been mine," Bertha said, "if that meddlesome fool Davidson hadn't come between us."

"He's a widower now," I said. "You can still have him."

"No," she said, "not with *her* child. I'll find me another beau and make Zeb die of jealousy."

"You're talking foolishness." Bertha was homely as a mud dauber. I never could understand what Zeb saw in her.

"Am I, though! I can do a lot of things. You'd be surprised."

"Maybe I would," I said.

Bertha rolled her bad eye up into her head so that only the white was showing (a trick she did when she got riled) and stared at me out of her good eye. Like always, it made my skin crawl. Sometimes I hated her, sometimes I pitied her, other times I felt she could have been the sister I never had. We were both the same age, lonesome, without friends, and Bertha, when the mood suited her, could be kind. "You should have gone to stay with the Perrys or the Loefflers instead of us," she said once. Was she feeling sorry for me? I asked. Maybe, she answered, but she wouldn't say why. She told me she had dark "powers," but I thought it was her fancy. If she had powers, why couldn't she fix that ugly eye of hers?

"All right, then," Bertha said one afternoon. "I'll show you what I can do."

She took me up to her room and closed and locked the door. Then she drew the blinds. It was a quiet afternoon. Mrs. Covington was napping in the parlor, and Judd and Eli had gone to the mill. The girl who had taken Janie's place (Mimsie, a black girl sent up from Charlottesville) was out in the yard boiling the week's wash.

"Sit over there," said Bertha, pointing to a spindle-legged chair.

"What—what are you going to do?" I asked, suddenly turning cold. Only a thin band of light showed at the bottoms of the drawn blinds, and amongst the shadows Bertha's face was like a white blob.

"You'll see." Bertha sat on the edge of the bed. "You notice that book on the bureau?"

"Yes," I said, "what of it?" trying to make my voice easy.

"I'm going to move it over to the washstand without touching it. Now—you must be very quiet, because if you speak, it will break the spell."

I stared at the book, holding my breath, my eyes popping. Minutes passed. Nothing happened. More minutes. The tightness went out of my spine. Why, I thought, she can no more move that book than I can fly. I peeped at her. Bertha's chin was lifted, her eyes half-closed. Beads of sweat had broken out on her flat, pale forehead.

Suddenly I heard a faint rustle, and my eyes snapped back to the bureau.

The book was moving!

Inch by inch, it jerked itself along like a dumb, lame creature—inch by inch, faceless, limbless, dragging itself toward the edge of the bureau. Cold prickles rose on my skin. I shut my eyes. The *thing*—what else could I call that creeping horror?—had reached the edge and was teetering there, teetering like something alive struggling hard not to fall.

Bertha groaned. And the book fell to the floor with a thud.

"Out of practice," said Bertha, wiping her brow with a handkerchief.

I stared at the thing on the floor—an ordinary book bound in brown vellum, the size of one of Eli's cigar boxes. Had the book really moved, or had I imagined it?

Bertha said, "Let me show you what else I've been practicing."

"No," I said quickly. "You don't have to." I didn't like being in that dark room with her, the door locked and the cold feeling running up my spine.

"Scared?" she said.

"No . . . I . . . I was going—"

"You weren't going to do anything. Now sit there and be quiet."

I sat. She went to the mirror and stood before it, looking at herself, studying her face feature by feature, then the whole of her body.

When she seemed satisfied, she returned to the bed and lay down full length on her back. She closed her eyes. The house was quiet, not a stir or a rustle or a movement to break the awful silence. After a minute or two the color went out of Bertha's face, and her chest, which had been moving up and down with her breath, became perfectly still.

She's died! I thought wildly, she's died right in front of my eyes!

But I went on sitting there, unable to move. Frozen and scared, just as Bertha had said.

I don't know how long I remained glued to my chair in that dim, soundless room. If Bertha and me and the furniture had floated up into the black night sky, we could not have been more alone, more distant from the living world.

Suddenly a strange light, a white glow, began to hover over Bertha. I blinked. The light was still there. Gradually, ever so slowly, the light thickened, and—as the Lord in Heaven is my witness!—the light thickened into an image of Bertha. The dark plaits, the white skin, the arms in full sleeves, the narrow gray skirt, and the feet in black leather boots. Two Berthas. One above, one below!

Again I felt the hairs on the back of my neck prickle all the way to my scalp. I tried to speak, but my tongue had gone dry. Dear Lord! I thought, this time I've really gone out of my mind.

The image glided out over the foot of the bed. Two Berthas. She has died, and her hant is moving into the spirit world, I told myself. *So plainly, so real! I don't want to see it.* But I kept looking. Like someone in a dream, the floating Bertha slowly came upright, drifting down, her feet touching the floor. She turned and looked at me, her eyes like pits of darkness.

I wanted to scream, but all that would come out was a choking sound. And the *other* Bertha still lying there on the bed.

After a long while, the standing Bertha turned and rose up in the air again. The ghost body bent back and back until it lay flat in midair. Then it moved over the bed. Slowly it descended until it melted into the other Bertha.

Somehow I found my legs and stumbled to the door. My hand shook so, when I pulled the key from the lock it dropped from my quivering fingers to the floor.

"Do you believe me now?"

I whirled. She hadn't died. She was sitting up on the bed. I shook my head, I nodded. I couldn't find my voice to answer.

"That's called astral travel," she said, just as calmly as if she were saying my skirt is gray or pass the salt, please. "I read about it in a book."

"Y—yes." I was afraid of her. Not even Skilly could have done such a trick. Was she a demon, a witch?

"Don't tell Mama or Papa," she said.

"N—no . . ."

"You aren't afraid of me?" She laughed.

"Oh . . . no . . . no . . ." But the smile I tried for wouldn't come.

"Makes no difference," she said. "Everybody else is."

I could see it now. I had thought Eli and Margaret were soft with Bertha because they felt sorry for her. Their ugly duckling. But it wasn't that at all. They were afraid, just as Mr. Bradley, the storekeeper, and Astoria were.

"I never hurt anybody," she said. "It's all just for fun."

I looked at her sitting there on the bed, a plain girl with two dark braids and a funny eye. She could shift books without touching them, move herself through the air like a hant, and cast spells. "For fun," she had said. But was it?

Chapter 7

FOUR years had gone by since I had opened the creek gate and walked barefoot up the path to the Covington house. I was a young "lady" now.

"We must see to getting you girls husbands," Eli said, pouring us each a glass of blackberry wine that New Year's Eve. "Here's to eighteen seventy-one."

Bertha held her glass to the light. "I've chosen single blessedness," she said. For all her clever talk and her "powers," no one had come to call on her since Zeb Ryland.

"Nonsense," Eli said. "Every woman should be married."

Margaret Covington sighed. "Eli, there's plenty of time for the girls to think of husbands."

But Bertha and I were twenty—spinsters—and no man in sight. I was not even sure I wanted one. Tyson was still with me, in my thoughts and in my dreams.

Then one day Judd, who seldom spoke, said, "Kate, you ought to get married."

I looked at him in surprise. I didn't think Judd had taken much notice of me—or anyone else, for that matter. He seemed to live apart from us in his own little world.

"You ought to find you a young man," he said, "and have a home and children."

"And where would this young man be?" I wanted to know. There was no one I had seen in Stone Mill, no boy or man who came near to moving me the way Tyson had.

"Leave Stone Mill Hollow, then," he said.

I laughed. It was winter, and there had been an unusually heavy snow. Drifts were piled to the door.

"I'll take you," he said, as if reading my mind. "This is just a freak storm, and the snow will soon melt."

We were at the dining table having a late breakfast. For some reason I can't remember, the others had already had their meal, and Judd and I were alone.

"Where will I go?" I asked, still smiling. "What will I do?"

"You can go to your friend, Mrs. Jennison."

"But she lives in Roanoke!" Was he teasing, "pulling my leg," as Eli would say? Only, Judd never teased.

"Roanoke isn't the end of the world."

I looked down at the table—a crumbled biscuit, a pat of soft butter, a dab of berry jam, my knife lying flat and lady-like across the plate. "And you reckon I'll find a husband there?"

"You're a pretty girl," he said. "Why not?"

I shook my head.

He leaned forward. "If you take my advice, you'll go, Kate," he said in a low, earnest voice. "You'll leave Stone Mill Hollow far behind."

I looked into his eyes and saw darkness there, a darkness which frightened me. "Why . . . why should I go?" I whispered.

"For your own good, Kate."

Could he see into the future? "There's something here," I said, and my lips trembled, "something you feel is bad for me?"

He did not answer at once but studied my face for a long moment. "No—no, Kate. I'm sorry, I did not mean to frighten you."

"But you must tell me why. . . ."

"I have nothing to tell," he said, pushing his chair back. "I'm sorry. Perhaps things will work out for the best here in Stone Mill." And he left me sitting there—alone, wondering.

I think it was soon after our conversation that I began to notice the funny way people in town behaved toward me.

"Good morning, Mrs. Covington, 'morning, Miss Bertha, 'morning, Miss Kate," Mr. Bradley, the storekeeper, would say, his smile passing over Margaret and Bertha, lingering for a moment on me, a wary smile, a pondering one. Is this Kate Rawlins? it seemed to ask.

Folks would stop speaking when I approached, hemming and hawing a greeting, embarrassed until I left them, as if they couldn't wait to start talking about me again. At church I could feel them staring at me, and if I happened to catch their eyes, they would look away quickly.

Had I grown thin-skinned? Why should people want to talk about me, Kate Rawlins—I, who was nothing but a far shadow in their lives?

* * *

One Saturday evening we were invited to a candy pull at the Loeffler place. Margaret Covington was in the habit of refusing such invitations, but Eli had persuaded her to go. He was interested in buying a stand of timber from Tom Loeffler and thought it best they accepted. "Good business," I heard him say.

Bertha and I, excited because this was the first party we had been to in years, primped for hours. I curled her hair, and she curled mine. (It was strange how every now and again Bertha could be so ordinary, just like any other girl. Times like that, I would forget her "powers" and wish she'd stay ordinary always.)

When we got to the Loefflers, someone was playing the fiddle and singing "Barbara Allen."

> " 'Twas in the merry month of May.
> The green buds were swelling,
> Poor sweet William on his deathbed lay
> For the love of Barbara Allen."

Sad songs about lovers dying were my favorites, and I wished the singer would give us another verse. But we had scarcely shrugged out of our coats when the fiddler laid by his bow and we were told to gather 'round a big tub of warm syrup.

"Choose your partners, boys," said Mr. Loeffler, a roly-poly man with a clay pipe stuck out the side of his mouth. "Choose your partners."

Kenny Dawson chose me. His father was Eli's right hand at the mill, and Kenny worked there, too. A towheaded boy, he had pink eyes and a mouth full of teeth. (Bertha said he reminded her of a rabbit.) Kenny's hands were sticky warm as they took mine. "You an' me," he said. His breath smelled of corn whiskey.

Mrs. Loeffler gave each couple a buttered dish, while Amy Perry handed 'round a small tub of lard so we could grease our hands. Then, when the syrup had cooled down, all the boys dipped into it with their hands.

"Here," Kenny said, holding up the mess, "start pullin'."

Well, we pulled back and forth, back and forth, pulled the syrup into long strings. I started to giggle, then to laugh outright when Kenny got some of the syrupy candy on his nose and, in trying to rub it off, got a big blob running down his mouth and chin. I laughed and laughed until I happened to catch Mrs. Loeffler watching me. Her eyes held such pity, such sorrow, it drove the smile clean from my lips.

Why does she look at me that way? I thought, growing cold. Was it my likeness to a dead girl that made some of the others draw away? It set me to wondering all over again about Francine. Maybe she had done something terrible, something unforgivable. I was a stranger in Stone Mill Hollow, and no one would tell me.

The folk who lived in Stone Mill didn't take to strangers, people whose people had not been born there. I could understand that. We would have felt the same in Hickory Cove had a body stumbled into our mountain hollow and wanted to stay.

Why didn't I go back to Hickory Cove, then? I thought of it often at first, but as time passed I felt I could no longer "fit in" at the Cove, either. All the girls my age would long since have married; they would have families by now. Tyson and Lizzie, too. Tyson and Lizzie. No, I couldn't go back.

Even Preacher Pearce Davidson spoke against outlanders. A bandy-legged man with a huge nose and fierce eyes, he held revivals once a month in addition to his regular Sunday meetings. It was at a revival meeting one night that he gave a sermon on the "roots that bind homefolk together" against outsiders who were natural enemies.

"The Lord says," he bellered, "we cleave to one another. Trouble comes, we close our ranks. Everyone in Stone Mill is his brother's keeper. *Everyone,* do y'hear me? That's somethin' an outlander won't understand 'bout us hyar. Vengeance on mine enemies, the Lord has written!"

Then he went on to speak of sin. Sin was a favorite topic with the preacher. "The clan," he said, leaning forward over the pulpit, shaking a finger at us, "is only as strong as hits weakest. Now, we hyar have sinned—oh, yes, the Lord knows hit—we're SINNERS!"—and the word snaked over our heads like a bullwhip—"and sinners must be punished. For 'em who does wrong, hellfire will follow sure as fallin' rain."

I stole a glance at Margaret and Bertha. They sat stony-faced, stiff as boards, paying heed to every word, as did Eli, who sat across the aisle with the other men. Judd never came to church. I suppose Preacher Davidson had already damned him.

I never knew what to make of sin, of fire, and Hell and damnation everlasting. At Hickory Cove we knew very little of the Bible and less about regular religion. We believed in the Lord—didn't everybody, except Mrs. Covington's missionary heathens? But we did not fear Him. We were afraid of the dead, of storms, of ghosts, of forest fires, and such—and sometimes the Devil.

". . . if you don't aim to be roasted in Hell, y'mind the Lord, d'you hear? Atone!" He threw his arms heavenward. "Ahhhtone!"

The sharp, pleasant smell of raw plank tickled my nose, for the church was new, built this past year by the congregation. Eli Covington had given the lumber, Mr. Bradley the "window lights," the men and boys their labor. The plank benches were full; everybody came (except for a backslider or two like Judd), even babes in arms, hushed and rocked in their mothers' arms.

". . . in wickedness, saith the Lord, for I will bring evil 'pon ye in the year of punishment. . . ."

I twitched, shifting my feet and refolding my hands, impatient, hoping the preacher would be done soon and get on to the revival. The revival was scary but exciting, and I enjoyed it much more than the preacher's sermons.

At last he had finished, and we all rose to sing "Jesus, Jesus, Rest Your Head" and "Lazarus" and "Blood of the Lamb." As our voices swelled, the night looked in through the windows, and the lamp hanging from the rafters threw our shadows against the wall.

"Jesus died for me!" someone shouted, and the stamping of feet and clapping of hands commenced. Softly at first, then louder and louder, the Ryland boys keeping time with guitars and tambourines. The music beat out—clap-clap, clap-clap, stamp-stamp-stamp! I clapped along with the others, excitement rising from my toes, tingling up all through my body. Louder and louder, faster and faster. A flush stained my cheeks.

"Salvation!" Preacher yelled, and Ned Loeffler sprang to his feet, arms outstretched. "Salvation! Oh, Lord—oh, Lord, save me!" The veins stood out on his neck. "SAVE ME! SAVE ME!" And we all shouted with him, "SAVE ME! SAVE ME!"

". . . this the year of our Lord, the year the Lord receives his due. . . ."

A woman, old and skinny (I never knew her name or where she came from, but she was always at revival), tottered out into the aisle, her head shaking, her eyes boggling. She began to hop, first on one foot and then the other. "I hear you—oh, Lord, I hear you!" Her shadow leaped to the wall, and above her the great lamp swung to and fro. "I hear you!" Ned Loeffler squeezed his way past the standing people and joined the old woman. Cass Davidson, Bradley's sister, Reba Perry, Mrs. Preacher, Donald Bradley—all came forward, hopping and jumping and shouting hallelujah. One by one the congregation slipped into the aisles hollering and skipping, while the clapping got wilder and wilder.

And then I was amongst them, twirling in that crazy dance, everything forgotten—my thoughts of Francine and Bertha and the things Judd had said to me, and my loneliness, that terrible, empty loneliness, the sweat pouring into my eyes, the tightly packed bodies moving with me, my stepped-on feet and elbow-jabbed ribs—everything forgotten in those moments when I came so close to the Lord, so close to joy.

When it was over and we left for home, worn out, limp as dishrags, I felt strangely content, though I never could understand why. Between revivals, though, I did not think very much about religion.

Margaret was cool toward revivals, and I guessed that Eli felt the same, but he respected Preacher Pearce Davidson. "He's a self-made man," Eli would say. His father had come out of the deep mountains years before with a tired, played-out wife and a parcel of children. Old Man Davidson moved into a tumbledown cabin on the edge of town, and after he'd settled his woman in the kitchen and himself on the front porch, he sent the older children out to work. The preacher was the second son and, according to Eli, the smartest of the bunch. He taught himself to read and write. ("Not that he ever became a scholar," Eli said, "but he knew his letters.") When a kindly traveler stopping over in Stone Mill gave him a Bible, he got the call. "He was seventeen then," Eli told me. "Brought himself up out of that mess to be a preacher. Fine man."

Pearce Davidson and Mrs. Preacher were two of the few people invited to supper at the Covington house, and the preacher sermonized at our table just as he did in the pulpit.

And we listened, quiet and respectful, just as we did in church. He seemed to fear no one, neither the Lord nor the Devil (nor Bertha). The folk in Stone Mill looked up to him, too—Mr. Bradley, Colonel Perry, Mr. Ryland, all of them.

He seldom spoke directly to me, but one night when he had come to supper, he said, "Are you prepared to meet yer Maker, little lady?"

"I . . . I reckon so." I hadn't really thought about it.

"Because if y'ain't, you'd best hurry. Yer goin' to meet the Lord God sooner than you planned." His eyes went through me like cold blue ice, and I flinched.

Eli said, "Now, don't take it personal, Kate. We all meet our Maker sooner than we think. Right, Preacher? Ha! Ha!"

Margaret, as usual, said nothing in the preacher's presence, nor did she try to correct his grammar, as she had once done with mine.

Winter moved with fits and starts into spring. The buds swelled on the branches, the pussy willows burst from their jackets, the creek ran faster. Logs that had been sledded down from the mountain were stacked high in the sawmill yard. The men worked late, and we could hear the whine of the saws far into the evening. Eli did not mention husbands again, nor did Judd. The days were endless. Bertha, Margaret, and I had finished the quilt for the heathens and had started on knitting socks.

One morning I awoke to see the gum tree outside my window fringed with leaves. A black-and-orange bird perched on a limb, a wisp of straw in its beak, the first oriole of the season.

Spring at the Covington house meant Mimsie shoveling the ashes from the fireplaces and sweeping the spiderwebs from dark corners, airing mattresses and storing winter clothes in camphor. It meant taking up the carpets and hanging them on the line, raising great clouds of dust as they were beaten.

It was then that Margaret Covington put on an old pair of gloves and a large sun hat and said, "Garden time. Come along, girls, make yourselves useful." Gardening was ladies' work.

She got Artie Clarke (grown into a beanpole now) to do the heavy jobs, pruning and spading and carrying broken tree limbs back to the woodshed. Only the garden in front of the house was tended; the rest grew wild. I sometimes wondered why, since both Eli and Margaret were such tidy people. Goodness knows they had money enough to hire it done. When I asked Bertha about it, she said, "They don't care to go down by the creek. I think something bad happened there once. It's a spooky place."

"You mean it's haunted?"

Her eye wandered away. "Could be."

"Are you *afraid?*" I asked.

"Certainly not."

"Sure?"

She looked past me to the wind-ruffled trees, to the rank vines and wild, crowded bushes.

"I dare you," I said, feeling I had at last found Bertha's weakness.

"You don't have to *dare* me. You forget I have powers and nothing can harm me. All right"—she took a few steps—"are you coming, too?"

Everything had grown so in the four years since I had come up this same path, I hardly recognized it.

"There used to be a swing here when I was a little girl," Bertha said, pointing to a huge, wide-spreading oak.

I looked at the tree, old and gnarled, and a sudden feeling of sadness came over me. Why, I thought, how strange. Yet it wasn't an unpleasant feeling, just a sad-sweet one, and I wanted to go and sit under the oak and think about Tyson.

"What are you staring at?" Bertha said sharply.

I didn't answer, for it seemed to me that I was in the wilderness again, in that long-ago forest, walking away from Hickory Cove barefooted and heavyhearted. I hadn't known the names of the trees and flowers and birds then, and it had been September, not April, but I remembered how I felt everything so keenly—the smell of the wind and damp leaves, the taste of the little spring's water, crystal clear, so cold and sweet. I remembered the sky and the mist, the dark night and my fear.

I once overheard Mrs. Covington say to Eli, "She doesn't show much emotion. Mountain people are that way. I suppose they aren't educated to feel as deeply as we."

It had bothered me to hear that. It just wasn't true. What has schooling or place of birth got to do with a heavy heart or a lonesome feeling inside?

"The gate's almost rotted away," Bertha said. We had come to the moss-covered wooden fence along the creek. An old, crooked bench covered with bird droppings stood on the other side.

I stopped to pluck a branch from a blooming spice bush. "Violets!" I exclaimed, glimpsing the purple-blue faces peeping out from under a patch of leaves.

"I don't like this place," Bertha said, hugging her arms. "It's cold, it's nasty."

"I can't feel the cold."

She gave me a scornful glance. A bird whistled, a lonely, sad sound. "Why did they take the swing down?" I asked.

"Because we got too old for it."

The creek ran high, flowing swiftly, its muddy waters carrying dead leaves and twigs, lapping and swirling over the footlog. To my right, back through the overhanging branches, the tangled mass of leaves, past the tumbling, rock-strewn falls, back, back over stones and thorn, through sassafras and yellow-foot shrub was Hickory Cove.

The bird called again, shrill and sweet.

"What happened here?" I asked in a dreamy voice.

"I *told* you, I don't know"—irritated, angry. "Let's go back to the house. It must be dinnertime."

The third week of April, we had a visitor from Charlottesville, the son of an old friend of Margaret's, a young man with fluffy side-whiskers and apple-red cheeks. He took a fancy to me, I think, for he asked if he might call.

"I don't mind," I said, "but I think you ought to speak to Mr. and Mrs. Covington first."

I never knew if he did speak to them, as he left for Charlottesville that evening without saying good-bye.

Bertha was outraged, not at his hasty departure, but because he hadn't paid any attention to her. She came into my room early the next morning, her eyes red-rimmed, her mouth drawn into an angry line.

"Well!" she exclaimed. "You made a perfect show of yourself."

"I—what?" I sat up in bed, pushing the hair from my eyes.

"Throwing yourself like a hussy at that young man."

"I did no such thing!"

"Liar!"

I said nothing. It was best to hold one's tongue when Bertha fell into one of her black, ugly tempers.

"Liar!" she repeated, thrusting her pale, flat face at me.

I got out of bed and began to pull on my stockings.

"You came here . . . you came here a poor nothing. *Nothing!*"

I tore my nightdress up over my head and quickly got into my shift, my dress.

"Barefoot, dirty, and stinking!" she ranted. "*Stinking!* You had to have a bath. Yes, Mama took you in, took you in out of the goodness of her heart. . . ."

I began to look for my coat. She followed me to the wardrobe. "She gave you the clothes on your back, a roof over your head, food to eat, treated you like a lady when you—you no-good harlot—you should have been working in the kitchen. And you—you bending over, showing your bosom. 'Would you like another helping of sauce?' " she mimicked, " 'another biscuit, maybe?' Why didn't you do that to your Tyson? Maybe he wouldn't have thrown you over. . . ."

I fled from the room and down the stairs. I saw Judd's face through a mist of tears as I tore out the front door. I found myself on the stone path, the wild growth surrounding me, the hated house lost from sight. I paused, a sob catching in my throat.

The morning sun glistened on the leaves and touched the lingering fog with warm, loving fingers, touched my cheek and my hair. As I stood there, the tears dried on my lashes, and peace and quiet folded over me like a bird's wing.

I began to walk slowly down the path, past the oak tree—the sad, beautiful tree. The dogwood was now blooming, a mass of white and pink blossoms against the dark green of oak and spruce. The mist stirred in the wind, stirred and floated lazily, melting into the slanting rays of the sun.

Suddenly I stopped. A man was sitting on the crooked bench near the creek. The mist swirled and hid him for a moment; then I saw him again. I shivered as a cold finger of fog crept under my collar.

He turned his head. "Oh . . . ," he said, getting to his feet. "I had no idea people still lived here. The garden looked so deserted." He had a pleasant, friendly voice.

"The Covingtons live here," I said. "In the house—up there." Motioning with my head.

"And who are you?"

"Kate Rawlins," I said.

"Ah—and for a moment I thought . . . ." He came closer. "You are a very pretty girl, Kate Rawlins." And he smiled.

"And what is *your* name?" I asked.

"Clayborne," he said. "I'm a Clayborne."

But the name came to me without meaning. I looked into his eyes—deep, dark eyes, sad ones.

"You are unhappy," he said. "And you seem so lonesome."

Why, he knows me, I thought, he knows exactly the way I feel.

"I was just passing through," he said in his deep, gentle voice, "and thought I'd stop to do a little fishing."

"Fishing?" I asked, and noticed a pole stuck in the clay bank. "I didn't think there were fish so close to the mill."

"There aren't," he said, making a face. "But I like to sit here." He looked up at the trees. "It's so peaceful."

"Yes," I agreed.

He was a young man, the same age as Judd, I would guess; handsomer, though. He had light-blond hair and a firm mouth and a dimple at the side when he spoke.

"Why don't you sit a spell?" he invited. "And we can get acquainted."

"I . . . ." Would Bertha say I was too forward? "I believe I will."

We sat down on the bench. He was wearing a dusty blue jacket.

"Are you from hereabouts?" I asked.

"I'm a native of Stone Mill," he said. "But today, as I said, I'm just passing through. And what about you? Where are you from?"

"Hickory Cove," I said.

"Well, well, you sure don't look or talk like. . . ."

"An ignorant mountain girl," I said with a crooked smile.

"There, now, don't take on. I didn't mean to put it that way." He reached out and touched my hand—just a light touch, yet the blood rushed to my face. It surprised me. I didn't think any man could make me blush that way again. And yet here I was, not only blushing but suddenly yearning to touch him, too.

"You do stare," he said.

My face flamed as I lowered my eyes.

"I don't mind, I don't mind at all," he said agreeably. "You visiting the Covingtons?"

"No, I live with them." I told him how I had come to Stone Mill to look for work because there had been too many mouths to feed at home. Somehow I didn't feel like telling him I'd left mainly on account of Tyson. "I think the Covingtons took me in because I look like their daughter—the one who died, you know. Francine."

"No, I didn't know. You see, I've been away."

"Well—she died. Oh, about seven years ago. They never said what ailed her. So young, she couldn't have been more than twenty, same as me, and. . . ."

But he seemed to have lost interest. He was staring at the creek where the water bobbed and eddied, foaming over the rocks. It was almost as if he'd forgotten I was there.

We sat for a long while without speaking, and then I said, "Would you care to come up to the house and join us for some breakfast?"

"Thank you kindly," he smiled, "but not now."

I got to my feet, and he rose. "They'll be missing me," I said, "so I'd best get back."

He held out his hand. "It's been a pleasure meeting you, Miss Kate Rawlins." He took my hand, and I found myself looking into his eyes again. Such a nice man, a fine man, so handsome . . .

"Are you sure you won't change your mind?" I asked.

"No. I can't come now, but I'll be back someday soon." There was a twinkle in his eye. "I'll be back to marry you."

"Marry me!" And we both laughed.

He took up his pole and opened the wooden gate for me. "Good-bye, Kate." The gate squeaked on its hinges. I watched him crossing the creek on the footlog. He turned and waved and, a moment later, was gone.

Chapter 8

BERTHA was contrite. "I don't know what came over me," she said. "I'm sorry, Kate." I wondered if her mother or Eli had asked her to apologize. "I won't do it again."

I did not want to think of the names she had called me, the things she had said. "It's all right."

Mrs. Covington, sitting across the breakfast table, smiled at Bertha, at me.

"There, you see?" Eli said in his hearty, morning voice. "Everybody's made up."

Mrs. Covington said, "I do want you girls to be friends—sisters."

"We are," said Bertha, tapping her boiled egg with a spoon. "Aren't we, Kate?"

"Yes," I said.

Bertha began to peel the egg. "Where did you go?"

"Down by the creek," I said. "And—there was a man fishing there."

"Fishing?" Margaret Covington said. "On our property?"

Eli wiped his mouth with his napkin. "I see no harm in someone fishing. Who was the man, Kate?"

"He said his name is Clayborne. I didn't catch his first name."

"What . . . ?" Margaret dropped her fork, her face white as the cloth. "What . . . ?"

"His name is Clayborne," I repeated, and then smiled, remembering. "And he said he wants to come back to marry me."

Mrs. Covington pushed her chair out, gasped as she tried to stand, and would have fallen to the floor if Eli hadn't caught her.

"She's fainted," Bertha said in surprise.

A flustered Eli said, "Judd! Where's Judd?"

"He's gone out," Bertha said.

"Well, don't just sit there, for God's sake! Help me get your mother into the parlor where she can lie down."

We carried her to the horsehair sofa. Eli began to rub her wrists while Bertha ran upstairs for the salts.

"What did I say?" I asked, very worried. Mrs. Covington's lips had turned blue. "Is it something I said?"

"Margaret's set her heart on you marrying Judd," Eli said.

"Judd?" I asked, astonished. "Why, he's hardly spoken to me."

"You know how mothers are. . . . Here, Bertha, give that to me."

Eli put the bottle under Margaret's nose, and a moment later her eyelids fluttered.

"I don't understand," I said, hovering at the foot of the sofa. "What is it I said to make Mrs. Covington faint? He— Clayborne—it was only a joke about wanting to marry me."

"The Claybornes have a bad reputation," Eli said.

"But he looked like a gentleman."

Bertha's lip lifted in a sneer. "They can look any old way they want. A Clayborne ran off to fight with the Yankees, and no one here at Stone Mill speaks to them. No one."

I thought of Clayborne's deep-set eyes and the way the dimple came alive when he smiled. I thought of the creek and the woods and the smoky mist lingering in patches and the touch of Clayborne's hand on mine. "Is that why we never see any of them in town, why they never come to church?"

Eli said, "That's why."

Margaret Covington stirred.

"Shhh," Eli cautioned. "Let's not talk any more about it. Margaret . . . ?"

He got some brandy and had Margaret sip a little. "Feeling better, dear?" She looked terrible, her face drawn, the little wrinkle lines she was always careful to cover with powder showing in webs at the corners of her eyes.

"Did . . . did I faint?"

Bertha took my arm. "Come outside," she whispered.

Closing the parlor doors behind us, she said, "That was a nasty thing to do."

"What? What did I do? I only . . ."

The door opened, and Eli poked his head out. "Bertha— your mama wants to speak to you."

Bertha went in, and I had a glimpse of Margaret Covington's pale face propped up on the sofa pillows. "Excuse us," Eli said with a smile and shut the door again.

I felt left out, hurt and bewildered. Such confusion! And all because I had said I had met a Clayborne. Were the Covingtons and Claybornes feuding? But I couldn't imagine Eli carrying on a feud with *anyone*—Eli who tried so hard to be liked, Eli who smiled and shook hands with the whole town. Maybe the Claybornes were feuding with the Rylands or the Bradleys, or maybe they stayed clear of Stone Mill for other reasons.

Why Eli felt Margaret Covington wanted me to marry Judd, I couldn't imagine. *She* had never said anything to me about it. Nor had Judd. I remembered him telling me to find a husband, but he hadn't offered himself, hadn't seemed interested.

After that day, I began to pay more attention to Judd, watching him closely. But his behavior was no different than usual—he ate hurriedly, said little, and spent most of his time away from the house. " 'Morning, Kate," " 'Evening, Kate," Same as always.

And as for Clayborne—though I went down to the creek several times, I did not see him again.

In early May, just as the apple trees were in full bloom, we had an unexpected cold snap, and Mr. Loeffler, owner of the largest orchard in Stone Mill, was froze out. It was a mean blow, since he had no other cash crop and would be hard put to support his family until his trees could produce again. He came to Eli to borrow money. "He asked Papa," Bertha said, "instead of Mr. Bradley, because Papa doesn't charge the high interest Mr. Bradley does."

Somehow the storekeeper got wind of Ned Loeffler's financial arrangement, and it made him mad as a hornet. Bertha and I happened to be in the store one afternoon when the two men met face-to-face. Mr. Loeffler was inspecting some harness, Bertha and I were sniffing Roses Red, a new toilet water, when suddenly Mr. Bradley came out of his office like a jack-in-the-box. He reached up and clapped Ned on the shoulder.

"I'd say you have brass!" Mr. Bradley said, his eyes blazing, "thinking I'll do business with you after you've gone behind my back."

"I ain't gone behind your back," Ned Loeffler said. "I just

took money where I could get it cheaper."

"*Everyone* borrows from me—that's part of storekeeping. *Everyone!*"

"Maybe that's why everyone owes you an arm and a leg."

Mr. Bradley's face turned a deeper shade of red. "Git—git out!" he sputtered. "Git out! I'll throw you out with my bare hands if you don't git . . . !" Mr. Bradley, who came up to brawny Ned Loeffler's chin, began to dance in front of him like a turkey-cock.

"Why, I could break you in two and have you for breakfast," Ned said. "Pipsqueak!" He threw down the harness and stomped out of the store. In the silence that followed—everybody in the store had stopped to listen—we could hear Ned's boots clumping across the wooden porch.

When Bertha told Eli about the quarrel he said, "If I had known lending Ned money would cause bad feelings, I would have pledged him to secrecy. I don't like it"—shaking his head. "We've never had bad feelings before in Stone Mill."

But—I wanted to say—what about the Claybornes?

Two weeks after Mr. Loeffler and Mr. Bradley had their set-to, a fire burned the Perry house to the ground. They blamed Granny Perry for it, forgetting the family owed their lives to her. Seems she had the toothache that night and couldn't sleep. Around eleven her jaw had swelled up the size of a goose egg, so she got out of bed and went into the kitchen to look for a piece of pork fat to "draw" the swelling and the pain. Needing a light, she unhooked one of those new kerosene lamps (advertised at Bradley's as "safety") from the wall and put a sulfur match to the wick.

"Thank goodness the Lord gave me the wit to jump aside," she told us on the church steps that Sunday, "because the damned ornery thing exploded and caught the kitchen curtains and a chair afire."

Forgetting her toothache, she hobbled into the bedroom faster than she had moved for forty years anc wakened the family. Everyone got out through a window, the other children upstairs shinnying down a rainpipe. As the family watched from the yard, the house went up like dry tinder, leaving nothing in the end but the chimney and little heaps of smoldering ashes.

* * *

The following Sunday, Preacher Davidson announced a house-raising for the Perrys. "If folk'll pitch in," he said, "we'll have the Perrys snug under a roof again."

Everybody went—all the men and boys to work, and the women to watch and later to cook a big supper. I had seen one house-raising in Hickory Cove, but the houses there had been log cabins, small ones, nothing like the house planned for the Perrys. There must have been fifty men helping, and they went about their business, each one knowing what to do. Some hauled and stacked lumber, some framed and measured; one bunch sawed and notched, and another hammered.

"Don't matter if it ain't matching," Colonel Perry said when they had come to laying the plank floor. Before we knew it the roof was up, with only the shingles left to set. Close to sundown it looked like the house would be ready, when it happened. I saw it, can still see it when I close my eyes.

Foxy Dawson (they called him Foxy because of his red hair) was splitting a log for the new fireplace, when the ax slipped. I saw the blood and heard Foxy scream. He had cut his right foot clean off at the ankle. Mrs. Preacher, the handiest woman in Stone Mill with a tonic or splint, tried to staunch the flow of blood, to no avail. The men carried Foxy to a wagon, but before they could bring him to the doctor in Novotno, he died.

The next morning the pall which had settled over the town could be felt at our breakfast table. For once, Eli didn't laugh or make jokes. Margaret sat staring straight ahead, not touching her food. She looked scared.

"I hope we've seen the last of misfortune," Eli said.

Bertha twisted in her chair. "They say bad luck comes in threes."

"Pray the Lord, you're right," Eli said. "There's been three already, and maybe that's the last of it."

But he was wrong. Four weeks later, almost to the day, Timothy Bradley, the youngest and brightest, the apple of Mrs. Bradley's eye, was thrown from a horse and killed. What made it worse was the way Mrs. Bradley took on. She wouldn't allow that Timothy had died. She refused to help with the laying-out, refused to go to the funeral. She wouldn't cook or clean or sew or tend store. She'd sit on a rocker on the store porch and rock and rock. "Waitin' for Timmy," she'd say.

The summer of '71 was a hot one—the hottest yet, old-timers said—and not a drop of rain since mid-June. All day, every day, the blinding sun beat down from a cloudless white sky. The creek shrank to a trickle, and the mill became silent. Cracks formed in the dry, parched earth. We had to drag cans from the pump in the early mornings to water Mrs. Covington's flower beds, but even so, they'd be wilted again by noon.

Judd was the first to sicken with fever. He had a splitting headache, he said, as he excused himself from supper one night. The next morning, he complained his face and limbs were on fire. Mrs. Covington fussed and carried on so, Judd said, "All right, send for the doctor. I'm going back to bed. I'm too sick to care."

The doctor fetched by Eli from Novotno was an elderly man named Caldwell with a snuff-stained white moustache and a hitch to his walk. He said there was nothing to do but keep cold compresses on Judd's forehead and the fever would go down of itself.

A few days later Mrs. Covington took to her bed with the same ailment. Only worse. She didn't know who or where she was, didn't recognize faces. Eli sat by her, day and night, fanning her cheeks. Bertha and I could hear her talking, her voice going up and down like notes on a scale. Delirious, Eli said, his face white and drawn. He would not let either of us go near her.

The white-moustached doctor came again and said "Cold compresses," just as he had done before. "Is it catching?" Bertha asked. "Indeedy, it is," he answered.

At least in that, he gave a sound answer. For a few days later, Eli fell ill. Poor Mimsie had to climb the stairs all day, carrying trays, changing beds. Bertha and I wanted to help, but Eli said we'd catch it for sure if we came near.

We caught it anyway. First Bertha, then me. I had never been sick a day in my life, never ailed, never suffered with bad teeth or a running ear. When the headache came suddenly, as I sat reading a book in the garden, I thought, It's the sun. Too much sun. So I moved back further into the shade, but the pain was worse, like an ax buried in my skull. Then I turned cold all over, and the boiled collards we'd had for dinner came up in a sour ball on my tongue. The sky was so blue, the trees so green, they hurt my eyes.

I got up, and my legs were like rubber. Judd was standing on the veranda steps. "What is it, Kate . . . ?" He had felt well enough that day to be out of bed for the first time. "What is it?" His voice clanged like brass pans in my ears. "What is it?"

I don't remember how I got to my room or to my bed. I saw Mimsie's face, her frightened eyes. "We'se all goin' to die," she whispered. "All."

A hot bandage lay across my forehead. A branding iron. I could feel the sweat running down my cheeks like tears. Then a cool hand touched my face and took the bandage, and the next moment there was a cold one in its place. I opened my eyes and saw Judd. His face seemed a long way off. "Get well, Kate, dear."

Did he say *dear?*

"Marry-me, marry-me," a bird sang in the tree. "Marry-me, marry-me"—an echo under the cool, sad oak. *Clayborne, why don't you come back?*

The shades were drawn, but I could feel the fire of the sun at the windows, angry, clawing at the glass, trying to get in. My arms felt swollen, then light, larger, then smaller.

"Am I going to die?" I asked. The dry dust rattled at the panes.

"No, child, you'll be all right." Eli? Judd?

They moved Bertha into my room. It was easier to care for us, and poor Mimsie had her hands full. I began to mend a little, enough to be conscious of things around me, but I was still weak, very weak.

"If you have powers," I said to Bertha, "why can't you cure us?"

Bertha turned her face to me—an old face, shrunken, the eyes deep in their sockets. "I have no power against this," she said. "Not against this."

"Do you mean the fever?"

"No. The fever is only part of it. There is another power here—in this town, in this house."

"But"—my voice caught with fear—"what? Whose power?"

"I don't know," she said, rolling her head to the side. "They won't tell me."

Chapter 9

OTHER families in Stone Mill had caught the fever, too. Clem Dawson, Eli's assistant at the sawmill, dropped by one evening to give us the latest news. His own wife and children, the Clarkes, the Bradleys, and even Preacher Davidson's family were among those who had taken to their beds. "A blight," Mr. Dawson called it. But Bertha said it was the plague. "The black plague, the same one that killed all those people in Europe," she claimed knowingly. "Carried by rats, ugly black rats."

By the third week in August, Judd and Eli had recovered enough to help Mimsie care for us. Though our fever had gone down somewhat, we three women were still ill. And Judd and Eli looked far from robust. For some reason Mimsie never caught the fever. She said it was because she recited a special prayer every night, but wouldn't repeat the prayer, though Bertha and I tried to coax it out of her.

Then, just as Margaret Covington got better, Judd suddenly had a relapse. From down the hall I could hear Mrs. Covington weeping. All that night she wept. I wanted to weep, too. It seemed that it would go on forever—the damp, warm cloths, the smell of the sickroom, half-eaten, liquidy custards, baffled sunlight at the blinds; and always the heat, the heat pressing down, choking, dry heat. And no rain. Not a sign of rain in the hard blue sky.

Preacher Davidson came to call. His booming voice reached all the way up the stairs to our bedroom. "He doesn't sound ailing to me," Bertha said. She got out of bed and, crouching down, put her ear to the floor. "He and Papa are in the parlor," she said. "He says they've been mighty sick at their house."

Margaret Covington opened the door. "What, pray God, are you doing, Bertha?"

86

Bertha got up quickly—so quickly, she staggered and almost fell.

"Please, darling," Mrs. Covington begged, "please, get back into bed. You'll have a relapse just as Judd did." She looked terrible—thin as a rail, the whites of her eyes yellowed. "I'm going downstairs," she said, tucking Bertha in. "Perhaps the preacher will come up to have a word with you."

As soon as Mrs. Covington left the room, Bertha said, "I want to hear what they're saying." But when she sat up she got so giddy she clutched the side of the bed and had to lie down again.

"Why don't you try astral travel?" I asked, forgetting that I had long ago decided that scene in the bedroom had been my imagination.

"I can't," Bertha said. "I have tried and tried. It doesn't work anymore. I've lost my power." She pulled the covers up over her head, pretending to be asleep.

Preacher Davidson stayed a long time downstairs, talking to Margaret and Eli. Once I heard Margaret crying. I wasn't curious, like Bertha, to know what they were saying. What did Preacher Davidson have to do with me? He'd had plenty of Sundays to pray to the Lord to make us well. And his own family sick, too. His "power," if he had any, was no better than Bertha's.

I must have fallen asleep, for when I opened my eyes, the room had grown dark. Downstairs the talk was still going on. My mouth tasted of brass, and reaching over to the side table for the pitcher, I found it was empty.

I rang the little bell, the silver one Mrs. Covington had left for us in case we needed Mimsie, the same one she used at the supper table.

I waited a few minutes, and when no one came, I rang the bell again.

Bertha groaned and rustled the bedclothes. "Are you awake?" I asked.

After a moment she said, "Yes."

"Preacher Davidson is still here," I said.

"I can hear him. I've been listening."

"What's he been going on and on about?"

"I can't tell you," she said.

"Why? Why can't you tell me?"

"Just that. I can't tell you. But it's worse than I thought."

"*What's* worse? The fever? Has everybody in Stone Mill got the fever?"

"No† everybody. Not the storekeeper Bradleys or the Loefflers or the Perrys or Foxy Dawson's family."

"They've already had their misfortune, I reckon."

"Yes. That's just it."

Preacher Davidson's voice got louder. He was standing in the hall. "See to hit, then. The whole blessed town'll be damned if y'don't." The front door opened and slammed shut.

A few minutes later I heard light footsteps coming up the stairway—Mrs. Covington's. (Funny how lying in bed day after day, you get to know people's footsteps—Mrs. Covington's, hesitant and light; Eli's, quick and tripping; Judd's, solid and heavy; Mimsie's, running.)

Mrs. Covington opened the door. "Are you awake, girls?" —coming in and putting a match to the candles on the bureau. "Hasn't Mimsie brought your supper?"

"No," Bertha said. "I don't care for any."

"That's no way to speak," Mrs. Covington said, her voice sounding more cheerful than I had heard it in a long time. "Preacher Davidson says we're all going to get well."

Bertha groaned.

"Now, Bertha. Take my word. A day or two and you'll be up." She sat down on the bed by my side. "The preacher has made me see things I couldn't see before."

I ¬anted to ask her what things. But suddenly she fell silent and sat staring into the candlelight with a faraway look in her eyes. The tree tapped at the window. Downstairs a door closed, dishes rattled. "Supper!" Mimsie called.

"Kate . . ." Mrs. Covington's hands fluttered over the covers, touched my arm, fluttered away. "Kate, dear, I owe you an apology. I'm sorry I was so upset with you about the Clayborne boy."

Upset? She hadn't been upset, she had fainted dead away.

"Of course he's welcome here," Mrs. Covington went on. "Any time you wish to invite him. The past is the past, as Preacher Davidson would say. All is forgiven."

What was forgiven? Who forgave who? And why? "You mean because one of the Claybornes took the Yankee side?" I asked. "But Mrs. Jennison said that a good many mountain folk fought with the Yankees."

"Not those in Stone Mill." Her hands, like thin, white

birds, flitted over the covers again. "But it makes no difference now, does it? Any Clayborne—whoever—is welcome
here." She lifted her chin. "Welcome!" she said loudly.

How strange, I thought. "He said he was just passing
through," I told her.

"Oh, he'll come back." She leaned forward and touched
my cheek with her finger, a cold finger. "I think he was
quite taken with you. He'll be back."

Unbelievably, it rained the next evening. Poured. It had
been so long I'd almost forgotten the sound—rain beating
with a hollow tattoo on the roof, rain drumming against the
windows, tinkling in the gutters, sweet, sweet music. I
wanted to run out in it, turning my face to the sky. Wet, cool
rain.

"Phew!" Bertha exclaimed, throwing off the covers.
"Ring that bell, will you, Kate? I do believe I'm hungry."

In a day or two we were out of bed and dressed, Judd
also, trailing down the stairs for our first meal in the dining
room in so long.

Margaret Covington said grace, a prayer that went on and
on, thanking the Lord and Preacher Davidson. When she
had finished, Eli rubbed his hands and looked around.
"Glad to see everyone right as rain again. Right as rain. Ha!
Ha!"

I felt so weak, so terribly weak, my heart thumping painfully in my chest. It had been too much, all those buttons
and the shoes and combing my hair with leaden arms, and
then coming down the stairs.

Judd said, "Will you be going to the mill today, Papa?"

Eli wrinkled his nose. "Lord knows what the help has
moved off the place. Ha! Ha! But you needn't go, Judd. You
look mighty peaked."

Mrs. Covington said, "Well, Judd did have the fever
twice."

Upstairs, getting out of bed, I had thought I was hungry.
But now the mess on my plate turned my stomach.

Mrs. Covington rang the little silver bell. "Coffee, Mimsie,
if you please."

Bertha got to her feet. "I'm going back to bed."

I meant to follow her, but I felt too weary to climb the
stairs, so I went into the parlor to rest for a few minutes.

The blind-drawn room looked strange and unfamiliar with

the furniture dust-sheeted and the carpets rolled up against one wall. Outside, the rain still beat against the windows. I thought of the garden and the wet leaves and the damp earth and how fresh it would smell, not closed in and musty like this room.

"Sitting alone in the dark?" It was Judd.

"For a spell," I answered.

"Mind if I join you?"

So formal. " 'Course not."

He'd taken off the dark coat he usually wore, and somehow his face looked younger above the white shirt.

"Ahhhhh," he sighed, sinking into a chair, stretching his long legs. He leaned his head against the cushions and closed his eyes. "A long siege," he murmured, "a long siege."

It wasn't necessary to make conversation. Over the years, I had learned that Judd preferred silence. Now he sat very still, almost as if he had fallen asleep. I leaned back, looking up at Francine's picture. She favored her mother—fair and blue-eyed—the only one of the children who did. The artist had painted her standing in front of a tree. Funny—I hadn't noticed it before, but it was the large oak in the garden. Francine had one hand clasping a rope. I squinted my eyes. It was the rope to the swing that Bertha said had hung under the oak tree.

I stared so long it seemed I could see the oak leaves tremble in the wind and a wisp of Francine's hair lift from her cheek. In another minute, I thought, I will get up and walk across the room right into the picture. And Francine will take my hand and say, "I've waited so long for you to come. Would you like to take a turn on the swing?" I would lift my skirts and sit down, and she would get behind and push. I would go up and up, higher and higher, right through the leaves to the blue, blue sky. A light-haired man would be waiting there, a man with deep-set eyes and a dimpled smile. *Will you marry me, Kate? Oh, yes, yes . . .*

"Kate . . . ? Kate?"

I opened my eyes. "I was dreaming," I said.

"Were you?" Judd had moved his chair close to mine. He was leaning over, looking down into my face. "I thought you said yes."

"Yes? Yes to what?"

"Why, that you will marry me. I . . . I thought. . . ."

"You want to marry me?" I asked in surprise.

"Would I have asked you if I didn't? Didn't you hear?"

"No . . . I . . ." I clasped my hands tightly, for they had begun to tremble. "I don't understand why you would want. . . ."

He took my hand and touched his cool lips to my fingers. "Because I care for you. Because I think you are the only girl I will ever care for. Because—but, Kate, you know I can't make pretty speeches." A slow smile, a painful one, crossed his face.

"But I didn't reckon . . . I hardly thought . . . you haven't said much to me . . ." I stumbled.

"I told you I can't make pretty speeches."

"You haven't even *looked*. . . ."

"But I have. From the very first. And from what I saw . . ."

"Too shy?"

"Yes." He kissed my hand again.

"I don't love you, Judd," I said, although I wasn't too sure anymore what love meant. I had thought I loved Tyson, but since then I had met Clayborne.

"Love comes with time," Judd was saying.

He was a nice-looking man and would make a fine companion—steady, decent, a good provider, a good husband. Did I want to live my life in "single blessedness," as Bertha had said? " 'Tain't natural," I could imagine Ma saying, "for a woman to be without her man."

Judd was saying, "I don't expect you to give me an answer right away. Just promise me you'll think it over." He touched his lips to my cheek. He smelled of shaving lotion, a pleasant smell, but it might have been Bertha kissing me—or Eli—for all the excitement I felt. It was awful to be that way, because Judd's proposal would have made any girl happy.

"Yes, I'll think it over," I said.

He looked at me, his face very close. Such sad eyes, I thought, such sad eyes.

"Kate, I know my shortcomings. I know you aren't in love with me. But I swear you will never regret saying yes. I swear. And, Kate . . ."

"Yes?" How serious he was!

"If you don't marry me, then you must leave Stone Mill."

"You've said that before, Judd. And I don't know why."

He put his finger to my lips. "No matter. Think about marrying me."

* * *

I said nothing to the rest of the family of Judd's proposal. Think about marrying me, he had said. But it was hard to think on anything. I was always so tired, so listless. Like a half-person I drifted from room to room, through the dim and silent shadows, moving in a heavy mist that never seemed to lift.

"Why don't you lie down for a bit?" Margaret Covington would ask, appearing suddenly on the stairs, in the parlor, her face white, her eyes staring in fright. They all watched me, fretting, I reckon, because I'd been poorly for so long.

"Who's going to church?" Eli asked one morning.

Was it Sunday already? "I don't think I'll go," I said. Even talking was like lifting weights.

"You needn't if you don't feel up to it," Eli said. "You rest. Rest, the preacher would say, is good for the soul." And he laughed.

They left an hour later—Eli, Margaret, and Bertha. Judd had ridden off on the mare hours earlier without saying a word. He hadn't said much of anything since his proposal. Maybe he had changed his mind, or maybe he was giving me time to think. It was hard to know with Judd.

When they had all gone and Mimsie had retired to her shack. I felt suddenly, wonderfully relieved. I was alone at last, and could do as I pleased. No one to say go to bed, get up, you'd best eat something, take care. No one to watch, to ask where are you going, did you sleep.

Wrapping a shawl around my shoulders, I went out the door and down the stairs into the garden, taking the stone path to the creek, walking slowly, tasting the fresh September morning. The first leaves were beginning to color, yellow and burnt orange and scarlet. Some of them had already fallen to the ground. I went past the oak tree, listening for the bird who sang that one sad note, but he must have gone away, for there was only the sound of the wind in the branches.

When I got to the creek I saw Clayborne sitting there on the bench. Somehow I wasn't surprised. He was wearing a funny blue cap, and as I came nearer, he turned his head.

"Kate . . . !" he said, his face lighting up. "Kate . . . !" I never thought anyone could put so much feeling into my name.

He came through the gate. "Oh, Clayborne, you've come

back!" I said, and suddenly nothing else seemed to matter except that he was there.

"Just like I said." He held my hands.

"I love you," I said, and wondered where the words had come from.

He drew me into his arms and kissed me, a far different kiss than Judd's had been. "I know you do," he smiled down at me.

"Judd asked me to marry him."

"Ah, Judd. The Rebel Judd. And what did you say?"

"I told him I didn't love him, but I promised to think it over. But I can't marry him. I can't marry anyone but you."

He drew me closer and kissed me again, and it was just like in my dream—going up and up in the swing, up so high I thought my heart would burst. When he let me go, he said, "I can't stay now, but I'll be back to make you my wife."

"But when . . . ?"

"Soon. Some evening when the sky is red. Tell them to get Preacher Davidson and have everything ready."

"But Judd—what shall I say to Judd?"

"That you're going to marry me. He'll understand."

"I don't know. . . ."

But he kissed me again and then, without saying good-bye, went out the rusty-hinged gate.

"Don't go!" I shouted after him, suddenly afraid. "Please don't go. . . ."

But he didn't turn, and I watched until he disappeared.

I must have stayed a long time in the garden, for when I got back to the house the others had come home. I removed my shawl and, carrying it over my arm, went quietly up the stairs. Margaret Covington's door was open, and I heard her talking to Judd.

"Do you want to throw this family to the wolves?" she asked. "You can't marry that girl."

"I can, and I will," he said. "I have no intention of letting *you* throw Kate—*that girl,* as you call her—to the wolves."

"I told you what will happen if you go ahead with this scheme," Margaret said.

"Nonsense. Superstitious nonsense."

"Do you call tragedy, disaster, illness—nonsense?"

"No, but I don't call it the will of the Lord or the will of whoever you care to name."

"Your blasphemy will be the ruin of Stone Mill."

"I don't believe it."

Margaret didn't answer.

I stole into my room and carefully shut the door. So Margaret Covington did not want me to marry Judd. Then why had Eli told me that she had set her heart on it? Had Margaret changed her mind? I might have known my marrying Judd wouldn't set too well with a person like Margaret Covington, always putting on airs about her kin in Charlottesville.

"Do you want to throw this family to the wolves?" she had said to Judd. That hurt. That really hurt, especially when I remembered all the sweet talk she had given me these past four years. "Please call me Mama," "Consider yourself part of the family." The Katie-dears, the honeys, the smiles, the goodnight kiss on the cheek. All false, all lies. She'd said she wanted to make a lady of me, and now she didn't care to have me as her daughter-in-law. Kate Rawlins, a Hickory Cove girl, too far beneath the Covingtons.

Or so I thought.

Chapter 10

THOUGH Margaret Covington liked to play the frail lady-fine, she could be hard as nails when she had a mind to, and I admired Judd for standing up to her. If it hadn't been for Clayborne, I think I'd have gone to Judd and said, "Yes, I'll be proud to be your wife." But I couldn't. I loved Clayborne; I was promised to him. And it worried me how to break the news to Judd, the quietest and gentlest of men.

All that night, however, I dreamt of Clayborne, and in the morning when Mimsie woke me, I could think of no one else.

"Ain't you fixin' to have breakfast, Miss Kate?" Mimsie complained. "It's awful late."

"No . . . no. . . ," I said, my mind still fastened to my dream. "I'm not hungry."

I remained abed all morning, thinking I must get up now, I must get dressed, but the old weakness, the drowsy, dazed feeling had come over me again.

At noon Bertha came upstairs to help me into my clothes. "They're waiting dinner," she said impatiently. "You can't be sick again."

I followed her down to the dining room, moving slowly. When I spoke I wondered that no one noticed the faraway sound of my voice. But if they did, they said nothing.

"Judd has gone away for a few weeks," Mrs. Covington said.

"Judd? Oh . . . !" I said, and saw that his place at the table was empty. "I can't marry him, you know."

"Yes, Kate, dear, I understand," Margaret Covington said.

"I thought you would." I had never really liked her, even when she had been kind.

"We all understand," Eli echoed, staring at his plate (no ha-ha's this morning?). I felt Bertha's good eye fastened on me. When I looked at her, she turned quickly away.

"I don't want to ruin the family," I said.

Margaret exclaimed, "Why, Kate! What a thing to say! You know we only wish for your happiness."

A lie.

"We must get Preacher Davidson," I said. "For I'm promised to Clayborne."

Nobody said a word. For a long time we sat there without speaking, a roomful of silent ghosts, the food on our plates uneaten. Then Eli cleared his throat. "Congratulations, Kate," he said in a false, hearty voice. "I'm sure you will make a good wife."

After dinner I wandered into the parlor. The blinds were still drawn, the carpets still rolled up like gray sausages. A dreary room. The whole house was dreary. I had never felt easy in it—too large, too many rooms, not snug like our cabin in Hickory Cove had been, though Mrs. Covington would have complained at the crowding and bad smell. But sometimes a person gets comfort from a crowd, especially when that person is lonely and afraid.

But I had Clayborne now, and in my dream he had told me that I mustn't be afraid or unhappy anymore.

The dream. Which was dream and which was waking? Was this, now—lifting one foot after another, climbing the stairs slowly—the dream? And the other—the oak tree and Clayborne saying last night, "Don't be unhappy"—real?

I found myself in the garden, although I couldn't remember going out the front door. It had rained the night before, and there were little puddles along the walk. I stepped carefully from stone to stone so as not to get my shoes muddy. The leaves dripped, drop by drop, and the yellow chrysanthemums bowed their wet heads, while, overhead, dirty gray clouds frowned down upon the trees.

The garden I had loved for its peace and quiet seemed suddenly different, heavy, full of danger. I felt as if someone were watching me from behind every tree trunk, peeking out at me from behind wind-tossed shrubs.

"Bertha . . . ?" I called, thinking she might be spying upon me. "Bertha . . . ?"

But no one answered. I passed the oak tree, and the leaves quivered, shaking wet drops on my hair and face. No shadows here, just the gray light. I stepped over a fallen branch, swarming with ants and grubs. Was the tree dying, shedding its arms one by one? This is a place for hants, I thought, shivering. Why don't I go back?

The path descended steeply until it reached the creek bank. I looked over at the bench, but no one sat there. "I'll be back," he had said, "one evening when the sky is red."

The creek below mumbled and complained, speaking, as it hurried along, in a strange, queer tongue. The rain must have been a heavy one, for the creek water had covered the footlog and washed out a part of the bank. I leaned over the sagging gate and saw a shoe. It was sticking out of the side of the washed-away bank—an old, rusty shoe with a large hole in the bottom. Thunder growled overhead as I opened the gate and stepped closer, my heart beating like a caged bird's.

Lord Almighty, the shoe had a foot in it!

I slid down, holding to a rock. Even now, so many years later, I can see that half-eaten face, the eyes gone and the skin rotted to a dead gray.

Tyson—Tyson dead and buried, and his soul haunting the creek and the garden.

The tired, half-awake feeling I had moved through for weeks suddenly dropped from me like a bucket shooting down a well. I didn't cry out, I didn't scream, though I wanted to do both. Instead, I leaned over sick, choking and gasping for breath. Then I staggered to my feet and, without looking back, stumbled up the path to the house.

No one was home except Mimsie. "You look lak a ghost," she said, her eyes going wide. "What ails you, Miss Kate?"

"I just saw"—looking about me wildly—"where is everybody?"

"Gone out," she said.

Forked lightning glimmered in the darkened hall. The mirror under the hat rack gave back my face, white as milled flour. I stood there and stared at the thumbprint circles under the scared eyes. Tyson had come back to fetch me as he'd promised. And while I'd sat in the green-striped chair someone had met him in the garden and killed him.

"Yo' shore y'aint seen a ghost?" Mimsie asked.

"I've seen Tyson," I said.

Thunder bounced and echoed through the house. "Tyson? I don't know no Tyson," she said, her eyes gleaming in the dimness.

"He was my first love," I said.

Oh, Lord in Heaven, it hurt so to think he'd wanted me after all and I had thought he'd deserted me. Jilted, Margaret Covington had said.

"Where is he?" Mimsie asked.

"He's dead."

And why? Who would want to kill him? Once, long ago, Ma's brother, Isham, was killed, shot through the chest by a man who ran a still in Angel's Hollow and mistook Uncle Isham for a revenuer in the dark. But how could anyone mistake Tyson? I had told the Covingtons I was waiting on him. And no one in town, far as I knew, had quarreled with Tyson. Strangers came and went in Stone Mill, and unless they made themselves unwelcome, no one bothered.

"Daid? Where daid?" Mimsie's eyes got bigger.

And I never heard him cry out that night, never heard a sound.

"You seen him daid . . . ?"

"In the garden," I said, "down by the creek." The hot tears brimmed, burning my eyes, spilling over, running salty and bitter down my cheeks.

A few minutes before Bertha and Mrs. Covington came home, the storm broke. I was sitting in the parlor, dry-eyed now, watching the wind in the trees.

"We looked for you," Mrs. Covington said. "We thought you might want to go down to Bradley's."

"I was in the garden," I said. "Tyson is there."

"Who . . . ?" Mrs. Covington asked, working the gloves from her fingers. Mrs. Covington always wore gloves when she went out, no matter if it was just to the front gate. "A real lady, once she steps outside her door, is as good as undressed without gloves," she would say.

"Tyson McAlpin, the boy from Hickory Cove."

Mrs. Covington's face got very white. "My dear Kate—" catching her breath.

Bertha said, "What's he doing here? Changed his mind after all these years?"

"He's dead," I said, and I wondered how calm my voice was, not breaking, not tearful. "And someone buried him down by the creek."

Mrs. Covington put her hand to her mouth. "You must be mistaken."

I shook my head slowly. "No, he's there. I saw him less than an hour ago."

Bertha said, "Show me. Come along and show me." But it was pouring rain now, and we couldn't go out.

It was still raining when Eli came home that evening. Bertha told him about my finding Tyson, and it seemed, as she talked, his face got white, too.

"Are you sure, my dear Kate," he said, "you haven't imagined this . . . this grave?" And he and Mrs. Covington gave each other a funny look.

"He's buried on the other side of the gate, where the bank has washed out."

"Buried?" Eli raised his brows. They had turned gray this last year like his hair. "I see. . . ." He took out his watch and studied it. "It's late now and still raining. First thing in the morning we'll go down and have a look."

I didn't sleep much that night. As soon as white streaked the morning sky, I got out of bed and dressed. Once downstairs, I sat on the bench in the hall, waiting for Eli.

"Let's have breakfast first, shall we?" he said, rubbing his hands together.

"I'll wait here," I said. "I'm not hungry."

"Now, Katie, dear, you *must* eat to get your strength back. You want to look nice for your intended, don't you?"

My intended! Clayborne! I hadn't wanted to think of him. I felt so bad about Tyson—almost as if Tyson had been my husband and I had flirted with another man.

"I don't think I can eat anything, thank you kindly."

He took a long time at breakfast, or so it seemed to me, sitting there in the hall, listening to the tall clock, the dishes rattle, to Bertha's voice, to Mimsie's giggle. A long time. But finally Eli came through the dining-room door. "Would you rather wait until noon?" he asked nervously. "It's still wet out, and the mud. . ."

"I don't mind the mud," I said, rising, "and the sun's out."

"All right, then."

And Bertha said, "I'm coming, too."

I led the way. Water sparkled on the hydrangeas and the rhododendron bushes, crystal drops shining in the sun. But under the trees it was dark and dank. No one spoke as we went down the path, brushing aside branches and wild, creeping vines. When I got to the gate I hesitated.

"Where?" said Bertha, peering over my shoulder.

"It was right about here." But I could not see the washed-out place. Along the side of the creek the bank looked as it always did.

"Wait," I said, "there's the rock I held onto." I slid down, not caring about getting my dress dirty. But there was no hole, no shoe, no body. Only brambles and wild cress.

"Katie, dear," Eli said, standing on the edge of the bank, looking down at me. "Perhaps you imagined. . . ."

"No. No, I saw him as plain as your hand. He's here, I tell you." And I began to dig in the mud with my fingers.

"Kate—don't, my dear," he said distressed. "I'll have Bertha run up for a spade."

While Bertha was gone, Eli talked to me as if I were a child. "You've had a bad fever, my dear, the kind that takes a long time to heal, the kind that sometimes makes one see odd things."

"You mean I've gone off my head?"

"No Kate, dear, you've just let your fancy roam."

"I haven't," I said. "Tyson's buried here."

When Bertha came back with the spade, Eli gave her his coat and rolled up his sleeves. He dug up the cress and the vines. He dug here and he dug there, the red-yellow clay slipping and sliding with a splash into the creek. But there was no body, no shoe with a hole in the sole, no staring, eyeless head, no Tyson. Nothing.

I wept as Eli helped me up the bank and the stone path to the house. They put me to bed and, drawing the curtains, left me alone.

Maybe I had gone crazy; maybe everything was a dream, would be a dream always until the end of my days. And in the years to come, people would say, "There's Katie Rawlins, snag-toothed old witch, crazy woman."

But I had seen Tyson. *I had seen him.* And if I was crazy, so was everyone else. He had been murdered and buried on the creek bank, and something had happened to his body between the time I had found it and the time I had taken Eli and Bertha back to the spot. I didn't know how Tyson's remains had disappeared, didn't know why anyone would have wanted to kill him. Poor, darling Tyson.

The Covingtons, of course, thought I had fancied the whole thing. It made me wonder if they had believed me years earlier when I had told them that Tyson wanted to marry me, to take me back to Hickory Cove. He hadn't come up to the house that day. They had never laid eyes on him. It would be easy for Bertha to say, "She made him up."

But *someone* in Stone Mill must have seen and talked to Tyson. Else how would he have found me? Someone. The storekeeper, or the Rylands at the smithy, or maybe even Preacher Davidson, whom Tyson had gone to fetch.

"Good morning, Katie," Eli said in his hearty voice. "You look as pert as a cricket. Ha! Ha!"

"I feel fine," I said, smiling, helping myself to biscuits and eggs, forcing myself to eat. "I think I'll pay Preacher Davidson a call."

"Why, Kate, dear," Margaret Covington said, "are you up to going out?"

"I'm all right," I said. "And I want to have a little talk with the preacher."

"About what?"

"Why—about marrying Clayborne."

Mrs. Covington looked at Eli, that same funny look going between them. "He knows about the wedding," she said. "The date has been fixed. Two weeks from Saturday."

"But how . . . why hasn't anyone told me?"

"I was going to broach the subject this morning," she said. "You asked us to speak to the preacher, and we did."

"But Clayborne . . ."

"Knows about it, too."

I thought it all very strange. Still, if that's the way they wanted it done, I had no argument. "May I go and speak to the preacher, anyway?" There was Tyson. I had to know about Tyson.

Again that look between Eli and Margaret. Eli cleared his throat. "Of course, dear Katie, if that's your wish."

Preacher Davidson lived on the far side of town on a small, three-acre plot which he farmed in order to supplement what he got from the Sunday collection plate. His wife helped to stock the family larder through her services as midwife. Folks hardly ever paid her in cash, but were generous with chickens and hams, not to say eggs and butter and produce in season. They ate well, the Davidsons, a whole lot better than folks in Hickory Cove, even though the preacher claimed he had taken a vow of poverty.

When I arrived, Mrs. Preacher invited me into the house. The preacher was out in the barn talking to Ned Loeffler about a milk cow, and wouldn't I like a cup of coffee while I waited?

We sat in the kitchen talking about the fever and how glad we all were it was over. She complimented me on the coming wedding. I said yes, wasn't it nice, never stopping to think that I knew so little of Clayborne, never stopping to question why he never came to the house or why no one seemed curious as to why our courtship had been so short.

When the preacher came in, after scraping his boots on the porch stair, he looked somewhat surprised to see me, but greeted me pleasantly enough. "Glad to see you this fine day." Away from the pulpit and in his own home, he did not look quite so stern. "Yore to be a new bride," he said. And turning to his wife, "Min, I believe I'll have some of that coffee, too."

Coffee was poured, and the preacher busied himself with cream and sugar. "Y'needn't fret about a thing," he said. "We'll take care of everythin', Kate."

"Thank you." There was a long silence, and I said, "Preacher—I thought you might be able to help me on another matter."

"What's that, girl?" His eyes were like sharp pieces of blue glass.

"Do you mind when I first came to Stone Mill? About four years ago?"

"I do mind, yes."

"A boy—Tyson McAlpin was his name—came down from Hickory Cove to fetch me back, and he went out looking for you so you could marry us beforehand."

"Who?"

"Tyson McAlpin. He was a little taller than me." I showed him with my hand. "Sort of reddish hair, freckles . . ."

"Tyson McAlpin. No, never seen him."

I turned to Mrs. Preacher.

"Now, let me think," she said, puckering her brow. "Four years . . . hmmmm. That be the year our Lonnie war born. Carroty hair, y'say? Freckles. Now, I do believe some'un like that come to the door. . . ."

The preacher rumbled, "Y'never seen him." He glared at

her. "I swear you'd say yes to anythin' that's asked, without a thought."

Her cheeks flushed up, and she turned away. She *had* seen Tyson, I knew it in my very bones. And I had a feeling the preacher had, too. But why should he lie? And make his wife lie? A preacher.

"It means a whole lot to me," I said. "You see, I . . . I found him dead."

The preacher looked surprised. "What? What's 'at?"

I told him about the grave. "Somebody must have moved the body, though, because when I brought Eli to it, Tyson was gone."

I saw the look of doubt in his eyes as I talked, and finally in Mrs. Preacher's. I couldn't blame them. It did sound strange, the story of a disappearing corpse told by a girl who'd barely recovered from a fever. "Maybe someone else in town remembers seeing him," I said hopefully. "Tyson said he'd gone all around asking people before he'd found me."

"Mebbe," Preacher Davidson said as he went toward the door. "But why don't y'sit a spell with the missus? Have y'another cuppa coffee and some of her good apple pie."

"Thank you, but . . ."

"No call to rush off," Mrs. Preacher said. "Y'ain't mad, are you?"

"I'm not mad," I said, resigning myself to the pie.

While Mrs. Preacher cut the pie, I looked out the window and noticed the preacher speaking to one of his sons, a boy of twelve or so, mounted on a mule. A moment later the boy urged the mule through the yard gate and, giving it a whack with his hand, galloped off. "Going somewhere in a hurry," I said to Mrs. Preacher, nodding my head toward the window.

"Oh, him?" she said. "Always in a hurry."

She brought the pie and a fork to the table. "Did you know the Claybornes?" I asked.

"Yes," she said shortly.

"You don't like the family?"

"I didn't say that. How's the pie?"

"Very good," I said. "And the coffee, too."

A half hour later, after I'd thanked Mrs. Preacher and said good-bye, I made the rounds of all the places where I thought Tyson might have stopped—Bradley's store, the

Ryland smithy, the Loeffler farm. Nobody—not one single person—had seen him.

It had been four years, easy to forget. But somehow I felt they were all lying, just as the preacher and Mrs. Preacher had.

Chapter 11

W HEN I got back to the house, I went upstairs to my room, my mind buzzing with a dozen worrying questions that had no answers. Why had Tyson been killed, and why had his body been moved? Why did Preacher Davidson lie to me? And what about Francine? And people looking at me, then quickly away? And Astoria saying, "This house is cursed"?

I did not know. I couldn't even begin to guess. There was something strange about Stone Mill, had been all along, but now, for the first time, it truly scared me. I wished that I could speak of my fear to Clayborne—or to Judd.

One morning I woke before dawn with the strong feeling that something terrible was going to happen to me unless I left the Covington house. But how foolish, I thought, what could happen? Yet as I lay there, the dark shadows seemed to whisper together in the corners, "Kate . . . Kate Rawlinsssss. Don't—ssssstay." Finally, unable to stand it, I got out of bed and began to dress. Maybe, I told myself, Clayborne will come back today.

I put on a shift, a petticoat, a plain muslin dress, and shoes, and, wrapping a warm shawl around my shoulders, crept down the stairs. I slipped through the front door and out into the dew-wet garden. Down the stone path I went, passing the mist-shrouded oak, where little heaps of dead brown leaves lay among the gnarled roots. I waited at the bench, hoping to see Clayborne. He would take me away. I did not care about having the preacher. We could be married somewhere else—somewhere, anywhere but in Stone Mill. ("Go away," Judd had said, "for your own sake, get out of Stone Mill.")

The bench was wet with dew, and using my shawl I wiped some of it away. I sat down on the edge, gripping the damp

105

wood with my hands, listening for the sound of a twig breaking, a vine rustling, yearning for the sound of a step on the path. The Covingtons had not wanted me to leave with Tyson four years ago. Would they be angry if I went with Clayborne now?

A finger of sunshine came down through the trees, melting a patch of fog. Up at the house Mimsie would be rattling her pots and pans in the kitchen. Presently they would descend the stairs one by one to the dining room. "Where is Kate?" Mrs. Covington would ask.

I looked across the creek, willing Clayborne to appear among the trees. "We'll go away, Kate," he would say. "Don't be afraid." But he did not come, and my fear grew and grew.

Finally I got to my feet. I slid down the muddy bank, not looking at the place where I had found Tyson. I crossed on the footlog and turned right, following the trail upstream. If Clayborne loved me, he would find me.

I was going home, back to Hickory Cove.

For all my new ways, my fine speech, my pretty clothes, the Cove had never left my heart. I realized that I wasn't meant to live anywhere else. It seemed like these past four years were a pretend time, a dream. I never belonged in Stone Mill. Tyson's death had shown me that. Ma might not care, and Clem might be mean, but I had other kin in Hickory Cove, cousins and aunts and uncles—and the McAlpins. Not one of them would look down on me; not one would call me "that girl" or "ignorant."

Home. Going back was as simple as leaving it had been—just follow the creek.

A half hour after I'd started, my feet began to burn and blister. I slipped out of my shoes, tied the laces together, and, carrying them in one hand, walked on. But my feet had become tender, and the stones and twigs cut cruelly. Let them, I thought. After a bit they'll harden up. As I walked I breathed deeply of the air, smelling the damp leaves and black loam. Autumn had come to the woods, something I'd scarcely noticed while at the Covingtons'. I saw where the witch hazel was blooming golden, and how the leaves were changing on the maples and sourwood, the red-gold intermingled with the pretty yellows. Ah—it was good to be free again.

It was when I stopped to pick a clump of branch lettuce

that I first heard the dogs. Someone hunting, I thought, and paid them no mind. But as the sound of barking grew closer, I began to wonder. Would the Covingtons set dogs on me?

Hitching up my skirt, I slid down the bank and took to the water's edge, hurrying, splashing along, my feet slipping on the muddy bottom. A few moments later the dogs gave tongue, and my heart jumped to my mouth as the baying echoed through the trees. *Yes,* dear Lord, yes, the Covingtons were using dogs to smell me out.

I tried walking faster, but the water was getting deeper, the current strong, which meant the falls were close at hand. I looked around at the alders hanging over the stream and, finding a likely branch, pulled myself up into a tree, climbing as high as I could.

Sitting in the fork of the tree, frozen, so still I could count my heartbeats. Lord, I was afraid! And the dogs kept getting nearer and nearer, baying in that blood-chilling way they do when they are onto something. Now I could hear them crashing through the brush.

"Halloooo! Hallooooo! This way!" a man called.

I clung to the tree, my eyes staring in fright. Suddenly, a quarter mile downstream, I saw the pack break through.

"Hallooo . . . !"

The dogs loped along the bank in my direction, then stopped short a few yards from where I hid. They began to mill about at the water's edge, three spotted, one yellow, wagging their tails, trotting down to the water and up again, and back, whimpering. I held my breath, but my heart went on beating louder and louder.

"She cain't be too fur. . . ."

It was the preacher. He appeared in a moment, coming through a stand of beeches. He was followed by Eli and Ned Loeffler. The three of them stood watching the dogs.

"I hate this," Eli said, taking off his hat and mopping his brow. His hair stood up in untidy peaks, and his neat trousers were splattered with mud.

"If y'd kept an eye on her, y'wouldn't have to git yoreself dirty," the preacher said in a disgusted voice.

Ned said, "Well, they've lost the scent. Now what?"

Preacher Davidson looked around, and I shrank behind the tree trunk, making myself as small as I could. For one terrible moment I thought those eagle-blue eyes were staring up at me, but then he turned away. Stooping to scratch one of the dogs behind the ear, he said, "Never seen the critter could fool this one, eh, Bell? We'll catch her smell agin, further up the crik."

Ned Loeffler leashed the dogs, and the men started up toward the falls, disappearing in among the trees.

I waited a long time, wanting to make sure they were out of earshot. Then I shinnied down to the lowest branch and swung into the water. I started to walk back toward Stone Mill, thinking to find another tree and maybe baffle the dogs even more. I was sure they had all gone on to Hickory Cove to look for me. Well, they wouldn't find out much. Even if I had managed to reach the Cove before the hunting party, the people there would say nothing. Hickory Cove folk did not take kindly to strangers asking questions.

But I needn't have worried my head about where the men had gone or what they would find, for I had taken only a few steps when the preacher suddenly stood up from behind a spicebush.

"Ha! Reckoned you war hidin' up in that thar tree."

I ducked around him and began to run, splashing, slipping, stumbling in the fast-moving current.

"Halloooo . . . !"

The dogs suddenly broke through ahead of me, jumping into the creek, baying with evil joy as they leaped and ran toward me.

I whirled, tripping over a stone. The preacher had my arm before I could catch my breath.

"Now, y'll get hurt if y'keep stubborn," he said. "Be good. We don't aim t'harm you."

Eli and Ned were standing on the bank. "Eli," I begged, gasping, holding the stitch in my side, "I want . . . I want to go back . . . back to Hickory Cove."

Eli took off his hat. "My dear Kate," he said with that dear-Kate smile on his face, "the fever has left you unreasonable. Why should you want to return to a place, to kin that don't care?"

"I want to go home."

"You *are* going home. Margaret is so worried about you."

"I want to go home."

The preacher's hold tightened. "The good Lord says we must mind our elders."

"No," I said. "Not when they hunt you with dogs like an animal."

"None of your sass"—the preacher's blue eyes flashed.

"You can't make me go back. I'm not a slave," I said, thinking suddenly of Astoria. But *she* got away, didn't she?

The preacher clucked his tongue. "Y'do go on." And he nudged me up the bank, his fingers still gripping painfully around my arm.

Ned leashed the dogs again, and we started back to Stone Mill, the preacher holding my arm, Eli puffing behind us.

"Now—*puff*—why should you do—*puff*—a fool thing—*puff* —like running away?"

I kept silent. I had already spoken too much.

Margaret was waiting on the veranda. "My dear child, my dear child"—wringing her hands—"whatever possessed you?"

Not a muscle moved on my face as she put her arms about me and kissed my cheek. She might as well have kissed a stone.

They led me into the dining room and set something to eat in front of me, but I refused to touch it. Then they took me upstairs to my room and locked me in. A few minutes later I could hear them talking in the parlor below. I kneeled down as Bertha had once done and put my ear to the floor.

"Hit's only six days," the preacher was saying, "and then hit'll all be done with."

A coldness came over me. Six days until what? Six days— why, that would be Saturday, my wedding day. Clayborne . . . ! But what had happened to him? Had he left Stone Mill, gone away, forgotten me? Or had he been murdered too?

"The Lord works in mysterious ways," the preacher continued in his pulpit voice. "Yes, the Lord shore does . . . he's testin' us. . . ."

Margaret murmured, "Preacher . . . your voice . . . little pitchers . . ."

The preacher lowered his voice, so I could only catch a word here and there. Something about forgiveness, atonement. Once I thought I heard Clayborne's name. A chair scraped, and then the preacher was in the hall, saying, "S'all right if you want to send Bertha away. Ain't no call for her to be here when th'time comes."

What time? Dear Lord, what were they going to do with me?

That night when I was sure everyone had gone to bed, I opened the window and climbed down the tree. It was a dark night. Lightning flickered in the black sky, and a storm was coming out of the east. But it didn't matter. I'd rather be out in the thunder and rain, I thought, out in the dark with the wind moaning through the trees like hants, than to be a prisoner in the Covington house.

I went around the side of the house, and as I passed the veranda, the lightning flashed—a dazzling, white moment—and I saw a man sitting in the shadows.

"Kate," he said.

It was Clayborne! I ran up the steps and into his arms. "Oh, Clayborne! Oh, Clayborne, I never . . . I never reckoned on seeing you again. I was running away. . . ."

"Running away?" His face was a pale shadow in the darkness. "Running away without me?"

"You didn't come. I waited. And I had to get away. Something—in six days—something awful is going to happen."

"And where were you going?" he asked, not heeding, a little angry.

"Back to Hickory Cove. I thought. . . ."

"I see. So you broke your promise."

"No—oh, no! But I was frightened."

"You broke your promise," he repeated. "And when someone breaks a promise, it's the same as betrayal."

"No, no! I do love you, Clayborne," I was crying. "Please take me away. Please."

"I told you I would after we married."

"Now," I begged. "Take me away now."

Suddenly a light went on in the house and the door opened. "I thought I heard voices." Eli stood there in his dressing gown. "How did you get out?" His face was white, sick-looking. "Come upstairs at once."

I turned to Clayborne.

"Do as he says, Kate. I'll be back."

"No . . ."

But he disappeared into the night.

Eli had my arm. "Please don't argue, Kate. I'm not well, and I can't bear arguing."

Margaret Covington stood at the head of the stairs. "Take her up to the attic," she said.

"The attic?" Eli was sweating. The yellow lamp on the hall table shone on his damp forehead. "But that would be . . ."

"The attic," Margaret Covington said. "Do you want her to get out again?"

She spoke as though I wasn't there.

I had never been to the attic. Even if I had been curious (which I was not), I couldn't have gone, since the attic was always kept locked. It was a fairly large room, bare except for a few chairs and a pallet on the floor—a cold room, a dark room, a room that for some reason raised goosebumps along my arms.

"I don't want to stay here," I said.

But Eli closed and locked the door.

I lay down on the pallet and, turning my face into the dirty mattress, cried myself to sleep.

In the morning Mimsie brought me a chamber pot. " 'Mornin', Miss Kate." She didn't look at me.

I said, "Set it down near the window," pointing to the high, round window—a small one, not big enough for a body to squeeze through.

Mimsie trotted dutifully across the bare floor with the chamber pot, and quick as a wink I went out the door.

But Eli was waiting for me at the foot of the attic stairs.

Neither of us spoke. I turned and went back up the steep, narrow staircase. Mimsie, pressed against the door, let me pass, her face a blue-gray. No sense in asking *her* for help. Poor Mimsie.

An hour later when she brought my breakfast, I slipped out the door again, and again Eli was waiting for me. It was a weekday, but I must have been more important than his work at the mill.

After that first day, Mimsie didn't come anymore. Maybe she had run away, like Astoria, or maybe she was just too frightened.

Different people came to empty the chamber pot, to bring food. One morning it was Mrs. Covington; another, Mrs. Preacher; and on still another, Mrs. Loeffler. None of them spoke except the preacher, who came twice, advising me to be a good little lady, telling me to pray.

I didn't ask questions. What was the use? Their answers would be lies, all lies, and more lies.

I had lots of time to think. Most of it I spent trying to figure a way out of the attic. Hour after hour into the darkness of night, my mind would go around and around like a squirrel in a cage. The window? I piled several of the broken chairs one upon the other and climbed up. Too small, just as I had thought earlier. The door? Eli or someone else was always watching. I did manage to prize a board loose from the floor. I had worked one whole day on it, breaking my fingernails, bruising my hands, and when I got it up, cried with joy. But while I was picking away at the second board, Preacher Davidson came in. He called down the wrath of the Lord and ordered Eli to tie me up.

After that, I lost hope. I was convinced now they had killed Tyson—and Clayborne. Why they had, why they were holding me prisoner, I did not know. I was scared, deathly afraid. When Mrs. Covington brought my food and untied my hands, I couldn't eat. I turned my face to the wall and couldn't eat. "Only two more days," I heard her say to someone as she carried the tray through the door.

That night I had terrible dreams, dreams of crashing through the creek with a pack of foaming hounds at my heels. One leaped at me, catching hold of my arm, worrying it, shaking it.

I opened my eyes. "Kate . . . Kate"—a hoarse whisper.

"Who . . . ?"

"It's me, Judd. Shhh!"

It was dark, but I could see a white bandage around his head. "Are you hurt?" I asked.

"Shhh!" He cut the ropes around my ankles, around my wrists. "Can you walk?" he whispered.

"Yes . . . but . . ."

"Don't talk."

He took my hand and led me through the door. A stair squeaked as we started down, and Judd froze, waited a few moments, and then went on. At the bottom, asleep in a chair, I recognized Ned Loeffler. A gun lay across his lap. My heart was hammering so loudly I was sure it would wake him. But he slept on, his chin sunk on his chest. We crept past him, past the Covingtons' room, and down the long stairway to the hall. It was late—the tall clock said two. The parlor doors were open, and a strip of moonlight lay across the bare floor. The carpets hadn't been put down yet.

Suddenly Judd squeezed my hand. Footsteps on the veranda and the next moment a pounding on the door and the preacher calling, "Open up! Open up, Eli!"

"The damn fool's found me gone," Judd muttered. He

whisked me through the kitchen and out the back door before the lights went on. Judd's gray mare was tied to a gate. He swung into the saddle. "Here we go!"—leaning down, taking my hand, pulling me up behind him.

We rode at a gallop through the dark streets, past the silent, sleeping houses, while the moon overhead followed along the treetops.

"Judd . . . ?" I said in his ear. "How did you know I was in the attic?"

"I knew," he said, turning his face to me, away from the wind. "And I would have come sooner, but they were keeping me prisoner, too."

"Why . . . oh, why?"

But he didn't answer.

When we reached the edge of town, a man mounted on a dark horse was waiting for us under a tree. "You must go with Erle," Judd said. "He will take you to a family I trust in Front Royal."

"But aren't you coming along?"

"I can't," he said. "It will mean never returning to Stone Mill again."

"But . . . you said. . . ."

He touched my cheek with his finger. "That I wanted to marry you? I did. I do. But we are a blighted people in Stone Mill—the Covingtons most of all. I can't have you, Kate, darling, they would never allow it. And I can't leave here, because—well, because my father, my family would suffer more than they already have."

"What is it?" I asked. "What is happening here?"

"It would serve no purpose to tell you." He dismounted and brought me down, holding me for a long moment in his arms. "God bless you, Kate, darling," he said, this kind man, Judd, who would never go inside Preacher Davidson's church. "God bless and keep you."

I never saw him again. I never saw the Covingtons or Clayborne or anyone from Stone Mill, never heard from a soul. It was as though that part of my life had been lived by someone else.

Now I am old. I have five children—three boys and two girls—and ten grandchildren. The grandchildren like to hear me tell mountain stories, tales of bears and berrypicking and hants, stories of my days spent in Hickory Cove. I did not speak of Stone Mill but once. I let drop that I had lived there, and they pressed me, wanting to know all about it. Since I couldn't bring myself to tell them the truth, I made up a pretty tale, one that I almost came to believe myself—almost. For as time goes on, memories of Stone Mill keep crowding back, and the faces of the Covingtons—of Clayborne—have taken to haunting my dreams again.

Part III

SARAH COVINGTON
(1906)

Chapter 12

MY mother and father died when I was four. "They've gone away on a long journey," Grandfather Judd explained at the time. But as the months and years went by and they still hadn't returned, Grandfather, pressed, finally admitted that they had succumbed to mountain fever. I thought it very strange. I could not recall their illness—I could not recall either of them being sick for a single day. No hushed voices, no drawn blinds, no invalid trays tiptoed upstairs. Mama and Papa were there one evening and gone the next.

"Children have poor memories," Grandfather said. "They tend to forget unpleasantness."

"That's not true," I remember countering. I hadn't forgotten New Bedford, and Lord knows it was unpleasant enough.

"New Bedford," he said. "That was a mistake."

My grandfather brought me to that Northern town shortly after my parents had gone on their "journey." A cousin of my mother's lived there, and Grandfather, feeling unable to cope with a small girl, thought I would do better with the Needhams. Of course there was my great-aunt Bertha at home, but she had never married, and grandfather, I suppose, felt that a spinster would not do as a substitute mother.

Molly Needham, on the other hand, had not only married, but by the time I arrived in New Bedford was well into motherhood, having given birth to five children (five hateful monsters) in quick succession some years earlier. James Needham, their father, I rarely saw, but Molly was ever present, a Puritan disciplinarian who had the ability to inspire sheer terror. Her twin gods were thrift and neatness. She had a square jaw and smelled of lye soap, a harsh contrast to the memory of my own mother's soft cheek and trailing scent of mimosa. I could not understand how two such dissimilar people as Mother and Cousin Molly could belong to the same family. Actually, the Needhams were very distant kin, related through some tenuous, intertwined bloodline to my mother's family, the Dawsons of Stone Mill. But even this vague relationship was a puzzle. The Needhams, to me, may as well have been creatures from the moon, and I daresay they thought the same of me. My Virginia mountain accent brought ridicule and mockery, while my grandfather's service in Lee's army evoked scorn.

Yet in all fairness I must say I was treated no differently from Cousin Molly's own children. Our routine never varied. The five little Needhams and I, regimented into a corps of obedience, were out of bed each day in the gray light of morning, washing in cold water, making our beds (even the toddlers must learn, and woe if our corners were not turned precisely!), then down to prayers in the dark-paneled dining room, kneeling on the splintered, bare boards. Breakfast—porridge, flabby, burned bread called toast, and watery milk. Prisoner's fare, nothing like the hot biscuits and honey and fried ham old Mimsie served. Playtime (games of learning without merriment), study time, prayers, dinner, naps, prayers, supper—each activity pigeon-holed to the minute.

Above all, I remember the cold, the damp chill wind blowing in from the sea, the gray houses huddling together, the unheated rooms, the meager fires in the grates.

In the spring when Grandfather came on a visit, I cried bitterly, begging him to take me home. "There's nothing at home," Grandfather said, "except two old people in a big, empty house. Give it a chance, Sarah. You'll soon get to like it here."

I couldn't tell him that I bore black-and-blue marks from Cousin Arthur's pinching, that hunger gnawed at me constantly, that the gown I wore was not mine, but hastily borrowed from Alice for the occasion (my clothes were too patched and mended to be presentable), because Molly Needham stood by all during Grandfather's visit.

The next time he came, however, I managed to get him alone in the back garden. There, between the dog kennel and the washhouse, I poured out my unhappiness—a long, tearful tale of injustice, of humiliation, of misery. Grandfather said nothing to me—and what he told the Needhams I never knew —but by noon of the next day he and I were on the train, rattling through the countryside on our way south and home.

I was seven, going on eight, when I returned to Stone Mill. Somehow the home I had longed for so painfully did not seem quite the same as I remembered it. Perhaps Grandfather was right. Memories sometimes do screen out the unpleasant. I couldn't recall the house being so somber—large, yes; many-roomed, yes; but not dim, not always in shadow. Perhaps it was the huge tree outside my window, its star-leaved branches filtering out the sunlight, or perhaps it was Mimsie's habit of keeping the blinds drawn. Sun never touched the front hall, where a tall, ivory-faced clock ticked the hours away, nor the staircase disappearing up and up into shadow. The dining room—the brightest room—admitted light only on early summer mornings. So perpetual hung the twilight within that stepping outside into the sharp light of day was often a shock.

I was not encouraged to play out-of-doors. The garden, untended, grew wild. "Snakes," Aunt Bertha would say. "Snakes all over the place." Aunt Bertha was full of alarms. She spoke of haunts, of little people, of fire-eating demons and of elves, most of them malicious, waiting to pounce upon the unwary. Her bedtime stories wouldn't have been acceptable even before the turn of the century, for they were enough to curdle anyone's blood, especially mine, timid and fearful child that I was.

One of Aunt Bertha's favorites was the story of the maiden who lived in the waterfall a mile up the creek. She had long white hair and lured people, calling them to come near, and when they approached, pulled them under the water, holding their heads until they drowned.

"Why is she angry?" I would ask Aunt Bertha.

"Because she's hateful. Beautiful and hateful."

Bertha told me of the Devil and the Devil's wife, the nine pretty girls and four little demons who danced to fiddle music at Skilly Pendergast's house. Aunt Bertha's one good eye would gleam behind her spectacles when she spoke of the Devil, the same Devil who came driving a coal-black cart to fetch the souls of the wicked. I heard of strange glows that appeared on the mountain, balls of fire, the spirits of the departed reluctant to leave earthly life behind.

"I had the power once," Aunt Bertha said. "But it all left when I caught the fever."

It was no wonder I looked upon the world outside as a fearful place, one to be avoided whenever possible. Church, however, could not be avoided. We, Bertha and I, went every Sunday, rain, snow, or shine. (Grandfather Judd did not attend. It was years before I ceased to expect the thunderbolt Preacher Davidson promised would strike backsliders to fell Grandfather.) There, in the newly enlarged clapboard building, redolent of pine shavings and stale sweat, Preacher Davidson, an old man with a shock of white hair and angry blue eyes, would harangue us hour after hour on the Devil. His stories were not quite the same as Aunt Bertha's, but they served to enlarge my vision of a doomed and guilt-ridden world.

Between the house, Aunt Bertha, and Preacher Davidson I should have hated Stone Mill, should have thought more kindly of the gray though superstition-free New Bedford I had left behind. But, strangely, I didn't. I belonged in Stone Mill; it was my home. And of course I had Grandfather Judd, whom I adored.

He was a sad man; even I, as a child, could sense it. A brooding, withdrawn man; quiet, rarely speaking. Not until I was grown did I realize that the odd odor on his breath was corn whiskey. He must have imbibed behind the closed door of his room when I was small, for I can't remember ever seeing him take a drink then. Years earlier he had sold his father's sawmill to my mother's family, the Dawsons, retiring, as he said, from business. Yet he was absent from the house a good deal of the time. Where he went or what he did, he never said.

In the fall of my eighth year I was sent to school—a wrenching experience. I cried a good deal beforehand, and on the appointed day clung to Aunt Bertha after we arrived at the schoolhouse, refusing to let go of her skirts.

"You're a big girl now," Aunt Bertha said. "Aren't you ashamed to carry on so? And in front of the others."

Conscious of some twenty pairs of eyes staring at me, I buried my head in her apron.

The teacher, Miss Davidson, taking my hand, said, "Come along, Sarah, and meet some of your classmates." She was not at all like her stern father, the preacher, though she had his blue eyes and large nose. She spoke gently, the preacher's harsh mountain twang muted in her voice.

I shared a desk with Elsie Clarke. She had hazel eyes and a front tooth missing and a thousand freckles. We became instant, intimate friends—a heady experience for one who had never anything but cousin-enemies or an old-maid aunt for a companion.

That noon we exchanged tidbits from our dinner pails, Elsie giving me a preserved pear in return for my pickled watermelon. Thank God for Elsie! She was not only exceedingly bright and affectionate, but a practical soul as well. Through her I began to see Bertha's spooked fantasy world in a more realistic light.

"Why, there aren't any fireballs," Elsie pooh-poohed. "That's lightning or gases, my pa told me. Besides, when you're dead, you're dead. If everyone who was dead came back, Sarah, the world would be so crowded with spirits you and I wouldn't have air to breathe."

Logical, very logical.

Or, "Why should the Devil be so busy in Stone Mill when he's got the whole of North America, South America and all those other places in the geography book to take care of? He can't be *everywhere* at once, riding around Stone Mill in that black cart, gathering souls, dancing in Skilly's parlor, calling on his witches, and tending to things down below, too. Don't you see? He probably don't get to Stone Mill but once every hundred years."

It made sense, good sense.

As for the white-haired maid in the waterfall, she scorned that outright. "My pa and brother fish there all the time. No maiden ever called or tried to drown them."

I believed her.

Gradually, as the months wore on, I began to shed many of my fears. I made friends with other children besides Elsie, and for the first time learned how to play, learned the real meaning of laughter—childish, carefree laughter.

I still remained timid, however, still took care not to let a gray cat cross my path, still concealed my finger- and toe-nail parings, still wouldn't look in a mirror or comb my hair in the dark of the moon. And my fear of night continued. Night meant dreams, and mine, peopled with black, long-tailed devils and fanged witches, would wake me and send me screaming from my bed. As I grew older, the dreams became less frequent, but vestigial nightmares were to haunt me well into maturity, and it was years before I could go to sleep without a night-light.

One Friday afternoon Elsie invited me home with her. "I've got a new dollhouse," she said. "Please come. I want you to see it."

Aunt Bertha, whose habit it was to fetch me after school, was reluctant to give permission. She wouldn't say why. But Elsie and I kept badgering until she finally agreed. "Just for an hour, mind," she said. She refused Elsie's invitation to come into the house.

Mrs. Clarke looked surprised when she saw me, though she tried to hide it, I think, by offering me doughnuts and apple cider. I had the feeling that my presence worried her for some reason. She came into the room—the sewing room where we were playing with the dollhouse—several times, eyeing me, smiling brightly whenever I happened to glance in her direction, in a guilty sort of way. I wondered if she thought I would steal something.

I wanted to ask Elsie to my house in return, but Aunt Bertha said noise gave her a headache. No one ever came to our house. No one. It was not that people disliked or snubbed the Covingtons. At church, at Bradley's store, on those rare occasions when we ventured out, the people of Stone Mill greeted us and spoke politely enough, but like Mrs. Clarke's politeness, theirs was the stiff, wary kind.

I was ten before I realized what the people of Stone Mill thought of Aunt Bertha. I had run over to Bradley's during the school dinner hour to buy some stick candy. There was no clerk at the counter, and with my penny clutched tightly in my hand, I went in search of someone to wait on me. Passing between the dry-goods and ready-to-wear tables, I heard a woman say, "Seems a shame to allow a young one like Sarah to be raised by a maiden aunt." Mrs. Ryland?

" 'Tis so. And the woman a loony."

"Eh, law! Always been queer in the head."

I was shocked. Bertha a loony? Maybe that explained the wry glances people gave us at church, Mrs. Clarke's strange behavior toward me. Aunt Bertha "queer in the head," an object of common gossip at the general store. I remember standing there stunned, anger, fierce loyalty, resentment— all churning sickly inside. Self-pity, too. I was an orphan with a grandfather who did not mingle in society and a demented great-aunt who was shunned.

It was no use telling myself that I had an identity of my own. In fact, I didn't. I lived in a town where kin gave status. You were the Ryland boy, the Loeffler youngster, the Clarke child. And though the Dawsons were related to me also, my name would always be linked to the Covingtons. Always. Not even marriage could cancel that out.

Despite the terrible blow to an already timid self-esteem, I didn't take sick, didn't go into a decline, didn't die. I survived. I had my friends, and school, and the day-by-day bits of fun, boredom, laughter, and girlish gossip to keep me from brooding overmuch about my sorry inheritance or my great-aunt Bertha.

So the years went—not unpleasantly, as I look back—and then—suddenly, it seemed—I was fifteen. By that time I no longer attended school. There had been some desultory talk between Aunt Bertha and Grandfather about sending me to "finishing school in Charlottesville," where my great-grandmother's people, the Gordons, lived. But nothing came of it. So I remained home, filling the long days with sewing and reading or whatever came to hand. For a time I developed a great passion for gardening. Having lost my fear of the outdoors, I hired one of the Davidson youngsters to clear the overgrown flower beds, and there I planted a succession of perennials and annuals, bulbs, and a rosebush or two. But the thrips, snails, and cutworms creeping slowly in from the jungle of vines and trees beyond dampened my enthusiasm, and after a while I gave the whole project back to the wild.

Oh, the interminable afternoons and evenings I spent braiding rag rugs, embroidering tablecloths, tatting handkerchiefs. If it hadn't been for Elsie, I think I should have become a recluse like Bertha, growing older and dottier, or like Grandfather, retreating more and more into a shell. But Elsie managed to persuade Grandfather to allow me to attend an occasional quilting or church supper, and sometimes, if properly chaperoned, a candy-pulling. Dances, it went without saying, were strictly forbidden.

It was at one of those church suppers that old Hattie Dawson (a great-aunt) said to me, "My my, aren't you getting to look more and more like Francine."

"Am I?" I answered smiling. "And who might Francine be?"

Letty Ryland gave Aunt Hattie a nudge. And Hattie said, "No one in particular."

It was exactly the sort of answer to arouse my curiosity and make me wonder.

When I got home that night, Bertha and Grandfather were sitting in the parlor waiting for me, their habit whenever I went out for the evening.

"You're late," Aunt Bertha said—same words, same tone, no matter what the hour might be.

"It's only half-past nine, Aunt Bertha."

"Clock must be slow, then," she grumbled.

Grandfather said, "Did you have a good time, Sarah?" lifting somber eyes from his book. I often wondered if Grandfather knew the meaning of "a good time," if he had ever enjoyed himself in his entire life.

"Yes, Grandfather. Harry Loeffler bought my box supper."

"Oh, the Loeffler boy. Nice lad."

Bertha's good eye glinted behind her spectacles. "I hope you behaved like a lady. You know, my mother always said, 'Act like a lady, and you will be treated as one.' And where's your gloves?"

"I took them off to eat. "They—they're here in my bag."

"Hmmm. How much did Harry pay for your box?"

"Fifty cents." I sat down on the chintz-covered chair. "Aunt Hattie said a funny thing to me."

"Hattie?" Bertha pursed her lips. "Wouldn't be surprised."

"She said I resembled Francine. Did we have someone in the family by that name?"

Her face froze. Silence. I looked at Grandfather. His face, too, had turned to stone. They were both staring at me with a frightening intensity, as if they were seeing me for the first time.

"What is it?" I asked, bewildered.

Still they did not speak. They went on staring, their faces drained of color in the lamplight. A board creaked. I could hear the clock ticking away in the hall. Each tick a heartbeat.

"Was she the black sheep of the family?" I asked brightly, unable to endure the strained silence any longer. "She must have been a relation if Aunt Hattie said I looked like her."

Grandfather wet his lips. "I think, if you'll excuse me,

I'll . . ." He got up and went out, closing the parlor doors behind him.

"You mustn't mention her name," Bertha said angrily. "See how it upsets your grandfather?"

"But . . ."

"She was our sister—and she died. And that's all you have to know."

My curiosity now, of course, was fanned to flame. Francine. The name intrigued me. My great-aunt Francine, a sister of Bertha's and Grandfather's. Her existence had been kept a secret; her life, her death a mystery. Perhaps Francine had done something to displease Grandfather. Perhaps, as I had hinted, she was a skeleton in the Covington closet.

I confided this puzzle to Elsie. At my request she tried to pry information regarding Francine from her own family. But they couldn't (or wouldn't) tell her more than what Bertha had told me. Elsie and I spent one whole rainy afternoon inventing imaginary identities for Francine. Had she been a "scarlet woman," a mistress to some man of high rank? "No," said Elsie, "I think she was a spy during the War Between the States, luring men with her beauty to tell secrets." We fancied Francine in the role of smuggler, highwayman's sweetheart, notorious actress—in as many characters as our fertile minds could invent.

"She might have died of a broken heart," Elsie said.

"Might," I agreed. "Do you think she haunts this house?"

"I don't believe in haunts, remember? Besides, you would have heard or seen her by now. And you haven't, have you?"

"No . . . ," I said, trying to sort out in memory a store of tangled fact and fiction—Bertha's tales, dreams, and reality. "No . . . I don't think so."

But she was there—Francine was there in the house.

I saw her.

Only once.

It was a clear day in late September, one of those bright, burnished days when the mountains stood out, etched in black against a hard sapphire sky. So there was no call later to blame what I saw on fog or evening shadows or night. I had spent the morning at Elsie's house, helping her hem a dress, and I was returning home, coming down the path from the front gate, when I happened to look up at the house—up at the round attic window, to be exact.

A face was pressed against the glass. Even across the distance which separated us I could see that it belonged to a girl or a young woman, and I could see, if not sense, the terror in her eyes.

I remember standing very still, clutching my sewing basket, the hairs rising along my arms, the cold ice creeping up my spine.

But there are no ghosts. No ghosts. Elsie says there are no ghosts.

The face continued to look out—a blurred face, one that seemed vaguely familiar.

Perhaps someone had come to call (who? when people rarely called) and had wandered upstairs and got locked in the attic by mistake. It was a highly unlikely explanation, as unlikely as the ones I had invented about Francine, but I forced myself to believe it.

I hurried into the house and up the stairs to the attic door. Locked. I stood there for a moment, biting my nails, then ran down to the kitchen. "Shhh," Mimsie warned, "your aunt Bertha is napping."

"Do you have the keys to the attic?" I asked.

"Attic? I ain't seen . . ."

I opened the pantry door and grabbed the bunch of keys which hung there. Then I flew back up the stairs.

Trying one key after another, I found the right one, unlocked and flung open the door. A few broken chairs, dust everywhere, dust and cobwebs. Somehow, deep inside, I had expected nothing more.

"What in God's name are you doing here, young lady?"

I turned. Grandfather stood in the doorway.

"Answer me!" His eyes were blazing. I had never seen him angry, never with that awful look in his eyes.

"I . . . I thought I saw someone up here"—quailing before that fierce gaze—"and . . . and I thought. . . ."

He moved from the door, a tall, burly stranger, wrathful, frightening. "Look around and answer me," he commanded, taking my shoulder and turning me.

"No, Grandfather"—swallowing hard—"no, I must have imagined it."

"Yes," he said, the anger draining from him, "yes, you imagined it. There never was anyone here. Never."

Chapter 13

TWO weeks later Grandfather and I left for Charlottesville. It had been decided in a hurried exchange of letters and telegrams with our relatives, the Gordons, that I should go to finishing school after all. The school, a day and boarding establishment run by two maiden ladies, had the portentous title of Southern Gentlewoman's Secondary Institute and catered to families of "good social standing" who could afford the high fees. For all its snobbery, the Institute, I was later to learn, afforded a fairly sound education, considering contemporary Victorian standards. But at the time of my enrollment I was too young and flighty (like most of my fellow-students) to be concerned with such mundane things as "standards" or academic criteria of any sort.

The Gordons' own two daughters had graduated from the Institute, subsequently finding prominent, well-to-do husbands. It was hoped, Aunt Fay Gordon hinted to Grandfather, that I would do the same. "You needn't worry, Judd," were Aunt Fay's parting words to Grandfather. "You shan't recognize the child when you return."

Her words may have soothed Grandfather, but they had the opposite effect on me. Mindful of my last unhappy exile from Stone Mill, I anticipated the worst.

It took only a day or two, however, to dispel my fears. The Gordons were quite different from the Needhams, their home a far pleasanter place. Aunt Fay, an aristocratic, poised woman, and Uncle Cary, sandy-haired, blue-eyed, could not have been kinder. Their one son at home (the other son, Vincent, was at Annapolis), Joel, a bachelor of thirty who closely resembled his father, except that his hair was a more fiery shade of red, put himself in the agreeable role of big brother. "It will be nice to have a sister again," he told me. His two sisters, married, were now living in Richmond.

127

Fay Gordon's one passion was fine clothes. Uncle Cary, part owner of the local woolen mill, could afford to indulge her fancy, I suppose, for she had an extensive wardrobe and I rarely saw her come down to supper in the same gown twice. So I was not surprised when, looking over my own rustic apparel, she registered shock. She took me in hand at once, bringing in her own dressmaker who was put to work measuring, cutting, snipping, and basting for three solid weeks. From her nimble fingers there emerged (besides the necessary school uniforms) day gowns, evening dresses, a dancing frock (dancing!), and two riding habits. All for me. "Your grandfather was most generous with an allowance," Aunt Fay assured me when I asked several worried questions. At home, though we weren't miserly, Grandfather dealt money out with a sparing hand.

I was especially taken with a blue velvet riding habit, the skirt slit at the sides to reveal blue velvet trousers tapering down to the ankle. With the outfit came suede boots and a porkpie hat sporting a pheasant quill. I remember my delight trying it on. Turning and twisting in front of the mirror, I thought it far more becoming than the formal black hunting habit with its silly black bowler.

"Admiring yourself?"

Blushing, I turned from the mirror.

"You shall become very vain," Joel Gordon said. But I could see the hint of a teasing smile in his eyes. I had heard from the upstairs maid, a gossipy, pretty mulatto, that Joel had been jilted by the belle of Charlottesville a year or two back. But if that were so, he certainly did not seem to be grieving.

I liked Joel. I liked Uncle Cary—and Aunt Fay, too, though she had a tendency to fuss rather irksomely over my clothes, my hair, my grammar, my walk. *Proper* was her favorite word. I took all her advice to heart, however, and tried to do my best, for I sensed her basic kindness, her wish to do well by Margaret Covington's great-granddaughter.

Uncle Cary had no memory of his great-aunt, Margaret Gordon, who had married and gone to live in Stone Mill when he was a small child. But, surprisingly, he did recall Francine. She had spent one winter with the Gordons long ago, and he remembered her as shy, pretty, and exceedingly homesick. "She was in love with some boy in Stone Mill," he said, but the name eluded him.

I pressed him, of course, wanting to know all about Francine. Of what had she died? "I don't know," Uncle Cary told me. "The Covingtons never explained."

Of my own parents, the Gordons knew nothing. Apparently a coolness had developed between the families several years after Francine's death. "Something to do with a colored maid, Astoria," Uncle Cary said, but couldn't remember details of the quarrel.

Did they have a picture of Francine, a portrait?

"We couldn't take pictures then as we can now," Uncle Cary explained, "but I do believe my sister, Beth, who was dabbling in watercolors, painted a likeness of Francine."

Could he show me?

Uncle Cary and Aunt Fay exchanged a look of mild surprise. "It's just silly curiosity," I apologized.

How could I explain to these people the deep, angry silence Francine's name evoked at home, or the haunting memory of the white, frightened face pressed to the attic window, or Aunt Hattie's "You are looking more and more like Francine"?

"It might be among Aunt Beth's belongings in the attic," Uncle Cary said.

So we went up to the attic. No hesitation, no locked door, no forbidding scowl here, as I had experienced at home. This was an attic crammed with boxes and trunks and dressmaker's dummies, old lamps, rusting bedsprings, outmoded chamber pots, and stacks of musty books. An attic, a storeroom—ordinary, reassuring—not like the empty, cobwebbed, dusty room at Stone Mill with its single high, round window, its cold, haunted aura.

The picture was found. "Beth wasn't much of an artist, I'm afraid," Uncle Cary said.

The paper had yellowed and the execution had been crude, yet I could see the resemblance Aunt Hattie had commented on. Francine's hair, a light blond color, was drawn back from a white forehead and tied with a large pink bow. Her eyes, a violet-blue, stared out unsmilingly through fringed eyelashes. Straight nose, small mouth.

"Do you think I look like her?" I asked Uncle Cary.

He took the picture from me and studied the painted face. "Possibly. Just possibly. But I think you're a whole lot prettier." And we both laughed.

If I was fond of the Gordons, I was dazzled by their

house, Highfield, a two-storied, red-brick building occupying a slight rise in a vast sea of well-kept lawn bordered by neatly clipped boxwood. A slender-columned, double-decked portico graced the entrance. Inside, the woodwork was painted a warm ivory, and the plaster ceilings in each room were decorated with differently carved motifs. Crystal chandeliers, ivory doorknobs, a view of the Rivanna River from my room, light-colored hangings—and everywhere sunshine, glorious sunshine. Such a contrast to my own gloomy house!

It would be untrue to say that I sprang into my new life without a backward glance at Stone Mill. I missed Elsie from the start, and very soon began a long-winded copious correspondence with her. I missed Grandfather, silent and stolid, even missed Bertha and her cranky garrulity, and—wonder of wonders!—Preacher Davidson's fire-and-brimstone sermons. At least with the preacher we knew where we stood, whereas the Gordons' enlightened Methodism left one with a vague feeling of uncertainty.

In spite of these occasional nostalgic twinges, I was happy at Highfield, happy with my new school. The Institute was run rather strictly by the Misses Lewis (said to be indirect descendants of Meriwether Lewis, of Lewis and Clark fame). Both ladies were Anglophiles, doting on all that was British. The sisters having lived in London with their father (who had been attached to the American Embassy there) for many years, their Virginia accent had been replaced by an English one. However, an attempt to purge our own speech of its regional idiom met with only partial success (" *'Escort,'* girls, not 'carry!' "), and we never could rid ourselves of the famous—or infamous—Southern drawl.

Literature, music, art, grammar, and mathematics. The schoolhouse in Stone Mill had ill-prepared me for advanced learning in these subjects, and so I was far behind the others. But Althea Lewis, the younger of the two sisters, tutored me privately. A model of patience, she gradually brought me up to the point where I could hold my own in class, though I never became more than a rather average, plodding student.

We worked hard at the Institute—the Lewis sisters demanded it—but there were compensations: songfests, side trips to the university for concerts and theater, when suitable, and last, and best, dancing lessons. That our instructor was a woman and no longer young did not matter. Folke was her name, Mrs. Folke. Tall, white-haired, she exuded the exotic, forbidding fragrance of cigarettes mingled with essence of violet, and was partial to loops of glass beads and gowns of long, trailing chiffon. She brought an air of romantic elegance into our lives, and as we two-three-ed about the Institute's tacky dining hall, we dreamt of gay formal balls, jeweled women, handsome, frock-coated young men, and champagne. Ah, Mrs. Folke—how we adored you!

That winter we worked very hard at our dancing in preparation for Louise Ann's coming-out party. A dark-haired, pretty girl, Louise Ann was to be presented to society in the spring, and everyone at the Institute had been invited. To me, who had never been to a formal dance, let alone a ball, spring seemed a century away.

Aunt Fay said I might have a new dress for the occasion, and when winter (at long last) passed, the little dressmaker was called in again. She outdid herself. I can close my eyes now and still see that lovely white gown of organdy, tulle, and eyelet with ruffles on the sleeves and a deep flounce at the hem. "You shall be belle of the ball," Aunt Fay said. "I wish I still had the waist to wear something like that."

Joel offered to be my escort, a rather stodgy one, I thought. But I was too young to have an outsider, and Vincent, home from Annapolis, would be escorting (not 'carrying,') Josephine Barett. At any rate, Joel and I would be going with Uncle Cary and Aunt Fay, so the business of an escort made little difference. As it happened, when the appointed day and hour finally arrived, I was glad of Joel's steadying arm. The minute we walked into Louise Ann's house and the manservant took our wraps and announced us, a terrifying stage fright struck me. I stood leaning on Joel's arm, looking at that sea of strange faces, a multitude of raised brows and inquiring eyes, and could well imagine one dowager whispering to another, "Is this the little relative from the country?" And another answering, "I believe she's from someplace in the mountains—an orphan with a loony great-aunt, I hear. What a pity."

When the violins and piano struck up a tune and the dancing commenced, I clung to Joel just as I had clung to Aunt Bertha on my first day of school. Except for his name, my dance program was blank. At that moment the prospect of sitting on the sidelines as a wallflower was as terrifying as being whisked off by a total stranger.

But no sooner had we finished that first waltz than a blond young man approached—Louise Ann's brother—and asked, "May I?" After that, I lost my shyness. Others asked for the pleasure, and I danced every dance.

The only incident to mar an otherwise perfect evening occurred during the seventh dance. I had been waltzing with a young man, a rather dashing, hard-breathing partner who smelled faintly of whiskey. "It's rather stuffy in here, don't you think, Miss Covington?" (Oh, we were very formal in those days.)

"It is a little warm," I said. His face was flushed, and his forehead, I noticed, was beaded with perspiration.

"Shall we walk out to the garden and cool off, then?"

"Oh—all right."

With his hand on my elbow, we threaded our way across the dance floor and out the long glass doors. The night was warm, a balmy April night, the sky sprinkled with thousands and thousands of stars.

"You're a very lovely girl," he said, taking my arm and leading me down the terrace steps into the dark, hedge-bordered garden.

"Thank you, sir," I said.

"You're not going to curtsy, are you?" he asked and laughed. He had very white teeth.

I didn't know what to say, so I fumbled with the corsage at my shoulder. Three pink camellias, the petals turning brown.

"Now, I've embarrassed you," he said apologetically, taking my gloved hand, kissing it.

"No," I said. "Of course not."

He kept holding my hand. It was so dark I couldn't see his eyes.

"Sarah," he said in a low voice. "Sarah . . ."

"Yes . . . ?"

He began to stroke my arm above the glove, his hand warm and pleasant.

"You mustn't," I said.

"I can't help it. I'm in love with you. Madly in love."

"How could you be," I asked, "when we've only just met?"

"Have you ever heard of love at first sight?" His arm

went about my waist. "You dance beautifully." And his lips touched my cheek, searching for and finding my mouth.

My God—I thought—I'm being kissed!

The next moment we were torn apart.

"You cad!" Joel's voice hissed in the dark. "You cad! I'll have you whipped through the town for this."

"Now look here . . . ," my dancing partner began.

"Sarah, go back inside," Joel said in a tight, angry voice.

"But, Joel . . ."

"Go inside at once before anyone notices you've gone. Do you want to ruin your reputation, girl?"

"No . . ."

"Then go! Well—what are you standing there for? Go!"

I went. I don't know what Joel said to the young man, but he did not reappear at the dance, nor did Joel speak of the incident again.

That summer Grandfather came for a visit. He looked older to me, though his hair was still dark, with only a brush of gray at the temples. He was very pleased at my progress, at my various accomplishments. I played the piano for him, and he smiled, one of his rare, ghostly smiles. But his eyes were sad. Now, because I was happy, I noticed them more than I had before. Poor Grandfather, I thought, was it any wonder he rarely smiled and never laughed? He had suffered more than his share of grief, losing his own wife, his sister, my mother and my father, his only son.

Bertha, he told me, was poorly. Rheumatism in her back. She sent her love.

When he left Highfield, nothing was said about my returning to Stone Mill. I had another year at the Institute, and after that, Aunt Fay was planning to bring me out. "The bachelors will flock," she teased, "and then you can pick and choose which of them you'll have for a husband."

The Institute reopened that September with the news that the Misses Lewis were adding a new member to the teaching staff—a riding master.

"Some of you deport yourselves rather awkwardly in the saddle," Miss Althea Lewis told us. "Sidesaddle, I'm speaking of, the only sort of saddle a real gentlewoman finds appropriate."

I had the feeling she was speaking directly to me. In Stone

Mill we rode merely to get from one place to another. And since coming to Charlottesville I had done very little riding at all. The one hunt I attended had been a fiasco. My horse had balked at the first fence, and instead of urging her on, I had turned about and cantered back to the house. Part of the problem, I believe, was my lack of enthusiasm for fox hunting—all that mob charging down upon one small animal seemed a silly pastime. Thank God, the Gordons seldom participated.

But now, it seemed, all that would be changed. Our new instructor would not only teach the backward pupils like myself the finer points of riding and jumping, but an appreciation of the sport of fox hunting as well.

Mr. O'Rourke came to the school the first week in October. Mr. O'Rourke. Dennis. I thought him far too handsome to be real—the black curls clustered about his well-shaped head, the gray-blue eyes, the cleft chin, the charming hint of an Irish brogue. Every girl in the Institute fell madly in love with him. How could he help not being vain? I even suspected Mrs. Folke of being infatuated with him, and I wasn't too sure of the Lewis sisters, either. Why else would they hire a man when they had never done so before?

Well, I thought, watching him from under my lashes that first afternoon as he went from one student to another adjusting reins and stirrups, I shan't be a sheep and do like the rest. I don't want a man every woman in the world throws herself at.

"Miss Covington, don't slump, please."

I squared my shoulders and stared straight ahead.

"I promise you, Miss Covington," he said in his soft brogue, "that these lessons will not hurt in any way, so you needn't wear that pained expression."

Everyone laughed. I hate him, I thought triumphantly, I hate him!

That evening at supper when Joel asked me how the day went, I told him all about Mr. O'Rourke. "He's arrogant," I said. "And not as young as he pretends. Up close you can see the wrinkles around his eyes."

"Oh?" Joel smiled. "And since when does arrogance go with wrinkles?"

"I didn't say that—or at least I didn't mean it in that way. It's just—well, you ought to hear and see the silly things the girls do. Simpering and fluttering their eyelashes at him, asking him to sign their grammar books. And today Molly Blaine *stole* his handkerchief."

Uncle Cary said, "And how does your good Mr. O'Rourke react to all this adulation."

"Vain, with his nose in the air."

Joel said, "I should think he *would* keep his nose in the air. It would be his job if he didn't."

Three weeks went by. We were riding up into the hills, five of us with Mr. O'Rourke, on the kind of autumn day that reminded me of Stone Mill. Though most of the trees had shed their leaves, others were still aflame with copper and scarlet, a sharp contrast to the dun-colored hills. Riding slowly, I looked back and saw a gray-slate farmhouse nestled in a small valley. Smoke was rising from the chimney. I thought suddenly of Grandfather Judd and the garden at home and wondered if the maples there were still showing their autumn finery. I thought of Elsie. She was walking out with Matt Ryland now, and. . . .

"Miss Covington." I jumped, startled out of my reverie. Mr. O'Rourke had ridden up beside me. "You're lagging behind again."

"I—I'm sorry."

"You don't seem very much interested in riding," he said.

"I—well, yes, I am."

"Then what's the trouble?"

"I—no trouble." I did not look at him.

The path narrowed, and his sleeve brushed my arm. "Is it me? You don't like me, do you?"

My cheeks turned hot. I kept my eyes on a spot between the horse's ears.

"I guessed right, then. And it's my fault. No—no, it is. I insulted you that first day. Not intentionally, but I did. I apologize—sincerely."

"You don't have to. . . ."

"I insist. Please, won't you accept?"

By now my face was on fire. I did not know what to say.

"Miss Covington . . . ?"

"Yes"—forcing myself to look at him. "Of course."

His eyes were the color of gray smoke. I had never seen such black-fringed lashes on a man.

"Sometimes I forget myself," he said. "You see, I taught at

a boy's military academy for a long while, and I got into the habit of being brusque, I'm afraid."

"Oh, but the girls here don't mind."

"The girls . . ." He turned away, but not before I saw the crooked smile on his lips. So, he did not think much of the others. "The girls are very kind."

Up ahead, Molly Blaine turned in her saddle. "Which way, Mr. O'Rourke?"

"Straight on," he called. "I'll be up there in a few moments." He turned to me. "If you think you'd rather be excused from riding . . ."

"Oh, no," I said. "I'll try to do better."

"Well—for a starter—here." He reached over. "Loosen up a bit." His hands were brown and strong. "That's better. Are we friends now?"

"Yes," I said, "yes."

That night I dreamt of Dennis O'Rourke. We were dancing, he and I, at Louise Ann's ball. "Will you come into the garden with me?" he invited. "I don't mind if I do," I answered, taking his arm. I wore a red dress, cut low in the neck, and carried an ivory cigarette holder. The boxwoods threw long shadows in the moonlight. "May I kiss you, Miss Covington?" He put his hand on my shoulders—strong hands, brown hands. "I was afraid you'd never ask," I said, throwing myself into his arms, kissing him passionately on the cheeks, on the mouth.

I awoke then, trembling with excitement and shame. How could I? Even in a dream. I was no better than Molly Blaine. Worse.

At our next riding lesson, I found it hard to meet Dennis O'Rourke's eyes. Each time he spoke to me I wondered if he could guess my shameful dream. But he did not seem to notice anything unusual, and I soon realized what a simpleton I was to imagine he would.

I found myself thinking about him at odd moments of the day. In history class, where we were reading the recently published firsthand account of Lewis and Clark (for some reason, long delayed), I wondered if Mr. O'Rourke thought Virginia a wild and unmapped country. At geography class while Althea Lewis intoned, "Albemarle County is the home of the famous pippin, Queen Victoria's favorite apple," I wondered if he liked apples. I listened intently now when the girls gathered to gossip, hanging about on the fringes, but I learned nothing new of Dennis O'Rourke except that he lived in a small house at the end of Brand Road. Molly Blaine had wormed that from the postman.

One late October afternoon I borrowed Joel's horse and went riding alone. Drifts of brown leaves lay in the road and under the trees, leaves now dead, bleached of their once lovely reds and yellows. Gray clouds scudded across the sky, and the wind had a fresh nip to it.

When I reached Brand Road, a fine rain began to fall. I pulled up the collar of my riding jacket (the blue velvet one I loved so much) and rode on. Presently, through the curtain of mist, I saw a horseman approaching. My heart leaped in my throat as I recognized Dennis O'Rourke.

"Why, Miss Covington!" he exclaimed. "I did not realize you took my lessons so seriously. And in this weather."

"I ride often," I lied. "Almost every day. But I believe I have lost my way."

"Where do you live?"

"Out on Rugby."

"Hmm. Well, seems to me you are going in the wrong direction. Here, let me. . . ."

At that moment the sky literally opened, and the rain sluiced down in buckets.

"You'd better come inside until this is over," Mr. O'Rourke called above the downpour. "Come along, I live only a few steps away."

It was the little house at the end of the lane. He lifted me down from the horse and carried me across the small yard already flooded with brown water. Setting me on the doorstep, he went back to tether the horses.

Then, with his hair and face streaming water, he unlocked the door, and I stepped into the room he called his parlor-kitchen.

"I'll have a fire going in a minute," he said, kneeling on the hearth.

I hung shyly back, watching him kindle a flame.

"Take off your jacket, Miss Covington," he said, rising. "Or you'll catch your death."

Exactly what Aunt Bertha would say. Or Aunt Fay.

I worked the sodden jacket from my arms, and he took it and put it on a chair near the fire. "Come, sit," he said. "I'll make some tea to warm you."

I sat down before the fire and removed my hat, the feather all wilted and drooping.

"You will excuse the mess, I hope, Miss Covington," he said, pumping water into a blackened kettle. "But I didn't expect a guest."

He seemed nervous, ill at ease. I leaned back in the chair. "You needn't apologize, Mr. O'Rourke." He looked my way, and I smiled.

"Well, then—let me see. . . ."

The tea was hot and strong. "I have no milk or lemon to offer," Mr. O'Rourke said.

"That's quite all right. Do you have a spot of whiskey?"

A startled look flashed into his eyes.

"Grandfather says. . . ." I sneezed. "Grandfather says a spot of whiskey will ward off a chill."

"By all means, by all means. I hope you are not. . . . Your blouse, Miss Covington, is soaked through. Here, I have an old sweater. Why don't you go behind that curtain and change? Then we can dry your blouse, too."

I went behind the curtain. The sweater smelled of tobacco and shaving lotion, smelled of *him*. It was much too big, much too long in the sleeves. Oh, if Molly Blaine could only see me now! I giggled.

"What is it?" Mr. O'Rourke asked rather sharply.

"Nothing," I said.

I could taste the whiskey as it went down, warm and pleasant. My eyes watered. I wiped my nose absently with my sleeve. Mr. O'Rourke hadn't noticed, though. He was staring into the fire.

"May I have another cup of tea?" I asked.

"Certainly. But no more whiskey."

His hand brushed mine as he took the cup, and I shivered.

"Still cold?"

"No."

A strand of hair had come loose and hung damply on my neck. I removed the pins from the looped bun at the back of my neck and shook my hair out. Then I stood on the hearth, shaking my hair to catch the warmth of the flames.

Suddenly I became aware of an odd silence behind me.

I turned.

Mr. O'Rourke was staring at me, his gray-blue eyes staring, staring. . . . If I had been born innocent, born yesterday, I would have known that look.

"Dennis . . . ," I said. Perhaps it was the whiskey, I don't know, but my shyness had vanished completely. I wanted him to go on looking at me that way forever. "Dennis . . ."

"Your hair . . . ," he said.

And I was in his arms, feeling his mouth hard against mine, and the kisses of my dream were as nothing to those he rained upon me now.

"No . . . ," he said, pushing me away. "No."

But I flung my arms around his neck. "Don't say no, please, don't say no."

He held me for a long time, just held me. It was such a warm, safe feeling, and I thought, He loves me, and I'll never be afraid of anything again.

"It's stopped raining," he said.

When he set me on my horse, he said, "I'll be riding out near the farm on Friday afternoon." I said nothing, only smiled, but I knew that he knew I would be there.

The following Friday I told Aunt Fay I had promised to help Molly Blaine crewel some seat covers she planned to give her mother as a surprise birthday gift, and would be gone several hours. Aunt Fay and Molly Blaine's mother weren't speaking that year—I don't remember what they had quarreled about—so there was no danger of my lie being discovered.

That was the beginning of my compounded lie, my deception, the first of my Friday afternoons. Ah, the sweet guilt of those Friday afternoons! Getting into the blue riding outfit, the hat set just so on my hair. Walking out the door casually, smoothing my gloves down, the riding whip held jauntily under one arm. "I shall be back in time for supper"—to Jones, the manservant. And my heart beating impatiently, wildly. Oh, Dennis—Dennis . . . !

We rode those afternoons far into the hills under the naked-branched trees, through empty apple orchards, across paths, along streams, climbing higher and higher, taking the rarely frequented ways.

In a secluded meadow we would dismount, and he would gather me in his arms and kiss me, my shoulders, my neck, my cheeks, my eyes, my mouth, and I would return kiss for kiss hungrily, passionately.

One cold Friday afternoon he took me home with him. Watching his strong back, the black curls clustering at the base of his head as he built the fire, I thought, This is meant to be, everything that happens here is meant to be.

"How old are you?" he asked.

"Seventeen."

"God," he said. "God!"

"I love you," I said, going to him. "I don't care about anything except that you love me, too."

"I do," he said. "God help me, I do."

His hands shook as he unbuttoned my jacket. I grasped his fingers, kissing them one by one. He laughed then, and everything was all right.

I can close my eyes now and see the firelight shining on the brass bedstead, can feel his body heavy and urgent, the sudden sharp stab of pain, his mouth covering mine. And his arms around me, holding me, holding me. . . .

"We'll go away," he said. "The two of us. Just you and me."

"Do you—do you want . . . ?"

"To marry you? Yes, my darling Sarah. But you mustn't tell anyone. The Gordons would not permit it—someone like me. . . ."

"Oh, Dennis, I can't see why not."

"My sweet"—kissing me—"you've so much to learn."

And he drew me close once again, kissing the hollow in my neck, kissing my breasts, his strong hands moving gently over me, moving until the flame on the hearth and I, suddenly, in one miraculous instant, became one. "Dennis . . . please . . ."

I wanted to stay forever in the warmth of his arms, not have to leave, not have to wait. "Can't we go now, Dennis?" I asked.

"No, sweet"—brushing the hair from my face. "Next Friday. Friday afternoon as usual so no one will suspect."

He would hire a trap, and we would ride to Lexington, there catching the train for New Orleans. He had a friend in that city who would find him employment.

"Take nothing but a handbag," he cautioned.

Such a long time until Friday, such an eternity! I worried for fear my face, my shining eyes might betray me. Couldn't they see I was no longer a virgin? Couldn't they see how completely, how wildly in love I was? I found it impossible to sit still. School was a torture, facing the Gordons every day even worse. Evenings I spent in my room walking the floor, simmering with suppressed excitement.

Five, four, three, two, and the last day, the longest, counting the hours, my heart fit to burst.

At two o'clock I began to dress, choosing a gown instead of my riding habit. The house was very quiet. Everyone had gone out, except the cook. Uncle Cary and Joel were at the mill; Aunt Fay was visiting old Mrs. Reeves. I was putting on my hat when someone knocked at the bedroom door. "Who is it?" I asked, surprised.

Joel opened the door.

"You're home early," I said.

"Yes. Going out?"

"To Molly Blaine's," I said, stabbing the hat in place with a long pin.

"You're not going to Molly's," he said coolly. "I happen to know that Molly Blaine has never seen you this past month on a Friday afternoon."

I turned slowly from the mirror.

"I also happen to know," he went on, "that you've been riding out with Dennis O'Rourke. Don't try to deny it, Sarah. Several people have seen you."

"Who? Who's seen me?" I might have known some snoop would spy upon us.

"Does it matter? You were observed in a rather compromising situation."

My face flamed.

"And I understand, too, that O'Rourke has hired a trap for this afternoon."

I stared at Joel, big, homely Joel, standing between me and my happiness. Was I going to allow it? Was I going to let fear, submissiveness, timidity destroy my life?

"He has," I said boldly, trying to control the tremor in my voice. "I love him. We are going away to be married."

"You fool!" he exclaimed. "You little fool!"

"I love him," I said, more firmly now—and angry. "And there's nothing you can do to stop me."

I picked up my bag and started toward the door. He caught my arm and whirled me about. "You're not leaving this room!" His face was white, his eyes blazing.

I tried to wrench myself free. "Let me go! Let me go!"

"Not on your life!"

I lifted my bag and struck him across the face. To my astonishment his hand rose and he slapped me—hard.

"Let me go!" I sobbed, beating at him with my bag. "I want him! I want him! Oh, Dennis . . ."

"Listen to me, Sarah!" He grabbed hold of my shoulders and shook me until my teeth rattled. "Listen! He can't marry you. He's already married. Do you understand? *He's already married!* He's got a wife and three children in Atlanta."

"No," I said. "No! You're lying! You're lying, lying, *lying* . . . !"

"I'm not lying." He reached in his coat pocket and brought out a letter. "This is from his wife, Nancy O'Rourke. I wrote, making inquiries. Would you like to hear what she says?"

"No! I don't care. I tell you, I don't care if he's married, if he has a dozen wives. I love him. He loves me. Nothing else matters—I DON'T CARE! Do you hear me? I DON'T CARE! I love him! I'll go to Hell with him. . . ."

He hit me again.

"Let me go . . . let me"—sobbing wildly—"let me go!"

He pulled me over to the bed and threw me down on the pillows. I heard the door slam shut, the key turning in the lock, and I thought, I want to die. Oh, Dennis, I wish I were dead!

Chapter 14

SOMEHOW—I don't think it was Joel's fault—the scandal broke loose. Dennis O'Rourke was immediately sacked, and I was sent back to Stone Mill Hollow in disgrace.

Joel had wanted to marry me (against the heated opposition of his parents). He swore he loved me, but I have often wondered since if his proposal was genuine or merely the prompting of a compassionate heart. Perhaps I would have accepted him if I had found myself pregnant. But I didn't. No one, I think, knew I was a despoiled virgin, although Joel might have guessed.

Grandfather met me in Front Royal. He kissed my cheek and held my hand for a long moment, but he asked no questions, made no comment. We had been on the road for a half hour when he spoke for the first time. "Your aunt Bertha is just as cantankerous as ever. But confined to her bed, poor soul, and sometimes a little wandering in her mind. We've both missed you. It's good to have you home." And that was all.

The garden had grown more wild, if that was possible, but the house had remained the same. Dim, gloomy, shabby, it folded over me as if I had never been away.

Listlessly, without heart, I took up the old routine. Sewing, tatting, crewelwork, reading, gardening. The flower beds were hopeless, but I managed to spade up one of the smaller ones and to plant some spring bulbs. Elsie and I renewed our friendship. I told her about Dennis O'Rourke (but not that he and I had become lovers—I couldn't), reliving my painful loss all over again, crying bitterly as I spoke.

"You mean you still love him?" Elsie asked incredulously. "After he lied to you? Him with a wife and family! How could you?"

"You don't understand," I said, nursing my pain like a swollen tooth. "You *can't* understand."

143

Elsie was promised to Matt Ryland. They would be married in March. By that time, Matt would have finished the house he was building on a piece of land he had bought out on Clear Springs Road. He would plant corn and tobacco and perhaps start a herd of cows. Within the year, according to local custom, Elsie would have her first baby. Their house would be snug and tidy and a red rose vine would climb up over the front door. Elsie would cook and bake and tend the chickens and a small kitchen garden, and Matt would run the farm. The Stone Mill pattern—unchanging, safe, and secure. There might not be the flicker of firelight on a brass bedstead, perhaps never a moment of unbelievably wild passion, but they would have each other. And that must count for something, mustn't it?

We worked on Elsie's hope chest, hemming sheets and pillowcases, embroidering towels and nightgowns, I remembering once too often the seat covers I had never creweled for Molly Blaine.

"You can't go on pining forever," Elsie said, biting her thread with strong teeth. "Come to a box supper tonight. Oh, come on! You've *got* to get out."

I had Mimsie put up the box for me. Mimsie, growing old, her knees creaking, still giggling like a girl. How she managed to retain her good humor in the face of Judd's somber silence and Bertha's sour tongue was a mystery. "Fried chicken," she said, wrapping the box in butcher paper and tying it with a ribbon bow, "always goes big at them suppers."

Harry Loeffler bid highest for my box, as he had done years earlier. He was a comfortable sort of person, a man of twenty now, with a tanned face and light hair streaked with sun.

"Pa's thinking of sending me away to study law," he said as we sat on a wooden bench eating Mimsie's fried chicken.

"Would you like that?"

"Better than farming. Yes, I think I would." He licked his fingers.

"Where would you practice, then?"

He looked at me with some surprise. "Why here—in Stone Mill, of course. The town's growing."

"I don't see it," I said after some reflection. "The same old people live here. No one *new* ever comes to settle."

"Stone Mill is growing, Sarah. Just amongst ourselves. Kids have kids and more kids." He smiled. "And there's a need for someone to draw up legal documents, handle a suit, whatever, instead of consulting old Bradley or having to go to Novotno for a lawyer."

"I'd think we could use a doctor more."

"Mrs. Preacher and Mrs. Dawson seem to be able to handle the doctoring along with their midwifing. Folks tell me they like it that way."

Harry asked if he might call on me. I said yes, I didn't mind. After I got home I thought about it. In Stone Mill a boy didn't ask to call on a girl unless he was serious. I liked Harry, but I knew I could never love him. Maybe—if there hadn't been Dennis. . . . But what was the use of that? I didn't want to be a spinster. The thought of ending my days like Aunt Bertha—old and stooped and ugly-tempered—was frightening. If I had a husband and young ones about me, perhaps the emptiness I felt inside would go away.

Grandfather and Bertha were both delighted to hear Harry Loeffler would be calling. It surprised me. All the years they had been so protective, watching over me like two brood hens—and now this smiling approval. I suppose it was because they trusted Harry—a steady fellow, decent, one not given to drinking or chasing girls.

"His father is sending him off to study law," I said.

The three of us were in Bertha's bedroom, Grandfather and I on chairs, Bertha propped up on pillows.

"What?" Grandfather said in surprise. "Why, that will take a year or two at the least."

Bertha said, "He surely can't expect you to wait, Sarah."

"Wait for what?" I asked.

"Why, to marry you."

I laughed. "Aunt Bertha, he hasn't even asked me."

Grandfather chewed on his pipe. (He had taken to pipes since I'd been away.) "You can't spend your time with a young man," he said, "unless there's marriage in the offing. Most girls here in Stone Mill have husbands by the time they're eighteen."

"I'm sorry to disappoint you, then," I said sourly. So, my disaster in Charlottesville did rankle.

"No need to boil," Bertha grumbled. "Life's been damned easy for you." (*She* had taken to cuss words.)

"I only want you to be happy," Grandfather said. "I'm not going to live forever. I want you to have a home of your own, babies, a good man to take care of you."

"The sooner the better," Bertha said.

I looked at her in astonishment. The thought suddenly struck me that the two of them were trying to get rid of me. New Bedford. Charlottesville. And now Harry—or anyone. The sooner, the better. I wondered if it was because they found me an encumbrance, a nuisance.

"Bertha," Grandfather said sternly. "You do go on. What your aunt means, Sarah, dear, is that one shouldn't fritter one's youth away."

"Exactly," Aunt Bertha said. "Look at me. I had beaus by the dozen. Too picky, and pretty soon they all got tired of waiting and married someone else."

"Well," I said after a short silence. "Well . . . I honestly don't feel like marrying anyone." I was close to tears.

"Now," said Grandfather, "there are plenty of fine young men in Stone Mill. You'll change your mind."

Bertha cackled, "Maybe Harry will change his and won't want to study for the law."

Grandfather wasn't home when Harry called. He had gone off without a word, the way he usually did. I never asked him where he went—I knew instinctively he would resent it—but I did wonder. Sometimes he would take the buggy; sometimes he would ride his horse. Often he would stay away for days, coming home late at night, waking me with his heavy step upon the stair. Once, creeping out of bed and cracking open the door, I watched him as he climbed to his room, his clothes rumpled, his beard ragged, his eyes bloodshot. And as he passed I caught a strong whiff of whiskey.

Surprisingly, Bertha, an inquisitive gossip, never spoke of Grandfather's absences. Perhaps it was because she thought he went off somewhere to get drunk, I would reason, and she was ashamed, though it wasn't like Bertha to be ashamed. I myself imagined Grandfather had a secret lady love somewhere—a romantic notion, though not out of the realm of possibility. Grandfather, though getting on, was still a well-setup, fine-looking man.

Harry brought me a small basket of glazed fruit. He courteously offered Aunt Bertha—who had dragged herself down to the parlor to "chaperone"—the first piece. She had taken a sugared orange slice and, after eating it and licking her fingers, had fallen promptly asleep with her mouth open.

Harry pretended not to notice, even when she began to snore. I liked him for that.

We talked easily. He told me about several changes that had occurred in Stone Mill, and some that he foresaw. "The mill can't last long," he said. "All the commercial lumber has been cut. And no one had the brains to reseed the forest."

"What will the Dawsons do, then?"

"Oh, they've plenty of money. There's talk of them opening a barbershop or a bakery."

"A bakery? When every woman in Stone Mill bakes her own bread?"

"There's quite a few who'd like to be free of that chore. You'd be surprised. Times are changing. The town's expanding. One of the Dawson boys has been thinking of acquiring the Clayborne property."

"Clayborne?" Their house out on Burnham Road was a weed-choked, blackened ruin. The family had moved long before my time, and the fields lay fallow, the apple orchard half-dead, a forest of gray branches.

"Just talk," he said.

Harry called all that winter. He took me to church socials, to dances. At Christmas he brought me a bottle of French perfume, and for my birthday a toilet set—a flower-backed hand mirror, glass-stoppered bottles, a comb-and-brush tray, all decorated with the same painted red rose and green fern. Bertha said it was cheap-looking, but I thought it lovely.

On my birthday he asked if he could kiss me.

Astonishingly, it was a very thorough kiss. On his part. As for me, I could only think of Dennis, think and compare, think and feel pain.

"I can't ask you to marry me now. . . ."

"Let's not talk about it," I said, turning away. I should have to go to bed with him if he became my husband. Could I? "Shall we have some of this birthday cake?" I asked brightly.

One Sunday afternoon in early spring, Harry and I decided to gather morel, a sponge mushroom which grew on the forest floor. I hadn't seen Harry for several weeks. He had been busy helping his father with the spring planting, and his appearance on that particular Sunday was a welcome surprise. Cooped up for so long with Grandfather and Ber-

tha, and with Elsie unable to visit much because of her fast-
approaching marriage, I had missed Harry more than I suspected I might. He looked healthy and sunburned, such a
contrast to us three Covingtons with our winter pallor.

"Get me some birch bark, while you're about it," Bertha
instructed as we left the house, each armed with a basket.
She claimed birch-bark tea helped her rheumatism.

There had been a shower that morning, but the sky had
cleared to an opal blue. A lovely day with a light, chill wind.
"Let's go down by the creek," Harry said.

The path through the garden had long since disappeared
into a wilderness of bush and vine. I followed Harry as he
beat a way through the damp, woody undergrowth with a
stick.

"Look, Sarah!" He paused, pointing. "Now, there's an
oak!"

I had never noticed the oak before, having rarely gone
down to the creek by way of our garden. The oak had a tre-
mendous spread—the trunk, old and twisted, would have
taken three men, arms outstretched, to span its girth.

"Some tree!" Harry said.

"It looks rather sad," I said. A shiver ran through me, and
suddenly I was thinking of Dennis and of time and how slowly the days sometimes went. And the long, sleepless nights.
I thought of the countless mornings when I woke with a start
and that first stab of fear, of loneliness. . . . Why should it
all come back to me at this moment—the pain and the tears?

"That's a funny thing to say about a tree," Harry said.

"Yes, isn't it?" Why should I feel this way when only a
minute ago I felt happy?

"Let's have a look," Harry said.

The dead leaves piled high under the tree were a favorite
ground for morel, but we did not find any.

We hesitated at the creek, its banks brimming with rushing water. I could not shake my depressed mood. The dark,
brooding trees, the thick vegetation, the absence of sunlight
only deepened it.

"I don't like it here," I said, shivering in the gloom.

"Oh, Sarah . . . !"

"There might be snakes," I said, looking fearfully down
at my feet.

Harry laughed. "I've got this big stick." He put his arm

about my shoulders. "I'm not going to let anything hurt you."

I wished with all my heart it could be true.

Within an hour we were deep in the woods, our baskets almost full. We had sat down to rest on a rock a little way from the stream, when we heard someone approaching. A few moments later, much to my astonishment, I saw Grandfather leading his gray mare through the trees along the bank of the creek.

Harry was on the point of speaking, when I put my finger to his lips. "Shhhh . . ."

"But—it's your grandpa, isn't it?" Harry whispered.

"Yes . . . I wondered. . . ." I told him about Grandfather's frequent disappearances. "Let's follow him," I urged impulsively.

"But—that would be spying."

Dear Harry, such a good, "proper" man. "I'm curious. And I can't see any harm in it, can you? If we're very quiet, he won't know."

He grinned at me. "All right, then."

We left the baskets under the tree. Harry dug his stick in the mud at the creek bank to mark the place.

We could hear the horse up ahead of us. Our own footsteps we carefully muffled by walking along the muddied part of the bank. The path was well used by fishermen, for the creek at that time still yielded trout, but we met no one.

Harry touched my arm. "Wait. . . ." He listened for a moment. "He's turned off."

Proceeding slowly, we went another few yards, then Harry took my hand and made a sharp turn.

The trees grew close here, dense, interspersed with an occasional evergreen, and only a faint animal track going through to guide us. Suddenly we heard the horse whinny, the sound startling us as it echoed through the silent forest. Harry drew me quickly behind the trunk of a sycamore. "Do you suppose he's onto us?" I asked, my heart beating wildly. It was crazy—and wrong—to be sneaking after Grandfather, but it was exciting, too.

"I don't know."

We waited a few minutes and then went on until we came to a small clearing. The horse had been tethered to a tree, but Grandfather was nowhere in sight.

"Where do you suppose . . . ?" I began.

"Shhh . . . !" Harry cautioned. I heard nothing but apparently Harry, who knew the woods well, having hunted them as a boy, had heard a telltale sound.

He took my hand. "Try not to step on a twig," he whispered.

Fortunately the forest floor was still damp from the rain. We had gone a little distance when we came to the edge of a deep, wooded ravine. Peeping over the crest, I saw Grandfather making his way to the bottom. He was carrying a rifle.

Hunting, I thought, feeling a little foolish and disappointed.

Grandfather stepped over several rocks, then paused, looking around. We quickly ducked out of sight. When our heads rose again, I saw Grandfather removing branches from several old washtubs, a galvanized oil drum, and a large, oddly shaped kettle with a closed hood. The kettle was resting on a pile of blackened rocks.

"Moonshine," said Harry, drawing in his breath.

"Are you sure?" I asked, astonished.

"Look . . . ," he said.

Grandfather was setting containers at the mouths of several coiled pipes. Then he proceeded to build a fire under the raised kettle.

"Must be the first running-off," Harry said knowingly.

"I never thought Grandfather would break the law."

"Pshaw!" Harry said. "A man's got a right to make his own whiskey."

"Does your father?"

"No. He hasn't the time—there's plenty to be bought fairly cheap. Besides, Pa's not much of a drinking man."

"Grandfather likes his corn whiskey," I said. So *that* explained his strange absences, the rumpled clothes and reddened eyes. Grandfather ran a still. Did Bertha know? Well, it didn't matter. Poor Grandfather.

"That's a fair-sized still," Harry said. "Your grandpa couldn't drink that all by himself. He must sell some of it."

"In Stone Mill?" I wondered if he had taken to moonshining for money or just for something to do.

"If he does, he keeps it awfully quiet," Harry said.

Suddenly one of the stones under my hand broke loose and went rattling down the steep side of the gully.

"Duck!" Harry warned.

A split second later, a shot rang out. A little puff of dust raised itself a yard from our hiding place.

"He thinks we're revenuers," Harry said.

"We can't tell him it's us," I pleaded.

"Won't do much good, anyhow. The minute we raise ourselves, he'll shoot and ask questions later."

"What shall we do?"

"Lie still for a spell. He might think it was just a squirrel."

We remained there on the damp ground, our bodies tense, waiting, waiting. Then another shot zoomed through the forest. And after that, a long silence.

"Come on," Harry whispered. "We'll have to crawl."

On our hands and knees we cautiously left the gully's rim, creeping over dead leaves and spongy, damp moss.

"Far enough," Harry said, helping me up. Then, holding hands, we both began to run.

Chapter 15

WE had walked some distance when Harry removed his hat and dabbed at his forehead with his kerchief. "Should have come to the creek by now." His eyes held a worried expression.

I turned cold. "You mean we're lost?"

"Reckon."

"*How?*" The trees suddenly took on a brooding menace. I hated being lost, especially here in this trackless, dark forest.

"We've been going due east according to the sun," Harry said. "Unless the creek took a sudden bend."

"Maybe we got turned around?" I suggested hopefully.

"Don't think so," he said, squinting up through the trees.

"But—I thought you knew your way." *And you said you would take care of me.* I wanted to cry.

"If the creek were close by, we should be able to hear the falls," Harry said.

The falls, home of the white maiden. My uneasy mind flew back to childhood and Bertha's stories. What was it she used to sing about the white maiden?

> For six of the King's daughters I have drowned,
> And you the seventh shall be, be, be. . . .

"It's all right, Sarah," he said, taking my hand. "Don't worry."

But I went on worrying. I had heard of people losing their way in the woods, people who should have known better, wandering around in circles for days and weeks. Some never came back. "The woods are full of goblins," Aunt Bertha had warned. Elsie had said it was all silliness, but how would Elsie really know? *She* had never been lost in this dark, trackless forest.

"Please don't worry, Sarah."

More firs, a giant tulip tree soaring high above, oak and maples, and still more firs.

"Do you think we'll find our baskets?" I inquired in a bright, high voice. Be practical, like Elsie. Don't dwell on misfortune, disaster—being lost.

"Sure." Did his voice lack conviction?

We seemed to be climbing a ridge. At the crest we paused. A rustling, sweeping sound made us look down. A woman dressed in ragged clothing, hatless, her hair disheveled, was foraging for firewood.

"She'll know," Harry said, urging me down the slope.

The woman did not look up until we had almost reached her.

"Heigh ho!" Harry said, using the old mountain greeting. "Fine evening"—removing his hat, smiling.

The woman looked from me to Harry. Her eyes were a curious milky blue.

"We're from Stone Mill," Harry said. "And we've lost the way. We'd be much obliged if you'd tell us how to find the creek."

The woman's eyes narrowed craftily. "Why do you want to know?"

"We're lost," Harry repeated, still smiling. "I'm Harry, and this is Sarah."

" 'Evening," I said.

Her dress was of faded green muslin, an old-fashioned shapeless dress and not very clean. Over it she wore a brown man's sweater, frayed at the sleeves and out at the elbows. "Is that so?" she said in a husky voice. "We had beans for breakfast, beans for supper. I'm so tired of beans." She shook her head. "And no end in sight. They took him away, and no end in sight."

"Pardon?" Harry asked politely.

"No end in sight."

Harry whispered in my ear. "She's a loony."

I looked at her wild hair and her lower lip, trembling now, and saw that Harry was right. Yet there was a touching sadness about her, her white, ravaged face, the deeply grooved lines between her eyes, as if she were perpetually trying to recall something—a person, a place, a voice—misplaced in time.

"What is your name?" I asked.

"Christy," she said and smiled, and for a moment she looked beautiful.

"Christy . . . ? Why, that was my mother's name. Christy what?"

"Just Christy. The beginning and the end."

"Christy . . ." I looked at Harry.

"There are lots of Christies," Harry said. "Two in Stone Mill."

"My mother had blue eyes—and light hair."

"Your mother's dead, Sarah."

She was buried in the churchyard next to Papa. We seldom visited their graves—twice that I could remember. Preacher Davidson did not hold with "decorations," the yearly communal memorial services celebrated by other hill towns for their dead.

The woman, Christy, touched my sleeve with a bony finger. "You're a pretty girl," she said. "Your eyes are like violets. They're blooming now, you know." Her own eyes suddenly filled with tears. "If only I could see them again."

"Where do you live?" I asked.

She cocked her head, narrowing her eyes, inspecting me closely, suddenly crafty again. "Hickory Cove, though it's not my home."

"Hickory Cove? Why, that's back up the mountain." We almost never saw people from Hickory Cove. They preferred to keep to themselves. "Worthless and lazy," Bertha would say of them. "Ignorant." Stone Mill folk agreed with her. "No wish to better their lot, won't work worth a damn. Birthin' and spittin' is all they'll do."

"You don't talk like a Cove woman," I said, having once overheard a Cove boy at Bradley's store.

Christy threw back her head and laughed, a laugh that mounted into a wild, crazy scream.

Harry took my arm. "Come away, Sarah," he said uneasily.

"No—wait. . . ."

The woman grasped my wrist with her thin claw. "I know you," she said, bringing her tortured face close to mine. "I know you." There was nothing threatening about her words —only a kind of pain in the way she pronounced them.

"How do you know me? From where?"

"I don't remember," she said. A tear formed in one eye and slowly slid down her cheek. "I don't remember."

Harry said, "Come away, Sarah."

The woman's clasp tightened. "Don't go. You mustn't leave. I promise—I promise. . . ."

Harry, looking thoroughly alarmed, unloosened her hand and pulled me away.

He urged me up the slope. Looking back over my shoulder, I saw her watching us.

"Harry . . ."

"Never mind *her*. It will be dark soon, and then we'll be in real trouble."

We hurried along, stumbling over stones, climbing over fallen tree trunks, brushing aside spiked undergrowth. It was getting darker; the wind whispered in the trees—a silky, sly sound. I forgot about the woman and began to get afraid again.

"Are we still going east, Harry?"

"I think so. Sooner or later—there! Can you hear it?"

"Hear what?" Faintly on the wind I heard the muted roar. "The falls!" I said, smiling. "The falls!"

Harry had me wait at the place he had marked with a stick. "I don't care about the mushrooms," I said, ashamed to tell him I was afraid of the growing dusk, afraid that he wouldn't return.

"Won't it look funny if we come back late without anything?"

It was dark when we reached the house, long past suppertime. Aunt Bertha was fit to be tied. She had heaved herself out of bed, down the staircase, and was waiting for us in the hall when we came in.

"What do you have to say for yourself, young man?" she demanded, banging her cane on the floor.

"I'm sorry, Miss Covington," Harry said rather sheepishly. "We got lost."

"Lost! You, a Stone Mill boy, lost in the woods? A likely story." She gummed her mouth, giving me a look, a sneering look which brought a hot flush to my face. "You'll have to answer to Sarah's grandpa . . . carrying on. . . ."

"*Nothing* happened, Aunt Bertha," I said, unable to look at Harry. "*Nothing!*"

"Huh . . . !" And her good eye raked me from head to toe.

"We just got lost," Harry said. "But if you must know, my intentions toward your grandniece are honorable."

Honorable. I wondered if he'd read that in a book. Oh, Harry, going to study for the law. So sweet. Why couldn't we just be good friends?

"Tut, tut," said Bertha, inspecting the baskets. "Where's my birch bark? Forgot my birch bark, did you?"

Two days later, Grandfather returned. I wanted to ask him about the strange woman I had met in the woods but was afraid he might guess that I had come upon his still. The woman haunted me. "It's not my home," she had said of Hickory Cove—yet why would a person of refined speech choose to live there? Married to a Cove man? Unlikely, unheard of. Except for a rare person who ventured out (as I had tried to do), we married among ourselves. If a man chose a bride from another community—rare also—he always brought her back to Stone Mill Hollow. And no woman in Stone Mill would ever marry a backwoodsman.

One afternoon, catching Bertha in a rare good mood, I told her about Christy.

"You met her going on toward sunset, did you?" Bertha asked.

"Yes."

"And she talked queer?"

"Yes, Aunt Bertha."

"Well, Sarah," she said, chewing on her gums, "do you mind what I told you when you was just a snip?"

We were sitting in her bedroom, I on a chair, she in bed. "You told me a lot of things, Aunt Bertha."

"I told you to keep out of the woods. Now, didn't I? Didn't I?"—her finger wagging.

"You said there were snakes. . . ."

"And haunts—and the Devil roaming about, doing his mischief."

"Aunt Bertha," I said. "I don't believe in haunts anymore." At least not here, not in the rosy glow of lamplight. "That was just to scare me when I was little."

"What?" Her bad eye rolled up into her head, the way it did when she got angry. "What? I never heard such fool's talk. Don't believe! The woman you met—now, who d'you suppose she was? Who? Answer me"—waving her cane at me. "Who?"

"She said her name was Christy."

" 'Course she did. Think she was going to come right out

and say who she really was." Bertha leaned forward, her nose pointed sharply over her chin. "The Devil's wife is who she was. Come to bemuse you, Sarah."

"No—she wasn't."

But I remembered the woods bathed in somber hue, the bony claw at my wrist, the mad eyes. . . .

"The Devil's wife, Sarah. A witch!"

"No . . ." And suddenly the years washed away, and I found the cold creeping through my limbs, my soul shrinking once again in childish terror. "No . . ."

"Yes," her whisper probed without pity. "A witch!"

My skin prickled, rose into an icy fur. "You old woman!" I shouted in baffled anger and in fear. "Why do you still torment me? You are just as mad as she. An ugly old maid . . ."

She shook her cane at me. "Damn you! Damn, damn you! Who torments who? Damn you, with your simpering, pretty face. How would you like to be ugly? Huh? Answer me! How would you like it? I had the power once—but now—God, if I had it now, I would . . ." Her eyes started from her head. "Damn . . . d—d—" Her breath came in choking gasps.

"Aunt Bertha . . . !"

"D—d—" Her face turned blue. I reached for her as she collapsed on her pillow, her one good eye staring at me. An eye that haunts me still. She was dead.

That night the church bells tolled fifty-nine times. Fifty-nine. I had thought Aunt Bertha so much older than that. Ancient, I had thought her. But she had not yet reached sixty. And now she was dead.

Mrs. Preacher, Tessie Ryland, Alice Dawson—our neighbors, the good wives of Stone Mill—came one by one for the laying-out and the "setting-up." They closed Bertha's eyes and put a nickel on each eyelid to keep them shut. Then they stripped her of her nightdress and began to wash the thin, shrunken body. I cried. Mrs. Preacher dressed Bertha in a long, old-fashioned gown Bertha had made herself. "She always told me," Mrs. Preacher said, "she wanted to be buried in this gown."

Later, when Grandfather came to my room, I said, "I killed her."

He sat by the window, puffing his pipe, a somber man

wearing black. "Sarah, my dear, she lived her life. Her time was due."

"But I quarreled with her. I called her an ugly old maid," I sobbed, wanting to be absolved by punishment.

"She was different," he said as if he hadn't heard. "It's hard to be different in this world." And I did not know if he was speaking of Bertha or of himself.

"I killed her," I repeated. Would her soul become a haunt? I wondered.

"What's that?" Grandfather said. "Sarah, Sarah," he sighed, settling back in his chair, "please, my child, don't dwell on it."

The bell tolled slowly—ding-dong-ding-dong. Fifty-nine times it tolled, fifty-nine.

"She's at peace," Grandfather said.

But I wasn't. I could have forgiven her for making me afraid, for the nightlamp I must always have at my bedside to keep the goblin-shadows away, could have forgiven her my nightmares of the Devil—if only *she* would forgive me now for bringing on that fatal stroke.

"Some do it with a bitter look," Grandfather said in a low voice, "some with a flattering word. The coward does it with a kiss. . . ."

"Grandfather . . . ?"

"A poem, my dear, by Oscar Wilde. 'Each man kills the thing he loves. . . .'"

"Oh, Grandfather. I didn't mean it! I didn't mean it!"

Grandfather turned abruptly, blinking. "Ah . . . What? What? Do I wander? I was thinking of the past, my dear, the long, long ago."

But I was too overcome with guilt and grief to wonder who he had killed with a word or a look or a kiss.

The next morning Joe Ryland brought the casket that he and Elmer Perry had fashioned during the night. It had been lined with white canebrake, the outside covered with black cloth. Donald Bradley had contributed the new brass handles. The house for the first time in memory was full to overflowing. People who had hardly been civil to Bertha—women like Mrs. Perry, who had called her a loony—were there, eyes moist, wearing long faces. They meant to be kind, I suppose, bringing baskets of food, hams and chickens and pies and freshly baked bread. But I couldn't help feeling that the people of Stone Mill had instilled the somber occasion with an air of festivity. They sang all night and all day, sang hymns and ballads and rondels while the Ryland boys strummed their guitars.

Mimsie, thin and ailing, sat in the kitchen and cried into her apron. Grandfather, for the most part, remained in his room. Never able to abide crowds, he simply made himself scarce, not caring what others would say. I suspected he had a jug of corn whiskey to keep him company, for when the mule-drawn wagon arrived at the gate for the cortege, Grandfather was too "sick" to attend. I could not find it in my heart to blame him.

Harry went with me, giving me his strong arm to lean on. He did not remark upon Grandfather's absence, and for that I silently thanked him.

The casket was set up below the pulpit, and Preacher Davidson read a chapter from the Bible. He talked about Bertha, saying what a good churchgoer she had been, how she could now meet her Maker fearlessly, ". . . a good woman, pure in spirit and mind." I couldn't remember my parents' funeral, though I squeezed my eyes shut, trying to. The one funeral I could recall was that of Willet Dawson, a young cousin who had gone up to Winchester to look for work. He had been killed riding the freight train, and his body brought home. The family had taken on so at the church, hollering and keening, tearing their hair, I became violently ill, and Bertha had to take me home.

I kept hoping no one would do the same now, kept waiting to hear the first moaning wail. But the preacher's voice went on uninterrupted, extorting, warning everyone to prepare for his Maker. I was the closest kin, of course. Any wailing to be done would be done by me. But everything I felt—fear, guilt, and loss—was bottled up inside.

After the preacher had finished, everyone filed up front to take one last look at the body before the casket was closed. Poor Bertha, looking so old and weaseled for her fifty-nine years.

The grave had been dug next to Great-grandmother Margaret's. The preacher said a few more words, and then Mr. Ryland and Mr. Perry took up shovels and filled the yawning hole. So there was Bertha resting next to her mother and father. And there were my own parents, too. All Covingtons.

But someone was missing. Francine.

The adjacent plot belonged to the Bradleys, and the one on the other side to the Dawsons. And though I looked, I could not find Francine's grave among them.

Had she died and been buried elsewhere? But I could never bring myself to ask.

Chapter 16

BERTHA's will, written in her own crabbed hand, named me as her sole heir. She had left a small legacy my great-grandparents had bequeathed her (some railroad bonds drawing interest in a Raleigh bank), her clothes, a few trinkets, and books. Among the latter I found a tattered volume, *Astral Voyages*, by Nikomes, and intrigued, I leafed through it. A weird book, it was all about people projecting their spirit bodies through space. The text was illustrated by graphic drawings of ghostly figures rising from beds or walking through walls and doors.

". . . after death," it read, "the soul around it (the corpse) becomes its own created power." So that was why Bertha spoke so much of haunts. She really believed there was life after death. Not in Heaven, as Preacher Davidson had promised, but here on earth—in Stone Mill Hollow. I wondered, with a sudden cold chill, if she was watching me now, that one good eye of hers staring down. . . .

But that was nonsense. Nonsense. I read on.

"I withdrew from my prone body upwards like drawing a sword from a sheath," one person testified, "using my phantom arms to lever up the top half of my phantom body. . . ."

I closed the book with a shudder and hid it in a drawer under a pile of underthings.

In Bertha's satinwood handkerchief box I discovered several aging photographs. One, an old-fashioned daguerreotype, I recognized as that of Eli and Margaret Covington, for there was a similar portrait in the parlor. Another pictured a young girl, large-eyed, her light hair drawn back and tied with a bow. I would have known her anywhere. It was Francine. The third photograph was of a young man in Confederate uniform—Grandfather, by the look of those dark, scowling brows.

When I went down to the parlor and showed him the photographs, Grandfather passed quickly over the ones of Francine and his parents, but stared at his own, a ghost of a smile in his eyes. "I was at Vicksburg," he said reminiscently.

After a short silence I asked, "What was it like?"

"Like?" He looked at me for a moment with a quizzical expression in his eyes, then frowned. "Thank God, you will never have to know, Sarah."

"Was it that bad?"

"Worse." He stared down at the picture, sucking at his pipe.

"Tell me about Vicksburg, Grandfather."

"Nothing much to tell except that I came out alive—no credit to my skill, just good luck."

"Preacher Davidson would say it's the will of God."

"Ah—Preacher Davidson." He struck a match, and I watched as he touched the flame to the bowl of his pipe, noticing how craggy his face had become.

"It was a siege, wasn't it?" I said, dredging up my vague memory of history.

"Yes, the Union had us holed up in that godforsaken town for a month and a half. A mystery why we lasted that long. They outnumbered us, you know, by far." He puffed on his pipe, lost in the past. "A stalemate, I guess you'd call it. The Yankees got so close we could see into their trenches. Funny thing did happen. There we were, face-to-face, week after week, cheek by jowl, so near we began to recognize each other. One day one of our boys stood up on the parapet, and someone from the Union line yelled, 'What are you standin' up fer?' And our boy said, 'Because you are.' Then the Union man said, 'I'm comin' down to the ravine to shake hands with you.' He ran down to a little creek which divided the two sides, and our boy ran to meet him. Then two, three more did the same thing. And more and more followed. Soon there were hundreds of men from both sides, shaking hands, talking"—he shook his head—"and you'd never believe it, some of them were picking blackberries. Picking blackberries!

"Well, I was junior officer, and as I watched, I couldn't help but smile to myself and wonder, too, what on God's earth we were killing each other for. Then the captain came along to see what the commotion was about. He got mad as a turkey-cock and raised hell. He read me up and down and said if I and the other officers didn't order our men back, we'd face court-martial. We rounded the men up in short order, and two minutes later the killing commenced again."

"And . . . ?"

"We lost Vicksburg. We were meant to lose it all along. A futile cause." He sighed. "I never really knew exactly *what* cause. Seems . . ."

"Were you taken prisoner?"

"What? Oh, prisoner. No. Grant decided against taking prisoners. As it was told to me, the Union general reckoned that sending thirty-one thousand Southerners to a prison camp in the North was far too expensive. So he had us turn in our guns and sent us on home under parole—our word of honor we'd not fight again. It was a word he calculated would be kept. You see, most of us were pretty disheartened by then."

"And you came home?"

"Came back to Stone Mill." He sucked on his dead pipe. I had never heard him speak for so long about anything.

"Did you tell that Vicksburg story to my father when he was a boy?"

For a moment he looked at me with a slightly startled expression in his eyes. "Your father? Robbie? Oh, yes, yes. He liked that one."

"What was . . . my father . . . Robbie like?"

"Like? What do you mean, 'like'? Oh, he looked a bit like me, I suppose. Ugly"—a faint smile. "He was right smart though, right smart. Invented a little gadget to speed up the making of commercial apple butter. Sold it to an outfit in Winchester."

"Why, I didn't know that. Did he invent other things?"

"Nothing of consequence. He didn't live long enough." A spasm crossed his face. He got to his feet abruptly. "All this talk's raised a thirst."

"Grandfather, does it hurt to talk about him?"

"Yes. Yes, Sarah, it does."

He left me sitting there in the gathering gloom, holding the three photographs, listening to the clock ticking in the silence.

It was on Easter Sunday that Harry told me he had changed his mind about studying law.

"Why, Harry, I thought you were so set on it!"

"Not anymore. Pa's willing to give me some of the upper

acreage. Fine place for apples, and I can grow corn and tobacco until the trees begin to bear."

"But, Harry, wasn't it you who said that sweating hard for a living was fool's work when a man could do just as well with a pencil behind his ear?"

"Law is chancy."

"So is farming."

"And I'll have to go away"—this with a direct, penetrating look.

We were sitting on the veranda swing. He was holding my hand. "So, you're giving up your studies for me?" I said after a moment.

"I'd give up a whole lot more for you," he said, his arm going around my shoulders, drawing me close. "Sarah, you'd not want. Pa's set money by for each of us boys." The Loefflers were well-to-do—probably the most prosperous farmers in and around Stone Mill. "And Lord knows I love you."

"Harry! Not here—Grandfather . . ."

But his hungry, eager mouth silenced me. And all I could think of was Dennis and his smoke-gray eyes, his black curls, and a song he sometimes whistled:

> For I wouldn't give a kiss from the gypsy's lips
> For the sake of you and your money, O . . .

The swing creaked. I pushed him away—but gently.

"Say you'll marry me," he pleaded, "if you'd just say it."

"Oh Harry, can't we talk about it some other time?"

He swallowed and took my hands, turning them up, inspecting them. "You've said that before." He spoke with forced patience. "Tell me yes, and I'll talk to your grandfather—do it the right way."

I looked down at his hands, roughened by sun and work, the short, stubby fingers, not the brown and supple ones I remembered so well.

"Don't you love me?" he asked.

"I'm very fond of you." I said it sincerely, with all my heart.

His Adam's apple worked.

"Can't we go on like this—being friends?" I could never tell him about Dennis. Never.

"There's no call for staying single. The two of us are free, we're old enough. Is it on account of my being just a farmer, not educated like you?"

"Oh, no, Harry."

"You wouldn't have to work like some. Alfred"—his younger brother—"would help me out in the field. And we could live with Ma and Pa—they have that big house—if you didn't feel like running your own place."

Everything for pampered Sarah. Everything a good man could give. And hadn't I told myself I must marry sometime —hadn't I? The clock was ticking away, measuring out the empty hours, the empty years. It was now or never. Harry would not wait too long.

"Yes . . . yes, Harry," I said, taking the plunge. "Yes, I'll marry you."

He kissed me, and I tried—Lord knows I tried—to give back some of his passion.

Smiling, happy, he asked, "When? Today, tomorrow, next week?"

Laughing, "A girl has to get her hope chest together."

"After harvest, then. That should give you plenty of time. Next October."

October seemed a long way off, and I said yes, that would be fine.

Harry spoke to Grandfather, who kissed my cheek and said he was mighty pleased with my choice (relieved, too?). The Loefflers had me to Sunday dinner twice in a row, and our engagement was announced at Elsie's wedding, the date set for October second.

I had all summer, then, to put my lingering memories of Dennis away for good.

It was during the last week of June that a great debate raged in Stone Mill over the proposed extension of the railroad up from Front Royal and through our town. The Bradleys and Dawsons were all for it. They spoke of mining mica, or feldspar, which had recently been discovered in the neighborhood. "Won't be worth a damn," Donald Bradley said, "unless we can get it out of Stone Mill. Mules and wagons won't do. We need the railroad."

Kenny Dawson agreed. A railroad would bring prosperity to Stone Mill. "Put the town on the map," he asserted.

Ned Loeffler was one hundred percent for the project be-

cause it was part of his land the railroad company wanted
to buy.

The town meeting was held in the church, and Grandfather attended, the first time I'd ever seen him come through
the church door.

"Can't see further than your noses," he said when he got
up to speak. "Mica this and mica that. Have you been over
the mountain to Shelton lately? Looks like a giant ground-
hog's been on the loose. Gouged-out holes all over the countryside, and big gray scars on the side of the mountain where
they've dynamited. Ugly scars. Can't farm worth a damn in
that place. Furthermore, now they've got all that money in
their pockets they've commenced fighting and feuding
amongst themselves over claims. Mica and railroads! A
mess."

Old Preacher Davidson agreed with Grandfather. Age
had leeched the fire from his speech (Hilliard, his oldest son,
had taken over most of the Sunday preaching now), but he
could still work up some steam.

"Judd's right," he said, standing behind the pulpit. "You
folks hear 'bout the riot they had over to Shelton? Read hit
in the Novotno paper. They been buildin' them tunnels over
thar, the railroad, y'know, through the Ridge. And the railroad brought in all them furriners, gangs o'them. 'Tallies"—
Italians—"Rooshans, and niggers. Well, sir, they got t'fightin'
'mongst themselves, and Cap'n Cross—he's a railroad man—
took some men and put the fight down. Killed five of them
furriners, mebbe six. And Cap'n Cross had to go to trial. A
big to-do, let me tell you. Now, we don't want that here, do
we? Way I see hit, hit's best to be by ourselves. No outlanders!" Shaking his fist, his voice suddenly rising with the
old zeal, "The Lord'll forsake y'all, I swear hit on the Bible.
Forsake you if you don't stick to the old tried-and-true. Bring
in the railroad, and the town'll go down, drowned in the
Devil's own blood. This year is *the* year, 'member? Nineteen
aught six."

From the corner of my eye I saw Grandfather get up and
quietly make for the door. I caught up with him outside.

"Going home?"

"Yes."

"Is it all right if I join you?" I had come to the meeting
with Elsie and her husband, as Harry had gone over to
Novotno on some farm business that day.

"If you don't mind riding pillion."

He helped me on behind him. We had left the church well behind before he spoke. "I hate for that old bigot to agree with me." And that was the only comment he made about the meeting. But Preacher Davidson and Grandfather carried the day. I learned later that the community had voted almost unanimously to keep the railroad out. "Let the rest of the world go by," someone had said, as good a motto as any for Stone Mill, I suppose.

One morning I happened to be in Bradley's waiting for the clerk to fill my grocery order, when a boy of twelve came in. He was dressed in ragged clothes, a torn shirt too big for his neck and arms, and crudely patched trousers. His feet were bare.

"I got 'sang," he said to the clerk, pointing to a gunnysack at his feet.

The clerk looked down at the boy over the rims of his spectacles and pursed his lips.

"See?" The boy opened the sack. Ginseng roots, like dried, spindle-shaped potatoes, peeped out.

"I'll have to talk to Mr. Bradley," the clerk said.

Ginseng grew wild in the woods and was a source of income for some of the more enterprising mountain folk. The 'sang root was highly valued by the Chinese for its medicinal as well as aphrodisiacal qualities, and I believe the Indians once found it useful, too. Stone Mill housewives, however, though they were great believers in herbs, did not think much of ginseng.

"Where is your home?" I asked the boy.

"Hickory Cove," he said, edging the gunnysack between his dirty feet.

Hickory Cove—I looked at him with interest.

"Do you know a woman called Christy?"

He scratched behind his ear. "Shore, I know Christy."

"Are you kin to her?"

"No, I ain't."

Mr. Bradley came through the swinging doors of his office. " 'Mornin', Miss Sarah. Now, now, what have we here?"

He opened the sack and began to poke through it. "Give you five dollars for the lot," he said to the boy.

I had no idea what ginseng fetched in the market, but I had a feeling that Mr. Bradley's profit would be at least triple that.

" 'S'all right," said the boy.

Mr. Bradley said, "Would you want to take the five dollars out in trade?"

"I wuz figgerin' on that. Ma tole me to git coffee, 'baccy, baking sody, salt, and . . . and a hat for herself."

Meanwhile, the clerk had gathered my order together—some staples, bacon, thread, and a length of poplin.

"Shall I charge it to your account?" the clerk asked.

"Yes, please."

Mr. Bradley was waiting on the boy, who, having discovered the jars of peppermint sticks, was gazing at them. "Why don't you throw in a few of those candies?" I asked Mr. Bradley.

"His money won't stretch."

I thought of the stooping and digging that had gone into that sack of 'sang. The whole family had probably worked at it, even the small children, dragging the heavy sacks along, up- and downhill. And then the days and weeks of drying.

"I'll pay for it," I said.

Mr. Bradley made a wry face. "You spoil these folk, and they'll be down here like a swarm of locusts."

The boy stared blankly at the wall.

"I'd like to buy some of that candy," I said.

"I'm not a cheapskate," Mr. Bradley said glumly. "Keep your money." And he threw a few of the peppermint sticks into the bundle he was making up for the boy's sack.

Outside, I spoke to the boy again. "You have a long walk home, don't you?"

"T'ain't much," he said.

"How far is Hickory Cove?"

"A good piece," he said, hitching the sack over his shoulder.

On sudden impulse, I said, "I'd like to go with you."

He blinked his eyes.

"I mean it. I want to . . . want to talk to someone."

He said nothing.

"If you guide me there and back, I'll pay you. I'll give you the same as Mr. Bradley gave you for the 'sang."

He thought me mad. Maybe I was, but Christy had been on my mind ever since the day Harry and I had met up with her.

"What do you say?" I urged. "I'll take the horse. You can

ride behind me, and then you won't have that long walk home."

I had Mimsie fix me a take-along lunch while the boy waited in the garden. "I'm going for a little ride," I told her. "If Grandfather should come home before I do, tell him I'll be back in time for supper."

It was eleven o'clock when we started, the boy using his sack of groceries for a cushion as he rode behind me. He was chewing tobacco, not eating the candy I had thought he wanted. ("Them's for the young 'uns," he had explained derisively when I asked.) He exuded a strong, rancid odor, the stench of the unwashed, but he was a friendly soul once he'd gotten over his initial reserve.

His name was Ty McAlpin, he said. He'd never been to school, and after I had told him about it, decided he didn't think he cared to go. Sometimes I had difficulty in understanding him ("Hope Ma likes her fotched-on"—store-bought—"hat," he said), and I guessed that a good deal of my conversation made little sense to him, either. When I thought we'd been riding for an hour, I unwrapped Mimsie's lunch and, without dismounting, shared it with Ty.

He seemed to know exactly where we were going, directing me to follow the creek, which, above the falls, had a disconcerting way of branching off in many directions. I trusted his ability to find his way, since the forest was his home. My only concern was the distance we seemed to be covering. I had had no idea that Hickory Cove was quite that far from Stone Mill. "Are we almost there?" I kept asking, thinking of the miles I must travel on the way back.

"Just another piece," he'd answer.

As we climbed higher, the course of the creek became more rocky and tortuous. Here the sourwood tree was at the height of its bloom, a mass of fragrant, creamy blossoms, and the chestnut, too (one day, alas, to be blighted forever from our woods), and the tall Turk's-cap lily.

When we topped the rise, I saw smoke in the distance, rising in a dense column between the pine trees. "Yonder," Ty said.

The path leading downward was steep and slippery with pine needles. I thought it best to dismount and, guiding the mare, followed Ty, who scrambled and slid his way toward the bottom, the gunnysack bumping along behind him. In a moment he was out of sight. The horse slipped, giving my heart a jolt, but she managed to regain her balance, and with hands clinging to her bridle, slowly, step by step, we finally reached the floor of the gully.

Ty was nowhere to be seen. "Ty! Ty!" I called, the woods echoing with his name. I called again, but there was no answer.

I stood there listening to the wind soughing through the dark trees—a mournful, desolate sound. A bird fluttered noiselessly up from a bush, while all around me the forest frowned, brooding and mysterious.

Why have I come? I asked myself, cold with sudden panic. What am I doing in this place?

It had seemed like an adventure, a way to satisfy my curiosity back in Bradley's store, but now, here in the shadowed gully with the restive horse and the great moaning silence and all those dark, unknown miles between me and home, it had become a wild, pointless folly.

"Miss . . ."

It was Ty. Thank God! "I thought you'd gone on without me." My voice trembled.

"Nope."

We came to a log house. A man sat on the sagging, narrow porch, his chair tilted back against the clay-chinked wall. " 'Evening," I said. He nodded. "I'm looking for a woman named Christy."

After a long moment he shifted his head and spat a thin line of tobacco juice expertly into the bushes. "Lives wi' th' widder Cora. Ty'll show you."

The widow was hoeing potatoes in front of a small, unpainted cabin. I said to Ty, "You can go on home and tell your mother you're here, while I stop to talk a little."

Ty dropped the gunnysack, squatting on his heels. "Ain't no need. She knows I'll be a-comin' back sometimes."

Cora, an elderly lady wearing a shapeless hat, leaned on her hoe, watching us.

"I'd like to see Christy," I said to her. "Is she at home?"

"What you wantin' her fer?" she said, eyeing me suspiciously.

"Just to talk."

"Ain't no sense in that." Shrugging, she went back to her hoe.

"But I've come all the way from Stone Mill," I protested.

Someone behind me laughed, and, turning, I saw the madwoman framed in the doorway.

"It's you," I said, going up to her. "Christy."

She laughed again.

Cora said, "Plumb out o' her head, can't y'see?"

"Christy," I said, taking her hand, "I'm Sarah. I met you in the woods one day several months ago. Do you remember?"

Her brows came together. "You're lying," she said. That crazy laugh again. "My love is dead. He had a dimple when he smiled. Now, don't you think that's unusual for a man?" She fixed me with her savage, mad eyes.

"Yes"—embarrassed. "I brought you something." I got a scarf I had snatched up at the last moment and put in the saddlebag. She took it in her rough hands, caressing the silk.

"Thank you. Come in, won't you, while I put it away?" she invited, just as sane, just as courteous as any Stone Mill hostess.

"I'll tether the horse first."

I tied the mare to a tree. Cora was watching me. "She's not from Hickory Cove," I said to her. "Where did Christy live before she came here?"

She worked her gums. "A gennelmun paid me t'keep m'mouth shut."

"Do *you* know?" I asked Ty.

He shrugged.

I went inside. The one, high-raftered room contained two beds, two chairs, a table, a cookstove, and a chest. Christy was sitting on the bed, stroking the silk scarf, putting it up to her face, smiling.

"How did you come here?" I asked.

She did not answer, so I repeated my question.

She eyed me slyly.

"Don't you have any relatives—a sister, a husband . . . ?"

"Shut up!" she suddenly screamed at me. "Shut your filthy mouth!"

Shocked, I turned rigid.

"Shut up!" She rose from the bed. "Shut up! SHUT UP!"

Her madness seemed to fill the cabin. Terrified, I backed away.

"SHUT UP!"

A shadow darkened the doorway an instant later. I was

stunned to see Grandfather Judd. "Grandfather . . . !"

Christy pushed me roughly aside and rushed at Grandfather, grasping him by the arms. "Have you brought my baby?" Looking past him, "Where is she? Where is my Sarah?"

Chapter 17

GRANDFATHER did not say a single word on that long journey home through the dusk-shadowed forest.

He rode on ahead, a black-coated figure straight in the saddle, his broad back, the tilt of his head a silent reprimand. My escapade in Charlottesville had not hurt him half as much as what I had done now. I had committed the unforgivable. By prying open his secret I had caught him in a lifelong lie.

My mother was alive. She was mad.

"Go into the house," Grandfather said when we reached home. "I must take care of the horses."

"Grandfather . . ."

"Do as I say."

Mimsie came out from the kitchen. "Where have y'all been?"

"Riding."

"I kep' supper for you," she said.

I sat at the dining-room table. But not alone, for a company of ghosts had joined me. They sat ringed about the table—my father, vague, featureless; my mother with her white, ravaged face; Bertha, her one good eye peering through the shadows; Great-grandfather Eli; Great-grandmother Margaret; light-haired Francine—my phantom family.

"I've made black bean soup," Mimsie said, bringing out a steaming tureen. "Yore grandfather with you?"

"He's bedding the horses down."

That frayed sweater, Bertha spoke from the shadows, out at the elbows, and the faded dress . . .

I heard Grandfather open the front door, heard his step in the hall, but he did not come into the dining room.

The soup was too salty. I drank some lemonade and had a bite of cold chicken pie.

The wild hair, my father said, and the milk-blue eyes . . .

"You ain't ate a thing," Mimsie complained. "Now, here's somethin' you like. Pie. Plum pie."

The unpainted cabin, and the widow leaning on her hoe . . .

"No, thank you, Mimsie."

Better to be dead, said Bertha.

I went out into the hall where the tall clock ticked, and started up the stairs.

"Sarah . . . ?" Grandfather was standing in the parlor doorway. "Come down, please. I've something to tell you." He didn't sound angry—only very tired.

I sat on the chintz-covered sofa, he in his favorite chair. A small table next to him held a cut-glass decanter and a glass half filled with a colorless liquid. Corn whiskey. He doesn't care about hiding it anymore, I thought.

I folded my hands and waited. He sucked at his pipe, frowning at the carpet.

"I'm sorry, Grandfather," I said in a small voice.

He roused himself with an effort. "How did you come to be in Hickory Cove, Sarah?" Still not angry.

I told him, leaving out the part about discovering the still. Although what did the still matter now?

"I see," he said, and fell into another silence.

Again I said, "I'm sorry, Grandfather."

He lifted his head. "There's nothing to be sorry for. It all happened so long ago."

"My father—is he . . . is *he* . . . ?"

"Dead? Yes. And that you can believe. You see . . . you see"—he looked away for a moment—"you see, Sarah . . . be brave, dear child . . . *she* killed him."

The room was very cold. In July? I thought—how strange. Yet I could feel the cold creeping up my ankles, up my legs. So many years. I remembered the scent of mimosa and the swish of silken skirts, the bent head. She had killed him. She was mad.

"It's a long story, and not a pretty one," Grandfather said. "But I feel you are old enough to hear it." He chewed on his pipe.

"Does—does anyone else know?"

"Bertha did. No one else."

Bertha. Part of the conspiracy—no, partnership, a partnership of silence. But she was dead now, and I wondered

if I hadn't come upon Christy in the woods—just by chance
—if I hadn't found her in Hickory Cove—just by chance—if
Grandfather hadn't come there at the right moment—just by
chance—would he have gone to his grave without telling me?
Grandfather, my rock, my one secure rock . . .

"Your father married very young," Grandfather began.
"He fell in love with Christy Dawson and was determined
to have her. She was a pretty girl and had many beaus—I
suppose he was afraid of losing her. They were married in
the church, and afterward the Dawsons put on quite a
spread—a big wedding. I think everyone in Stone Mill came.
I was only sorry your grandmother couldn't have enjoyed
it. She loved big dos. God knows, we had very little of them
here. Very little occasion to have them." He drank from his
glass. His hand, I noticed, had a slight tremor.

"They came to live here," he went on. "Robbie had set
up a workshop in the toolshed where he could tinker at his
inventions. I told you about the apple-butter device, did I?
Well, yes. He thought he was on the way. Going to make a
million." His lips twisted into a rueful smile. " 'I won't need
your money,' he said. As if I minded.

"We got along well, all of us, including Bertha, for a wonder. She seemed to have mellowed somewhat, got used to
being an old maid, I guess. And I'll say this for Christy—
for all her flighty ways, she was a loving girl—to Bertha, too.
That took a lot of doing. But Christy wanted to love everyone and for everyone to love her. Trouble was, it irked Robbie. 'You're too free with your smiles and your hugs,' he
would say. 'Must you make over old Ryland so?' And she
would toss her head, 'What harm is there in it? You mustn't
be jealous, Rob, darling. It's you I love most of all.' She
adored parties and would give one at the drop of a hat."

"Parties, here?" I asked in surprise. There never had been
a real party in the Covington house as far back as I could
remember.

"Yes, here. Christy would get extra help for Mimsie.
She'd have a side of beef or a piglet brought in for a barbecue in the garden. Once even had a mess of oysters and
clams delivered specially. . . ."

I tried to imagine the wild garden tamed, long tables covered with cloths, a piglet slowly turning on a spit. . . .

"At first," Grandfather went on, "Robbie went along with
the parties, wanting to please his new bride. But, poor fel-

low, he was like me, I'm afraid—serious, not a partying man. Made him uncomfortable, he said, all that yammering and fiddling, feeding all those people who turned around and talked behind your back. So the parties got fewer and fewer and finally stopped."

I asked, "Did Christy mind?"

"Didn't seem to. Or didn't let on—I don't know which. And then when she knew she was expecting you, she seemed to bloom. If only I could describe how happy both she and Robbie were when you arrived. Robbie said he wanted a boy, but secretly, I think, he was tickled to find himself the father of a daughter.

"You were not quite five weeks old when Christy took to her bed. Couldn't tell us what was wrong, where she hurt. 'The baby blues,' the doctor we fetched from Novotno said. 'Happens to mothers sometimes. She'll come out of it in time.' And he was right. She did, but"—he paused, staring past me with pain in his eyes—"now that I think on it, that was the first sign. The first sign." He refilled his glass from the decanter.

I unclasped my hands and wiped them with a handkerchief. The first sign. I tried to imagine the Christy in Hickory Cove as the same girl Grandfather was describing, but could not.

"She liked to dress you up in frilly little gowns she had made herself, and take you to church on Sundays. And afterward she'd visit with her sisters. They didn't come here very often—they all had families, you know."

Did no one come? Had the silence and the brooding and ticking of the tall clock in the hall depressed them?

"Your father got interested in the new horseless carriage—motorcar, I guess, is what they call it now. He'd decided to try his hand at building one himself. I reckon he got his mechanical inclination from your grandmother's side of the family. The Rylands were always tinkering at something. Your father, whenever he took up a new project, was like them—nothing else mattered, he went into it lock, stock, and barrel. So if it was motorcars, he must journey up to Michigan to visit this fellow by the name of Ford to get his opinion. He came back loaded down with blueprints and cartons of gadgets, and first thing he did was enlarge the toolshed. Took to working fourteen, sixteen hours a day out there."

Grandfather shook his head. "I might be old-fashioned. out of step, not one whit romantic, but I know a marriage—any marriage—falls apart when the wife is shunted aside. I hinted as much to Robbie. But he was too far gone with his motor to listen or to understand. But then, Christy seemed content, never complained. She had you. A time or two I'd catch her staring into the fire, sad-like, but I told myself that everyone has their moments.

"Then, a few months after your fourth birthday, she seemed to bloom again. Rosy cheeks, that beautiful sparkle in her eyes, the light step, humming as she ran up the stairs. She's expecting again, I thought. I didn't ask. It wouldn't be right. I waited for her to tell me. But she didn't. I waited for Robbie to tell me. But nothing happened. A secret, I thought. She's going to surprise the two of us anytime soon.

"She did surprise me, but not in the way I thought.

"One summer evening—August, I think it was—a hot, airless evening, I went out and started down toward the creek, where I thought I might catch a breeze. In those days we had an old bench sitting on the bank just outside a fence. As I got closer to the creek I heard Christy say, 'But I do love you. I swear I love you. And I *will* go away with you just as soon. . . .'

"I stopped dead in my tracks. I knew it wasn't Robbie she was speaking to, because I had just looked in on him for a moment in the toolshed before commencing my stroll." Grandfather frowned into his glass.

I asked, "Did you know who it was?"

"No . . . no, not then." He drained the whiskey in one convulsive gulp. "I went to Christy and told her I had over-heard her. 'I won't ask who the man is,' I said, 'but you are heading for disaster.'

" 'Father,' she said, 'Rob doesn't care for me anymore. He's in love with that motorcar—not me. I've got to have love, or I'll die.'

" 'You're his wife,' I told her.

" '*I* know that, but does he?'

" 'I'll have a talk with him,' I said, 'but you must promise not to see the other again.'

" 'I don't know if I can keep that promise,' she answered.

"I went to Robbie. I made him listen. Sat him down and made him listen. I didn't tell him Christy was seeing another man. 'She's a delicate thing,' I told Robbie. 'Like a flower. She needs comforting and company.'

" 'She's got the baby,' he said.

" 'It isn't enough,' I told him, 'if you get my meaning.'

"Right away I could tell I had said too much. He looked at me, his eyes all suspicious. 'Has she been fooling around?'

" 'No,' I lied. 'No. It's just that she might take it into her head to leave and go back to her family.'

"He didn't believe me, I could tell he didn't, but he didn't say anything. After that, he took to watching Christy. I would see him in the evenings standing in the shadows in the garden. It made my blood run cold.

"Then one morning I heard them quarreling. Their voices were so loud. 'I'll kill you!' Robbie shouted, 'and I'll kill him, too.'

" 'Please, Rob,' Christy begged. She was crying. 'I promise I won't ever see him again.'

"But I suppose. . . ." Grandfather sighed. "I suppose she couldn't keep that promise no more than the creek could run uphill. I don't know"—another heavy sigh—"I should have sent her away. Far away. I should have done something, not just let things happen. There were so many should-haves, but what's the use?" He poured the last of the whiskey from the decanter into his glass, and lifted it. "So many should-haves." His eyes had a terrible look.

"Grandfather," I began, "you mustn't blame yourself. You did everything you could."

But he had not heard me. "It all came to a head a week later. There was a moon that night and a cool mist rising from the creek. You know the way it does, Sarah. All white and ghostlike?"

"Yes, Grandfather."

"I was sitting here in the parlor, just sitting, when I heard Christy scream in the garden. I ran out, ran as fast as my legs could carry me down the path. Robbie and Christy were struggling over a gun—my rifle, if you please, my hunting rifle. 'Don't, you fools!' I shouted. And the gun went off! God damn, the gun went off!" There was a sob in his voice. Sweat beaded his forehead. "It went off!" he repeated dully.

And it was as if I were standing there myself, the white mist swirling and shifting wraithlike under the black trees, the wet dew falling, the creek talking to itself, and the sudden shot, shattering, exploding the night into a thousand fragments.

"He was dead," Grandfather said. "I knew it the minute I knelt by his side and lifted his hand. 'He's gone,' I said to Christy. She was wearing a blue dress and carrying a small case. Blue was her favorite color. 'Robbie's gone,' she repeated, and she began to laugh—that terrible laugh you heard in Hickory Cove. I took her up to the house. I don't know why she didn't wake you, she was screaming and carrying on so."

Maybe she did, I thought. Or was it in a dream I heard that shrill laughter?

"Bertha was up, though. She helped me get Christy to bed, and between us we managed to get her quiet.

" 'What are we going to do?' Bertha asked. She was frightened, and your great-aunt Bertha very rarely got frightened.

" 'She's killed Robbie,' I said. 'But we can't turn her in.'

" 'We'll have to,' Bertha said. 'I don't see how we can hide it.'

"And while we were talking, all that time I thought of Robbie lying dead in the garden, the blood flowing from his shattered head and the white mist moving slowly over him. I thought of his motorcar and how he had hoped to make a million dollars." Grandfather covered his face with his hands. I wanted to touch, to comfort him, but I didn't know how.

Presently he went on. "We had no sheriff in Stone Mill. 'I'll have to go over to Novotno,' I said, 'but I can't do it. He's dead, and nothing will bring him back. They'll put Christy away in one of those awful madhouses, an asylum. I can't turn her in.'

" 'But what will we do?' Bertha asked.

" 'I must think for a spell.'

"I sat down in this chair, and it came to me almost at once. 'I'll have you go into Bradley's for some quinine tomorrow, Bertha. You say that Robbie and Christy have come down bad with the fever and that I've already sent for the doctor. This town's so afraid of fever, won't anybody come near the place.'

" 'Then what?' Bertha said.

" 'Why, they'll die. I'll make the coffins myself.'

" 'You're not thinking of doing away with Christy?'

" 'Certainly not. I couldn't. Even if I wanted to, I couldn't. I'll send her away, pay someone to take care of her, someone who won't talk.'

" 'But where? Who?'

" 'I'll think of something.' And after a bit, that came to me, too. Hickory Cove. No one ever went up there, and Cove people rarely ventured into Stone Mill. I'd met one or two Covers who had worked a short time at the mill. Close-mouthed people, especially to strangers.

"So while Bertha sat with a corpse and a crazy woman and tried to keep you and Mimsie from suspecting, I went up to Hickory Cove. It wasn't easy convincing the widow Cora. Money didn't mean much to her. But when I promised to keep her supplied with tobacco—they're all addicts, you know —and with staples and whatever else she thought she might need, she agreed."

"But, Grandfather . . . ," I said, dismayed, remembering the tumbledown cabin and its meager furnishings.

"I know what I gave wasn't much. They're proud folk, Sarah. They have their own standards. Cora would fall in the eyes of the community if she had a good deal better than her neighbors. 'Risin' above her britches,' they'd say, mocking her. And the same went for Christy's clothes. I wanted, of course, to make sure Christy was dressed decently. But Cora pointed out that Christy would be a figure of fun if her costume were different from the others'. Don't you think it breaks my heart to see her that way? But when I think of how she would be in an asylum, locked up, not cared for properly, beaten, maybe. . . ." His voice trailed off.

"Do you think she's very unhappy?" I asked after a short silence.

"Who can say what goes on in that pitiful mind of hers?"

"Would it help if I went to see her again?"

"I doubt it, Sarah. She remembers you as a small child. Now you are just another stranger to her."

"And no one suspected the empty coffin?"

"No one," he said.

He brought out his pipe and tapped it on the edge of the empty decanter.

"Did you ever find out who the man was?" I asked him.

He reached for his leather pouch and carefully began to dribble tobacco into the bowl of his pipe. "I wasn't able to find out until after . . . after . . . when she was screaming the name Clayborne."

"Clayborne? But I thought they were long gone from Stone Mill."

He took a long time lighting his pipe. "They are. But every now and again, one of them comes back."

"To look at their property, I suppose," I said.

There was one more question I had to ask. "What happened to—to this Clayborne?"

"I don't know," he said. "I—I don't rightly know."

Chapter 18

LONG ago I had heard a rumor that Old Man Bradley, the storekeeper, had killed his first wife, Mary. She was supposed to have been fat and ugly and rich, and when Mr. Bradley fell in love with another woman and asked Mary for a divorce, she wouldn't give it to him. It was then, so the story went, that he poisoned her. "All those poisons a storekeeper has handy to him," people whispered.

Sometimes I wondered if the people of Stone Mill were whispering about us, too. Had Grandfather really fooled them into thinking my parents had died of fever? I did not know. I never discussed the tragedy with anyone—not with Harry, not even with Elsie.

I doubt that we and the storekeeper were the only ones in Stone Mill who kept a dark secret or a skeleton in our closets. It was quite possible, too, that some families might not even suspect the presence of such a skeleton, not in their closets but parading around them as respectable. A family like the Loefflers, for instance, as staid and conservative a tribe as could be found in Stone Mill. I am almost certain that no one had an inkling of Minna Loeffler's colorful past. It was only through chance (and a shrewd calculated guess) that I found out about it myself.

I met Minna at the Loeffler family reunion, an annual affair which drew the members of the huge Loeffler clan from all around Stone Mill, and a few, like Minna, who had moved away, from other parts. Minna was a contemporary of Grandfather's, a great-aunt to Harry. In her youth she had met and married a harness salesman, a drummer, Isaiah Logan. When he was alive she traveled with him—"all over the South," she said—and after his death she opened a boardinghouse in Jackson, Mississippi, which she ran for a good many years. Recently she had sold her business and was now looking around for a "little place" to retire. "We always come back to Stone Mill," she told me with a smile. "No matter how far we may roam." She was a short, dumpy woman with lively eyes and a warm, outgoing manner, the kind of woman I had always imagined would make a perfect aunt.

She was delighted to hear about Harry and me. "None of the Loeffler boys have ever had the good sense to marry a girl so pretty," she said. I caught a strong whiff of Boudoir as she kissed my cheek, and thought it a rather daring scent for a widowed Loeffler.

So many overnight guests had crowded into the Loeffler home, many of them were forced to sleep in the barn. On impulse, I invited Minna to stay with us. "There's just Grandfather and I rattling around in that big place," I said. "And I'm sure *he* won't mind."

"Maybe you ought to ask first," she suggested.

Grandfather couldn't recall which Loeffler Minna had been. "There were quite a few sisters," he said, "but it doesn't make any difference. Of course she's welcome here."

Minna arrived with two large steamer trunks, three boxes, and two portmanteaus. "It's all I own in the world," she said sadly.

I gave her Bertha's room. "Lovely!" she exclaimed. "Lovely! Your aunt Bertha and I were chums, did you know that? A fine person, Bertha, a fine person."

When Minna was a girl, she had known nearly everyone in Stone Mill, and she loved to gossip about them. But of the three people who interested me the most, she knew little. She had been married and gone by the time Francine died, and my parents she knew only vaguely. But she remembered the Claybornes.

"Old Asa was a bull of man," she said. "Nearly killed the storekeeper with his bare fists—would have, too, if the preacher hadn't stopped him. Asa did have a temper."

"What did they quarrel over?"

"Asa claimed Bradley short-weighted him, and Asa wasn't a man to mess with, I tell you."

"The Claybornes weren't very popular, were they?"

She gave me a surprised look. "Didn't you know?"

"Know what?"

"Why, that Gilman Clayborne went off to fight for the Yankees, and. . . ." She bit her lip. "On the other hand, I don't reckon it's my place to tell you."

"Tell me what? What, Aunt Minna? What about Gilman Clayborne?"

"Never mind. Wasn't much. Here—help me with this box, child."

When Grandfather came into the dining room that night, Minna said, "Hello, Judd, it's been a long time," and Grandfather turned white as a sheet.

"I'd plumb forgotten," he said, looking uncomfortable as he pulled out his chair and sat down.

"Forgotten what?" I asked.

Minna, calmly unfolding her napkin, said, "Why, that your grandfather and I met up during the war. I was running that boardinghouse. Near Vicksburg, wasn't it, Judd . . . ?"

"Please, Minna," Grandfather said. "I don't like to talk about the war. Not at the table, not anywhere, if you must know."

I thought he was being rather curt with her, but put it down to his being in one of his dark moods.

Minna settled in quite happily. She seemed to have forgotten her wish to search for a "little place," and began to give out all sorts of hints to Grandfather on "redoing" the house and garden.

Now, Grandfather, on the whole, was a generous man, but there were some areas where he remained stubbornly stingy. The house, for instance. His reluctance to replace worn-out furniture, to install gas—piped into Stone Mill this past year (and there was already talk of the new electricity, heaven forbid!)—or new plumbing, or to reroof had been a bone of contention between him and Bertha. "If this house was good enough for my parents," he would tell her, "it's good enough for me."

But Minna kept pressing him, and at last he agreed (so she said) to let her start with the garden. She got several of the local lads to come in and clean up the jungle, a herculean task, especially on those hot, humid days of August, and when they got as far as the large oak tree, they quit—all of them. Too hot, they claimed.

Undismayed, Minna ordered outdoor furniture from Bradley's. How she got Grandfather to agree to this expenditure, I had no idea. At first I believed that he had taken a fancy to her, perhaps with marriage in mind. I thought he might want someone with whom to share his old age. But I soon realized that, far from being fond of Minna, he disliked her, a dislike which he sometimes barely concealed. Yet he never spoke of it to me or to her, never hinted that she might be happier elsewhere.

Minna drank—not openly, for she would politely refuse Grandfather's offer of sherry before dinner. But her breath often smelled of whiskey despite the peppermint candies she devoured by the score. Sometimes she got a little tipsy, and her tongue would go on and on. It was then that Grandfather, I think, disliked her the most.

Yet I continued to be fond of Minna. She was good humored, cheerful, pleasant company, and the house seemed brighter for her presence.

"Minna," I said one lazy afternoon as we sat on the new, green-cushioned lounges in the garden, "did you know my grandfather well when you lived in Stone Mill?"

"No," she said, fanning her flushed face with a handkerchief. "I was barely acquainted with your family."

But what about you and Bertha being chums? Minna was that way, though. She'd often forget what she'd said only an hour or two earlier.

"No one knew the Covingtons well," she said. "They didn't mingle socially. And your grandfather never came to church." She reached over to the small table, where there were two pitchers of lemonade and two glasses. "I had Mimsie make mine up separately," she said as she poured lemonade into a glass. "I don't care for a whole lot of sugar."

Hers had whiskey in it, of course. I could smell it from where I sat.

"What was he like?" I asked.

"Your grandfather? A dour man—yes, *dour*'s the right word. Not much for dances or parties. Kept to himself. But it was all a front, my dear, don't you know. A front. I got to know him better in Jackson."

"Did he stay at your boardinghouse there?"

"My dear, did he ever!" And she burst into laughter.

I should have known then, but I went on in my clumsy, naive way. "Grandfather is dignified even when he drinks."

"Well, he dropped his dignity in Jackson, just like he dropped his . . ." She paused and gave me a roguish smile. I could tell she was tipsy. "He liked the redhead best," she said, pouring herself another glass of lemonade. "Lisette was her name. Said she was from Paris. But she was no more from Paris than her hair's true color was red." She laughed again.

I felt suddenly hot, uncomfortable. She must have noticed, for she said, "My dear, I do go on. But it is nothing to be ashamed of. Every man must sow his wild oats."

Was Grandfather ashamed of those wild oats? Had he allowed Minna to stay on, to do pretty much as she pleased, because he was afraid she would speak of this episode in his past?

"It wasn't a boardinghouse you ran, was it?" I said boldly, not liking her very much anymore.

"Sure it was," she said, slurring her words.

"Not an ordinary boardinghouse." I knew of those places. They had had one on the outskirts of Charlottesville. The girls would whisper and giggle about it. "And you were a . . . a madam."

She raised one eyebrow in mock disdain, then laughed. "So what if I was?" Her laugh was so merry, so devil-may-care, I couldn't go on being angry.

"What a big thing people make of it," she said, filling her glass again. "An honest profession, my dear, an honest profession. And what was I to do when Isaiah up and died? There I was in Bypass, Mississippi—now there's a mudhole—with only a few dollars to my name, and the horrible war going on, and no way of getting back to Stone Mill. I made the best of it, the best. Isn't that s'much s'anyone can do? Pardon me, dear. . . ." She belched into her handkerchief. "The best."

"I suppose," I said. "But couldn't you have taken in washing or something like that?"

She whooped. "A washerwoman? M'dear, thass darkie work. 'Neath my dignity."

She patted her face and plump neck with a limp handkerchief, the rings on her short, pudgy fingers glinting in the sun.

"Have you been blackmailing Grandfather?" I asked suddenly.

"What? What's that?" She held the handkerchief in mid-air.

"Have you threatened to tell on Grandfather if he didn't agree to your fixing up the garden and buying new furniture?"

"Why, what a preposh—preposterous notion. I never heard

of such ... such"—a belch which she didn't bother to hide—"a thing. Why, he knows I'm the shoul—soul of discretion."

Minna Loeffler Logan, a boardinghouse madam, I thought, and wondered what the church-guild ladies would say if they knew.

"Minna ... ," I began after a few minutes, turning back to her.

But she had fallen asleep.

Preacher Davidson died in late August on a hot Saturday afternoon. He'd been ill of a stroke for several weeks, so we were not surprised when the church bell began to toll, ringing out seventy-five times for his seventy-five years.

Hilliard Davidson, who had taken his father's place, spoke at the funeral and, much to everyone's surprise, rose to the occasion with a resounding sermon. Until then, he had been a pale replica of his father, but it seemed as if the old man's death had released a secret, hidden Hilliard. "He's even gotten to look like the preacher," Elsie, expecting her first child, whispered to me as we sat side by side in the church.

Hilliard, short, heavy-jowled, his hair so light it looked as if it were white, waxed more and more emotional as his talk progressed. Banging his fist on the pulpit, he shouted, "My father always listened to the word of the Almighty Lord!"

"The Almighty!" voices suddenly chorused. We hadn't heard vocal response of that kind in the church for a long time.

". . . the Almighty will reward the good and punish the sinners. But here—here we are all sinners, and we must atone, must drop to our knees. . . ."

". . . to our knees . . ."

Minna, sitting on my right, her face shining, joined the others in a loud, clear voice. But Elsie said nothing, looking as uncomfortable as I felt.

"My father promised Heaven to those who obeyed, and I fully intend . . ."

Someone in the front row—Esther Perry, I think it was—began to moan. Then Hattie Dawson jumped up and, stumbling to the open coffin, threw herself on it. Several people commenced to keen. The wailing sound cut through me like a knife.

"I can't stand it," I whispered to Elsie, my heart thumping in my breast. "I can't stand it when they do that."

I got to my feet and pushed past the others to the aisle. I had taken only a few steps when Hilliard Davidson thundered, "And where might you be going?"

The congregation suddenly became silent. Necks craned, feet shuffled, a hundred pair of eyes turned on me, pinning me down in frozen terror.

"Where may you be going, Sarah Covington?"

My throat worked, but I couldn't answer.

"Where?"

"Home," I managed to squeak. Then turned and fled.

After that Sunday I had no desire to attend meetings again. When I spoke to Grandfather about it, thinking he would back me up, he said, "Do as you wish, of course, Sarah. But I wonder if you want to be marked as—well, as a dissenter, different, the way I've been marked."

"I don't mind." But even as I said it, I knew that I did. I lacked the courage for the kind of indifference Grandfather carried off so well.

"And you must remember," Grandfather pointed out, "that you will be living in Stone Mill the rest of your life, as Harry Loeffler's wife. You have him to consider."

"Yes." I had almost forgotten.

Preacher Hilliard came to our house the following Wednesday afternoon and was closeted a long time with Grandfather in the parlor. I had some notion that he had come to speak about me, and so I skulked about the hall pretending to adjust my hair at the mirror. But all I could hear was Grandfather saying, "Superstitious nonsense!" before Minna caught me listening.

"Come outside," she whispered. "If that old firebrand catches you eavesdropping, he'll have you roasted in Hell for sure."

We sat on the cushioned lounges.

"I'll say this for Hilliard, he preaches a lively sermon," Minna said. "I like my religion with lots of get-up-and-go."

I looked at her in surprise. "I should think you, of all people, would resent the preacher's harping on sinners."

"Not at all. I don't take it personally, my dear. You heard what he said—we're every one sinners. It's salvation in the hereafter that's important, not what we poor clods do here down below."

"It seems to me that if we believe in the Bible, in the Ten Commandments. . . ."

"Now, wait a minute, Sarah. Hold on. Isn't there something in the Bible about casting the first stone?"

I turned away from her questioning eyes. What a hypocrite I had become.

"It doesn't matter," she said. "I tell you one thing, though. If I was a young girl living in Stone Mill, I would leave."

"You *did*," I pointed out.

"I was lucky." She leaned over in her chair. "Why didn't you stay in Charlottesville?"

"I . . . I got homesick. Besides, I wouldn't be marrying Harry if I hadn't come back."

"Good thing—the sooner the better. This house is no place for you. I'm surprised your grandfather. . . ." A shadow fell across her face, and, looking up, I saw Hilliard Davidson standing behind us, his thin mouth set in a stern line.

"May I have a word with you in private, Minna?"

She got up and followed him to the veranda. They stood talking for a long time.

The next day, Minna moved back to the Loefflers', taking her trunks, her boxes, and her two portmanteaus. I had tried arguing with her, but she had remained stubbornly silent. She would not say why she was leaving, would not say anything except "Good-bye and thank you," in a rather brusque way.

Grandfather disclaimed responsibility for Minna's hasty departure. "She could have stayed," he said, "but I think Hilliard felt she belonged with the Loefflers."

"Why?" I asked.

"Oh—some damn fool notion."

But more than that he wouldn't tell me.

Chapter 19

BECAUSE of a long, dry hot spell, harvest came earlier that year and I saw little of Harry. He worked like a fool from sunup to dusk at his father's farm, and after dark running up to our piece of land, clearing as much of it as he could by lamp and moonlight.

I hardly ever went into town anymore, and no one came to see us. Elsie, as a farmer's wife also caught up in the rush of harvest, was too busy to visit with me. So there was only Mimsie dozing in the kitchen and Grandfather sitting in the parlor to keep me company. Grandfather must have given up the still, because he rarely left the house now. I asked him if he ever saw Christy, and he said yes, she was doing fine. I thought of riding up to Hickory Cove myself, but somehow I never did. I pitied Christy, the woman with the wild hair and mad eyes, yet I could not think of her as my mother. I was a stranger to her, Grandfather had said. And to me she was the same. My real mother remained fixed in memory as a shadow figure, rustling through the twilight, pressing a soft cheek to my face, leaving behind her sweet fragrance.

The house had never seemed so somber, so silent. Grandfather would sit in his chair hour after hour, silently staring at the wall, his glass and bottle and dead pipe on the little table beside him. Sometimes I wondered if he were going mad. Then I would run out into the garden and pace up and down the stone path, or fling myself into one of the lounges, or hurry down to the swing Minna had put up the day before she left. Anywhere—just to get away from the house and its air of haunting gloom.

I got to like the swing, a child's swing. Minna had thought it went "just perfect" with the oak tree. And it did. The swing belonged there—it looked as if the stout knotted ropes and the wooden seat had been dangling from the branch for years. And what a marvelous sense of exhilaration I got pushing myself up and up ("How would you like to go up in a swing/Up in the air so blue?"), higher and higher, until the tips of my toes brushed the leaves. The garden would reel below me, the ground so far away. I remembered Bertha's stories and how I used to be frightened of the garden, how I had imagined it peopled with all sorts of demons, but now it was fast becoming a refuge.

Sitting on the swing, shaded by fretted light, I thought of Dennis a great deal. Instead of putting him out of my mind as I had promised myself, I relived those long-ago (had it been less than a year?) October weeks—the rides, the kisses, the firelight playing on the brass bedstead. I wondered where he was, what he was doing. Had he gone back to his wife? Perhaps they were separated, perhaps she—his wife—had deserted him. Had Dennis loved me? Was he thinking of me now? Or was there some other young girl? And the old song came to me:

> If I ever promised to marry you,
> It was all in a merry mood. . . .

But no, I couldn't believe that. I couldn't.

One afternoon Mimsie tapped at my door. "There's someone here to see your grandfather," she said, "and I tole him he was restin', but the man won't go away."

I went down to the parlor and found Zack Bradley sitting in Grandfather's chair. Zack, a dapper young blade sporting a close-clipped moustache, clerked for Old Man Bradley, his grandfather. His own father, Donald, being the eldest, would someday inherit the store. And no doubt Zack was anticipating the day the Bradley emporium would come to *him*. He was that kind of forward-looking, enterprising young man.

"Good afternoon, Sarah," he said. "I came to see your grandfather. Your servant here says he's napping, but as this is important business, most important. . . ."

"I'll go upstairs and see what I can do, Zack," I said.

Grandfather was lying across the bed, fully dressed, his face flushed, snoring loudly. The room reeked of whiskey. I shook his shoulder, and he mumbled, "Kate . . .?"

"Grandfather, there's someone to see you," I said, bending over him.

"Kate . . . ? Kate, darling?"

I stared at him for a long moment. My grandmother's name had been Wilma. I didn't know a Kate. Perhaps she had been some girl he had once courted.

Returning to the parlor, I said, "He's not feeling well. Could you come back tomorrow?"

"We're busy at the store, and I can't be spared," he replied haughtily.

"Would you care to leave a message?"

He frowned, adjusting his coat sleeves at the wrists. "I suppose I have no choice. Well, yes. You might tell your grandfather his credit at the store has been stretched to the limit, and we won't be able to extend it further unless he pays his bill."

I was shocked, more shocked than I had been to discover Grandfather had visited Minna's boardinghouse. "Are you sure?"

"I can show you the ledger." He had a mouth like a steel trap.

"I'll speak to him."

"If you will, Sarah"—getting to his feet, pulling at his cuffs. "Good evening."

Grandfather's voice shook with anger. "Damn that impudent monkey! He'll go far, I've no doubt. Credit overextended! Why the impudent . . . !" Words seemed to fail him. "Mimsie? Mimsie . . . ! Bring me the bottle."

Mimsie brought the bottle, and Grandfather poured himself a tumbler of whiskey. "Credit! My credit is a damned sight better than his. Every single bill paid up, except for that blasted garden furniture. I told Old Man Bradley I didn't want that rubbish, asked him to come out and take it away. . . ."

"I thought you said it was all right for Minna . . . ," I began.

"I did nothing of the kind. Minna decided to buy those chairs on her own, and the Bradleys, like damn fools, charged it to me."

So Minna *hadn't* been blackmailing Grandfather. And the preacher hadn't spoken to her about it, as I had supposed. Then why had she left in such a hurry?

"The more I think of it," Grandfather was saying, "the madder I get. I'll be damned if they're going to make me pay for something I don't want." I had not seen him so angry since he had caught me in the attic. "Damned storekeeper! Petty, petty, petty . . ." His hand trembled as he brought the glass to his mouth.

"The Bradleys have too much say in this town," he went on, "more than they should. They don't like me, never have, but if they think they can make me eat humble pie at this late date, they're mighty mistaken."

I wondered silently, for I daren't speak of it, if part of the Bradleys' enmity wasn't due to Grandfather's corn whiskey. The Bradleys sold whiskey, legitimate brands, all duly tax-stamped and therefore costing much more than moonshine, which, according to Harry, outsold store-bought whiskey every time.

"I'm not the most well-liked man in Stone Mill by any means," Grandfather said, "but the Bradleys aren't so all-fired popular, either."

"Why do you stay in Stone Mill, Grandfather?"

"Stay?" He looked at me in surprise. "Why, this is my home. I'll be damned if I'll let anyone chase me from it."

Grandfather poured himself another drink. "Seems the storekeeper and the preacher run Stone Mill," he grumbled. "And it's easy to see why. No one has the means of gathering information on folks like those two. The preacher hears confessions—oh, not like the Papists, I mean, but you've seen for yourself how eager people are to tell all at church meetings. And the storekeeper gathers secrets, too. Credit—now that's a powerful weapon. Withhold it, and you got most folks by the scruff of the neck. And there's more than that. Why, Bradley is a financial wizard—he drafts notes, holds mortgages, deeds of trust, liens, rental contracts. The preacher himself is probably indebted to Bradley, since Bradley's the one who collects the money for his salary." He lifted the tumbler, stared at it for a moment, then drank.

I said, "There's talk of the Bradleys putting in one of those new telephones."

"Wouldn't be surprised. What better way to keep tabs on his creditors? That and the post-office concession. Next thing you know, he'll be arguing for incorporating Stone Mill as a town and then make himself mayor."

It came true, as Grandfather predicted, except that Colonel Perry became our first mayor.

One afternoon Elsie dropped by. She hadn't lost her figure yet, nor had she grown rosy and plump as they say expectant mothers do. Instead, she looked pale and tired. "Could I get you something cool to drink?" I asked.

We had gone out to the garden, moving the lounges (over which the Bradleys and Grandfather were still disputing) under the shade of the gum tree.

"No, don't bother," Elsie said. "Hot, isn't it?"

"It isn't too bad if you sit very still."

She fanned herself with her hat. "Sarah, there's something funny going on in this town."

"You mean Bradley trying to incorporate?"

"No," she said after a moment. "I don't think it's that. I don't think they'd be secretive about it."

"Secretive? How do you mean?"

She leaned over and said in a low voice, "They held a meeting last night in my folks' house. I had dropped in to see Ma. She was out, but I heard men's voices through the closed door of the parlor. The preacher was talking. 'It's been seven years,' he said. And your grandfather—I'm sure it was him—said, 'Superstitious nonsense.' "

"He's always saying that," I told Elsie.

"Well, that's what he said, and the preacher came back, 'Now, none of you talk about this. Tomorrow'—that's today —'we'll have another meeting. Can we use your barn, Clarke?' Pa said, 'Yes, I guess so,' like he wasn't too happy about it. 'Well,' said the preacher, 'we'll have to have a bigger place for the womenfolk and a few of the younger ones we can trust. . . .' And then I left, because I could hear someone coming to the door."

We were silent for a few minutes, staring at the leafy trees bordering the walk. "What do you suppose they're meeting for?" I asked at last.

"I have no idea, but I'd sure like to know."

"Would you?" And after a pause, "What time are they going to hold their get-together?"

"Eight o'clock, I think they said." And she suddenly smiled, the old lively look coming back into her eyes. It made me wonder, seeing her face light up, if she had found marriage dull. "We could listen."

"But that would be spying," I said.

"I suppose you could put it that way," said Elsie.

"I don't know as I dare," I said, not worried so much about the spying as being caught at it.

"They'll never know," she said. "We'll hide in the loft."

"But supposing Grandfather asks where I'm going?"

"Say you've promised to pay me a visit. Look, Sarah, you know you're just as curious as me. Come on, don't be scared. What's the worst that can happen? We'll get a scolding, that's all. Anyway, they won't find us."

Persuaded, I agreed to meet her at seven o'clock. We were to dress in dark clothing and wear "squeakless shoes." It seemed like a lark as we made our plans ("The same as old times," Elsie said, her eyes snapping with excitement), but when I got to the Clarkes' back lot, with the sun just setting and Elsie nowhere in sight, my heart started to flutter, and I began to wonder why I had ever allowed her to talk me into such a harebrained scheme. I was thinking of turning back and going home (I had left the horse tethered among some trees down the lane), when Elsie came past the house. Clinging to the shadow of the fence, she made her way quickly around to me.

"Hurry," she urged, "before anyone sees us."

The loft smelled of hay and manure. Elsie closed the trapdoor after us, and it soon became oppressively hot. On one side a tiny, glazed, fixed window overlooked the cow pasture, and on the other were double half doors which when opened allowed for the hay to be tossed down into the yard. I said to Elsie, "If we don't get some air, we'll suffocate."

"Well," looking dubiously at the half doors, "just a teensy."

She unbarred and inched one of the doors out on oiled hinges.

"Elsie," I said, "how are we supposed to see?"

"There's a couple of knotholes in the trapdoor," she said.

We stationed ourselves, each at a knothole, lying flat on our stomachs. I looked over at Elsie in the half gloom and giggled. "You don't act like a married woman who's 'childing.' "

"Shhh—someone's coming."

I put my eye to the hole and saw Elsie's mother and father coming through the barn door, toting a long bench between them. Elsie's older brother, Artie, and his wife, Polly, followed, each carrying several ladder-back chairs. They were arranging these when Hilliard Davidson, accompanied by his wife and the ancient, widowed Mrs.

Preacher, arrived. "I don't think we'll have enough chairs," Mrs. Clarke said in a worried voice.

"Don't matter," Hilliard Davidson said. "Some of them can sit on milk stools or on the floor. Our bones ain't that brittle."

Artie laughed nervously.

For a while it looked as if no one else would come. Then the Perrys (Everett and Dorothy and their oldest daughter) and my prospective in-laws, the Ned Loefflers, arrived. The colonel couldn't come, Everett Perry said—"Not feeling up to it." A minute later, the blacksmith, Joe Ryland, and his wife, Tess, and their son, Joe, Jr., and *his* young son, Will, the one who played the fiddle so beautifully, were followed by three generations of Bradley's, Grandpa Bradley and his wife, Donald and his wife, and Zack fussily arranging his shirt cuffs beneath his coat. Then all together, it seemed, Dawsons, Clarkes, and more Loefflers poured into the barn. Most of them, I noticed, were the older people of Stone Mill, nearly all related by blood or marriage. The young folks, the few who were present, were usually the eldest of the children in their respective families. Serious business, I thought, not a social gathering.

Minna was there, but not Grandfather. And not Harry.

"Close the doors," Hilliard Davidson ordered, rising to his feet. "Artie? Please." Kerosene lamps had been lit, and their yellow light shone on the upturned faces, some already shining with sweat.

"Now," said Hilliard, rubbing his hands together, "no need to tell you why we're gathered here this evening. Nineteen aught six is Stone Mill's red-letter year, and we're fast coming up to September, our red-letter month. . . ."

"Preacher . . . !" Grandpa Bradley was on his feet. "Preacher—with all due respect—oughtn't we to take up that certain minor account before we get to the main business?"

"What's that?—oh, yes." Hilliard stroked his chin, looking over the assembled crowd. A curious silence fell; no one spoke, no one coughed, no one moved.

In the dark, I looked over at Elsie. "What do you suppose . . . ?"

"Shhh . . . !"

"Well, now," said the preacher at last, cracking his knuckles, "we all know that once in a while we will have a blabbermouth amongst us. And that ain't good. Leads to all sorts of trouble."

Minna sprang to her feet, bright patches of red mottling her face. "Preacher, I take it you're meaning me." Though her chins shook, her voice was strong.

"Could be," the preacher said.

"I may talk more than I should. But I haven't given away anything. No secrets. I swear it to you." She turned appealingly to the others. "I'll swear it on a stack of Bibles."

There was a murmur of voices.

"Now, Minna," the preacher said, rapping for attention on the back of his chair. "You know well as me, I caught you just as you were about to . . ."

"No," she said. "I aimed to reveal nothing."

He stroked his chin. "You've been away a long while, so you don't know how strong we feel about this. We had a blabbermouth last time—Willet Dawson. He took sick sudden-like and died. Didn't he, folks?"

A chorus of "Right," "Yes," "Amen" echoed through the barn, striking a note of fear in my heart. Something funny, Elsie had said. Something terrible was more like it.

Minna's face had blanched to a ghastly white, and now her voice quavered as she spoke. "I haven't *said* anything. You can't. . . . You can't! It ain't fair, without giving me a chance."

"Nothing personal in this, Minna, y'understand. I'm only God's instrument. We'll have a vote."

Cass Loeffler, one of Stone Mill's midwives, jumped to her feet. She, like her sister, Reba Perry, the other midwife, had been a Davidson before her marriage, and her mother, Mrs. Preacher, was said to have been the best midwife Stone Mill ever had. "Can I speak a word, Brother, before we take the vote?"

"Go ahead, Cass."

"I want to put in for Minna. She's a woman with a heart of gold. She give twenty dollars to her nephew, my nephew-in-law, to have his appendix taken out down in Novotno, 'cause his folks didn't have the money. I could tell you other charitable things she done, y'know, like takin' care of that old man, Judd Covington, tryin' to make a decent home for him. . . ."

My ears burned. Why, Minna had done no such thing!

". . . so I say we give Minna Loeffler a chance."

There was a faint ripple of applause when Cass sat down. The vote, taken by hands, showed forty for Minna, ten against.

Minna rose to her feet again, her face dimpling. "I want to thank you good people here. And I promise . . ."

Grandpa Bradley broke in. "Let's get on with it. We ain't got all night."

"You're right, Mr. Bradley," Hilliard said. "Now . . ."

Suddenly the door which Elsie had opened earlier banged shut—not a particularly loud noise, but it caught the preacher's ear.

"Whoa, there . . . !" He held up a hand and tilted his head back. My heart froze. "Seems I heard a sound. . . ."

Elsie got to her feet and moved quickly to the door.

"It's only the wind," someone down below said.

"Best to make sure," the preacher argued. "We wouldn't want . . ."

"Hsst!" Elsie urged. "Come here." I crept over to the door.

"We've got to get out," she whispered.

From the barn I heard the preacher say, "If some of you folks will move your chairs, maybe Artie can climb up."

Terrified now, I said, "Elsie, how? We're trapped!"

"No," she said. "There's a ladder outside this door."

Before I could protest she opened the door wide, exposing the top rungs of the ladder. "I'll go first," she whispered. "Hurry . . . !" And she was on the ladder, nimble as she was in the days before approaching motherhood had caught up with her. I hitched up my skirts.

Suspended between two terrors—one coming closer in the person of Artie, the other a dizzy, perilous height from me to the ground—I hesitated. "For Lord's sake! Aren't you coming?" Elsie whispered in desperation.

Clutching my skirts tightly, I got out on the ladder with the cowardly thought that if I should fall, Elsie would be there to cushion me. She had probably climbed that ladder a hundred times as a child, and so was down at the bottom in a wink. "I'm holding it, Sarah," she whispered hoarsely. "Hurry!"

One step at a time (*Don't look down*), like a very small child, I cautiously felt my way. When I finally reached solid ground, my knees were so wobbly I could barely stand.

Elsie drew me into the shadows, and none too soon. We

heard the door above the barn open and Artie's voice, "I told 'em it was the wind."

We waited for several minutes, hardly daring to breathe; then, hand in hand, we scuttled across the yard into the safety of the tree-shaded road.

When I was able to find my voice, I said, "Elsie, do you think Preacher Hilliard meant it about Willet Dawson? I mean about his dying suddenly?"

"The preacher always means what he says." Her face had lost all its color. "Don't ask questions, don't tell anyone," she warned me.

"Not even Grandfather?"

She thought for a moment. "No—no one. He might let it slip that we were spying on their meeting. And mum's the word for Harry, too."

"But Harry's my intended."

"He's a Loeffler, and the Loefflers are related to the preacher by marriage. Don't trust anyone, is my advice."

Elsie and I discussed that strange gathering in the barn at great length, but neither of us could come up with a likely reason for such secrecy or for Hilliard Davidson's threat to punish Minna for "blabbing."

Chapter 20

GRANDFATHER had to go to Raleigh on business—something about banking and stocks.

"Why don't you keep your money here?" I asked. "There's talk that the Dawsons might open a bank instead of a bakery."

"Dawson's got a better head for gooseberry tarts," Grandfather said derisively. "I'll keep my business in Raleigh."

"Why Raleigh?" I asked.

"There's Covington kin there."

I laughed. "I thought I'd met them all—New Bedford, Charlottesville. . . ."

"Not all," he said. "These are cousins on a great-uncle's side."

After Grandfather had gone, Mimsie, who claimed never to have had a sick day in her life, took to her bed with stomach pains. When I found her still unwell the following day, I wanted to ride over to Novotno for the doctor, but Mimsie said no, if I had to get someone, why not fetch Cass Loeffler? "She knows more 'bout doctorin' than anybody."

Cass came, wearing the uniform of her trade, a clean white apron and white bonnet, and carrying her "tote" bag. "Nervous stomach," she told me when I described Mimsie's symptoms. She fixed a poultice of catnip and dock leaves.

Grandfather scorned midwives, or "granny women," as they were sometimes called. "I'd sooner have a witch doctor at my bedside," he once said. But Mimsie felt differently. Five minutes after Cass had applied the cold pack to her stomach, Mimsie swore she was on the mend. "I'll git up now and fix Miz Loeffler a cup of coffee."

"No, stay there, Mimsie," I said. "I'll do it."

Cass followed me into the kitchen and sat at the small table while I put the coffeepot on the stove.

"The first time I've set foot in this house," she said, looking around. "Y'do have a grand place."

"Thank you," I said.

" 'Course, Minna told me all about it."

"Yes," I said, remembering Cass's defense of Minna at the meeting.

I found some ginger cookies and put them on a plate.

"The Covingtons always kept to themselves," Cass said, helping herself to a cookie. "I hope y'won't do the same once you and Harry are married."

"Oh, no," I said. Cass would be kin, my sister-in-law. And all the other Loefflers, dozens of them, would be related to me, too. I would be Harry's wife.

"I hear there's some talk of taking out a town charter for Stone Mill," I said.

"We're a-goin' to try. That way, y'know, we got more control."

Control? Over their secrets, of course. The smell of boiling coffee filled the kitchen. I lifted the pot from the stove.

"We don't like strangers meddlin'," Cass smiled, exposing two prominent front teeth. "We like t'think Stone Mill's one big happy family."

But what about Willet Dawson? I wanted to ask—Willet, who suddenly got sick and died. And Minna standing there, her face blanched with fear. One big happy family.

"People will gossip," I said, and realized too late I had spoken aloud.

"What kind of gossip?" Cass's voice was sharp.

"Oh, nothing much. Will you have cream and sugar?" My hand shook as I passed the cream to her.

"What have y'heard?" she asked again. Her eyes—I had never noticed, but she had a cast in one just like Aunt Bertha.

"Silly things." She had seemed so harmless at the meeting, "putting in" for Minna. But now . . . "Things like, well, the talk about Mr. Bradley's first wife, and . . ."

"That!" she said, and laughed. Her laugh was like Bertha's, too. It gave me goosebumps.

"Aren't you having any coffee?" she asked.

"No—I don't much feel like it. Shall I keep changing Mimsie's cold pack?"

"Let her get up and do it. They get lazy, y'know."

"Mimsie's not lazy," I said.

She stirred her coffee, studying my face. "You're mighty

pretty," she said, just as Bertha would do, not as a compliment but more like a reproach. "I wonder your grandpa lets you outta the house." Again, Bertha's words.

Weird, I hadn't ever noticed the resemblance. Was it possible . . . ?

"Oh . . . !" I said, jumping up. "How much do you charge?"

"For that? I guess fifty cents would be fine."

I went to the dining room and got a dollar from the sideboard where Grandfather kept the housekeeping money.

"No, take it," I insisted when she said it was too much.

"Well, thank you, Sarah."

At the door she hesitated. Her eyes searched mine. "You'd best marry as soon as y'can and leave this house."

Everyone wanted me to marry and leave the house. Of course, I was getting on. Eighteen. I would have children, lots of children. More and more Loefflers. Harry would be their father.

"Don't you go a-wanderin' out in the dark of th'moon" were her parting words as she stepped through the door.

After she left, the house seemed cold and strangely empty. I went from room to room with a candle, lighting every lamp I could find, from the beaded chandelier in the dining room to the lamps in the parlor. Shadows sprang up as I moved with candle flame—distorted shadows thrown against the walls, gathering in odd corners. Shadows of what? The house echoed with the solemn ticking of the clock.

Suddenly I thought of the face I had seen years ago, the white, frightened face pressed to the attic window. I thought of phantoms curling like smoke under the thresholds of closed doors, and the book upstairs, *Astral Travel,* and of unseen eyes that watched in the night.

I stood in the hall, my hand to my mouth, listening to the clock, and I thought, If I stay here another moment, I shall scream. Snatching a lamp from the table, I fled from the house, down the stairs, and around to the backyard to Mimsie's little shack beside the shed.

"Is that you, Miz Sarah?" Mimsie turned her head on the pillow. The cold pack had slipped to the floor.

"Are you feeling better?" I asked.

"Yes, Miz Sarah. Much." Her eyelids drooped.

"Would you like some supper?" I asked halfheartedly, for how could I go back now to that deserted, ghost-haunted place?

"No'm." Mimsie's eyes fluttered.

"I'll read to you," I said brightly.

Mimsie nodded with closed eyes.

The only reading material in the room was a Bible, one that had been given to Mimsie by my great-grandmother. The pages were crisp, though yellowed. Mimsie herself could not read.

I opened the Bible at random. "Then Job answered;/How long will you torment me,/and break me in pieces with words?"

Does God torment people, I wondered, or do we torment ourselves?

". . . he has set darkness upon my path. . . ."

Why should I be so afraid? Of nothing. Nothing.

". . . have pity on me, have pity on me. . . ."

Mimsie had fallen asleep. Even so, her presence was warm, comforting. I turned the pages. "Man that is born of woman . . ." I blinked as the words began to blur. "He comes forth like a flower. . . ." I put my finger on the place, closing my eyes for an instant. " . . . he flies like a shadow. . . ."

I could hear the katydid's shrill chirrup, and down by the creek, the distant chorus of frogs. . . .

When I awoke, the kerosene lamp had gone out. It was morning, and Mimsie was shaking my shoulder.

Grandfather had not said when he would be back. I missed him terribly. The house, even with Mimsie bustling in the kitchen again, seemed lonely and deserted.

I spent most of my time in the garden. For some reason, I felt less anxious there.

One afternoon toward dusk, as I was sitting in the swing, I was surprised to see a man, a stranger, coming up the path from the creek.

"Good evening, miss," he said, removing his cap, "I beg your pardon. I didn't mean to trespass, but"—and he smiled.

He was a youngish man, handsome, with light hair. "I was wondering if this was still the Covington place," he said. For some reason he reminded me of Dennis, though there was no physical resemblance between the two.

"It is."

He turned his head, looking up in the direction of the house. "The trees have grown some."

"You know my family?" I asked.

"I did," he said in a low voice. "I'm a . . . Clayborne."

The name shocked me into silence for a few moments. "You've come back to look at your property?" I asked politely—though very curious.

"In a way," he said. "How is Christy?"

"She is very ill," I answered, trying not to stare. Was this my mother's lover?

"I'm much saddened to hear that. You are the daughter, then? And grown to be so pretty."

"Thank you" I added, "My name is Sarah."

"Sarah." He gave me another smile, a winning smile. "I suppose you are spoken for?"

"Yes. Harry Loeffler. We're to be married in October."

"The Loefflers. A good family." He leaned against the tree. "Are you in love with him?"

"No," I answered truthfully, and wondered why I should be confessing it to this stranger, a man who had been the cause of so much unhappiness for us. And yet he seemed so pleasant, so friendly, not at all like the devious seducer I had pictured. "But I have to marry someone."

"What? A charming girl like you? Someone? Why, you could have your pick."

"No," I said, "the only one I . . . I ever cared for was already married." How easy it was to say it, to speak of Dennis as though it no longer hurt.

"Blighted in love," he said. "But that was a first love. You still have a heart, I take it?"

"Oh, yes," I said, and we both laughed.

"It's good to have someone to laugh with again," he said. "I've been very lonely since your mother took sick. May I call on you sometimes?"

"I would like that, but . . . I don't think my grandfather would permit it."

"Then perhaps I can come and talk to you here in the garden?"

What harm would there be in that? I was so curious, so terribly curious about this man. Besides, Grandfather was not at home. "Yes," I said. "I spend a lot of time out-of-doors."

"Then, the garden it shall be." He looked up at the oak. "It goes on forever, doesn't it?" His voice had a strange, disturbing tone.

"What?" I asked, perplexed. "What goes on?"

"Everything." He removed his hands from his pockets. "So happy to have met you." I thought he would shake my hand, but he didn't.

He was waiting for me, sitting in the swing, when I came down the stone path the next afternoon. "I was afraid you wouldn't come," he said.

"Were you?" I hadn't really expected to see him.

"Because of your mother," he said. "But nothing passed between us that I need be ashamed of."

His admission surprised me, and I felt the color rise to my face.

"I can imagine what people in Stone Mill have been saying about the Claybornes," he went on.

"Not very much," I assured him. "There was some talk of a quarrel between Asa Clayborne and the storekeeper. And then ... then ..."

"Then Gilman went off to fight with the Yankees."

"Yes—but all that's long forgotten. It doesn't matter now."

"Doesn't it?" And I caught a note of bitterness.

"They don't like my grandfather, either," I said by way of consolation.

"Not Judd Covington, the brave Reb?" His voice was sneering, and suddenly I wondered why I had agreed to see him again. He was our *enemy*.

"Do you bear my grandfather a grudge?" Because of this man, my father was dead and my mother mad. What was he doing here in our garden?

"There are few saints in this world, Sarah, and I'm not one of them."

I said nothing.

"I apologize for my ill-tempered tongue. Come, don't be angry." He smiled, and my anger softened. "Am I forgiven? That's better. Come sit with me," he invited, squeezing to one side of the swing.

His arm went about my waist. "Let's push this high, as high as it can go." He laughed, stretching his long legs. He smelled of mint and river mist.

Up we went, slowly at first, then faster and faster, higher and higher, back and up, forward and up, the yellowed leaves rushing to meet us, and now the ground in a dizzying sweep. Up and back. My breath caught in my lungs. Higher and yet higher. "Enough ... !" I screamed.

He held me tighter and laughed.

"P—please . . . !"—gasping, terrified, wildly excited.

He braked the swing, slowing our climb, and we drifted lazily back to earth. "Oh—oh!" I panted, half laughing, half sobbing.

His face was very close to mine. He's going to kiss me, I thought. Do I want him to? He and my mother . . .

His lips brushed my cheek—and suddenly I wanted him, wanted him with a shocking, fierce desire, an emotion which hadn't swept me with such intensity since the afternoon I faced Dennis with the firelight at my back.

"Shall you come to meet me again?" he asked, his lips almost touching mine.

"Yes," I said, and then, "I can see why my mother fell in love with you."

He drew away, and I was sorry I had said it.

"It's getting late," he said, rising from the swing.

A thin veil of mist lay along the garden path, "Wait. . . ."

"I shall be here tomorrow, Sarah."

That night, Grandfather returned from Raleigh. "Mimsie tells me she was ailing," he said. "But you're looking well. Pink-cheeked and bright-eyed." It was his way of saying he had missed me. Dear Grandfather. I wondered what he would think if he knew I had been seeing Clayborne.

"How's Harry?" he asked.

Harry! Guilt brought a blush to my face. But Grandfather was pouring himself a glass of whiskey and didn't seem to notice.

"He's been busy getting in the harvest," I said. "And then evenings he's up at the place."

"Hmmm. Do you think you'll like being a farmer's wife?"

Last week I would have answered yes, or certainly. But now . . . What did Clayborne do? I wondered. Where did he live? In the city? On a farm? He was so soft-spoken, I was sure he had been educated somewhere other than Stone Mill.

"Sarah . . . ?" Grandfather was looking at me with curiosity. "Wool-gathering, are you? You didn't answer my question."

"I don't know," I said. I didn't want to marry Harry Loeffler, to bear his children, to live with him for the rest of my days. I knew that now, knew it with a clear, almost shattering certainty. I was fond of Harry—a good man—but fondness was not enough. I wanted to be in love—that insane, foolish, utterly wonderful, abandoned feeling, letting go. . . .

"Something wrong?" Grandfather asked.

Should I tell him? I couldn't. His son dead, and Christy mad. The name Clayborne anathema to him. "Nothing's wrong," I said.

He looked at me for a moment over the bowl of his pipe, eyebrows raised, but made no comment.

I saw Clayborne again the next evening. We sat by the creek holding hands, and talked. Soon, forgetting my promise of silence to Elsie, I found myself telling him about Hilliard Davidson's meeting in the barn.

"I've no idea what Stone Mill folks could be up to," he said when I had finished. "But"—and he touched my cheek with his finger—"do you really care that much?"

"No," I said—and suddenly I didn't. What did they—Hilliard Davidson, the Loefflers, the Bradleys, the Perrys—have to do with *me*? Stone Mill, everything, everyone seemed so far away.

"I may be leaving soon," he said, looking at me with a smile.

"Leaving?" I said, trying to keep dismay from my voice.

"Why don't you come with me?" he said, kissing my hand. "Just the two of us."

Exactly what Dennis had said. "I've had that offer once before." I had told him of my affair with Dennis; there wasn't anything about me he didn't know now.

"But I'm not married, sweetheart. I'm a bachelor, remember?" His arm went around my shoulders, and he drew me closer.

"I don't know very much about you," I said, realizing that until that moment it hadn't seemed so very important. Even his relationship with my mother had ceased to trouble me.

"I shall tell you everything, then," he smiled, and kissed me on the cheek. "Answer all your questions, and then you can decide if love is a matter of the heart or the head." He kissed my cheek. "Think it over, Sarah. Think about going away with me?"

I thought of him all the next day. In the late afternoon I wandered down to the oak to wait, hoping he would come.

As I sat there on the swing, the light suddenly grew dim, and, looking up through the branches, I saw that gray, ugly clouds had covered the sun. The wind rose in a sudden gust, whipping at the bushes and trees, scattering leaves all around. Summer's end, I thought with a queer pang. I waited a long time, but Clayborne did not come, and finally, chilled, with the wind plucking at my skirts, I went back up the stone path.

When I came into the house, Grandfather was sitting in the parlor. I stood for a few moments in the hall, watching him. He looked so sad and old, his face lined and heavy, and I was filled with pity. I can't deceive him, I thought.

"Grandfather . . . ?"

He roused himself. "Ah, Sarah. I must have been dozing."

I went into the parlor. It's now or never, I thought. I swallowed, but the lump wouldn't go away. "Grandfather . . . Clayborne's back."

"Who . . . ?"

"Clayborne. I met him in the garden—while you were gone."

The color drained from his face. His lips moved, but no sound came. The shocked, stricken look in his eyes frightened me, and for a moment I thought he would have a seizure, but then his hand reached out like a blind man's and grasped the whiskey decanter. The colorless liquid splashed into the glass.

"I—I know how you feel about the Claybornes . . . ," I began uncertainly, regretting my decision to tell him.

He shook his head, his hand trembling as he brought the glass to his mouth and drank. A few drops dribbled on his chin, and he wiped them away with the back of his hand. He shook his head again, muttering, "And just when I had convinced myself. . . ."

"Convinced . . . convinced yourself of what, Grandfather?" I asked bewildered.

His eyes were fixed on me, eyes filled with anguish.

"Grandfather . . ."

"Sit down, Sarah,' he said, "sit down, girl."

I sat on the chintz-covered sofa with a terrible feeling of foreboding.

Grandfather downed the rest of the whiskey and frowned at the empty glass. When he spoke his voice was low. "I had hoped you would never have to know, Sarah." Wasn't that what he had said when he told me about my mother and father? Could anything be worse?

"I don't know how—how to go about this. But I can't keep silent. Not now. *Certainly* not now. It—it all goes back a long, long time," he began, reaching for the decanter.

He talked and talked, on and on and on. He told it all to me, the truth, the secret the Covingtons—and God knows how many others in Stone Mill—had been hiding for years. He explained the white face at the window and the sad oak tree, his wish to see me safely married, and why I must put Clayborne from my mind. And as he spoke in that low, deep voice, my fear grew, a cold fear that soon turned me numb with horror.

"Sarah," he said when he had finished, "you realize that you cannot stay here any longer. Come, girl"—giving me his hand—"I shan't let anything happen. Get a few clothes together. We'll leave at once."

My mind was in turmoil as I put my things in a suitcase—an extra petticoat, a knitted shawl, my hairbrush, some ribbons. I took one last, backward look at my room—the calendar on the wall, the photograph of Grandfather on the bureau, my dresses in the wardrobe. But there wasn't time—no time. . . .

We left in the dead of night, with the wind howling down the chimneys and thrashing at the trees. No one, not even Mimsie, saw us go.

The darkened town slept under wind-tossed shadows—the church, the smith, the store, the mill all silent and shuttered like the houses. The wheels of the buggy creaked and clattered over the cobblestones, the horse gathering speed once we left the main street behind.

Grandfather brought me to the Covingtons in Raleigh. A few weeks later I heard that Minna had died shortly after my departure—and one of the Perry girls, too. My cousins in Raleigh didn't seem to know the cause of their deaths. Mimsie, old and ailing, died that Christmas, and Grandfather himself passed away in the spring. I did not go to the funeral. He left me all his money and property and a letter which said I was not to worry about Christy—he had made provisions for her. "And, Sarah, promise me you will not return to Stone Mill."

I remained in Raleigh for many years, too many to tell.

I never married. How could I, with that dreadful Stone Mill secret inside me, with a great-aunt who had been "loony," and a mother gone mad?

Long afterward, when I became old, I got homesick for Stone Mill and, thinking Grandfather's warning no longer mattered, I came back. I don't live in the old house, though, I bought a place in town. (Grandfather did well out of corn liquor.)

These days I keep to myself, read a little, work in the garden some, talk to my cats. I hardly ever think of what Grandfather told me that long-ago night. I don't *want* to think about it. Nor have I ever breathed a single word of his terrible revelation. This is one promise I intend to keep.

Part IV

ADDIE RYLAND
(1920)

Chapter 21

THEY wheeled him into the emergency room at half-past ten on a Sunday night, a young, blond-headed man, unconscious, with several knife wounds in the chest and on the arms.

"Cut up in Hell's Half Acre," the orderly said.

That surprised me. The young man didn't look like the type of tough who'd get mixed up in Half Acre fights. And Lord knows, Creesey Hospital had seen enough of *those*—the sailors and dockworkers, the drunks and the drifters attracted to the saloons and brothels of that district. *Notorious* was the polite way the newspapers described Hell's Half Acre. A murder a week.

"No vital-organ damage," Dr. Osmond said. The young man lay still as a corpse, his face a ghastly blue under the brilliant arc light. "Lost a lot of blood. Nurse, see if you can't get one of his friends out there to donate."

There were several nurses present, but because I was a student nurse, and low woman on the totem pole, the task fell to me.

When I came out into the crowded waiting room and asked Sylvia at the desk to point out the young man's friends, she told me they had left.

"Gave me his name—Will Ryland. Said they didn't know any more and stomped right out the door."

We didn't have blood banks in those days.

"Well . . . ," Dr. Osmond said, looking around, "which of you will it be?"

Mrs. Gorman, my superior, said, "How's about you, Addie?"

"Sure," I said, "I don't mind." Always a soft touch—stray kittens, beggars, old ladies crossing streets, a hand to the halt, the lame, and the blind. What other kind of person would be crazy enough to want to become a nurse?

213

The next morning when I came on the floor, I was told that Will Ryland wanted to see me.

He was sitting up, still pale, a nice-looking man with eyes that crinkled at the corners when he smiled. His chart said he was twenty-eight.

"So you're the gel who saved my life," he said.

"No," I answered modestly, "that was Dr. Osmond."

"You gave me your blood, didn't you?" He patted the chair beside the bed. "Can you sit?"

"Only a minute."

He smiled again, the kind of smile that makes a girl feel warm all over. Not very many good-looking men smiled that way at me. It seemed they always went for the cute, baby-faced girls, the bee-stung lips and flat chests and painted eyes.

"How did you get into such an awful fight?" I asked.

He looked down at his bandages and grimaced. "Some fella called me a hillbilly, and I took exception. He didn't fight fair."

"No, I don't reckon so. You looked like a scored ham."

He laughed. "What's your name?"

"Addie—Addie Svenson."

"Svenson?" His tongue twisted around it.

"Swedish," I said. "My folks came from Sweden. But I was born and reared here in Newport News."

"City gel, eh?" His eyes teased.

"Watch it, or I'll be calling you a hillbilly, too."

He laughed again. Those white teeth and the strong throat. Will Ryland was something.

"Where you from?" I asked.

"Stone Mill Hollow," he said.

"Never heard of it."

"It's up the mountain—in the Blue Ridge."

It might as well have been Cincinnati—or Timbuktu. I had never been further than a ferry ride across the Roads to Norfolk.

"How long they fixin' to keep me here?" he asked when I removed his supper tray that evening.

"I don't know, but I can find out."

He was to be released the next day. Will Ryland worked for the Newport News Shipbuilding and Drydock Company, a concern ahead of its time in that it provided medical care for its employees, but only for injuries received on the job.

Will was bitter about that. "Seems to me when they say medical services, they mean medical services."

"You can hardly blame them for not wanting to bear the cost of men who get roughed up in Hell's Half Acre."

"Hey, now! I don't want you thinkin' I go there regular. I was just havin' a look-see. Can't fault a man for being curious, can you?"

"No," I said, punching up the pillow behind him. "Would you like something to read? A book? A magazine?"

"Right nice of you to ask. A magazine—with pictures—would do fine."

That was when I first learned that Will Ryland could read—but barely.

It didn't matter. Now, that's a funny thing, I remember thinking, because I had been brought up to respect education. My mother and father had no sooner settled themselves in Newport News than they began learning the new language, going to a little night class conducted by an old German immigrant. It wasn't easy for them, since most of their friends and relatives had traveled on to Minnesota (my father had been promised a carpentry job in Newport News) and the German spoke a garbled Swedish, but learning was in their blood. There were five of us children, and my folks had managed through no little sacrifice to send each one through high school at the least. Education was held high by the Svensons, and when Will Ryland came to call that first time, my parents noticed his lack.

They never really liked him.

But I did. His merry eyes, the nose and the chin and forehead all put together just so, his laugh—everything about him tickled me pink.

Two weeks after he left the hospital, he invited me to a dance, a hoedown. "I brought my fiddle," he said.

Well, you know that ad, "They all laughed when I sat down at the piano, and then—?" That was how I felt about Will and the fiddle. But, Lord, how that man could play! Tucked up under his chin, a faraway look in his eye, he played it sad, he played it gay, he made it talk, giggle, and cry. People gathered round to listen as he put the other musicians to shame.

And Will could dance, too—light, tireless, smooth.

> "It's hey, pretty little black-eyed Susie,
> Hey, pretty little black-eyed Susie,
> Hey, hey, hey. . . ."

Swinging me to the center and right back, swinging me home. I'd never laughed so much, never thought I could be so happy.

We saw a lot of each other in the next few weeks, in spite of my folk's coolness, in spite of Nurse Gorman's lecture on half-awake students, in spite of me telling myself, Now, watch out, he's a love-'em-and-leave-'em man.

What did we do? We walked and we talked, we danced and we spooned, we watched the moon set and the sun rise.

He did not like Newport News.

"Why did you leave Stone Mill Hollow?" I asked him one night.

He was silent for a long time, unusual for Will, a man who, as a rule, couldn't abide a gap in the conversation. I had the feeling he resented my question.

But when he finally spoke, he said, "For a while there, Stone Mill got too much for me. You see, my sister Ellie-Mae died—suddenlike. And I thought I'd get out and see the world. But now"—he turned to me—"now I'm missin' Stone Mill. I miss the huntin' in the fall, and cold, cracklin' winters, and the good, clean well water. I miss my family, too."

More and more he spoke of quitting his job and going home. He had worked most of the war years helping to build ships, and the company had kept him on afterward when they converted to locomotives and turbines.

He wanted to go home. Well, I would think, what do I care? There are other fish in the sea.

His father was the town blacksmith, but Will hoped to persuade him to make the forge over into a garage. "Automobiles is the thing now. Why, Pa is still back in the last century. I've a mind to set him straight."

Spring crept upon us—a tight bud unfolding slowly here, a leaf there, a bird twittering, another pecking at new, tender grass. And then, suddenly, the bare-branched arches down the long streets were replaced by green canopies. Sweet-smelling lilacs, yellow daffodils, and ruby-red tulips bloomed on lawns and in backyards with a pain-stabbing loveliness.

By then, of course, I was madly in love with Will, and everything I looked at hurt.

"You're a sweet gel," Will would say, his arm about my waist. "Why you want to live in this godawful city beats me."

"I'm fond of it, just like you're fond of Stone Mill. This is my home," I would answer, while inside other words, other tunes played. *I'll go with you anywhere you ask, anywhere, anywhere. . ."*

One evening he called early. We were to attend a dance, and he carried his fiddle in its black case under his arm. His face was shining with joy. "They laid me off," he said. "They laid off a bunch of fellas."

I had been half expecting it. Pa said the war boom was over and business was bad. People were tightening their belts. But so soon—I didn't think it would be so soon.

"Then I expect you'll be going back to Stone Mill," I said.

"A-dancin' all the way." He gave me a bear hug, kissing me soundly on the cheek. "But first I aim to get me a partner."

I held my breath.

"Well, ain't you sayin' anythin'?"

"Who you got in mind?" My voice came out in a high treble.

"Didn't you know? 'It's hey, pretty little black-eyed Susie!' Some gel I met up in Hell's Half Acre."

He was teasing me, of course. But I took him at his word, thinking, So that's where he's been all those nights when he wasn't with me, gallivanting up at Hell's Half Acre. A black-eyed girl (my eyes were gray), painted, no doubt, with bee-stung lips, had sidled in and taken him away; just as easy as taking candy from a baby.

He put his fingers under my drooping chin and lifted my head so that he could look into my eyes. "You got a long face for a gel's just been proposed to."

"Will . . . I . . ." And I was in his arms, laughing and crying and saying yes, yes, yes. . . .

Ma and Pa tried to talk me out of it; my sister Inga, too. She was the oldest, married, mother of three, solid, sensible. "You don't know a thing about him," she said. "And where is this Stone Mill Hollow?"

"In Heaven," I said, starry-eyed fool that I was.

* * *

We were married by a Protestant minister on a Saturday morning. Will, anxious for us to be on our way, wanted no partying or fuss, so that afternoon we caught the C&O train to Front Royal. From there we hitched a ride up the mountain with a drayman carrying a load of Irish potatoes and flour to Bradley's store in Stone Mill. The man's name was Ralph, a brawny fellow, his unshaven face creased and reddened by wind and sun. He kept a mason jar of corn whiskey under the seat, and every now and then he'd reach down, haul it out, and offer a swig to Will before tilting it back and taking a long drink himself.

He told me that this was his first run to Stone Mill and he was glad of the company.

"I wonder if it's changed much," Will mused.

"Can't tell you," Ralph said. "But there's hard times along the countryside here. Bad freeze this spring, I been told, and then a bug just about wiped the new plantin' clean."

"Is that so?" Will commented.

The road grew steeper, and Ralph, cursing good-naturedly, urged the horses on. With ears flattened they strained in their harnesses while the wagon creaked and groaned. We passed a tiny hamlet—four or five houses clinging like limpets to the side of the hill. A dog dashed out from somewhere, a skinny, half-starved beast, and began running in and out under the horses, nipping at their heels.

"It's going to get hurt," I said anxiously.

"Serves 'im right," Ralph said.

A yelp and an awful crunch bore out my prediction. "Stop . . . ! Please stop!"

Ralph spat over the rim of the wheel.

"Please . . . ," I begged.

He brought the horses to a halt, and, turning, I saw the dog, a bloody heap. "Dead as a doornail," Will said.

A child burst out from the bushes and ran toward the dog. When he—it was a boy—reached the mangled corpse, he began to sob. I couldn't stand it. "Let me down."

He was very thin, very pale, dressed in tattered, ill-fitting rags. "Y'uns kilt hit," he accused, his grimy face stained with tears.

"I'm sorry," I said. "We didn't mean to. You see, he was chasing the horses."

A woman carrying a baby on her hip approached. Tall and gaunt with sunken cheeks, both she and the babe, as well as the boy, had the gray, drab look of poverty, the look of those who seldom have enough to eat.

"Are you the boy's mother?" I asked—a stupid question, but she was staring at me wordlessly and I had to say something.

"I'm his ma." She tugged at the boy's shoulder. "Listen at me and quit yore wailin', y'hear?"

"I'm sorry about the accident," I apologized, and then added impulsively, "I . . . I'd like to give the boy something." I ran back to the wagon and got the basket which held our lunch.

Will said, "What you doin'?"

"They're *hungry*, Will," I whispered.

"For Lord's sake!" he said impatiently.

I brought out several sandwiches and a piece of cake, wrapping them in a napkin. The woman, meanwhile, had come closer, and she stood looking at me out of tired eyes, as if to fathom the unknown world I represented.

"This," I said, holding out the linen-wrapped sandwiches, "this can't make up for the dog, but I'd like for . . ."

As the boy reached for the package, the woman put out her arm and barred the way. "We got plenty," she said.

I didn't argue. I knew pride when I saw it.

"Shiftless, ignorant," Will said when I got back in the wagon.

I thought of the woman's tired eyes, the work-worn hands holding the baby, the boy's rags.

Ralph said, "They ain't got much but a teensy few acres, a cow if they's lucky, a few chickens. End of winter's a bad time."

We stopped at a sun-bleached farmhouse called Grimshaw's to water the horses. Three or four men and a boy in overalls lounged on the porch watching us, their jaws moving over quids of tobacco. Will got down to talk to them. They had the same gaunt, hungry look as the woman. "Isn't easy for them up here," Ralph said, shaking his head. "Hard times."

But nature seemed so generous and giving. Will pointed out mountain laurel, flame azalea, the showy rhododendron, and stands of dogwood in pale bloom. What a feast for the eyes, what a show! Only the occasional mean log cabin we passed was a reminder that man had faired poorly.

We rode into Stone Mill Hollow just as an orange sun was

setting in the west. It threw a peculiar light over the trees, over the houses, over the town—a place much smaller than I had imagined. We jolted down a cobbled street flanked by a church, a school, a closed mill, a store; and then we were stopping at the forge. Was that it? I wanted to ask, *all* of Stone Mill?

"Thanks, Ralph," Will said as he helped me down. "Stop by the house for a bite of supper, once you get your business done."

"Thanks kindly, I believe I will."

A grizzled man wearing a black leather apron came out from the forge, his face alight with pleasure. "Why, if it ain't the old fiddlin' fool, Will, m'boy!" He clapped him on the back in a rough half-embrace. "Tess! Tess!" he called to an upstairs window. "C'mon out and see who we got here."

I stood modestly in the background among the boxes and suitcases, a nervous smile on my face, waiting for Will to introduce me.

"Well—lookeee . . . !" A woman with salt-and-pepper braided hair rushed down the side stairs. She hugged and kissed Will, and was joined a moment later by a younger woman who did the same. A young man came out of the forge and pumped Will's hand. "Welcome home, welcome home."

I stood and waited and waited, thinking, What about me?

Finally, Will freed himself from their embraces. "Hey! Wait a minute. . . . I want you all to meet my new bride. Addie . . . ?"

Silence. They stared at me, all of them in shock. Will hadn't told them. He promised he would, he said he'd write. But he hadn't.

My smile began to ache. "How d'you do," I said in a small voice. They didn't like me. I could see it in their faces. I wasn't pretty; I didn't have bee-stung lips; I was too old; I was too young. . . .

"You done got married?" Will's father asked incredulously. "Whyn't you say somethin'?"

"I thought I'd spring it on you," Will smiled.

And his mother said, shock still lingering in her eyes, "But she's an outlander!"

And that's what I was, what I always remained.

Chapter 22

AFTER the Rylands had finished digesting their surprise, inborn hospitality took over.

"Addie, dear, if you want a wash-up," Ma Ryland said as we went up the stairs, "there's a bathroom end of the hall. A new one. Pa just had it put in. And you and Will can have the boys' room. See here. . . ." The room was small, with two brass bedsteads, a marble-topped dresser, and an old-fashioned commode. "I hope you didn't mind us being so took."

"No," I said. "I didn't mind."

Of the Rylands' six children, one was dead (Ellie-Mae), three were married (counting Will), and two, Elizabeth and Roy, were still living at home. Elizabeth, eighteen, was the youngest, the "least one," a pretty girl with honey-colored hair and a pert nose. Her brother Roy, also light-haired, was a widower at twenty-one. His young wife had died in child-birth six months earlier.

"She should have had Cass birthin' her," he told me, "instead of going down to the doctor in Front Royal." Cass, as I understood it, was the local midwife.

When we sat down to supper that night, the table fairly groaned with food; no sign of starvation here. Chicken and dumplings, a "mess" of greens, gravy, snaps, canned beets, corn cake, biscuits, jam, pie—all were washed down with strong, bitter coffee. No wonder the Rylands looked so healthy, so thriving.

"Smithing must be a good business," I said to Will later, as we undressed for bed.

"So-so," he said. "But I've put a flea in Pa's ear. He's beginnin' to think on a garage."

There was this thing about Stone Mill folk I noticed the very first week—*Everybody* looked prosperous, jolly, rosy-

221

cheeked, happy, and except for a few oldsters, all hand-some. Among the young there wasn't a single homely person. Made me feel a bit out of it. Not that I'm ugly, but I wouldn't win a beauty contest, either. My nose is too small, my brown hair straight and fine (the perm I got just before the wedding had only frizzled it). I could hardly blame the Rylands when I thought of their shock, for I expect they looked for Will to marry a local beauty, some young thing with golden hair, like Elizabeth.

Neither spring freeze nor drought nor the bug had touched Stone Mill. "It's protected from the cold by the mountains," Will told me. "Same reason we get rain when other places might not have any." The town was in a hollow, just as its name said. You could see the mountains covered with dark trees all around, crowding close against the sky.

"Not everyone here raises their own food," I said to Will, still puzzling over the lack of hard times in Stone Mill. "Some are in business, and they're all doing well. Why?"

"Now, Addie," Will said. "One thing you gotta learn. Folks here don't appreciate busybodies."

We'd been married two weeks by then, and I was already beginning to see wedded life wasn't to be an extended honeymoon. Not that I had expected to be catered to and petted, or "dearied" and "sweetied" every minute—not with Will—but I didn't think I'd be called a busybody so soon in the game.

Furthermore, I didn't like living with my in-laws, though they tried hard to be kind. Too hard. There was nothing for me to *do*. Elizabeth and Ma Ryland cooked, cleaned, sewed, washed, and ironed. Even Will's clothes. It was as though I were some kind of tolerated guest just passing through.

"Don't fret," Will said. "There's a house I've had my eye on."

"Where?"

"You'll see."

That was another thing about Stone Mill. It had a funny effect on Will. No sooner had he come home than he be-came *secretive*. I don't mean he suddenly stopped talking—Will couldn't do that unless his tongue was torn out—but he just didn't *say* anything. Ask him a question, and he'd fend it off with a babble of words.

He had become ambitious, too. In Newport News he had seemed such a happy-go-lucky fellow, taking each day as it came, but now, suddenly, he seemed bitten with the "get-ahead" bug, working long hours in the forge, talking constantly garage, garage.

When a few more weeks had gone by and Will still hadn't said anything about a house, I decided to go out and look around myself. The older houses, built of wood, clustered near the center of town, were modest, two-story dwellings kept up to snuff with fresh paint and well-tended lawns. In one of these lived the mayor, Colonel Perry. I understand the title was an honorary one inherited from his father. I didn't think titles like that could be handed down from one generation to another, but nobody else seemed to consider it out of the ordinary.

Further out, Main Street made a little jog and became Tulip Avenue. Here stood four or five fairly new, solid-looking houses of red brick set back from the street under shade trees. Elizabeth had informed me that they were the residences of the more prominent citizens of Stone Mill, people like the Dawsons (bank) and the Bradleys (general store). None of them looked vacant.

I kept on walking. At the last large house was a little, unpaved street—more like an alleyway—branching off to the left. I turned the corner. Trees and bushes grew thickly on either side. A lane leading nowhere, I thought, until a sagging wooden fence suddenly appeared, running parallel to the lane. I peeped through the unpainted slats but could see nothing because of a dense screen of shrubbery. I moved along until I found a gate. Beyond was a forest of trees. I hesitated, then unlatched the gate, the hinges screaming in the silence as I went through.

The walk, once paved with stones and overgrown now with moss and creeping vines, led through a trackless jungle. I hadn't yet learned the names of these mountain trees and shrubs. But I recognized the tulip tree, the magnolia and dogwood. Countless others grew there, strange trees of every size and shape, crowded together, their branches intertwined—dark-green, jade-green, yellow-green—green everywhere, overpowering, blotting out sun and sky. Each tree and shrub capable of blooming seemed to have done so—showy, oppressive blooms, masses of them, perfuming the air with a heavy, almost sickening scent.

I can't breathe, I thought. What am I doing here?

But then the trees thinned, and a moment later I was standing before a house. Two stories high, it had an attic with a round window, and steps leading to a veranda. The outer walls had once been painted white, the shutters green; but the paint was flaking now, leaving strips of mottled gray. Shades were drawn across blank windows. A deserted house, empty, lonesome, silent.

The wind stirred a dead wisteria vine which had wound itself about one of the veranda posts, and it made a hollow, staccato sound like the rattling of dry bones. I wondered who had lived here, how long ago. There must have been a garden also, for I could still see the little looped wire fences marking out the beds where a few daffodils and iris had struggled up through the weeds.

Turning, I followed a stone path as it wound past the ruined garden and entered the thick forest again. It was very quiet under the trees—not a peaceful quiet, but the kind of stillness that holds its breath and makes you shiver. Wait, it seems to say, wait and see.

Why am I so uneasy? I wondered.

The path was barely visible as it trailed through the rank shrubbery and then disappeared altogether in a wild tangle of dogwood and thorny vines.

A bird called out—one long, high note, sweet and piercing—the first bird note I'd heard since passing through the gate. The silence quivered as it called again, and then I was standing under an immense spreading oak. From a thick, gnarled limb a child's swing dangled by one rope. A small breeze sighed through the leaves, causing the swing to sway lazily back and forth, its elongated shadow swinging with it over the ground.

Watching that dark shadow, a sudden panic seized me, and, turning quickly, I fled back up the path to the house.

And there I paused, ashamed of my ridiculous, stumbling flight. *Addie, get yourself in hand!* Clearheaded, practical Addie. Here's a house—empty, near town, certainly large enough for Will and me and the family we hope to raise. A little paint, a few repairs, and it will do fine.

It looks spooky, Addie, a little voice inside me said. Pooh —pooh! Show me an empty house that doesn't.

I went up the wooden steps and into the cold shadow of the veranda, my footsteps echoing in the awful stillness. The door was locked, and I crouched down, putting my eye to the keyhole. I saw a dim, dusty carpet and the bottom half of a clock pendulum, as if it had been frozen in time at the far end of a telescope.

I walked back down the stairs and around the house to the rear door. It was locked, too, but halfheartedly, as if the key had not turned the bolt all the way. One strong pull, and I had the door open. I went into the kitchen. Taps in the kitchen sink, not a pump, taps rotting and green with rust. In the pantry I found empty shelves, a few blackened cooking pans, a cobwebbed jar of moldy preserves.

The dining room was dominated by a large, old-fashioned kerosene-lamp chandelier. Under it stood a round table, and in a cobwebbed corner a walnut cupboard displayed rows of dusty plates.

Crossing the hall where the clock stood, I came to a parlor with a fireplace, several chairs, and a sofa. The rugs rolled up to one side revealed a wide planked floor.

Nervous, chilled by the dim silence, I hesitated at the bottom of the stairs. Then I went up. There were four bedrooms, two with fireplaces flanked by rusty firedogs, the hearth covered with a light powder of ashes. The bedrooms were furnished with outmoded four-posters made up with woven coverlets and fat pillows, and a confusion of old chests, tables, ornate, curled mica medallions, and spindle-backed chairs. In one room, shadowed by a large tree outside the window, there was a faded photograph of a dark-bearded man with a scowl. A calendar dated 1906 hung on the wall. It was as if I had stumbled into an old, forgotten museum.

I went to the dusty bureau and opened a drawer. Suddenly, without warning, the same panic which had gripped me under the oak took hold of me again. My heart began to pound, my knees to tremble. Now, Addie, I said. But it was no use. I could feel the ghosts of those who had lived here all around me, felt them watching, whispering among themselves.

Stumbling down the stairs, I fled from the house and up the stone path, shoving branches and bushes aside, kicking at vines which clung to my skirt, gasping for breath.

When I got out into the road, my fear left me as suddenly as it had come. I felt like a silly fool, standing there with my hair all mussed and my blouse riding out of my skirt. Running away from nothing, *nothing*. Yet I knew I could never live in that house.

That evening I asked Will about it.

"Why d'you have to go wanderin' 'round like that for? Didn't I tell you I'd find us a house?"

I knew he wasn't going to tell me a thing about that house, even if I asked until I turned blue in the face. So later, when I managed to get Elizabeth alone, I put it to her.

"It belonged to people called Covington," she said. "The place has been empty ever since I was little."

"Covington? Have I met them?"

"There's none in town. They're all dead, I reckon. No, wait—seems to me there was some talk of an old maid, Sarah, who lives in Raleigh now."

I had just about given up the thought of moving when a week later Will said he had rented a house and it would be ours the first of the month. I was so happy I could have cried.

"It ain't much," Will warned. "Belongs to one of the Davidsons. He's rose up a little in the world, and he's bought a larger place."

The house *wasn't* much. Though the outside had been painted to spruce it up a bit, it looked tired, sagging, like an old crone trying to hide her wrinkles with powder and rouge. Inside were two tiny bedrooms, a kitchen and parlor. I wondered where the Davidsons had all slept (there were eight of them). The plumbing was ancient, a pump in the kitchen sink, and across a flinty yard stood the outhouse, odorous, crowded with spiders.

Still, it was better than living with the Rylands, squeezed into a tiny room where our lovemaking could be heard through the walls, taking the pleasure from it. And the house wasn't really so bad once I got over my first disappointment. In the front yard a locust grew—in pink flower now—and there were lilacs and azaleas, too. The Rylands had promised us some furniture, and if I made covers and bright curtains for the windows and decorated the splintery walls with paper, I could pretty the place up. At least it would be *ours*.

As Will was the oldest son, he would someday inherit the forge. Meanwhile, he was not letting grass grow under his feet. He'd already persuaded his pa to let him do repairs on the few cars in town. People were only too glad to come to Will instead of having to go over to Novotno.

Every now and again, though, I could hear Pa Ryland grumbling and Will arguing back. "This here's a lucky year, ain't it?" I overheard Will say one afternoon. "Nineteen twenty. Everythin' fresh, everythin' gonna start new. Lucky."

"The old ways can't go by the board so easy," Pa Ryland said.

"I'm not talkin' 'bout old *ways*," Will said. "I'm talkin' business."

There was a short silence. "Seems like it took you long enough to come back to the fold," Pa Ryland said.

"I was a green kid. Didn't know any better. Ellie-Mae—her goin'—the way she went—hit me hard. But now that's all through with. . . ."

I wondered what he meant by "the way she went." Had she been ill a long time, in pain . . .?

"You shoulda wedded a Stone Mill filly," Pa Ryland said.

Standing in the shadows outside the forge window, my heart seemed to stop beating.

"Addie's a good gel," Will said. Not, "I love her, I was mad for her, she's wonderful." Addie, a good "gel." Like a smart dog or a steady horse. Good gel, Addie.

After a moment Will said, "We ought to keep an eye on Elizabeth."

"No need," came Pa Ryland's voice. "We already did for the cause."

Cause?

But they walked away from the window, and a moment later all I could hear was the clang of iron against iron.

We moved into our new house June 1—a Wednesday—and on Saturday we gave a housewarming. Since our little parlor wasn't big enough for the crowd invited by Will, the festivities took place in the yard. While Will, his father and brother set up tables on the lawn, Ma Ryland and Elizabeth helped me in the kitchen. People started arriving early, the women crowding into the house with covered dishes and baskets and pans containing food enough for an army. Coarse muslin was spread on the tables, and we scurried back and forth from the house laying out the feast.

The men stood together under the pink locust, spitting and chewing, talking, and I gathered from their loud laughter, passing the jug. The smaller children sat on the grass and watched with large eyes or clung to their mothers' skirts. The older boys chased and wrestled in the dusty road, calling out to one another, while the girls lolled under the lilac, giggling and whispering and pretending not to notice.

I had met most of our guests in church: Preacher David- son, a banty rooster of a man; Cass Loeffler and Reba Perry, the two midwives; Everett (Colonel) Perry, the mayor, and his wife, Dorothy; several Dawsons and dozens of Loefflers —people whose faces and names I couldn't quite put to- gether yet. Matt and Elsie Ryland arrived late. Matt, an uncle of Will's, a husky, well-setup man, and Elsie, a sweet- faced woman of thirty, were on the outs with my in-laws for some reason no one would explain. But they mingled that night with the others and seemed to be having a good time. When supper was served, the company crowded around, heaping their plates, eating with voracious appetites. I wouldn't have thought it possible, but within an hour most of the food was gone.

As we sat around, heavy-limbed, trying to digest our meal, the evening air carried the sound of musical twangs and plunkety-plunks. Will and Roy had taken out their fiddles and were gradually joined by others, some with fiddles, some with guitars or banjos. A few had brought harmonicas and tambourines. Jay Clarke had come with a dulcimer, of all things, a box with metal strings. He had bought it in Bath, Kentucky, from a man named James Edward Thomas, he told me, "the only good dulcimer maker in the whole U.S.A."

Looking at the men tuning up their instruments, I could understand why Will was so crazy for music. Every young male over the age of fourteen seemed to play something, even if it was just a gourd fiddle.

The night drew on, and lamps were brought out and set on the tables. Early moths came flitting around the bright flames. A pretty young woman sat down next to me. I had met her earlier but couldn't remember her name.

"Such a fine warming," she said.

"Thank you."

"I'm sure Will and you ought to be happy. He's a right good man."

The way she said "right good" made me look at her closely. She had lovely golden hair, a perfect little nose, and white, rosy-tinged skin. Just like a fairy princess.

Myrtle Loeffler. That was her name. Myrtle.

I went back to watching the men. "What will you have?" Will called.

Myrtle sprang to her feet. " 'Lord Thomas and Fair Ellen.' Sing that one."

A hush ran through the audience as Will began to play and sing,

> "Mother, O mother, come riddle to me,
> Come riddle it all in one;
> Must I marry fair Ellen,
> Or bring the brown girl home?"

I stole a glance at Myrtle. She was looking at Will the way a hungry dog looks at a bone. I felt sick.

> " 'Is this your bride, Lord Thomas?' she cried,
> 'I think she's most wonderful brown,
> When you could have married a fair-skinned girl
> As ever the sun shine on.' "

Elizabeth said, "I don't see why we can't clear the tables and dance. All this toe-tapping music going to waste."

"Yes," Myrtle echoed. "Here—some of you menfolk, push aside the tables."

The tables were shoved to one side and the benches made a square. A caller was found, Estes Clarke, and the dancing commenced. Myrtle made her way through the dancers to Will, and from where I sat I could see her talking to him.

I wanted to tear her blond hair out. Instead, I sat there, a frozen smile on my face. Don't look, Addie, don't look. Sooner or later you knew this would happen. All the pretty girls just waiting for Will to come home, married or not. I was just handy at the right time, the right place.

Will danced with me later, after he had finished whirling Myrtle through several sets. But by then my evening had been ruined.

Chapter 23

THOUGH he never spoke of it to me, I knew my husband felt his father ought to make out a legal will.

"It's true the forge comes to me, Pa," I once overheard him say. "But there's Ralph"—his married brother—"and he might have his feelin's hurt if it ain't in black and white."

"Ain't no feelin's involved," his father said.

"Maybe if you had somebody write it down . . ."

"I ain't writin' it. I make a will and first thing y'know I'm dead. Happened to Eb Clarke. Shot in a hunting accident two days after he'd been to Harry's."

Harry Loeffler was the town lawyer.

"But, Pa," Will pointed out, "Eb was ninety."

"Makes no never mind," he said stubbornly.

My husband may have had trouble with the printed page, but he was nobody's fool. "Look, Addie," he said to me one morning, "now that we're settled, we ought to have company for supper. I don't mean a big do—just a sit-down supper."

"Fine with me," I said. "Who you got in mind?"

"My ma and pa for one."

"I've been meaning to have them."

"And Harrry Loeffler."

I saw his plan. "Do you think he can talk your pa into making a will?"

He gave me a sharp look. "How'd y'know about that will?"

"I didn't think it was a secret," I said. Husbands and wives are supposed to share. My parents did.

"I don't like it talked about," he said.

"I'm not a talker," I retorted, hurt and annoyed.

"All right, all right. It's for Pa's own good as well as mine. Can you have a nice supper?"

"Yes. But you had better invite someone else, too. So it won't look too . . . too obvious."

We settled on Elsie and Matt, since it seemed they had

made up their differences with Ma and Pa Ryland.

I cooked all day, making the Swedish dishes I had learned from my mother. Brown cabbage soup, *slottsslek* (pot roast), stuffed cauliflower, beet salad with apples, and jam torte.

I could have saved myself the trouble. Harry Loeffler and I were the only ones who ate. The others pushed their food from one side of the plate to the other, uncomfortable at all the strange food. "No biscuits?" Pa asked plaintively.

I tried to make light of it. "Thought you folks would like a change from fried chicken and greens."

"Best vittles there is," grumbled Ma Ryland.

Harry leaned back in his chair. "I enjoyed it, Addie. Thanks."

I smiled at him. "How is it," I said after a moment, "such a good-looker like you is still a bachelor?" Harry, I judged, was about thirty-five, a pleasant-natured man with crisp, light-brown hair and regular features.

"Never found the right girl," he said, the usual reply, but coming from him it sounded forced.

"Not here in Stone Mill?" I asked. "With so many pretty girls, and you so handsome? Certainly there must have been someone?"

He looked away in embarrassment. No one said anything. There *had* been someone, then. Who? I wondered.

Ma Ryland said, "Addie, you must give me the recipe for this pie."

"Torte," I said. "It's called a torte."

They didn't want me to ask who. But why? At Harry's age couldn't he laugh about it? A jilted suitor or one who had changed his mind? What difference did it make?

The coffee I had brewed to Stone Mill's taste, strong with a pinch of chicory. I found some leftover corn pone in the cupboard and brought it out with a jar of strawberry preserves and a wedge of cheese. Pa Ryland fell on it as if he had been starved for weeks. I ought to feel guilty, I thought. Plain folks like plain food.

"I reckon I'll have a little bit of cheese, too," Ma Ryland said.

His strength now regained, Pa Ryland, a man who did not hold with verbal fencing, came right to the heart of the matter. No dummy himself, he had guessed the reason for Harry's presence. "Now, Harry," he said, "I ain't got no objection to you folks who read the law, but if you're thinkin' of talkin' me into a will, you gotta think twice."

"A written record is a good thing to have," Harry said. "Saves arguments, families fighting and splitting up."

"I don't give a boot who fights," he said. "That's the last word on it."

Pa Ryland, of course, didn't believe he was ever going to die. And that was another thing about Stone Mill—none of them did. When death came they grieved—or at least they seemed to grieve—but dying was a thing that happened to someone else. Not me. *You.*

"Will's not being grabby," Harry pointed out.

"No need for him to be. The forge's his, whatever."

Will said, "You could change your mind, Pa. I do mean to make it into a garage."

"No. I ain't a-changin' my mind."

One morning a child came to my door, a girl of ten, bare-footed but neatly dressed. She was greatly agitated.

"I'm Estie Dawson," she said breathlessly. "Ma's birthin' her baby, and neither Cass nor Reba is able to be there, and" —pausing to swallow—"and Ma says you been a nurse, and could you please, please come. She . . . she's hollerin' somethin' awful." Tears hung on her eyelashes.

During my student-nurse days I had watched enough births to know pretty much what to do. But suppose this one was breech—or the mother started to hemorrhage?

"Couldn't your father fetch the doctor?" The nearest one, I had been told, was in Novotno.

"He don't want a doctor. And anyways, there ain't no time," she said plaintively.

"All right. I'll get my medicine box."

Estie's family lived on the other side of Bradley's, handy to her pa's work as a store clerk, Estie told me. Theirs was one of the older wooden houses, two-storied, painted cream, exactly like the others along the street, except that it had a high, deep porch.

Mr. Dawson himself met me at the door with a nervous smile. "Much obliged you could come," he said. "Our two midwives wasn't able. Cass's down with her rheumatism, and Reba's out helping at her granddaughter's, and—" A scream pierced the air. "I'd best be taking the young ones out of your way." And with that, he herded three small children and Estie through the door.

"Mr. Dawson . . . !" I called. Another scream, and sudden fear, like stage fright, gripped me. "Mr. Dawson . . . !" halfway across the leaf-littered lawn, he turned. "I'll need help," I said.

"I aim to get you some. I'll send Lydia's sister."

But by the time Mrs. Dawson's sister arrived, so had the baby. He came, a robust boy, sliding headfirst into the world before the water on the stove had commenced to boil.

"As easy as falling off a log," I said, making the mother comfortable, feeling as proud of my solo midwifery as Mrs. Dawson felt of her new baby.

That night I said to Will, "There's no reason why I can't help others. Cass is laid up most of the time. There isn't a doctor closer than ten miles. . . ."

"You'd have to ask Cass and Reba," Will said. "You might be stepping on their toes. They like to keep midwifery in the family."

And that was another thing about Stone Mill—everybody was related to everybody else. Except me. I might be married to Will, but I had never been a Davidson, a Perry, a Loeffler, a Dawson, a Clarke—or even a Ryland distantly removed.

Still, in those days I had plenty of youthful optimism and bounce. If I'm an outsider, I remember thinking, it doesn't mean I have to remain one.

The next morning, carrying a small loaf cake wrapped in a clean towel, I paid Cass Loeffler a call.

She was sitting in a rocking chair by the window, looking out through the lace curtains, when I came up the porch stairs.

"Let yourself in!" she hollered.

She thanked me for the cake. "Can't get up, so you'll have to s'cuse me. Have a chair."

Her cane stood leaning against the sill. I noticed her fingers, the ones on her right hand, especially, were drawn up, the way severe rheumatics' hands are. And she had a cast in one eye—not a pronounced one, but it was there all the same.

"Heard you did right well by Lydia Dawson," she said. She was smoking a hand-rolled cigarette.

"That was nice of her to say so. Thank you."

" 'Course there's one or two things I'd've done differently."

I couldn't imagine what. There hadn't been much to the

whole procedure except to cut the cord and wash the baby. But I wasn't in Cass's parlor to nitpick.

"I expect it's always been easy for you," I said. "All the babies you must have delivered."

"One hundred and twenty-five," she said with an air of satisfaction. "Reba's done about two hundred."

Enough to populate a small village, I thought. "That's a record to be proud of."

She nodded.

"I . . . I was wondering," I began after a moment of silence, "if you could use some help."

"Help?" she repeated, surprised.

"I've had training as a nurse, and I thought, with you feeling poorly. . . ."

"I feel fine, pert as ever! A little rheumatism gets me down now and again, but there ain't no reason why I should need help."

"I'd like to," I said.

She squashed her cigarette in a tin can on the floor, her clawed hands trembling. "Reba and me do all the midwifing in Stone Mill." Her eyes blinked rapidly, angrily. "We don't need no help."

"But what about the people who live outside of town?"

"The farm folk? Why, they ain't that far. I got my horse and buggy, and so has Reba."

"But there are others," I said, suddenly remembering the gaunt mountain woman.

"Mountain folk," she said with scorn. "We don't mingle with them, they don't mingle with us."

"But who do they go to for their doctoring?"

"They do it amongst themselves, I reckon."

But what if they don't? I thought. What if they don't know how? And here I was with my medical learning going to waste, and all kinds of time. Cooking and cleaning took but an hour or two. And there was no sign of a hoped-for child on the way.

When I spoke of helping the mountain folk to Will, he thought it a crazy notion. "Gallivantin' 'round the country-side like a granny woman!" But he didn't say no.

One morning, two weeks after I had delivered the Dawson baby, I asked to borrow Pa Ryland's horse and buggy and rode over to Novotno. It was a fair-sized town, not as large as Front Royal, but it boasted several stores, a post office, a small bank, a tobacco warehouse, paved streets, and a railway station. And I counted six automobiles before I reached the frame house where Dr. Willoughby practiced and lived.

A little sign on his door said WALK IN, and a bell tinkled somewhere in the back as I opened it. I stepped into a room crowded with dark, heavy, clawed furniture. A three-legged coatrack stood in one corner, and on the wall a printed placard invited me to be seated. Voices reached me through a closed door. I sat gingerly down on the edge of one of the massive chairs and, picking up a magazine, began to flip through it.

Presently the door opened. "Just take care you don't get the wound dirty."

"I will, Doc. Much obliged to you."

A pause. "And what can I do for you, young lady?"

I lowered the magazine. He was much younger than I had thought. Much. "I'm Addie Ryland," I said. "Mrs. Will Ryland from Stone Mill Hollow, and I wanted to talk to you. . . ."

"Yes. Won't you come in, then?"

His desk, a wide, old-fashioned rolltop, was littered with bills, empty phials, pill envelopes, a stethoscope, a rubber hammer, journals—all the paraphernalia of a busy country doctor.

"I don't very often have patients from over Stone Mill way," he said. He had a face like a cherub, very pink and smooth.

"I'm not here as a patient," I said. "I've come for advice."

"Oh?"

"You see, I'd like to be a midwife." I went on to tell him the situation in Stone Mill (Reba and Cass's jealously guarded domain) and how I'd come within months of getting my nurse's cap. "I feel I'm qualified," I said, "just as much as the others."

"More so, I would think," he agreed.

"And I thought you could tell me if there was a need for a midwife somewhere close to Stone Mill."

"Good Lord, Mrs. Ryland, this country roundabout could use half a dozen like you. But I'm afraid none of the places I have in mind are within walking distance."

"Well—I suppose I might talk Pa Ryland into loaning me the buggy."

"Horseback is more like it. Can you ride?"

"I . . . I never have," I said. "I'm a city girl. Newport News."

"Hmmm. Thought you sounded a little citified." He gave me a smile. "Didn't know Stone Mill folk ever married outside the town."

"They don't as a rule," I said.

"In any case Mr. Will Ryland is a mighty lucky fellow. Where did you do your student nursing?"

"Creesey Hospital."

"Creesey? What a coincidence! I interned there in nineteen twelve. Tell me, is the old surgeon Dr. Osmond still there?"

"Oh—is he ever!" I laughed.

"Mean as the devil—and arrogant. But pretty good with the knife. And Mrs. Gordon?"

"Oh, yes, she was my superior."

We went on for the next ten minutes talking about the various people at Creesey, chatting like old friends.

"Have you been in Novotno long?" I asked him.

"Seven years. I came down from Winchester—that's my home—when Dr. Caldwell died."

"You knew Dr. Caldwell?"

"Never laid eyes on him. The town council here advertised. I was a fresh young doctor trying to decide where to set up practice—Winchester already had two—and what to use for money, when I read their ad. I'm not sorry, although I got a little jolt at the beginning."

"How's that?"

" I had the impression that Dr. Caldwell was an old man when he died. But he wasn't. He was the son, Abner, you know. His father had been doctoring here for many years and lived to a ripe old age. His heart finally gave out, and then Abner took over. Abner was the youngest of old Dr. Caldwell's sons, just thirty-two when he was killed. Thrown by his horse. Neck broken—at least that's the way they tell it."

"You sound skeptical. Don't you think it was an accident?"

"I don't know what to think. He was a man who had been in the saddle ever since he could walk—that's what his sister said. And the horse, from what I understand, was not an ill-tempered one." Dr. Willoughby moved his stethoscope aside, his chubby fingers tidying a pile of scattered papers. "He was on his way back from tending to a child down with a severe case of whooping cough. A Stone Mill child."

"Stone Mill?" I asked. "But I thought they never ..."

"They don't. That was the last time a doctor—from Novotno, anyway—has been called to Stone Mill. Dr. Abner Caldwell hadn't gone but a half mile from the town when the—the mishap occurred."

"And you think it might have been an accident on purpose?" I asked.

"I can't say. I may be all wrong." He spindled the papers on a long nail and then went on. "I've only been to Stone Mill once. Would you believe that? Ten miles away, and I've been once. It was when I first came to Novotno. I wanted to start out on the right foot. Make friends with the people who might be calling on me." He chuckled. "That's naiveté for you. No one told me, no one warned me." He paused. "Am I boring you with all this?"

"No, not at all."

"I can remember that day so clearly. A raw November one, with the wind howling down from the mountain. I rode up to the store—Bradley's? Yes. Well, I went inside and introduced myself to the men sitting around the stove. The minute I said 'doctor' everybody froze.

" 'We don't need a doctor,' a red-faced oldster said. And another chimed in, 'We got our own here.' A little man with a huge nose added. 'The Lord God is our best healer.' They didn't want me." He smiled. "Now, I'm talking like a child. Of course this has nothing to do with you."

He drew his chair closer and leaned his elbows on the desk. "You've come to ask my advice. All right. I don't see why anyone at Stone Mill would object to you helping at, say—he glanced at a map of the county on the wall above his desk—say, Hickory Cove. Yes, that's the nearest. They're in desperate need over there. The old woman, Cora McAlpin, who used to tend the sick and deliver the babies has died."

"Hickory Cove," I said, trying to remember if I'd heard of it.

"Truly isolated—about five miles from Stone Mill, as the crow flies. But there's no road. That's why I say you'll need ..."

"I'll go," I said suddenly. "I can't see where there's much to riding a horse. I'll get one and go."

"That's the spirit! Now, you'll need a bag and medicines. At the moment a license isn't required, so that's no problem." His hand went to the map. "Hickory Cove can be reached by following the creek. . . ."

That night at supper I told Will I was planning to midwife at Hickory Cove. He was so deep in his own news, however, I don't think he heard me. Seems that a man in Front Royal had offered to sell him an old Ford "dirt cheap," and Will was wondering how to haul it up to Stone Mill.

"Is it all right with you, then?" I asked.

"What? Is what all right?"

"Midwifing in Hickory Cove."

"Can't see any harm to it," he said expansively. "Just don't go rilin' Cass and Reba up."

Pa Ryland lent me his mare, and Will's brother Roy gave me some pointers on riding. "You'd best practice in short spurts at first," was his sage advice, "else you'll be eatin' off the mantel for the next week."

I hadn't asked Will to keep my Hickory Cove venture a secret, but on the other hand, I did nothing to advertise it. So, one June morning I set out for the Cove without any fuss, without a word to anyone, planning to be home in time for Will's supper.

I picked up the trail on the other side of the abandoned sawmill, following it easily until I got to the falls Dr. Willoughby had told me about. I chose the left branch of the creek as instructed, and almost at once the way narrowed, winding upward, sometimes so steeply I had to dismount a time or two and lead the horse. "Try to keep the creek in sight," Dr. Willoughby had advised, "or at least the sound of it."

Here the forest, like the deserted Covington garden, was suffocating. All those trees and vines and shrubs shutting out sky and sun seemed to squeeze the breath out of my lungs. The green light, the moving shadows, the twittering and creaking scraped at my nerves. I kept looking back over my shoulders. "There are no wild animals to be frightened of," Dr. Willoughby had said. "The game has almost disappeared. Hunted out."

Still, I had the creepy feeling that hidden in the shadows

small, bright little eyes were watching me with interest.

Suddenly a rabbit jumped out from a bush. The horse shied, and I nearly tumbled from the saddle. "Whoa . . . ! Whoa!" I had the sense to call in a voice of authority while pulling tightly on the reins. Fortunately the mare wasn't skittish, for I don't know what I would have done had she chosen to bolt. Even so, I found myself so unnerved I decided to dismount and lead the horse the rest of the way.

The path such as it was, topped a rise and then went steeply down. I guided the horse to the bottom. At the mouth of the ravine, rising through the trees, I glimpsed a chimney. Hickory Cove. A few minutes later I emerged from the wood and caught it full view.

I was not prepared for what I saw. Dr. Willoughby, who had been to the Cove a few times, had told me it was a poverty-stricken community, but I hadn't imagined any place could present such an ugly, dreary picture. The few miserable cabins, some built of logs, others of wooden slats, were tumbledown, weathered to a drab gray. Porches sagged, paneless windows gaped, refuse abounded. The barren ground, creased with rain gullies, supported only the hardiest of weeds, among which a handful of scrawny chickens pecked. The houses were scattered about the ravine—six that I could count from where I stood.

No one was in sight. Except for the occasional cluck of a chicken, an eerie silence hung over the settlement.

"Hello there . . . !" I called. "Hello there! Hell—"

I saw the rifle barrel poking around the corner of the house, and the next split second a bullet zinged past my ear, exploding the silence and scattering the chickens in a flurry of feathers and loud squawking.

Chapter 24

D R. Willoughby had warned me that the people of Hickory Cove might be a little suspicious and unfriendly at first.

But this? I thought, breaking out into a sweat. I clung to the horse's bridle, my eyes glued in fear on the rifle. *I'm going to be shot, and my body will be thrown into the dark-green, shadowy woods; or maybe they'll fling my corpse across the mare's saddle and send us home as a warning.*

ADDIE SVENSON RYLAND, THE DO-GOODER. I could see it written on my tombstone. Dead because she couldn't stay home and mind her own business.

Time stretched. The horse snuffled and nuzzled at my ear. The chickens clucked companionably among the weeds, and a dog, a hound with floppy ears, sauntered out from under the pilings of the house.

The rifle had not moved an inch.

At last, unable to bear the strain, I managed to squeak, "Please . . . please don't shoot." I swallowed. "My . . . my name is Addie Ryland, and . . . I . . . I've come . . ."

The rifle barrel was lowered, and a tall, gangling boy emerged from around the side of the cabin.

"Reckoned you war the school lady," he said.

I realized then that the large hat I had been wearing had shielded my face and that I had been mistaken for someone else. (The school lady, as it later turned out, was the county truant officer who had been bold enough to venture into the Cove the past winter in search of children who were not registered in school. The Cove's enmity was not so much a matter of their being against school attendance as a general resentment of authority, any kind of authority, from the outside world.)

I smiled brightly. "My name is Addie, Addie Ryland."

Go slowly, Dr. Willoughby had cautioned. "And I'm pleased to meet you."

The boy shifted a wad of tobacco from one side of his jaw to the other.

"I'm a midwife," I went on, "and I've come to see if any of you folk here need my help."

The boy's gaze went past me, and, turning, I saw a woman standing on the porch of the cabin, a bony woman with a face honed by wind and sun. She was very pregnant.

"This 'un says she's a granny woman," the boy explained.

The woman went on staring at me. Suddenly I remembered the midwife's white cap in my saddlebag. I got it out and put it on, smiling, feeling like a traveler in a foreign land who is trying to make contact with the natives.

"I'm Addie . . . ," I began once again.

"You got somethin' fer a cough?" she asked.

"Why—yes." I fumbled at the saddlebag for my medicine box.

"Hit's one of the young 'uns," she said.

I climbed the three high steps, the woman watching me. Not one word of apology from the son or from her for the bullet which might have killed me.

"Hit's Iday," she said.

If I had found the first sight of Hickory Cove depressing, the inside of the cabin appalled me. There was just one large room furnished with two double iron beds, a large, scuffed, knobless chest of drawers, a battered, stained sofa, a trestle table, and three crudely made kitchen chairs. A fireplace and a single window—paneless. Two children sat on the bed peering at me out of large, curious eyes; a third lay between them. Over all hung a powerful stench of unwashed bodies and urine.

Iday went into a fit of coughing. It was whooping cough. Not much I could do now but give her some cough syrup. The other children, of course, wanted some, too, and I dosed them each with a spoonful. To my horror I saw that their hair crawled with lice.

"Have the other children had the cough, too?" I asked the woman.

"Reckon not."

"Could you separate them from Iday?" It was probably too late but worth a try.

"Don't see how. Thar's four more young 'uns, my man, and Mama."

Ten people in that one room! "A neighbor, maybe?" I suggested.

She shook her head. "They's got their own t'look to."

I left the cough syrup. (A mistake, I was to learn. For medicine left—no matter how clear the instructions—was invariably all taken at one or two sittings.)

As I was packing my bag, the woman shyly said, "Do y'care to have some grub with us?"

I looked at the cluttered table, the food-encrusted dishes sitting there amidst a host of flies, and my stomach rolled. But I sensed that turning down the invitation would make me appear "biggety," and if I ever wanted to help these people (and I did now, more than ever), I had to gain their trust.

"I'd be proud to," I said.

Her name was Sadie, Sadie McAlpin. I said, "I could help to deliver your baby."

She smiled. "That's right nice of you." While she busied herself at the hearth, stirring a huge pot—snap beans with fatback, she explained—her husband, Brig, came in.

"This hyar's the granny lady," Sadie said by way of introduction.

"Howdy," he said, eyeing me suspiciously.

"Howdy."

Mama, her snagged, rotting teeth exposed in a tobacco-stained smile, hobbled through the door, followed by two small boys. She said she was mighty pleased to meet me.

The meal was served in haphazard fashion. Some of the children had to stand, since there were not enough chairs. Others grabbed their bowl or plate and went outside. Cutlery was at a minimum. One fork and three spoons. I, as a guest, was given a fork and a spoon.

It was the first meal I had at Hickory Cove, but not the last. I survived them all. Yet I often wondered how they did, for their diet was sparse and monotonous—fatback, corn pone, gravy, a few beans or cabbage and apples in season, sometimes honey when they could manage to rob a beehive. If they happened to earn some cash (by occasionally hiring out as laborers), they bought coffee and tobacco. Old and young alike—even the spindly children—had a passion for tobacco chewing, smoking, or sniffing.

When I finished the meal, I told the McAlpins I'd return in a week. "If your time comes before then, Sadie, send someone down to the store in Stone Mill. They'll know how to find me."

Before I left, I took a short ride up the ravine, counting the cabins, trying to estimate the number of people who lived in the Cove. Suddenly a woman rose up from a clump of dusty bushes at the side of a cabin.

"Wait . . . !" she shouted, running toward me. "Wait . . . !" She grabbed the mare's bridle. "Don't go," she pleaded, a wild-looking creature with white hair and a deeply grooved face.

"Can I help you?" I asked, disturbed. "Are you ill?"

"I want to go home," she said, her eyes filling with tears.

Her thin, ill-clothed figure, her lined face seemed so pitiful. "Don't you live here?"

She grasped my hand with a bony claw. "No," she said. "I live in Stone Mill."

"But how . . . ?"

Someone called from a doorway, "Christy! Christy! Come back hyar."

The woman clutched at my hand. "Where's Sarah?" she begged. "Why didn't you bring Sarah?"

She was mad, of course, mad as a hatter, poor creature.

One rainy Thursday afternoon, two weeks after my first visit to Hickory Cove, the gangly McAlpin boy came into Stone Mill to fetch me. "Hit's Ma," he said.

In less than fifteen minutes I had laid out Will's supper, left him a note, got my bag and cap, and was on my way with the boy riding behind me.

The rain poured in buckets, green forest rain thrumming through the trees, puddling the track, beating down relentlessly upon my head, drenching my cape in minutes. Thank the Lord, I thought, I wasn't summoned during the night. The falls roared in white, angry foam as we dismounted to climb the rocky ledge. I was grateful for the McAlpin boy's help, for the noise of the falls seemed to bother the mare, and she balked several times before we reached the top.

Brig had taken the children to his sister's, and no one was at the McAlpin cabin but the old grandmother, Marthy, and Sadie lying on the bed, her features carved in patient stone.

Suddenly Sadie's face broke into a terrible grimace, and she grabbed at the rope tied to the iron post of the bed, her body writhing in pain. But no sound came from her clamped lips. A veteran, I thought. No problem with her. It will be as easy as falling off a log.

It wasn't. Somehow the baby had become twisted and had to be turned. Dr. Willoughby had given me a pair of forceps but had cautioned me against using them unless the situation was desperate. "Best to call on me if there's a bad case," he said. I knew only too well how easily a fragile skull could be damaged by instruments. And I had received only minimal instruction with them.

"Marthy," I said to the old mother "you must get Brig."

"What fer? Birthin' ain't no place for a man."

Sadie moaned on the bed.

"Your daughter needs a doctor. The baby isn't coming right."

A muffled cry escaped from Sadie's lips, and she clutched at the rope until the veins on her neck stood out like blue, twisted cords.

Marthy wrung her hands. "Oh, Sadie, Sadie. What'll we do?" She hobbled to the trestle table and came back with a knife.

"What's that for?" I asked in horror.

"Hit's goin' 'neath the bed. That'll cut the pain."

"It won't cut anything," I said, exasperated, wanting to shake her. "Please, will you fetch Brig?"

He came in with her a half hour later, rain dripping from his nose, looking disgruntled.

"I ain't a-goin' fer no doctor," he said. "That woman's birthed seven without no trouble. Stands to reason she can do eight."

I could not persuade him. An appeal to fatherhood, husbandhood, the offer of my horse, of my paying Dr. Willoughby's fee, left him unmoved. When I suggested we send the boy, he said it was too far a ride. " 'Asides, hit's night, and he's feared of hants in th'woods."

It was up to Sadie, then—Sadie and me.

"Hold on," I said. "We'll make it all right."

Be patient, I told myself, patient and calm. Sometimes they'll turn themselves.

Sadie's labor dragged on, pain squeezing and relenting. The woman's endurance was beyond belief. For sheer human

courage I did not think I had ever seen the like. I was afraid
to give her anything (I had morphine) because I needed her
help.

"Do you reckon I'll die?" Her face was damp with sweat.

"Of course not. You heard what your husband said." How
could she help but hear—one room, no privacy for either
birth or death? "This one is just taking its time."

I sat by Sadie's side, wiping her brow. Why did they go
on having children? I wondered. Why repeat this excruciat-
ing ordeal over and over again? Even if it meant not having
one's husband make love to you again. And with someone
like Brig, I thought, Sadie couldn't get much pleasure from
the act.

Would she die—she and the child together?

I sat, holding her clammy hands, and gradually her pain
seemed to become my pain, her sweating, panting labor
mine. I suffered with her through each phase, from the onset
of the big rolling wave to the crashing, wrenching climax of
agony, the easing off, the momentary relief.

"How long?" she whispered.

I examined her again. The baby—unbelievable, but yes!
The baby was turning! Carefully, carefully, with my hands—
one last turn . . .

And it came in a rush of blood and gore—a child—headfirst. Thank God, thank God!

"It's a girl. A lovely princess!" I cried happily, forgetting
for the moment that girls were held in low esteem in Hickory
Cove.

I cut the cord and washed the baby and placed it in Sadie's
arms. She gazed down at the wrinkled, ugly mite, and a slow
smile lit up her pale, worn face, a smile that seemed to make
her hauntingly young again. "I'll name hit Addie," she said.

I could not speak for the sudden lump in my throat.

Hurrying out onto the windswept porch, I clung to a post,
and there, in the pouring rain, wept bitterly, not knowing
why, ashamed of my tears, yet unable to stop.

After that night, I was fully accepted in Hickory Cove,
and so felt freer to ask questions about the woman Christy.
I had seen her again on my second visit to the Cove, and she
had clung to me so tenaciously I could not get her out of my
mind. Where had she come from? From Stone Mill, I was
told, but no one seemed to know who had brought her. The

old woman, Cora, who had taken care of Christy, had died, and with her had gone the secret of the madwoman's identity. Years back, a man would come out from Stone Mill, Sadie McAlpin said, a dark man with a beard, to visit and to bring tobacco and extra food for Cora. Now a young woman came. But who she was, no one knew, not even Joanne Rawlins, who had inherited the role of caretaker.

People at home gradually became aware of my visits to Hickory Cove. They didn't think much of my medical endeavors—my "trippin' around," as Reba put it—but on the whole refrained from criticism. As for Will, he was so busy working on his motorcars, he hardly noticed my absences. As long as he had clean clothes on his back and a hot meal on the table, he didn't complain.

Unless an emergency arose I usually went up to Hickory Cove on Fridays, or if I was troubled about a patient, I would ride over in midweek. And that's how I happened to be heading for the Cove on a sultry Wednesday morning. Gare McAlpin had split his foot open by stepping on a rake, and though I had given him a tetanus shot, I worried about his keeping the bandage on.

As I crossed the creek, summer thunder grumbled over the treetops. Along the path the dark heat pressed in somber heaviness. I had never become accustomed to the forest, the murky greens, the massed vegetation, never felt comfortable on this narrow track hemmed in by hostile trees. Always I rode with the feeling that if I relaxed my stiff vigilance, even for a moment, something terrible might happen. What that something could be, I did not know, but it seemed that just beyond my range of vision, to the side or in the rear, a nebulous, cloudy Nemesis kept pace with me.

And today that feeling became so strong I found myself breaking into gooseflesh.

Something . . .

I reined the mare in.

Tickety-tock, tickety-tock. Horse's hooves, faint at first, growing louder and louder. And then nothing. Suddenly, as if the rider had paused to listen, too.

I slid from the saddle and led the mare into the underbrush, hiding myself, and waited with a beating heart.

Tickety-tock, tickety-tock. A halt, and, to my mind, the invisible rider peering ahead. Tickety-tock, closer, almost here now. Tickety-TOCK! Silence. I peeked out through a curtain of leaves. A hooded rider, a large black horse.

Overhead thunder muttered, and the wind in a sudden rush moaned through the swaying branches.

A phantom? One heard all sorts of stories, especially in Hickory Cove. Nonsense, of course, I reassured myself. All nonsense, Addie.

The rider turned in the saddle, looking behind.

And then—I might have anticipated it—my mare whinnied. The rider looked in my direction.

It was Elsie—Elsie Ryland!

Embarrassed, I thought of crouching down, hiding until she had gone on. But the horse whinnied again.

"Oh, Elsie," I said, coming out from the bushes, smoothing my skirt as if I had just answered a call of nature, "I wondered who it was."

She did not seem glad to see me. "I thought you went to the Cove on Fridays," she said.

I explained what had brought me out on a Wednesday. "And you?" I asked.

"Riding—just riding," her answer came reluctantly. She did not look at me. And that hood, I thought, on such a warm day—mighty suspicious, that. "I reckon I'll turn back now," she said.

"Wait—why don't you come on with me, and we can go home together? It won't take long to have a look at Gare's foot."

She pushed the hood back from her head. "Oh—all right." And as I remounted the horse she asked, "You doing much good at the Cove?"

"I think so."

She stared at me. Elsie was one of the few youngish Stone Mill women who was not what one would call pretty, though her eyes—hazel, a brown flecked with green—were beautiful.

"I lied to you," she said suddenly. "I'm not just riding. I'm going to Hickory Cove, too."

I wanted to ask why. But there was something in her manner which did not invite questions.

We rode on, Elsie in the lead on the narrow path.

"I expect you're wondering," Elsie said, so suddenly I jumped. We had reached the bottom of the ravine at the mouth of the Cove, and Elsie had fallen back to ride alongside me.

"Yes—yes I am," I said.

"Can you keep a secret?"

"Cross my heart and hope to die," I said earnestly.

"I can only tell you part of it. You must promise not to press me for more."

I promised.

"I come to see Christy"—she hesitated—"Christy Covington."

I tried not to look shocked. Covington! The house, that empty, haunted house, the jungle garden, the swing's shadow swaying back and forth, the wind sighing through the trees . . .

"Her father-in-law, Judd Covington, brought her here to the cove because he didn't want her to be put away in an asylum."

"Has she no family?"

"No," she said after a moment's pause, "none. And, Addie, remember you promised not to ask."

No family. It didn't make sense. Everyone in Stone Mill had family. Even if Christy was an outlander like myself, somewhere, someplace she must have a sister, a cousin, a maiden aunt. Why had she been *hidden* in Hickory Cove?

But I wasn't to ask questions. I wasn't to speak of it.

It was inevitable, I suppose, that Cass and I would come to blows. Unlike Reba, who could bend on occasion, Cass was stubbornly jealous of her rights as midwife. And I hadn't meant to challenge her or to intrude—in fact, had carefully avoided it.

Our differences came to a head over a silly thing like a toothache. Penland Dawson's. I met him one morning at Bradley's, his jaw blown up to the size of a grapefruit. "That's an abscess if I ever saw one," I said to him.

"Cass give me a poultice," he said, "but don't seem like it's doin' much of anythin'. My head is fair splittin'."

"That tooth ought to be pulled," I said.

"Cass says to wait. But I don't know as I can."

"There's a dentist in Front Royal," I said.

He didn't have a way of getting there, so I, doing good again, took him.

Cass heard about it the next day. And she came hobbling over to the house as fast as her cane and crippled feet could carry her. "You're courtin' trouble, you know, messin' 'round with my patient," she railed at me, her bad eye shooting out of sight.

"But he was in pain. . . ."

"Never you mind." She banged her cane on the floor in a fury.

"I'm sorry. . . ."

But she refused to be placated, and though we came to terms later, when her rheumatism incapacitated her completely, she continued to remain hostile, an enemy I could well have done without.

Chapter 25

M Y falling-out with Cass was not nearly as disturbing as the one I had with Preacher Davidson. A formidable man, he enjoyed an authority in the community which baffled me. Though the Bradleys were the "money men" of Stone Mill, carrying most of the town on credit at the store or the bank, it was the preacher they looked to for important decisions. He was consulted on a variety of matters—religion, morality, agriculture, education, town policy —his word always heeded. And I wasn't too sure he hadn't some say at the bank, too. Even the mayor, Colonel Perry, deferred to him. "Ask the preacher" was a byword; or, "Preacher Davidson says. . . ."

Will did not seem to think the situation unusual. "The preacher is a knowin' man," he would say.

Which could have meant anything, I suppose. There was no question the preacher knew everyone in town, knew them intimately, knew everything about them, the good and the bad. But he was uneducated, not an ordained minister, and his views were narrow. "A Fundamentalist," our own minister at home would have said.

"The sins of men's appetites" was one of the preacher's favorite topics—"drunkenness, fornication, pridefulness of spirit . . ."

He had a way of stirring and feeding the dark, secret fears inside a person with a relish and vigor that sometimes frightened me. And yet I kept going every Sunday to his church, not because I was entranced—or bullied—by his sermons, but because my absence might be noted and held against me. Bad enough to be butting in with Cass's patients, and tripping to Hickory Cove. An outlander had to be careful.

Preacher Davidson himself had remarked upon my Cove visits, but not in any way which could be construed as disapproval. "Passes the time, I reckon," he had said to me casually at Dee Perry's barn raising, "until your own family comes along."

Aside from that remark, he did not seem to take much notice of me until one Sunday in late June. As I stood on the porch after the meeting talking to Elsie and her husband, little Don Davidson tugged at my skirt. "Grandpa wants to see you inside, Addie."

It was a hot day, and the windows and doors had been left open during the service, but as I entered the preacher shut the door behind me and pulled the back windows shut.

"Please set," he said, motioning to a bench, his mouth drawn in a thin line.

I've done something, I thought, committed one of those terrible sins the preacher is always railing against. But which? So many sins to consider, so many . . .

"Addie, I've been studyin' you for some time now in church here," he began, and paused as if waiting for me to make a comment.

But I could think of nothing.

"Yes, Addie. And sorry to tell, but I caught you nappin'— nappin' in church." His voice was stern.

I stared at him in astonishment. Napping in church?

". . . now I'm not a vain man, but what I have to say here in this place of God is important, and I *will* have folks' attention."

"But I haven't been napping," I said, finding my voice at last. "How could I, when . . . ?"

"You namin' me a liar?" His blue eyes turned dark with sudden anger. "Shame to you! saith the Lord. Shame to you!"

"I didn't mean to. . . ."

"You do go on contradictin' me, don't you? Let me quote from Proverbs. 'There is severe punishment for him who forsakes the way. . . .'"

He was such a little man, an ugly man, one of the few homely people in Stone Mill. Uneducated, pompous. Inconsequential. And yet he frightened me.

". . . so I reckon it's best for all concerned that you stay away from church for the next few months."

He was chastising me, but it seemed more like a reprieve. His sermons bored me, roaring diatribes all cut from the same piece. Boring, boring, boring.

Yet later, when I began to realize the full impact of

Preacher Davidson's ban, I saw where I had been put even further outside the pale. The excuse had been trumped up (who, unless one were stone-deaf, could fall asleep in Preacher Davidson's church?). He didn't want me there, because . . . because what?

"He's kinda touchy about people fallin' asleep," Will told me.

"But, Will, I swear I never closed an eye." The men and women sat separately at church in the old-fashioned, biblical manner.

"You didn't shut your eyes for just a minute?"

"No," I said after reflecting a moment. "No. Do you think there might be something the preacher's planning to say on Sunday mornings he doesn't want an outsider to hear?"

Will laughed. "You're danged silly."

People still spoke to me, though, greeting me politely, stopping to chat at Bradley's. Nor was I excluded from the social events, like the big one coming up, the Fourth of July celebration held annually at Mill Park. The old mill itself, so the rumor went, would soon be refurbished as a town hall, but the surrounding area had long since been planted with shrubbery and set with picnic tables. A swimming hole had been created by rebuilding and enlarging the dam.

"Covered dish," Ma Ryland instructed, "just plain food." A hint to forgo, please, my "furrin' " cooking.

So I played it safe, and the day preceding the Fourth I baked traditional pies, berry and rhubarb. For good measure I also stewed a fat hen. When I fell into bed that night, it was to dream of Cass exclaiming to a crowd of happy-faced Rylands that I had baked the best berry pie in all the Blue Ridge and Preacher Davidson himself had pinned a blue-ribbon medal on my stewed hen.

I awoke at dawn with a feeling I had left something undone. Had I remembered to salt the hen, put cinnamon in the apple pie? Will stirred beside me and, sitting up, squinted at the red, rising sun. "Hot today," he said.

By nine o'clock the heat lay like a heavy, suffocating blanket over Stone Mill. Not a breath of air stirred; the leaves hung limp as rags, and the dog after lapping at his water bowl had refused his food, slinking under the house to find what coolness he could there.

"Maybe we'll have a breeze down by the creek," Will

said as I loaded the pies in the back seat of the Ford. The old car was in running order now, painted and polished to a glossy mirror luster. Will gave the hood one last swipe with a cloth, smiling, looking proud as a turkey-cock.

"Ain't you the one!" Will's brother Roy exclaimed as we drove up with a wild tooting of the horn.

The Rylands were all there—heavyset Ralph and his wife; the two oldest girls, Maude and Luella, with their respective husbands and assorted offspring. Elizabeth, looking pretty in pink, was shyly holding hands with Teddy Loeffler. Maude, rubbing down her muddied and dripping youngest with a towel, called, "Howdy there! Late, ain't you?" and Ma Ryland hurried to help me with the pies.

Everyone was in a gay holiday mood, the men cleanshaven in shirtsleeves and straw hats, the woman in light summer dresses, a bit long in the hem and unstylish, but cool-looking. Little girls wore ribboned pigtails, their older sisters garden hats, and their male counterparts starched overalls. The women talked and laughed and jostled one another as they unpacked the picnic baskets.

Harry Loeffler, wearing a dark-blue suit and a tie, despite the heat, pumped Will's hand and then mine as if he hadn't seen us in years. Grandma Perry, at our elbows, shouted, "Shoo them flies away from the baby, Ellen! Why, hello there, Matt, Elsie. Been a coon's age, Elsie. Where you been keepin' yourself?"

Elsie murmured something I did not catch. She looked paler than usual, her freckles standing out like a spattering of brown confetti across the bridge of her nose.

Irene Loeffler (mother of Myrtle, the pretty girl who had danced away with my Will at the housewarming), very pregnant, weighted down by a huge hamper in each hand, puffed her way across the greensward, followed by her brood —the smallest, a baby, riding on the hip of the ten-year-old. Each of them except the tiniest toddler carried a basket or a covered dish. Terrence, Irene's husband, empty-handed, had made a beeline for the old mill building, where it was rumored some of the men had gathered for a precelebration passing of the jug.

"That's a tribe to feed," Elsie commented in a low tone. "Eleven now, and one to come."

Ma Ryland, sharp-eared, never missing a trick, retorted, "Only doing her duty as a good Christian woman." This a snide reminder that perhaps Elsie, whose offspring numbered only two, might not be doing her part, and I, certainly, had failed completely.

Elsie, passing over the remark, said, "Irene's twins are pretty."

Myrtle had a sister Mary, an identical twin with the same blue eyes and golden hair. Mary, however, mute as the result of a childhood accident, was painfully shy, preferring to remain unnoticed in the shadow of her brash, outspoken sister Myrtle.

Preacher Davidson approached, and for a moment I quailed, clinging to Will's arm. But his greeting was friendly enough. "Glad y'could come," he said, including us both and passing on to speak to others.

Will nudged his father. "Comin' with Roy and me to have a little snort?"

"Sure thing," Pa Ryland said. The men ambled casually toward the old mill, meeting up with others headed in the same direction.

"They'll all be drunk as skunks before dinner," Ma grumbled.

We covered the dishes with tea towels as protection against the flies, who, sensing a feast, were now circling the tables.

"Speeches first," Elsie whispered. "Soon as they all get here."

In the languid heat I could feel the moisture gathering in my armpits. I stood for a few moments in the humid shade of a locust, wiping my brow. A group of small boys raced past, and a woman shouted, "Don't you go swimmin' yet. Just you wait."

The sun rose higher. Suddenly I felt isolated and strangely alone, although people were milling all about me. Now, why is that? I thought. Why should I feel so deserted?

At home in Newport News, Mama and Papa would be sitting down to cold dill soup and meat loaf. I missed the quiet stillness of our small dining room, the faded wallpaper, the acanthus in its earthenware pot. "Bless this food," my father would say as his face, all angles and pure line, bent in prayer. So familiar. So dear.

"You look like you just swallowed vinegar," Ma Ryland said. "Come ahead, they've started the speechifying."

We sat at the tables while Colonel Perry talked about the

Revolutionary War. He had a rusty voice, and I had to strain to hear him.

". . . came here in seventeen fifty. Some say the Claybornes were first, others the Loefflers. . . ."

I leaned over and whispered to Elsie, "Who are the Claybornes?"

But Will tugged at my arm. "Shhhh," he admonished, shaking his head.

Colonel Perry's voice rasped on. My eyes closed, and my chin sagged.

"For Lord's sake," Will hissed at me, "don't fall asleep."

"Who, me?"—popping my eyes open.

The colonel's face by now had turned a beet red, and he was fanning it with his hat as he talked. ". . . the brave mountain men who fought against the British and their allies, the perfidious Cherokees. . . ."

The unfortunate Cherokees had backed the losing side, I remembered from my history books, and they were eventually punished for it in a most terrible way. Their land was taken from them, and they were forced to march to Oklahoma, four thousand of them dying on the way. The Trail of Tears, they called it. But Colonel Perry made no mention of that.

I don't know why I had thought of this tragic incident, except that I was suddenly feeling bitter. Will had drawn away from me, and I caught him winking at Myrtle Loeffler. Her dress, I noticed, was far too tight, her breasts close to bursting through the cloth.

And she had winked back.

Colonel Perry finished his speech, and applause rippled through the crowd. When Preacher Davidson got up to speak, a hush fell over the assembly. Even the children ceased their play, sitting at attention. The preacher's sermon, unlike his Sunday ones, was short. "We've prospered and we thank the Almighty, we've sinned and the time has come again for atonement. Let us go forward this year to meet our obligation . . . to walk gladly the path Our Lord has seen fit to set before us. . . ."

Mumbo jumbo, I thought, my stomach rumbling with hunger.

The preacher sat down. Roy Ryland sprang up and led us in a resounding chorus of "Dixie." The echoes had barely died down when we were whipping the towels from the tables, and the passing and repassing of dishes heaped with food commenced. One thing about Stone Millers—they relished their food. Very little conversation took place during the next half hour. Then, first hunger satisfied, talk began to hum again. People got up to stroll around, the men disappearing one by one into the mill.

"Seems like they's had enough of that giggle water," Ma Ryland said sourly.

Elsie smiled tolerantly. "The strawberry pie was mighty good," she said.

"It's mine," I claimed proudly.

We scraped the leavings from the dirty plates onto newspapers and fed the dogs roaming under the tables.

Suddenly Ma Ryland said, "Where's Elizabeth?"

"Probably with Teddy," I said.

"No, she ain't," her mother said. "I seen Teddy go into the mill."

I got to my feet, feeling logy, wanting nothing more than to curl up under a tree and sleep. "I'll ask Teddy," I said.

Ma Ryland and Elsie followed me up the small slope. I paused for a moment at the open door, peering into the dust-shadowed interior.

"You dasn't go in," Ma Ryland said. An unwritten rule forbade females of whatever age from intruding upon men at the jug.

"Teddy . . . ! Teddy . . . !" I called from the doorway, "Teddy!"

The babble of voices stopped for an instant. "Somebody naming me?"

"Yes. Teddy, it's Addie. Could I see you?"

He came out into the sunlight blinking, his face flushed.

"Have you seen Elizabeth?" her mother asked anxiously.

"No, I ain't. She told me she was goin' for a walk down by the creek."

Ma Ryland turned pale. "Dang that girl! I told her not to wander off."

"She's grown now," I said. "She can take care of herself."

"That ain't the point," Ma Ryland said.

I couldn't understand it. Was there something wrong with Elizabeth? Was she afraid the girl would go off in the bushes with a man? Or was she worried that Elizabeth might fall in the creek and drown?

Elsie said, "Surely, Mrs. Ryland, you're not worried. There never has been two. . . ." And she stopped, throwing a quick look in my direction.

Two what? What on earth was she talking about?

"There's always a first time," Ma Ryland said.

Children, all sizes and shapes, were strung along the banks of the creek in various modes of undress, some in the water, splashing and screaming, others wading along the clay bank. Boys, holding their noses, dove into the dammed-up pool, rising in a froth of bubbles, swimming in long, awkward strokes to the wooden steps built along the side.

Elizabeth was nowhere to be seen.

"I'm going to fetch Pa," Ma Ryland said, "and Will."

Elsie said, "Me and Addie will walk up toward the Covington place and look."

We walked along the well-worn path in silence for a few minutes, and then, unable to keep my curiosity in check, I asked, "Why is Ma Ryland so worried about Elizabeth?"

Elsie hesitated before she answered, "It's a long story, Addie. And I don't feel free to tell it."

Mind your business, Addie. But said in a kind way.

The trees overhanging the path, the black shadows, and the silence broken by the murmur of the stream made it seem cooler.

"You having a good time today?" Elsie asked.

"Fine," I said. "Except"—and in a sudden rush of intimacy —"except I wish I would feel less like an outsider."

"I reckon that's hard." Then, after a moment, "Will shouldn't have brought you here."

I went cold. Elsie must have seen dismay on my face, for she said, "Look here, I didn't mean Will shouldn't have married you. I meant that you and he ought to have settled down in Newport News or somewhere else."

"He was homesick," I said.

She nodded.

"This town is full of secrets," I murmured. "Do you think I'll ever live long enough to know at least some of them?"

"You already know about Christy Covington," she pointed out.

"Yes, but . . ." I plucked at a leaf. "Today, Colonel Perry mentioned the Claybornes. Are they people I haven't met?"

"They moved away from Stone Mill ages ago, even before my time."

"That's odd, isn't it? Two whole families who have moved away. I thought they all stayed, except for a few of the young."

"No—not all."

We paused beside a clump of laurel. Elsie cupped her mouth and called. "Elizabeth . . . ! Elizabeth!"

"She's probably back at the park," I said. "Sound asleep under a bush."

"Probably."

We skirted the trees and went on, the path now a thin line through the underbrush. The banks of the creek became steeper, the woods thicker. At last we halted, and Elsie cupped her hands once more. "Elizabeth . . . ? Elizabeth . . . ?" The dark, oppressive forest swallowed the last echo of her voice as we waited, listening. The quiet was intense.

Suddenly a twig crackled, snapping the silence.

Elsie's body went rigid, her face blanching to a greenish pallor. The twig crackled again, and my heart jumped. Peering into the tangled mass of shrubs, I thought I saw the branches sway, but though I peered intently, they did not move again.

Neither of us spoke. The wind trembled in the leaves overhead, the creek babbled, the humid smell of muddied water, of damp loam, of moldering leaves, the odor of decay and death rose like a vapor, touching my cold skin, entering my nostrils, rank and sour. Looking past the dense greenery through an arch of ferns, I saw the gray, gnarled trunk of the immense oak tree, and I knew we were on the fringes of the Covington garden.

"Let's go back," I whispered to Elsie, and wondered why I felt it necessary to lower my voice.

"I pray to God. . . ." She took my hand, hers as cold as ice.

"Elsie, let's go," I begged. "There's something here, something awful. I feel it."

"So do I. Though I've never before. Oh, Addie . . ." There were tears in her eyes. I knew she was about to tell me something, something important, and I clung to her hand, staring into her eyes. But she turned from me and started back along the path.

We found Elizabeth sitting at the table with Ma Ryland. She had fallen asleep under Mary Lou Perry's umbrella.

"I'm sorry I caused you all that trouble," she apologized, "but you know Mama—she still treats me like a baby."

We started to gather our silverware, plates, and pans from the table. "Is this your dish?" Ma Ryland asked, holding up a blue-willow bowl.

"No," I said, taking it. "I think it might be Elsie's. I'll ask."

Elsie was standing near the old mill house in earnest conversation with Preacher Davidson. "We can't go on like this. It's murder," I heard Elsie say.

I hung back, pretending to search for something in the grass at my feet.

"You're to keep yore mouth shut!" the preacher hissed angrily. "Them's my last words!"

When I looked up, the preacher was striding away, and Elsie, her face half turned from me, was weeping.

Chapter 26

REBA sat in my kitchen polishing her spectacles on the voluminous white bib apron she wore. "I do believe I *will* have another smidgen of that pie, Addie," she said.

"I'm glad you changed your mind." I cut a generous wedge.

She replaced the steel-rimmed spectacles on her small nose and picked up the fork, her chins quivering.

"More coffee?" I asked. "Or would you like some cold buttermilk?"

"Buttermilk'll be fine."

Her face, round and plump, had the fresh, high color of a country girl's. Despite her stout, matronly appearance it was hard to believe she was the fifty she claimed, still harder to believe she was a Davidson, a family made up of lean, knobby people with twisted noses. Reba must have favored her mother, or maybe some distant, gentle-featured ancestor. Only the eyes were like the Davidsons', a bright, piercing blue.

"I'd like to have the receipt for this pie," Reba said. It always amused me the way they said "receipt" for "recipe."

"Be glad to." I got my card file down from the shelf, and a pencil and paper from the kitchen drawer.

Vinegar Pie, I wrote. *Two cups scalded milk.* She watched me over the rims of her spectacles. *One-half teaspoon grated nutmeg.* "It's much like custard pie," I said, "except for the vinegar."

"Hmmmm."

This talk of pie was just a formality. There was hardly a female on the Blue Ridge who didn't know how to make vinegar pie. Something besides sociability had brought Reba to my kitchen, but what it was I could not guess.

A half-cup sugar, one unbaked pie shell . . .

"You birthed many babies out Hickory Cove way?" Reba asked offhandedly.

"Two, so far," I said. "One I had to turn."

She nodded approvingly. "Good things been said 'bout you."

"Thank you." *One-half teaspoon salt, four eggs* . . .

"Cass is poorly again. Her hands is so crippled now she can hardly hold a fork."

"Oh, I'm sorry to hear that." *Two teaspoons vinegar.* "There you are!" I said with a flourish.

She took the paper, eyed it briefly, folded it, then tucked it in the pocket of her apron. "We—Cass and me—allus hoped one of our girls would carry on the family tradition. My ma, she's Mrs. Preacher, was midwife here. She learned Cass and me everythin' we know. And my daughter—the only one God saw fit to give me . . ." Her blue eyes filled with tears. "She died. Was only eighteen."

"How terrible!"

"Guess you might call it an accident," she said, dabbing at her eyes with the corner of her apron. "Yes, she went to her Maker fourteen years come September. Thank God, I still have my boys."

"And fine ones they are."

"Yes, ain't they? Married, but they still think of their ma." She paused to blow her nose. "Well, now, Cass—she's got two girls, y'know. The eldest, Tansy, married a Perry— no kin—well, she couldn't take to midwifing. And Peggy weren't t'all interested." Reba sighed heavily. "So, there's just me, y'know, and I can't be in ten places at once. So I was wonderin' . . . I was wonderin' should you . . ."

Here it comes, I thought with a sneaky feeling of triumph, I know what she wants.

"I was wonderin' should you be able"—her face turning very red.

"I'd be glad to help with midwifing," I said, releasing her from her embarrassment.

"Now, that's right nice of you, Addie."

"If Cass doesn't mind."

"Mind? She'd be pleasured."

Reba thought it best that I stop by the next afternoon. "So's I can give you a few things for yore bag," she said. "Stone Mill folks is used to certain ways. And they get fidgety should they think somethin' different's afoot."

* * *

Reba Perry's kitchen was large, high-ceilinged, the walls covered with paper whose pattern had long since melded to a dull, blurred puce.

"Come and set," Reba invited cheerfully.

She crossed to a glass-fronted china closet, brought a small key from her apron pocket, and opened the bay-windowed door. Shelves from top to bottom were lined with labeled jars. "Keep my medicines in here," she said, taking down several jars. "Some young 'uns get a hold of digitalis or the like, and there'd be real trouble."

She carried the jars over to the table. Jimson root, tannic acid, oil of thyme . . .

"Got you a paper and pencil?"

"Yes," I said, fishing in my bag.

"I suppose you never learned about these in your city hospital?"

"Not exactly. I recognize some of them, though."

"All right, I'll learn you about *all* of them. Take heed." She turned a jar so that the label was facing me. "Can you read my writin'? All right. This here's creosote. Comes from the wood tar of pine or beech. Use it for coughs. This . . . this be belladonna—you gotta be careful with it 'cause it comes from the deadly nightshade—just a bit will do wonders for inflammation and stubborn bowels." Her fingers, short and fleshy but surprisingly supple, twisted another jar. "Leopard's-bane for bruises and cuts, makes a fine poultice. Now, pokeroot is good for skin rash, jimson root for ulcers—a little pinch of that, mind you, jimson can be chancy, makes you see things that ain't there. Clover for salves, bloodroot for corns. All of 'em"—she waved her hand over the jars like a magician who has just pulled ten rabbits from his old hat—"all of 'em found in the woods here-abouts. All of 'em better than anythin' you can buy at the drugstore."

She fetched a split basket from the pantry and set the jars in gently, packing newspaper between each.

"Anyone in Stone Mill sick right now?" I asked.

"Em Loeffler's boy sprained his ankle at the Fourth cele-bration, but I tended to him, and there's Allie got a car-buncle, but I'll slice that off this evening, and Tess's baby has croup awful bad, but ain't much Tess can do other than what I already tole her. Guess that's 'bout it."

"It doesn't sound like there will be much call for me, then."

"Hold on. Just you wait. It'll all come at once. Irene's to have her baby in a few weeks or so, I reckon, and my daughter-in-law Winnie is to have hers, and there's Chatty and Beth and Mary. . . ."

I looked at her in astonishment as she ticked off the names. "All those women having babies?" I said, wondering how Stone Mill kept its population from exploding into the next county.

"This is a lucky year," she said. "Folks sort of plan for it."

"Lucky? But why? What's so special about nineteen twenty?"

"Why—it just is," she said, and a shutter seemed to go down behind those bright blue eyes.

Later, when I repeated what Reba had said to Will, he claimed she was a superstitious old fool.

"If she is," I said, "why does she choose nineteen twenty from all the other years?"

He didn't know. And why must I keep asking him so many questions? "Miss Nosy Parker," he teased.

Winnie didn't know, either. I had gone to her house in answer to an urgent message brought by her twelve-year-old niece—premature labor. I examined her, the baby hadn't dropped yet. "False pains," I said, smiling. This would be her second, she told me. She wanted another boy. I gave her a bottle of tonic. "Reba's," I said. "It works wonders."

She accepted the bottle, thanking me. "We can't pay you right now. . . ."

"No need. Seems like your baby will be born in a lucky year."

"Ain't it the truth?" She was a pretty girl, no more than twenty, with a pert nose and a mass of light-brown, curly hair.

"There aren't many lucky years, are there?" I said, casual-like.

She looked at me, and then her eyes slid away. "Enough in one lifetime."

Riddle me, riddle me. A philosophical riddle. But from a girl of twenty and not schooled beyond the sixth grade?

I was more direct with my sister-in-law Elizabeth. "Why do people in Stone Mill feel nineteen twenty is a lucky year?"

"Nineteen twenty?" She thought a moment. "I expect because it's the beginning of the twenties, don't you see?"

"I never thought of it that way." But somehow it made little sense. Why would the start of a new decade be reckoned as lucky?

I asked the same question at Irene Loeffler's, where I had gone to tend her "least one's" colic. "I never heard tell of such a thing," she said. "I've had my babies one a year, almost." And then, in a whisper, her face a beet red, "*I* reckon it's a lucky year when I don't."

I had to smile. "Would you like not to go on having babies?"

She looked at me in surprise.

"There is—something—a device your husband could use. He can get it at the drugstore in Novotno." I described a condom as best I could.

She shook her head. "He'd never agree to that. Never. He'd say I was tryin' to curb his manhood."

"But it wouldn't."

She was adamant.

"There are several things I can give you, then," I said. "But they won't work unless you use them. We can talk more about it after you've had the baby."

She was grateful, so grateful she insisted I take one of a litter of new kittens. "It's been weaned," she said.

It was a pretty creature, long-haired, white-and-black, with a pointed, heart-shaped face, and it purred so lovingly as I settled it in the crook of my arm.

"I'll send if I need you," Irene called after me.

I had left the mare and buggy at home, walking the half mile to the Loeffler house. Now I was sorry. The day had grown stifling hot, the heat rising in waves from the cobbled street. Though I kept to the shade, I could already feel the damp sweat between my shoulder blades.

I had reached the church when I heard a motorcar approaching from behind. I turned to look as it drew alongside me. "Howdy, Addie." It was Zack Bradley, the storekeeper's son.

"Give you a lift?" He raised his straw hat, a neat man, well-groomed, elegantly suited. His smile, however, I always found oily.

"It's only a step," I said. He drove an imported car—a

Rolls-Royce—the only one in town. Will, green with envy, had once remarked, "Can you imagine what that must have cost him?"

Zack, leaning out the window, said, "I can save you that step, and I'd be delighted with your company."

"Thank you, but no." The cat squirmed in my arms. "I'll cut across here and be home."

He smiled again but made no move to go on.

"Good-bye, then," I said nervously. The man gave me chills. He always looked at me as though he were toting up my assets, calculating what my face, my bosom, my arms and legs might amount to in dollars and cents.

I turned and cut across the front lawn of the church. I didn't look back, but as I got to the churchyard gate and went through, I could hear the car start up and drive away.

I never had used the cemetery as a shortcut, since a small sign on the gate warned against it: NO TRESPASSING UNLESS ON CEMETERY BUSINESS. But I was not eager to meet up with Zack (who might be lurking down the street) again, and I didn't think there would be any harm in it if I hurried through.

My bag had grown heavy, and as I shifted it from one sweaty hand to the other, the kitten suddenly sprang from under my arm, and an instant later had scampered off.

Wouldn't you know it? I thought, exasperated. "Here, kitty! Here, kitty!" I set the bag down and, tiptoeing over the thick, carpetlike grass, went searching for her. "Here, kitty!"

I captured her at last, poor little frightened beastie, lifting her from the base of a headstone where she had sought refuge. Then I happened to glance at the inscription. CHRISTY COVINGTON, it read. BORN 1869. DIED 1892. BELOVED WIFE OF ROBERT. MOTHER OF SARAH.

I read it again. Yes, I had been right the first time.

I mused over that tombstone all the next day and finally went to see Elsie. "I know I promised I wouldn't ask any questions about Christy," I said to her, "but I was wondering if there had been another Christy Covington in Stone Mill. One with a daughter named Sarah, too."

Her eyes met mine for a long moment. "You saw the headstone in the cemetery, didn't you?"

"Yes."

She sighed. "I could lie about it, I suppose. But there are

so many lies already." She stared down at her hands, then, raising her eyes, she said, "It's the same one, Addie. The coffin's empty."

"But why?" I whispered.

"Her father-in-law, Judd, wouldn't tell me. But when I went to visit Sarah—she's living in Raleigh now—she gave me some of the story. Christy accidentally shot her husband, and then she went off her head."

"But if it was an accident . . ."

"It isn't that simple. They were quarreling over another man. Christy's lover."

I looked at her questioningly.

"I can't tell you who, Addie."

In spite of my new medical duties in Stone Mill, I hadn't given up my weekly visits to Hickory Cove. Sometimes Elsie would ride with me. "It helps to pass the time," she said. "There's only so much quilting and cooking and washing a body can do."

It had rained the night before this particular Friday, and a warm, wet mist lay along the creek bed. We were passing the old Covington place when I saw a man sitting on the far bank. "Looks like someone's there," I said to Elsie.

"Where . . . ?" she asked, peering past me. "I don't see anyone."

"A man, wearing a cap . . . ," I pointed.

A swirl of mist obscured the view for a moment, and when it cleared, I saw that the man had gone.

"A tramp, most likely," I said.

"Most likely," Elsie repeated, and those were the only words she spoke all the way to the Cove, though I tried dozens of times to start a conversation.

We were crossing the creek by the old mill on our return journey when I said, "Elsie, are you mad at me or what?" She still hadn't spoken.

"No," she said.

"Aren't you feeling well?" Her face was white as a sheet, but then she always had a pale look, not unhealthy, just pale.

"Addie, I've got to speak to you in private," she said. "Come home with me for a few minutes."

She, Matt, and their two boys lived in a two-story red-brick house a half mile from the apple-packing plant Matt owned and ran. We went in the back way. Elsie hooked the screen and closed and locked the kitchen door. Then she pulled all the window shades.

"What is it?" I asked, my spine tingling.

"Sit down, Addie."

I pulled a chair up to the kitchen table.

"I don't know where to start," she said, clasping her hands together, her face shining palely in the dimness. "And I shouldn't be telling you. An outsider. Only the older people and a few of the young ones know." She paused, biting her lip. I sat very still. "But you saw . . . today, when you saw that man. . . ." Again she paused; then, taking a deep breath, went on, "You see, it all began long ago with the Claybornes."

"The Claybornes!" I exclaimed. "That's the family Colonel Perry mentioned. . . ."

"Yes, they once lived out on Burnham Road. An old place that's burned down. They didn't get along with the rest of Stone Mill. I don't rightly know why. Maybe because the oldest boy went off to fight for the Yankees. Anyway, this boy came back on leave one day. . . ."

She stopped suddenly, wide-eyed, listening. Then I heard it, too. A step on the porch. We stared at one another as the rat-a-tat of a knock echoed through the kitchen.

"Elsie! Elsie, are you at home?"

"It's the preacher's wife," Elsie whispered.

The knock came again, a knock made by a commanding fist.

"Do you think she listened at the window?" Elsie whispered. "If she heard me . . ."

"I don't know."

The knock sounded through the kitchen once more. "Coming!" Elsie called. "Addie"—in a low tone—"run, sit in the parlor—like you've been there all afternoon."

The preacher's wife had come over to invite Elsie (and, incidentally, me, now that she had me there) to a baby party she and a few of the other ladies were giving for the expectant mothers of Stone Mill. "A week Saturday," she said.

"That's right nice of you," Elsie said. "Seeing as how my sister, Chatty, is expecting, too. Shall we bring gifts?"

"Law, no!" Mrs. Davidson exclaimed. "There's too many. Just bring yourselves. Coffee and cake for refreshment. Well"—looking around, getting to her feet—"hot, ain't it? Coming my way, Addie?"

"Yes—yes, I was just about to leave."

I went back to see Elsie the next afternoon and was surprised to find Matt at the house.

"Is Elsie around?" I asked.

"No . . . ," he frowned. "I don't know where she's gone." Matt, at one time, had farmed, and he still had the rough, sunburned look of a man who worked outdoors. "She usually leaves me a note and my dinner on the table at noon if she's planning to be out, but nothing was here. And the boys hadn't seen her since morning. At the plant, I got to thinking. . . ." His voice trailed off.

"She might have gone over to visit with Chatty."

"I been there." His frown deepened. "Her horse came home without her."

"What?" I asked, sharing his alarm now.

"I sent the boys 'round to ask at the Loefflers' and the Clarkes'."

The boys returned in a half hour. No one, it seemed, had seen Elsie that day.

She might have gone to Hickory Cove, I thought. Not wanting to give Elsie's secret away and perhaps alarm Matt further, I said, "The boys could have missed her somewhere, at somebody's house."

"But the horse . . . ," he protested.

"Maybe she got to talking and didn't notice it was gone."

"Maybe," he said without conviction. "I'll wait a bit, and then if she don't get home, I'll get some of the men out to look. Thank you, Addie."

I went home and saddled up the mare. Crossing the creek, I rode up the trail I had followed countless times before. Today the dark trees seemed more forbidding, more silent than ever, their shadows moving ahead of me, sighing with the wind.

It wasn't like Elsie to go off in that fashion—no note for Matt, riding to the Cove one day after the next. And the horse coming home without her—that worried me, too.

"Elsie . . . !" I called, remembering how only a few weeks earlier she had shouted for Elizabeth in this same place. "Elsie . . . ?" And the silence mocked me.

I rode slowly, looking first to the left and then to the right. When I came abreast of the Covington place, I dismounted and began to lead the mare, searching for some sign along the way—recent hoofprints, a wisp of cloth, anything.

It was so quiet, so terribly, awesomely quiet, almost as if the silence were trying to speak. I turned my head and looked down at the running, trilling water.

She was there, her head nestled on a white arm, the water flowing over her pale, upturned face. Even before I slid down the clay bank and touched her icy hand, I knew she was dead.

Chapter 27

ELSIE, apparently thrown from her horse, had struck her head against a rock and been killed instantly. We had no county coroner, and even if there had been one, I doubt whether he would have been called. Stone Mill took care of its own.

"So young to die," the preacher's wife said sadly. In deference to Elsie's passing she had canceled the Saturday party. "Not yet thirty-five."

Among Elsie's effects Matt found a note addressed to me. *For Addie in the event of my death.* But it contained nothing more than Sarah Covington's address in Raleigh and the request that I contact her "should anything happen."

The day after Elsie's funeral, I paid a call on Dr. Willoughby. "It's been a long time," he said, shaking my hand. "How are things going in Hickory Cove?"

"Pretty good," I said. I told him my territory had been extended to include Stone Mill.

"So the old-time reactionaries are giving a little, are they?"

"A little. Cass, one of the midwives, is too crippled with rheumatism to work." I watched as he rolled himself a cigarette. "A friend of mine died the other day. Elsie Ryland, an aunt by marriage. She was thrown from a horse, just like Dr. Caldwell."

He struck a match and lit his cigarette. "It's not an unusual accident."

"I remember you telling me that the doctor's horse had been gentle. So was Elsie's."

Dr. Willoughby drew on his cigarette and slowly exhaled. "Are you trying to tell me something, Mrs. Ryland?"

I studied the framed diploma on the wall over his head. "There's something strange going on in Stone Mill," I said, meeting his eyes at last.

"Strange?" He blinked through a cloud of smoke.

"I hope you don't think me a fusspot," I said. "They're piddling things, but . . ." I told him about my falling-out with the preacher, about the "lucky 1920," about Ma Ryland's excessive worrying over Elizabeth, about the general secretiveness. "Maybe Stone Mill is just another small town. But Elsie was going to tell me something before she died. She said not everyone knew, only the older people and some of the younger ones."

"Sounds very mysterious."

"Yes. And then"—I lowered my voice—"I think Elsie was killed."

I don't know what I would have done had he laughed. But he said, "Did Elsie leave anything in writing that might indicate she was worried?"

"She did write a note to be given to me in case something happened. So she must have been uneasy, but there was nothing in the note that explained why." I went on to tell him that she had requested me to notify a friend of her death, omitting the complicated tale of Christy, which I thought was irrelevant.

"I've often wondered . . . ," he said, opening a desk drawer. He hunted around in it, finally bringing out an envelope. "Dr. Caldwell left some odds and ends—or rather, his widow did. And among them I found this."

It was a page torn from a prescription pad, covered with so many doodles of eyes and ears they nearly obscured the writing. "The girl's death troubles me," it read. "When I go over there to see the Bradley child, I must remember to inquire."

"It's not dated," I said, lifting my eyes.

"No. But he was coming back from his visit to the Bradley child when he was 'thrown,' in quotes, from his horse."

"You don't believe he was, do you?"

"Dubious. Let's say I'm dubious."

"That was fourteen years ago. Hmmm. Will's sister died fourteen years ago."

"Of what?"

"I don't know. They won't talk about it."

"Maybe she committed suicide," he suggested. "People often hesitate to admit a suicide in the family. That sort of death would have troubled Dr. Caldwell, too."

"I suppose it's possible. Only the people in Stone Mill—except for Elsie—seem so happy. And healthy."

"A smiling face can hide a lot sometimes," he said, smiling himself.

We were silent for a few moments. "I wish I could have had the chance to examine your friend," Dr. Willoughby said. "I might have been able to tell whether she was thrown, or deliberately struck by someone. Might, I say."

"Speaking of 'might,' I wonder if there's a murderer in Stone Mill, someone they're all protecting. Or maybe there's a feud going on and they don't want outsiders to know. They're all related in some way or other."

"Dr. Caldwell wasn't kin to anyone in Stone Mill," he pointed out.

"He could have been killed because he knew too much."

He gave me a bleak smile. "You've been reading those pulp detective stories."

"No—honestly, I haven't. It's just that the town is so odd. All that inbreeding and no village idiot." Christy was mad, but it wasn't the same thing.

"It *is* odd, but then they're not too sure anymore inbreeding causes idiocy."

I got up to leave. Dr. Willoughby said, "Won't you stay and have a cup of coffee with my wife and me?"

It was the first time I'd heard him mention a wife, and I don't know why, but I felt—well—disappointed. Funny. Dr. Willoughby wasn't at all my type. And me a married woman. "No, thanks. I'd best be getting home."

"If I can be of help, Mrs. Ryland, please feel free to ask. Anytime."

"Yes, thank you."

"And, Mrs. Ryland, do be careful."

"I will."

Don't tread on toes, Addie, don't ask so many questions, don't meddle.

But I did, anyway.

The next morning I went down the street to see Bert Dawson. He kept a small printing press in the back of his barbershop. Here he put out a gossipy biweekly, the *Stone Miller*, a higgledy-piggledy-put-together two-sheeter written in a cozy, down-home manner.

"Do you keep files?" I asked him.

"Sure do," he said. "Someone's kept them ever since the paper first came out in nineteen hundred."

"May I look through? There's a recipe for hearth bread Reba was telling me about, but she couldn't remember it. Said I might find it in a back copy."

"Help yourself." He indicated a wooden filing cabinet.

It didn't take me long to make an astonishing discovery. The obituaries consisted of only one line. So-and-so died on such-and-such a date, wife and mother, or husband and father, or daughter, or son. One line. No indication of age or what had caused death. No folksy little article to describe good deeds, affiliations, fine points of character such as one would find even in the Newport News's crowded paper. Death, in contrast to the bright, chatty attention to birth, received short shrift.

I learned one other fact from the *Stone Miller*. Through the years the same families were associated with the same occupations. Though neither Claybornes nor Covingtons were mentioned, other names appeared frequently. The Dawsons, who had once owned the mill, were now associated with the bank. Loefflers, of which there must have been a multitude, were mostly farmers, Rylands were smiths, Davidsons were preachers (or midwives), and so on.

But a small town is like that, I thought—isn't it?

"Find your recipe?" Bert asked, peering over my shoulder.

"No—not yet."

He stood there, not moving away as I had hoped, but breathing down my neck.

"Interesting—your paper," I said.

"So 'tis."

I turned a page—a church social, a barn raising out at the Loefflers', a recipe for Pennsylvania scrapple by Allie Clarke. "You don't write folks up when they die, do you?" I said in an easy, offhand voice.

"Don't see any reason to. Dead's dead." He spat at a brass spittoon, a thin stream of tobacco juice which hit dead center. "What makes you ask?"

"Just wondering." Then, suddenly, surprising even myself, "I was wondering about Ellie-Mae, Will's sister. She died so young, and I don't like to ask the Rylands why."

"Nosy, ain't you?" His eyes narrowed, and for some reason my heart skipped a beat. I guess it was the way the light had changed—the afternoon was passing on, and it had grown dim in the little back room. I remembered, too, that Bert was married to one of the preacher's sisters. Davidsons, more than any of the others, seemed to resent questions.

That night I asked Will, surely for the dozenth time, "Do you think I'll ever be an insider here in Stone Mill?"

"Sweetie pie—you haven't even been here six months. You've done right well, too. Hasn't Reba asked you to help with the midwifing?"

"She didn't have a choice. She needed someone. Besides, the people I see, though they're nice enough, seem so cool."

"Naw. You're imaginin'."

"I'm not. Folks at Hickory Cove are friends, real friends. They tell me everything, all their troubles, all the good things. . . ."

"Since when does spillin' everythin' make a friend?"

"It helps." I loved my husband; I thought he was my friend, too, yet I couldn't bring myself to tell him that Elsie had begun to confide in me before she died, couldn't bring myself to say, I think a murder's been committed.

The next afternoon, I decided to look in on Chatty. I had seen her at the funeral, and she was taking her sister's death hard, sobbing uncontrollably all through the service. Her baby was due in late September, Elsie had told me, and I knew the shock and the emotional upheaval wasn't doing her much good. To my surprise I found both Reba and Cass sitting at Chatty's kitchen table having cake and coffee.

"Join us," Chatty invited. She resembled her sister—pale, freckled face and light-brown hair. Her eyes, I noticed, were swollen and red.

"I didn't know you had company." I hesitated. Cass had managed to give me a cold look on the sly. She was still angry with me over Penland's toothache, and not very happy, I supposed, at my replacing her as a Stone Mill midwife.

"Come set," Reba said, waving her fork. "Come set awhile."

Chatty poured me a cup of coffee and cut a slice of cake.

"Chocolate cake was allus my favorite," Reba said appreciatively.

Chatty refilled her cup and sat down at the table.

No one said anything—Reba forking her cake into her mouth, Cass staring glumly into her cup, and Chatty staring at nothing. It appeared I had interrupted a conversation my hostess and her guests were loath to resume in my presence.

"I meant to get here sooner," I said to Chatty, "to tell you how sorry I am."

Tears welled up in her eyes.

Reba went on eating; Cass glared at me.

"It seems such a useless death," I burst out.

Cass's face flushed a mottled red. "Yore speakin' out of turn."

Reba sighed and wiped the crumbs from her chin.

"I'm reconciled," Chatty said in a tired voice, folding her hands over her swollen stomach.

"The Lord giveth, and the Lord taketh away," Reba said.

Cass nodded. "And that's the way t'will always be."

Chatty bowed her head. Compassion and anger choked me so that I couldn't speak. I didn't believe in a passive acceptance of fate. I didn't believe in letting things go on, in turning away from the unpleasant because facing up to it might make a few heads roll. (Or did I? Really? Why did I tiptoe around Will, then?)

"We like the old ways here," Cass said, apropos of nothing, it seemed, until I caught her sour look again. How she must hate me, I thought. "It's when folks forget the old traditions they get into trouble."

"What sort of trouble?" I asked.

There was a short silence. Chatty's head remained bowed. Cass's eyes flashed. "Just trouble."

I drank my coffee. Reba began to talk about a grandson who was selling homewoven baskets at the Well Springs resort. Ten minutes later I took my leave.

Chatty saw me out the door and to the edge of the back porch.

"Will you be all right?" I asked, looking up into her face, and for a moment it seemed a cold hand was squeezing my heart, she looked so like Elsie—pale, with those freckles across the nose.

"Yes—I think so."

"Something's wrong," I said in a low voice. "Can't you tell me?"

She lifted her head as though listening. The house had gone very quiet. "No—nothing's wrong." She gave me a weary smile.

Late-afternoon sun slanted obliquely through the trees, bathing the road in a dusty haze. I passed a field where the crickets and grasshoppers sang in the tasseled corn. Soon I came to the fork where Main Street crossed Burnham Road. I suddenly recalled Elsie's saying that the Claybornes had once lived there. On impulse I turned the mare, and we trotted down the wheel-rutted lane. We had gone a half mile when I glimpsed a chimneytop rising behind a neglected apple orchard. Sliding from the saddle, I led the horse up through the twiggy, sparse-leaved trees, and presently had a better view of the chimney—blackened, I noticed, as if by towering flames.

Drawing closer, I saw part of a wall leaning crazily against a dead, stunted tree. Except for the wall and chimney, the house had been burned completely to the ground. How many years ago? I wondered. Grass, timothy, and a host of unnamed weeds grew rampant, clambering over or concealing charred bricks and shards of timber. A button gleamed dully, and I stooped to pick it up—a tarnished brass button, worn smoothly by wind and rain. The brass button of a uniform? One of the Claybornes, Elsie said, had fought with the Yankees. But that was—when?—1862 to 1864?

Time enough for the ashes to have gone to soil, for the smoky air to have been cleansed by season after season of rain and pine-scented wind. And yet there hung about the place a peculiar odor, a stench, here, in this very spot, where the door must have been.

The grasses whispered and bent under a little breeze, rippling like water on a wind-harried pond.

I knew that smell—somewhere in the past it had stung my nostrils, that very same odor. And a sudden picture of Creesey Hospital's emergency room rose before me. I saw the scorched, blistered body of a boy wheeled in, a child screaming in agony. He had been playing with matches, his hysterical mother had said. . . .

Burned flesh.

The horse whinnied, a sound that shattered the eerie, whispering silence.

With cold, trembling hands I fumbled for the stirrup. Mounted, I gave one last, frightened look at the house and, turning the horse, galloped away.

Chapter 28

I had written to Sarah Covington informing her of Elsie's
death, explaining that because I made frequent visits
to Hickory Cove as a midwife, I knew her mother, too. It
was a fairly long letter, and I was hoping to receive an
equally long one in reply, perhaps even strike up a friendship and in the process learn more about Stone Mill. But all
I got was a formal note from Sarah Covington's lawyer
saying that his client would be grateful if I continued the
payments in kind to Mrs. Covington's caretaker and that I
would be reimbursed for my trouble. I wrote back telling
the lawyer I would be happy to see that Christy was taken
care of and that I chose not to be paid for it. Clearly Sarah
Covington wanted very little to do with anybody in Stone
Mill—or Hickory Cove. Her silence seemed, to me, cold and
heartless.

Christy herself, however, spoke frequently of Sarah, a
Sarah who still existed as a child. "Have you brought my
baby?" she would ask whenever I came. Sometimes she
seemed quite rational, and then I would try to question her
about the past. But she remembered very little of Stone
Mill—a few unrelated anecdotes of girlhood, her baby,
Sarah, and nothing more. Her marriage, the "other man,"
the shooting of her husband apparently were blanks in her
mind, for she never referred, even obliquely, to the tragedy.

She lived not only in her own mad fancy but in a place
worlds apart from Stone Mill. For Hickory Cove might as
well have been on the moon. Except for an occasional foray
to earn a little money or a rare trip to Bradley's for coffee,
tobacco, and rifle shells, the Covers never left home.

So I was surprised when old Marthy McAlpin told me
that she had a brother, Ty, who had gone to Stone Mill years
ago and never returned. "He went to look for his girl," she

said. "Kate Rawlins was her name. She run away to Stone Mill. Neither of 'em ever come back."

Kate Rawlins and Ty McAlpin swallowed up in Stone Mill? I doubted it. It was one more little oddity to add to the rest. Mad Christy and her mysterious lover, Dr. Caldwell and Elsie both killed in the same way, Ellie-Mae's death, Chatty's troubled silence. Were these things somehow related, keys to some secret tragic puzzle?

Probably not. Idle minds have idle fancies, my father used to say. And maybe he was right—for one morning I threw up before I could get to the outhouse, and, suspecting I might be pregnant, I forgot all about Stone Mill's peculiarities. Ever since I had come to live in the town, I had longed for a child, and I hoped with all my heart that now, at last, I had one on the way. But I wanted to make sure before I told Will, so I waited a few weeks, and then I went over and had Dr. Willoughby examine me.

"You've got all the right symptoms," he said. "Congratulations! I'd wait a month or two before horseback riding." He smiled. "Let the baby get well established."

"You're sure, then? Imagine!" I whooped. "A baby!" A girl, maybe, though I knew Will preferred a boy. Well, it didn't matter. It was going to be mine—whatever—*mine*. "I can hardly wait to give Will the news," I chortled.

That night I put on my prettiest dress, my wedding dress to be exact, a lilac chiffon gown, rather daringly short for Stone Mill, and I perfumed myself with Mon Amour (the girls at the hospital had given me a large bottle as a going-away gift). I cooked Will's favorite dishes and set the table with candles and a centerpiece of early asters.

As usual, Will ate as though someone were going to snatch his plate away at any moment. "Addie"—wiping the gravy from his chin—"Addie, there's a meetin' tonight, and I don't want to be late."

"But, Will, there's something . . ." Disappointment suddenly formed a lump in my throat. "There's . . ."

"Later, Addie." He squinted at the mirror over the kitchen sink as he slicked back his hair.

"What kind of meeting?" I asked, tasting gall. Of all nights!

"Town meetin'," he said.

"And I'm not invited?"

He didn't look at me. "Just a few of the old-timers."

"So—I'm outside the pale."

"Now, Addie . . ."

"Well—what kind of *old*-timer are you?" I retorted bitterly. "You're not yet thirty."

"It's a business meetin'," he said. "Addie"—turning from the mirror—"you got to understand. I have to be in good with the folks who's got a say in this town. I'm goin' to need money for the garage—there's equipment to buy. . . ."

"And you have to play toady, is that right? You have to kiss . . ."

"Addie! Hey, now, sweetie, watch your language."

He was out the door before I could find a stinging reply. "You—you . . . !"

He returned home late, smelling of whiskey and tobacco. Business meeting? I thought of Myrtle Loeffler, her breasts straining at the seams of her tight dress, her teasing smile. I'm a jealous wife, I realized without surprise, jealous of the pretty women in this town who are drawn to handsome Will and his fiddle like bees to honey. Yet there was no real reason to believe Will had been seeing Myrtle.

"Will . . . ?"

"Mmmmm . . . ," he muttered and rolled over, clutching his pillow in his arms.

"Will . . . ?"

A faint snore answered me. He was fast asleep.

When I went into Bradley's the next day, I felt a sparkle in the air. People smiling, talking loudly, effusively. "Howdy, Addie." "Where you been keepin' yourself, Addie?"

Somebody's brought good news, I thought. Or maybe it's the apple crop. September. Harvest time. Nineteen twenty, a lucky year.

It wasn't exactly what I would call a "gay" mood, but wherever I went that week I felt the same state of high anticipation. A current of nervous excitement was running through the town, the very air hummed with it.

"I can't explain what I mean," I said to Will.

"There you go," he said in a voice tight with annoyance. "Imaginin' again."

I still hadn't told him about the baby, still went on waiting for the right moment, and now I was beginning to wonder when that would be.

"What's happened to you, Will?" I exclaimed. "Don't you love me anymore?"

" 'Course I do."

" 'Course I do,' " I mimicked. "We're like two strangers. You and me. Two strangers. We were closer in Newport News before we were married than we are now. You don't tell me a . . . a damn thing."

"Addie—Addie! You're swearin'!"

"What do you expect?" I could feel the bitter saliva gathering around my tongue. But I couldn't stop. "I'm your wife. Husband and wife, remember? We're supposed to share. But no . . ."

"Addie!"—sternly.

"No. You and me. But you've been holding back, keeping secrets."

"Shut up!" he yelled.

My mouth fell open.

"Shut up," he said between clenched teeth, "or I'll smack you."

What had happened to my Will—easygoing, smiling, fiddle-playing Will?

"Will, if you'd only . . ."

"Don't bother me! Can't you see I've things on my mind?"

"What things? Oh, Will, if you'd only tell me."

He didn't answer, but strode out the back way, slamming the door behind him.

Two weeks later—on September 18, I think it was—Irene Loeffler went into labor. Reba had wanted to attend her—Reba and Cass both—but Reba had sat up two nights in a row with Beth, and she was in no shape to attend anyone. Cass had tried, but her hands were so crippled and the pain in her spine so bad she had to go home.

According to custom, Irene's husband had taken all but the oldest—the twin girls, Mary and Myrtle—to his sister's, the house had been swept, and Irene put to bed between clean sheets. I was surprised to find her frightened.

"This your twelfth," I said reassuringly, adding my stock in trade, the old saw "It'll be as easy as falling off a log."

"It's like dying," Irene said, clutching my hands. "I'm sure each time I won't live through it."

"But you do, don't you?"

"Maybe this time—this time . . . Oh, God! Here it comes again."

The baby was well positioned. Irene had a broad pelvis. The pain she experienced came irregularly and lasted all of one minute. "It might be hours," I said. "Try to relax."

Myrtle, who had been sitting at her mother's side, said, "You won't be needing me right away, then?"

"No, I don't think so." I tried not to think of her as my possible rival. She was just a girl of eighteen, a pretty girl who liked to flirt with men. Harmless, really.

"Is it all right if I go out?" she asked. "I won't stay more than an hour."

"I don't see why not."

"I'll change, then," she said happily.

I went into the kitchen where Mary, the mute, poured me a cup of coffee from the stained pot. Her hands shook a little, and she bit her lip as some of the hot liquid sloshed over the rim of the cup. I wondered if she was nervous about her mother.

"Your ma will be all right," I said, smiling.

She sat across the table, her wide eyes watching me. People might call her "dummy," but those eyes were far from dumb. And she was assessing me.

Myrtle came out of the bedroom wearing a blue dress of some thin material. On someone else the gown might have seemed demure, but on Myrtle it looked indecent. "I'm off!" she announced.

Mary took one look at her sister, sprang up, and ran to the door, barring the way.

"Get out of my way!" Myrtle ordered, pushing Mary roughly. Mary tried to hang onto her sister's arm, but Myrtle wrenched herself free and was out on the porch, tap-tapping down the stairs.

A little embarrassed by this sisterly spat, I said, "Mary, you can go, too, if you promise to come back within an hour."

She shook her head. She didn't want to go.

I started to fix some warm milk for Irene. I lit the stove, found the saucepan and the milk jug. Mary came and stood beside me. A moment later she touched my arm, and when I looked up, I saw her eyes were wide and compelling, be-seeching.

"Is something wrong?" I asked.

She nodded yes.

"Can you tell me?" I asked stupidly. Of course she couldn't.

I rummaged in my bag and brought out a small notebook and a pencil and offered them to Mary. She shook her head again.

Feeling frustrated, I went into the bedroom and spoke to Irene. "How do you manage with Mary when she has something to say. I've tried to get her to write. . . ."

"She don't write. She don't know how."

"But . . . but there's nothing wrong with her hearing. Surely her teacher at school . . ."

"She ain't gone to school. Well—what were the use? She can't talk, so what's the good in her learnin'?"

I was too angry to say anything.

Mary was waiting for me in the kitchen. I could tell she was still upset.

"What is it, Mary?"

She gesticulated at the door.

"You've changed your mind, then—you want to go out?"

No, a vehement shake of the head. She pointed to the door again, then her hands moved from high to low, describing a figure eight.

"Myrtle," I said. "You're angry with Myrtle."

Again the no, fiercer this time. She went through the figure-eight motion again.

I thought for a moment. "Something about Myrtle disturbs you?"

Her head bobbed in the affirmative.

It's like playing charades, I thought, amused, a game I hadn't played since I was at nursing school.

Mary clasped her hands to her heart.

"Myrtle? Myrtle is in love," I said triumphantly.

Yes, she mouthed, yes.

And then she began to make a series of wild gestures which were a total mystery to me. Grasping her forehead with one hand, her other hand going to her heart, while her body commenced to shake and shudder.

"I—I don't understand," I said, confused.

She tried once more, waving her arms, bringing her hand back to her heart, to her forehead. She repeated the performance again while I stood dumbly watching her. And a third time. A tear formed in her eye. But it was no use.

"Let's go in to your mother," I suggested. "Maybe she can explain what you're trying to tell me."

No, no! She didn't want to go in to her mother. She put her finger to her lips. "A secret?" I asked.

Yes. Again the series of gestures, the hand over the heart, and now a look of fear in her eyes.

"Ah ... !" I lowered my voice. "Myrtle's got a secret lover?"

I had guessed right.

"A married man ... ?" I hazarded. And in that moment between question and answer I had a vivid picture of Will embracing Myrtle in some tree-shaded corner. Will and Myrtle. Why else the late nights, that business meeting, the sly winks? And Will's recent bad temper—a cover for guilt?

No, Mary was shaking her head. No.

"Not a married man?" Just to make sure.

No. But she was afraid. She pointed, she arched her hands, she drew circles and curves. The more I struggled to get her meaning, the more urgent Mary's fear became. She was afraid, not for herself—that much I finally got—but for Myrtle. And it had to do with Myrtle's lover. Perhaps the boy was "planting his corn without building his fence"—a saying in Hickory Cove for hanky-panky without benefit of clergy.

Plainly she expected me to interfere in some way. "I'll talk to Myrtle," I promised.

Myrtle arrived, not one, but several hours later, when her mother was in the throes of serious labor. I was too busy to say much except, "Hang onto her shoulders, there, Mary," or, "Get me a basin of warm—not hot, please, *not* hot—water."

It was a boy. Irene took it into her arms, perfunctorily, I thought, and promptly fell asleep.

Tired, I had the girls help me change the bed sheets and instructed Mary to dispose of the afterbirth.

When she had gone, I said to Myrtle, "I want to talk to you for a minute. Your sister is worried. Are you doing something that's not on the up-and-up?"

Her eyes widened. "Like what?"

"Like seeing someone on the sly. Mary is scared, and she thinks you ought to be."

"Scared, huh! Pay no attention to her," Myrtle said scornfully. "I'm not scared of anything. Why should I be? A fine, handsome boy is courtin' me."

"Courting for play or for serious?"

"For serious. What d'you take me for? We're soon to be married."

"Funny, your mother hasn't mentioned it."

"We've not told her yet."

"Well, then, who is this fine, handsome boy?"

"You'll see," she said slyly.

Strange, when I think of it now, but at the moment I thought she was merely acting coy.

Chapter 29

MARY, the mute, had the truth locked in her head. And maybe that is what saved her, her affliction, her enforced silence, when the final days of reckoning and vengeance came.

Had I but known. Isn't that how heroines in books put it? But I sometimes wonder if it would have made any difference. I had taken Myrtle at her word, thinking she would publicly announce her marriage when she and the boy had fixed on a date. Maybe her suitor was trying to save money toward an engagement ring, maybe he wanted to wait until he had established himself in a job, a business, or a farm. There are any number of reasons why a couple prefers to keep their plans for marriage secret. Still, Mary's obvious fear continued to nag at me.

Meanwhile, Will and I made up our quarrel, forming a polite truce. If he had only taken me in his arms, kissed me, made love to me, I might have told him about the baby. But he had become a stranger, a polite, distant stranger, and I was angry with him because of it. Night after night he would crawl into bed and fall instantly asleep, while I would lie awake for hours, staring at the ceiling, silently hating him.

"If you have trouble sleepin'," he said one night, "why don't you take a pill? You must have all kinds in that bag of yours."

"I don't like to get in the habit of taking pills," I said.

But he must have slipped one in my coffee, for an hour later I began to drowse well before bedtime, and had hardly gotten undressed and between the sheets when my eyes closed. Funny . . .

And then someone was shaking me. I felt the hand on my shoulder, the bed trembling.

"No," I mumbled. "Go 'way, go 'way."

Fingers, sharply nailed, dug deeper into my flesh. With an effort, I pried my eyes open.

"Mary . . . !" It must be a dream. I closed my eyes.

Again the clawed fingers, and then a stinging slap across my face brought me up from the pillows. "Don't you slap me—you . . . !"

The bedroom lamp had been lit, and Mary's face, half-shadowed, looked gaunt and frightened.

"Oh, God," I groaned. "I feel like I've been hit by a lamp-post." I wanted to fall back on the pillows and pull the sheet over my head. But Mary's strong hands wouldn't let go. She peeled the covers from my body. Then she brought my chemise and dress.

"Get dressed?" I asked in astonishment. "But it's . . . it's the middle of the night! Eleven fifteen. Will . . . ?" I looked over at the pillow where Will's head ought to have been. And it wasn't.

Had he come to bed? "Will . . . ?" I called, craning to see through the bedroom door.

Mary shook her head. No, he wasn't in the house, he was gone.

Mary pointed to my dress.

"Something's happened," I said. She nodded yes.

I had all my clothes on in two minutes. "Is it your mother?" No. "The new baby?" No. "Someone hurt?"

Yes—oh, God, it was Will!

She went to the fireplace and got Will's gun down from the rack.

I picked up my bag, and when we reached the door, I discovered it was locked. "How did you get in, Mary?"

She pointed to a window where the glass had been shattered. And I hadn't heard, I hadn't heard a thing.

God, talk about fear!

We went out into the night, a windy darkness with a ghostly moon riding the clouds. The trees edging the street bent and swayed like mocking dancers, the leaves fluttering from their branches to be caught here and there in a whirlwind, a dervish dance of their own.

"Where is he, Mary?"

She pressed my arm.

We hurried along the cobbled streets. There wasn't a light to be seen anywhere; the houses stood silent, gleaming

in the shadowed moonlight behind their neatly clipped
lawns. Somewhere a dog barked, then began to bay, a
lonely, piercing sound.

"It's cold," I said. The wind whipped at my legs. In my
haste I had forgotten a wrap. "Do we have much further?"

Mary pulled at my arm, and we crossed the street cattycorner, turning left. There was no sidewalk, and the street
ahead was black as pitch.

"Isn't this the way to the Covington house?"

She urged me on. I heard the distant hum of voices and
through the trees on my right caught the flash of light.

I stumbled, and Mary's hold tightened. The hum of
voices grew closer. A fiddle scraped a bar of music as if in
practice, and stopped, scraped and stopped. *Here comes
the bride.*

Mary took my hand, leading me on until we came to a
gate. I knew it was a gate because it whined in the darkness.

We proceeded slowly, hand in hand, single file, Mary
slightly ahead, I on her heels, tripping over vines and roots.
Above us the wind thrashing at the trees soughed and
moaned. Another light winking like a firefly.

A woman laughed, hysterical laughter rising in a lunatic
scale, rising, rising, and suddenly breaking off. The fiddle
scraped that one bar.

Now I could see the moonlight through a break in the
trees, and in another moment we were out of the thicket.
The Covington house loomed over us, dark, secretive, sneering.

"Will's not hurt, is he?"

And in the ghostly light Mary wagged her head no.

"Then what . . . ?"

She put her finger on my lips. Then, taking my hand
again, she guided me along the walk, toward a glow which
shone faintly through the trees. The voices got louder.

She pulled me off the path into the wild, tangled undergrowth. She had no need to caution me. Instinctively I felt
that we must not be heard.

The light grew brighter, and Mary suddenly ducked us
both under an umbrella tree. Together we crept to the far
side, and she carefully pushed a frond aside. I was looking
across the small clearing where the giant oak stood. Its
branches were festooned with bright, gay paper lanterns, and
beneath them a large gathering of people stood chatting.

Stone Mill folk dressed in their Sunday best—Reba in her flowered print, Zack in a natty vested suit, Irene almost unrecognizable in long, trailing chiffon and a big picture hat, Roy Ryland stiff-necked in a paper collar and a tie tucked into his vest. And—I gasped—Will! Will, his fiddle nestled under his chin, looking handsome and splendid, wearing his wedding suit. A punchbowl rested on the far side of the circle, and Elizabeth, dazzling in yellow voile, passed among the throng with a tray of punch glasses.

It was almost ludicrous. I don't know what I'd expected—Will laid out with a severed jugular, or held captive by a mob of Stone Millers angry because he had married an outsider, or maybe some horrible rite, some witchlike gathering, a satanic revelry, but not this group of neighbors drinking punch and chatting. It was a party to which I hadn't been invited, a little strange because it was being held in the Covington garden and no one seemed to be in a particularly party mood. They looked so sober, even Will. Especially Will, who seemed downright sad. Maybe it was because he had been asked and not me?

I needn't feel bad, I thought. There are lots of others who haven't been invited: Chatty and her husband, the Bob Loefflers, the young Perrys, and, with a few exceptions, the young, single crowd of the town.

Will trilled on his fiddle and then commenced the "Wedding March" in earnest.

The gathering broke up and formed a line on each side, and Preacher Davidson walked into the light carrying a Bible.

A wedding! Why, of course. A wedding. And here *came* the bride—Myrtle in a white wedding gown, leaning on the arm of her father, her face smiling and radiant through a thin, gauzy veil. In the background Irene Loeffler sobbed quietly into a handkerchief.

Mary grunted and thrust the rifle—which I had completely forgotten—into my hands. I stared at it dumbly. What did she want me to do? Stop the wedding?

She was tugging at my arm, gesticulating wildly at her sister.

My God, did she want me to kill Myrtle, her own twin? Maybe she was in love with the groom. "No," I whispered heatedly. "Are you crazy?"

Tears came to her eyes, begging eyes, pleading eyes, desperate eyes.

"No," I said.

"Dearly beloved," Preacher Davidson began, "we are gathered here in the sight of Almighty God. . . ."

But something was wrong. Where was the groom?

"Where is he?" I whispered to Mary.

She shook her head no, no, no. And pointed again at her sister, drawing her finger across her throat. "I'll do no such thing," I hissed.

". . . the holy state of matrimony . . ."

It was all so weird and eerie. Suddenly Mary grabbed the rifle, and before I could stop her she rushed into the lantern light, pushing her way through the line of onlookers. "Watch it!" someone, Zack, I think, yelled, and the rifle went off in a cracking whine.

Mary's hand went up as the crowd converged upon her.

They had thrown Mary to the ground and were kicking her. "Stop!" I screamed, dimly aware of Will (not among the maddened throng, thank God!) staring at me from under the tree, his fiddle hanging slack from one hand, his face white and shocked.

"Kill her!"

They turned on me then, beating at me with their fists, pulling, pushing, scrabbling, sharp elbows and knees, angry claws tearing my hair, my dress, gouging my eyes. "Kill her!" Each one eager to have his share. "Kill the busybody!" "No!" It was Will trying to get to me. A fist in my mouth, and I tasted blood. And then I was down on the wet, trampled oak leaves, blood and dust stopping my mouth. A kick in the ribs, another . . .

"Wait! Wait, you fools!"

I lay panting in the silence. "The ceremony!" It was Preacher Davidson. "We must finish the ceremony! Tie her up and put her in the house."

I had a glimpse of Will lying motionless on the ground before they carried me off.

Trussed like a fowl, I lay in the darkness. A thin thread of light fell across my bound hands. A window. But I couldn't move. There wasn't a bone, a muscle in my body that didn't scream. The baby, I thought, what if they've killed the baby? Hot tears coursed down my cheeks. What was it all about? Why the savage frenzy? It was no use telling myself I had interrupted a wedding party. This was something else. . . .

I heard a noise, a slight scratching, sliding sound, and my body stiffened. A door opened and closed. Silence. Oh, God. This house with its frozen clock in the hall, the creepy ghosts, the feeling of tragedy.

"Addie . . . ?"

It was Will! "Oh, Will . . ."

"Shhh . . ." He was kneeling beside me, undoing the rope at my wrists, at my ankles. "You wouldn't listen," he muttered. "Stubborn as all get-out. Now see what you've done."

"Oh, Will, I'm so scared. Are they planning to kill me?"

He pressed me close. "Are you hurt, sweetie? Oh, Lord . . ."

"No— I'll live, but the baby . . . I'm going to have a baby, Will."

"Oh, Lord! Why didn't you tell me? I hate myself, hate myself for gettin' you into this mess, but I reckoned . . . It was for us, Addie, you and me, the kind of good life I wanted for us. And I reckoned if I can't fight it, might as well join. Dumb, the dumbest thing I ever did. And now the baby. Why didn't you tell me?"

"I tried, Will, but you always . . ."

He hugged me hard. "I love you, Addie."

And for the moment, the time, the place, the fear hanging over us didn't seem to matter. "Oh, Will"—trying to swallow the lump in my throat.

He kissed me again. "Hurry, change clothes. We've got to change clothes. He was out of his shirt and unlacing his shoes. "I'll stay, and you hightail it home and take the mare. Don't stop for nothing—nothing! Ride as fast as you can to Novotno. Do you think that the doctor fellow . . . ?"

"Willoughby."

". . . might take you in?"

"Yes, I'm sure of it."

"I'll come get you in a day or two. Here, help me get into this fangled dress."

"Will—exactly what are they doing out there?"

"Oh, Addie, for God's sake, don't ask me now. Just hurry."

I waited a day, two days, three, a week, secluded in Dr.

Willoughby's house, afraid to go out on the street. The doctor and his wife (a plump little woman with a lisp) were kind and sympathetic. I don't know how much of my garbled story they accepted, but they believed enough of it to suggest sending the county sheriff over to Stone Mill.

"No," I protested. "No, you can't. That would put Will in danger."

"But it's wrong to let people get away with beatings—and possible murder," Mrs. Willoughby said.

The doctor agreed with me, however. "Addie may be right dear. There's no real proof anyone has committed a crime. As for the threats and the beatings, it will be Addie's word against that of the others."

When another week had gone by and Will still hadn't appeared, Dr. Willoughby offered to ride over to Stone Mill and inquire. "I won't let you," I said. "That would be suicide. You know what happened to Dr. Caldwell."

The following day the *Novotno Register* carried a small item: "William Ryland, twenty-eight, of Stone Mill Hollow was killed early Monday morning, October 3, in a motor accident on Burnham Road when his car apparently went out of control. He is survived by a wife, Addie, and parents. . . ."

I didn't cry out, didn't exclaim, didn't weep. In time all of that would come, but for now an icy rage, a numb, paralyzing anger squeezed all other feelings from me. They had killed him. Whether in outrage or in trying to prevent him from leaving Stone Mill, I didn't know.

That afternoon Dr. Willoughby and I went to see the editor of the *Register*. The report, he told us, had been mailed. No, he didn't know who had sent it.

"If I remember," he said, "there were actually two items in the letter. One we didn't print because I didn't feel it was newsworthy. But if you would like to see it—just a moment. "Eddie . . . !" He got to his feet and called through the door of his glassed-in office, "Eddie! You got last week's file?"

The notice read: "Mary Loeffler, a mute, was severely injured on September 26 when she fell from a ladder while picking apples in her backyard. It is hoped well-meaning friends will do nothing to hinder her recovery."

The veiled threat was not lost on me. "If we call the sheriff in," I said to Dr. Willoughby later, "I'm sure they'll kill Mary."

The next day Dr. Willoughby put the OUT sign on his door, and he and his wife (such kind, good people) took me down the mountain to my home in Newport News. My family did not seem surprised to see me. "I never thought much of Will," my elder sister said.

"But I didn't leave because of Will!" I protested.

I tried to tell them what I *thought* had happened. But people laughed or turned away in embarrassment. Some said the high altitude had touched my brain, or that I had become tired of being married and had run away from my husband.

And how could I convince them of the truth when I wasn't sure of it myself? The only things I knew for certain were that the folk of Stone Mill Hollow were mixed up in something bad, something evil, and that my beloved Will had given his life so that I might escape with mine and his child's.

Part V

JEANINE STEWART
(1976)

Chapter 30

A S I stood under the great oak in the garden, looking
down at the creek, I was suddenly struck with a feeling
of poignant sadness. Nothing unpleasant—more like a bitter-
sweet nostalgia. But nostalgia for what? I had never seen the
house, the garden, or this tree before, never knew of their
existence until I had blundered upon them a half hour
earlier.

Déjà vu. It was an odd feeling, but then I had been subject
to so many odd feelings these past six months. Six months.
Sometimes it seemed like six years, sometimes like six minutes. Was it only last fall Vance and I went sailing on the
Chesapeake? October—yes. A Sunday in late October, and
the sky had been a smoky blue. He had lolled at the tiller,
dangling that phony cigarette from the side of his mouth
because he was trying to give up smoking. Last October.

Yesterday...

I walked down to the little creek carrying my pain carefully, a fragile, glasslike thing that might splinter suddenly
and stab and cut.

Yesterday...

"You must make an honest attempt to forget the past," Dr.
Ornstine had advised. "Live for the present."

I sat down under a tree and leaned my head back, looking
up through the fretwork of green.

Yesterday...

We had met in a very orthodox way, this unorthodox (or
so it seemed to me then) man and I. He was writing his doc-
toral thesis, "The Sociological and Psychological Character-
istics of a Typical Forger," and had come to the Treasury
Department for information. The bureaucratic hierarchy
had passed him along to me. We had a lively, wisecracking
conversation over a file cabinet drawer, a discussion which

had nothing to do with forgers or sociology. That night, he took me to dinner.

A week later, when my roommate left for an apartment of her own, Vance moved in. My folks might have been dismayed, but they were in Iran, where Daddy, an engineer, had been transferred by his firm a year earlier. So I had no one to scold or to naysay me. Not that it would have made any difference.

I was wildly in love.

What cornball philosopher once said that it was better to have loved and lost than never to have loved at all? A few moments of happiness, a handful of hours if you were lucky, and then it was over and the piper had to be paid and paid. And paid.

My friends envied me. Handsome, young, single, intelligent men were as rare as hen's teeth in Washington. Vance was charming; he had poise, he came from a wealthy family in Philadelphia. He called me his "genie with the light-brown hair." We went everywhere together. I never thought about tomorrow—or yesterday—then.

The first pinprick in the silver bubble I had inflated around myself appeared at Thanksgiving. Vance had to go home for the "feast," as he put it. "Boring—the biggest bunch of bores on both sides of the Great Divide. I couldn't subject you to an afternoon of my relatives." He kissed me. "It will only be for a few hours. I'll fly up and be back before ten tonight. We can celebrate then."

But it was ten the following night when he returned. "I had too much to drink and had to sleep it off," he explained sheepishly.

We made love and it was better than ever. I forgot all about my hurt, my wanting to meet his family, about being left out. He had dark-brown hair that gleamed copper in sun- and in lamplight, and a way of hooking his little finger in mine when we walked. (Up tree-lined Constitution Avenue on a cold, cold night, and the Reflecting Pool between the Washington Monument and the Lincoln Memorial, the water so still, like black glass.)

Yesterday . . .

He was gone a week at Christmas. The beginning of the end. But I refused to see it. I kept making excuses for him, for myself—he had to have more time, his family were bores, we would meet later. My parents had wanted me to join them, had sent me the air fare, but I had written to say I couldn't make it, hoping until the last that Vance would ask me to go home with him. He didn't.

He returned New Year's Eve, but for me fear, like frozen panic, had already set in, and not even the Scotch and champagne I consumed could bring me to a festive mood.

"I have to discuss my thesis with Professor Dodd," he said as he packed his suitcase the next afternoon. "It won't take but a few days. I'll call you."

He didn't call. The coup de grace came in a letter (doesn't it always?). "Dear Jeanine: This has not been easy to write. Before I say anything else, I want you to know I shall always treasure your friendship. We've had such good times together, such fun. . . ."

Good times. A lump formed in my throat as the hot tears burned my eyes.

But there was more. I blinked away the tears and read: ". . . I have known Allys for some time. In fact, she and I grew up together, and it was always more or less understood that she and I would someday marry. Allys . . ."

Allys. Who was Allys? I went back to see if I had missed anything. But no. ". . . we are to be married next month. And I thought I ought to write and let you know. . . ."

Angry, sobbing, I tore the letter into a thousand strips. He had known all along, known Allys, known that they would marry.

I went to bed and remained there for a week, not answering the telephone or the knocks on the door. After I had drunk every drop of Scotch and gin in the cupboard, I lived on crackers and peanut butter. Then one day my friend Sally persuaded the landlady to open the door. When she saw me she screamed, "My God!" She called me all kinds of a fool, a poor darling, a nut. It was she who took me to see Dr. Ornstine.

You must make an honest attempt to forget. . . .

I tried, Lord knows I tried. I went back to work. I went to the movies with the girls, to dinner with an old friend of my mother's. I met a man (bald and married) at a cocktail party and accepted his invitation to see a play. I let him hold my hand.

I tried transcendental meditation and self-hypnosis, and I signed up for a class in belly dancing, and another in pottery.

"I think I can lick this," I said to Dr. Ornstine. He gave me pills to make me sleep.

Then a well-meaning friend sent me a news clipping from a Philadelphia paper. "Mr. Vance Hartwell, son of the Langley Hartwells, was married to Allys Montrose, last year's most popular debutante, at a double-ring ceremony today. . . ."

I never finished the article, because I began to shake—not just the hand which held the scrap of paper, but my whole body went frighteningly out of control. I leaned against the sink, hoping to steady myself. But I kept shaking, my heart pounding like mad. I bit my lip, trying not to scream.

Terrified, I crept into bed fully dressed and pulled the covers over me, but the quivering and shaking got worse.

I sat up, reached for a book on the night stand, opened it, and tried to read. The words all ran together. My forehead, my hands were clammy with sweat, and my terror mounted and mounted. . . .

"I was afraid this might happen," Dr. Ornstine said. "You've come face-to-face with your rejection."

"I'm dying," I said. He had a long, sallow face resembling a yellow egg with black, painted eyebrows and mouth.

He said, "I'd better put you in the hospital."

"In the loony bin, you mean."

"I can't have you walking around in this state," he pointed out reasonably.

"I'm losing my mind. I'm crazy, is that it?"

"Of course not. But you need medication, someone to look after you. What about your parents?"

"They're in Iran," I said. And even through the fog that divided me from the rest of the world I saw what a disaster it would be to have Mother hovering over me with that I-told-you-so look on her face. *Men don't marry girls who give themselves freely.*

"I'd rather leave them out of this," I said.

"Have you a friend who can stay with you, or who will take you in?"

"I can't bother my friends."

"Then I see no alternative, but . . ."

"Sally," I said quickly. "Sally will take me."

She had a job at the Smithsonian, so I was alone in her apartment for most of the day, lost in a gray, hopeless void. Sometimes I felt like climbing the walls—literally. The antidepressants, the tranquilizers muted some of the fear, but not all. Then Sally's niece came to stay during Easter week, a vivacious high school girl on her first visit to the Capital, and it fell to me to show her the town. It—she—saved my life. I was forced to go out, to mingle with people, to plan a day for someone other than myself, to wrench my thoughts from brooding on my self-pitying misery.

Gradually I gave up the pills. Cautiously, like one easing into a hot bath, I slipped back into the old routine. But in the back of my mind I wanted desperately to get away. What I needed was a change. A whole new way of living.

Aunt Penny gave it to me. Crotchety, disagreeable old Aunt Penny died and left me eight thousand dollars. Bless her heart. I scarcely knew her, having met her only once, an occasion during which she had done nothing but grumble and find fault. But now I gladly forgave her bad temper. With Aunt Penny's generous gift plus the one thousand I had in the bank, plus what I could get for my furniture, I could have a year to do whatever I liked.

But where to go? Not abroad. I had lived in London and Rome and had traveled Europe extensively with my parents. California? Florida? I didn't know.

One Sunday afternoon in early June I decided to take a drive. "Why don't you go up to Shenandoah Park?" Sally suggested. "It's only an hour away, and right now the wild flowers and trees will be in bloom."

She gave me a map. "Sure you don't mind going alone?"

"No," I said. Sally had been invited to a cocktail party.

A half hour later I had left the city behind. It was the first time I had traveled this particular road and I found myself in a highly receptive mood. Everything I passed I noted with keen awareness. Colors and sights and sounds seemed to leap out at me—the barking of a dog, the jade of summer grass, the blue-gray hills in the distance. The displays of numerous open-air booths and country stores along the way were brilliant-hued—bouquets of yellow forsythia, blood-red roses, and pink peonies in buckets, bushels of rosy-cheeked apples, baskets of strawberries, emerald pea pods, and lime-green lettuce. FRESH EGGS, a sign read. SOURWOOD HONEY.

I drove slowly, stopping once for a cool drink, savoring the afternoon, impervious to the monoxide fumes and noisy traffic in front and behind me.

And so I came to the roadside stand and the screened-

porch cottage with its sign STONE MILL HOLLOW APPLES
HERE. This tourist-trade cluster seemed different from the
others I had passed. The buildings were freshly painted—a
barn red with white trim—and potted geraniums and tubs of
azaleas were attractively placed around them. Everything
looked spruced up; not a scrap of paper or a beer can littered
the parking lot or small lawn. I bought a quart of strawberries from a smiling blond girl who might have been an
advertisement for the plump berries she sold, pretty, pink-
cheeked, and blooming with health.

Inside the cottage, knickknacks, cuckoo clocks, oil lamps,
and cheap china from Hong Kong lay stacked side by side
with lovely quiltwork, creweled samplers, and animal figures
lovingly carved from cherry wood. The baskets, all sizes and
shapes, were not the flimsy, carelessly woven ones I had seen
elsewhere, but beautifully, expertly done. A rocker in one
corner, elegantly handfitted, was a piece of furniture that
would have lent grace to any room.

STONE MILL HOLLOW. I stood outside in the cool shade
studying the sign. Why, yes! Aunt Penny's father, my own
great-grandfather, had married Kate Rawlins, a girl who
had been born in a hamlet called Hickory Cove, but who had
also lived for a time in Stone Mill Hollow.

I found the town proper a mile west of the highway. It
impressed me very much. Instead of the clutch of gray shan-
ties and shabby houses, the unpaved streets and single gas
pump which had characterized a good many of the small
towns along the way, Stone Mill Hollow, behind its homely,
roadside facade, was a substantial community, small but
fairly contemporary, with a church, a school, a post office,
several shops (aside from the ubiquitous general store), a
café, and even a bank.

I parked the car in front of the café—empty, a CLOSED
sign dangling inside the glass door. I got out and began to
walk down Main Street, deserted except for a companion-
able dog who trotted along beside me. As I passed Ryland's
Garage, church bells began to peal, the resonant chimes
echoing through the still, tree-arched streets. I had almost
forgotten it was Sunday. Afternoon services were being held,
no doubt, in the steepled church. I liked the feel of the town
—quiet, peaceful, secure. I liked the houses, old but far from
scruffy, painted light blue or white, each with a good-sized,
well-attended lawn. I liked the lavender wisteria clambering

over the porches, the lovely old trees, the beds of roses and peonies. I liked the cobbled sidewalks, the way my shoes made a homely tap-tapping sound as I walked along.

Two blocks from the center of town, the wooden houses gave way to more substantial, red-brick ones, larger, more innovative in architecture. Here, too, the trees, the lawns, the flower beds made an attractive setting. If there was a slum or a ramshackle area, I didn't see it.

The sun was just beginning to set when I got back to my car. The CLOSED sign had been taken down from the café, and through the window I could see several people sitting at the counter.

I went in, flushing for a moment as heads turned, then sat down in a booth. The waitress came out from behind the counter. "What'll you have, miss?"—icily, without smiling, not at all like the girl in the strawberry booth or the elderly lady who had sold me the hanging basket.

"Coffee," I said, "and—oh, a Danish."

"We don't have Danish. Or doughnuts, neither."

"What do you have?"

"Pie—there's pecan, apple, strawberry, quince...."

"I'll have the quince."

During this interchange I was aware that the others—a white-haired man with a hooked nose, a young boy, and a stout woman in a felt hat—were watching me with interest.

I was a stranger in a small town—what did I expect? My illness had made me supersensitive. I was forever imagining people were staring at me or talking about me, whispering things like, "It was bound to happen to someone like her." Dr. Ornstine and I had long discussions concerning this paranoia of mine. "You're not that much of an interest to strangers," he said. "A pretty girl, yes. Why shouldn't men stare at you? But for the rest . . ." and I had said, "I'm working on it, Dr. Ornstine."

I forced myself to look out the window. Across the street stood a square-shaped building of stone and timber. TOWN HALL, read the inscription over the door. A woman and a child went by, a little girl with a white, ruffled dress and bowtie shoes. She was on her way to a party, I decided. I wondered if my little girl, the girl I might have had if Vance and I had married, a little girl with bouncing curls that had a copper sheen....

"Here you are, miss," said the waitress, plunking my order down. If only she'd smile, I thought, she might be attractive.

The pie was homemade and good. As I was eating, a man came in, a middle-aged man, sturdily built, prosperous-looking. He gave me a brief glance and sat down at the counter. "Coffee, Gladys, and lots of sugar and cream." Then, turning to the white-haired man, "That was a right fine meeting, Preacher."

"Thank you kindly, Donald."

"That ought to get us set," the prosperous-looking man said, stirring his coffee.

"I sure hope so. Folks always got to be reminded when the right year comes along. Though I do admit nineteen seventy-six rolled up mighty fast."

Nineteen seventy-six. They must be talking about the Bicentennial, I thought. Perhaps Stone Mill was preparing their own small celebration.

The young boy tapped the prosperous man's arm. "Mr. Bradley, is the store going to get some more of them skateboards?"

"No, Billy, sorry about that. Too many people been complaining they tear up the streets."

Mr. Bradley—storekeeper?

Outside, dusk had come. The rose-tinted light softened the lines of the town hall, creating pools of black under the trees. When I got up to pay my bill, I said to the waitress, "Are there any motels in town?" On an impulse I had decided to stay the night.

"No," she replied sharply, punching the cash register.

"An inn? A rooming house, maybe?"

"We don't cater to tourists," she said coldly.

"But . . ."

The hook-nosed man said, "Try the next town."

A chill followed me through the door.

I sat in the car, not moving, suddenly feeling bitter. Strangers might buy Stone Mill baskets, Stone Mill strawberries, and knickknacks galore, but they were not welcome in the town itself. The roadside stand, the cottage store would take a fool's money gladly and with a smile, but coffee at the café was served grudgingly and the outsider advised not to linger.

Bad luck. Was I going to sit there and feel sorry for myself all over again?

I looked up and saw them watching me through the window. Mr. Bradley said something to Gladys, and she nodded grimly. The boy shook his head.

I wanted to shout at them, stick out my tongue, shake my fist, but instead, I started the car, backing out quickly with a squeal of rubber.

I drove slowly down Main Street. The thought of joining the night traffic, the stream of bumper-to-bumper Sunday drivers homeward bound, depressed me. And I hadn't realized until that moment how bushed I was, so tired I could scarcely keep my eyes open. I took the car around the block and, turning off onto an unpaved side street, parked under a dark canopy of trees.

I leaned my head back, intending to take a short nap, but when I awoke I was astounded to find it was morning. Birds chattered and trilled and peeped cheerfully in the trees overhead, and the sun, sifting down through the leaves, made moving patterns on the hood of the car. I got out to stretch my cramped legs.

The street, or alleyway, was little used and heavily wooded on either side. I walked a little distance but could see no sign of habitation except for an old, rotting wooden fence half smothered with vines. I followed the fence until I came to a sagging gate. I looked for a posted NO TRESPASSING, but there was none. The gate grated harshly when I pushed it open, and a large bird flew up out of the clumped bushes with a whirring of wings.

At first it seemed all jungle with no discernible passage, but then I made out a faint break in the mesh of crawling vines and encroaching shrubs. I took a deep breath. Why not? If I was trespassing, I would find out soon enough.

Laurel and hemlock, pine and oak, beech and gum twisted their way upward for a share of sunlight and breathing space. The meager light dappled down indiscriminately, touching a rhododendron bush here, a dogwood there, lush in growth but ragged in bloom. There was a cathedral stillness about this tangled, overgrown place, a stillness which soothed the nerves.

I had not expected the house, and when I saw it appearing out of the trees, an odd sort of excitement took hold. Two stories with an oval-windowed attic under a gable, it sat dozing comfortably in the morning sun. A wisteria vine looped and twined over the shadowed porch, one part dead, the other riotous with fragrant lavender bloom. Weather had stripped the paint, rubbing the timbered walls to a mellow gray. An old house, a quiet house, charming, tree-shaded. I liked it. It was my kind of house. Some houses seem that way, though you have never seen them before—they say, Home, you've come home.

I went up the stairs and, cupping my hands, peered through a side window. I could see nothing but my own reflection, as the shade was drawn. The same was true of all the other windows I could reach—shades drawn or shutters closed. I tried the front and the back doors—both locked.

I stood on the worn steps for a few minutes, drinking in the sweet fragrance of the wisteria. A squirrel skittered across the weed-choked drive, stopped for a moment to observe me from unblinking, bright eyes, then, with a flourish of its tail, scrambled up a tree.

There was another path leading down through a different part of the wooded garden. I took it and came upon the huge oak tree then, a gnarled behemoth, its heavy branches spread wide, a tree as old and as primal as time. Somewhere high in the leafy bower a bird called, a single note, so sad and lonely it pierced me through.

I sat by the creek and went over all my yesterdays until I came to now, and suddenly I knew where I wanted to spend my year, maybe forever. Here. Here in that old, tranquil house above, here where the creek purred and sang as it lapped over the moss-covered stones, here in this peace and quiet. Here was where I would find myself again.

Chapter 31

THE hostility I had met in the café no longer troubled me. Since the house was so isolated (though only a mile from the center of town), I needn't have much to do with the natives if I didn't choose to. I could do my shopping or run whatever errands I found necessary in the next village, Novotno, say, shown as ten miles distant on the map. And who knew but that some of my closer neighbors might not prove tolerably friendly?

It was half-past nine when I drove back into town. Unlike Sunday, when the place seemed deserted, there were cars parked up and down the main thoroughfare, and a handful of people were out on the sidewalk. Not a bustling community, but alive, very much alive.

The post office was located in an annex of Bradley's General Store, a large, brick-fronted building with a high porch. Inside, I waited until a young woman had finished her business at the window, and then I stepped up to state mine. "I'd like to inquire about a house I saw this morning . . . ," I began.

"A house?" the postal clerk asked suspiciously. She was a woman in her late thirties, forty, maybe, even-featured, with a mass of golden hair. Good-looking, except for the scowl.

"I'm interested in renting it," I replied.

"There's no house for rent in Stone Mill," she snapped.

"It's an empty house," I explained, undaunted. "On an unpaved street. Near the creek."

"It's not for rent. There's no house for rent in Stone Mill."

"Are you the owner? No? Well, then, may I have the owner's name and address?"

"I'm not allowed to give out names and addresses."

A teenage girl standing behind me said, "I think she means the Covington place."

"Thank you," I said.

I found a telephone booth in the general store and looked up the name Covington. Fortunately there was only one—Sarah—and she lived at 312 Main Street, a few doors from the post office as it turned out, in a small, red-brick bungalow. The house was fronted by a tiny lawn on which a clump of silver-barked birches grew. A white-haired woman was rocking on the porch. She held a large gray cat in her lap.

"Are you Mrs. Covington?" I asked politely.

"Miss," she corrected. Her face was like a wrinkled apple, rosy cheeks lost in a furrowed web.

"Miss Covington—my name is Jeanine Stewart. . . ."

Her pale-blue eyes peered up at me from behind gold-rimmed spectacles with a look half-startled, half-curious.

"I happened on your house today," I said, "and fell in love with it." I smiled—and waited. She said nothing. "I haven't been well," I went on, "and I'm looking for a place where I can have peace and quiet. I—I wondered if you would rent your house to me."

She kept looking at me in that funny way. "How old are you?" she finally said in a dry, whispery voice.

"Twenty-three," I replied.

"You're too young to bury yourself in a place like Stone Mill."

"Just for a year," I said. "You see—I need a change."

"What ails you?"

"Unrequited love," I said, not meaning to be funny or melodramatic. It just came out that way.

I thought I saw the ghost of a smile in her eyes. Or was it pity?

"The house is not for rent," she said after a long moment. "Or for sale—or for anything."

I pleaded with her, saying I would be a good tenant, I would provide references, would pay the whole year in advance if she liked. I even mentioned that my great-grandmother had been an inhabitant of Stone Mill.

"No, I'm sorry. It's not for rent. And that's final." Hitching the cat under her arm, she staggered up from the chair. I made a movement to help her, but she brushed my hand away.

She went inside, hooking the screen and closing the door.

I stood there staring at the blank door, my eyes slowly filling with tears.

Back at the café I sat nursing my disappointment over a

cup of coffee while waiting for an order of scrambled eggs to fortify me for the long drive back. I had bought a copy of the *Novotno Register* and was deep in an article about the grafting of apple trees when I heard my name called. It was Mr. Bradley, the prosperous-looking storekeeper.

"Miss Stewart . . ."

He was standing over me, a tall man for all his portliness. I hadn't realized how tall. "May I sit down? Thank you." He slid into the booth. "Nice day," he said. I wondered if he was politely leading up to the question of why I hadn't left town yet.

"Yes," I agreed, folding the newspaper and putting it aside.

"I understand you are interested in the Covington house."

"Yes . . . ," I said hopefully because he was smiling.

"And you want to rent it?"

I nodded.

"You realize that it's rundown? The plumbing is very old."

"I don't mind."

"And there's no electricity."

"Oh? I wasn't aware of that. But I could use kerosene lamps." It seemed suddenly romantic, kerosene lamps and an old house.

"You still want it?"

"Oh—*yes!* Yes. Has Miss Covington changed her mind?"

He folded his hands on the table and began to twiddle his thumbs, large thumbs, the nails filed short. "It seems that she has."

"I'm so grateful. You don't know how much."

"She wondered if seventy-five dollars a month was too dear."

"Too dear?" I replied incredulously. "Oh, my, no, it's ridiculously cheap. Is the house haunted or something?" I laughed.

For a moment he looked startled, and then laughed, too. "There's an icebox, Miss Covington tells me. You can order ice from the store. We deliver, no charge." He went on to say that Miss Covington had given him permission to hire someone to clear the paths of vegetation. "The rest of the garden she leaves up to you."

"I don't mind. I rather like all those trees."

The waitress, Gladys, brought my eggs. "Hope they're done to your taste," she said with a warm smile.

Well, well, I thought.

Mr. Bradley twirled his thumbs again. "There might be a leak or two in the roof."

"I'd gladly pay to have it taken care of."

He held up his hand. "Miss Covington is a lady of means and of honor. As owner she feels it her duty to underwrite repairs."

I gave him a check. Four months in advance, he said, would be fine.

"When can I move in?" I asked.

"I don't know what has to be done. . . ."

"Two weeks?" I asked.

"I guess that will be all right. The inside is pretty much a mess, you understand."

"It looks like it's been empty for years. How long has it been since anyone lived there?"

He twiddled his thumbs again, staring out the window. "I don't rightly know. The house got too much for Sarah, so she moved out." He shook his head.

"It doesn't matter," I said. "Just curious."

He seemed to wince at the word. "I'd show you the house, but Miss Covington couldn't seem to locate the key just now."

"That's all right, I like what I saw."

He nodded. "We're friendly folk here in Stone Mill, once you get to know us. But we do like our privacy."

"So do I," I said, thinking how completely I planned to drop out. No telephone, no TV, no radio. And no one except Sally and my parents (who were still, thankfully, in Iran) to know where I had gone.

When I returned to Washington I told acquaintances that I planned to join my parents for a year. My boss offered to give me a leave of absence, but I said I'd rather resign. I wanted no ties, no pressure, no feeling I had to return to my former life, no feeling I had to *do* anything. I would take one day at a time, and when the year was up, then I would see what came next.

Mr. Bradley had sent me a list of furnishings still in the house. I was surprised to notice china and silver enumerated among the featherbeds, tables, and chairs. I wondered why Miss Covington had not seen fit to take these small and probably precious items with her, if only for sentimental reasons. As for myself, I sold or gave away not only my own tableware but most of my other belongings as well. Still, the car was pretty well packed with sheets and towels, my wardrobe, a hand loom (for the weaving I had always meant to do but never could find time for), and stacks and stacks of books.

As I crossed the Potomac I didn't look back once.

"Thought you'd be along," Mr. Bradley said, smiling broadly as he led me down the narrow, merchandise-crowded aisles of his store to his little office in the rear. "I want you to meet my wife, she's been waiting for you."

It was the snappish postal clerk, but now she was beaming at me, her hand shaking mine, shaking it with warmth. "Sorry I wasn't too polite when we met," she said, "but Miss Covington, you know, is very old and hates to be bothered. But everythin' worked out for the best, didn't it? I hope you'll be happy here."

"Thank you, Mrs. Bradley," I said, a little overwhelmed.

"Dora, call me Dora."

"Then you must call me Jeanine."

"The house is about as shipshape as we could make it. We made an old-fashioned house-raisin' bee out of it, you know. Everybody got together on a Sunday after church—some did the roof, some the broken windows and carpentry; the ladies took care of the dustin' and cleanin'. Then we had a supper; each of us brought a covered dish."

"Sounds like fun," I said. "I'm sorry I missed it."

"Oh, there'll be others," Dora assured me.

"I don't know how to thank you. You've all been so kind. Miss Covington . . ."

"She liked your looks," Mr. Bradley said.

He gave me the key, and Dora Bradley offered to go along and help (it was her half-day off at the P.O., she said), but I told her I could manage. I wanted to be alone, to savor my moving in without having to make polite conversation.

"The drive is 'round the back," Mr. Bradley said. "You can get in by an alley that turns off from Main, just after Tulip Street."

The trees in the alley were so low, their branches scraped at the roof of the car as I drove through. I felt nervy. Excited. There was a ramshackle building I hadn't seen before, a garage or stable. I drove past it and around to the front, noting that the bushes on either side had been sharply cut back.

My hand trembled as I unlocked the door. Inside, it was dim and cool, and a tall clock ticked beside the staircase. It seemed to say welcome, welcome, and the silence flowed around that homely sound like a benediction.

I went from room to room, from the double-doored parlor, the dining room, the kitchen, to the upstairs bedrooms, exclaiming, "I can't believe it! I can't believe it!" The entire house had been scrubbed and cleaned and polished to a fare-thee-well. And the furnishings! The carved Victorian pieces, the tasseled lamps, the marble-topped tables, the bedsteads—all in such good repair. Surely, I thought, these old things could not have survived many years of neglect without showing signs of mice and dampness?

But I wasn't about to look a gift horse in the mouth. Perhaps a few of the ladies had searched their attics and contributed some of the pieces, the quilted covers or the faded velour sofa downstairs, for instance. If so, I was grateful. Wasn't it lucky that Sarah Covington had liked my looks?

As I unpacked I began to find other tokens of the townspeople's thoughtfulness—a bowl of fresh flowers in the parlor, lavender sachets in the drawers, the walls of the turn-of-the-century bathroom newly papered, detailed, printed instructions as to how to work the kerosene cookstove, and a keg of oil in the pantry ("in case you have forgotten"). A lump formed in my throat as I thought of them swarming over the house, polishing and sweeping and hammering, tucking little sachets into drawers, and writing up the helpful notes, an unobtrusive, almost shy neighborliness. I must repay them, I thought—have them all to dinner or, better still, throw a large garden party.

As I arranged my books on the shelves of the alcove in the parlor, I remembered the many times I had packed and unpacked in my life, too many to count. As far back as I could recall, we had been on the move, following my father from city to city, from country to country. Packing and unpacking, settling down in different rooms, alien rooms, walking unfamiliar streets for the first time, entering the unfamiliar school, and those eyes, dozens of pairs of curious eyes staring at the "new girl." And always, it seemed, the moment I gained acceptance, the moment the unfamiliar became familiar, the moment I felt at home, the suitcases and trunks would be dragged from their hiding places and Daddy would be checking the railroad and airline schedules again. And now ...

I stepped back from the books to survey the room, my eyes traveling slowly over the bowl of roses reflected darkly in the polished wood, the worn carpet, the fireplace waiting to be lit, the curtains moving gently in the breeze. Already the house had a lived-in air. My home. At least for a year. And after that, who knows? I might even stay.

The room I chose as my bedroom must have been Sarah Covington's, for there was a faded photograph on the marble-topped dresser, a picture of a black-whiskered man, scowling slightly, and at the bottom the inscription "To Sarah." I thought it strange that Miss Covington would leave this personal memento behind, even if she did not care for her silver and china.

On the wall hung a yellowed calendar—September 1906, probably the month and year Sarah Covington had left. She must have been a young girl then, yet I'd got the distinct impression from Mr. Bradley that she had moved because of her advanced age. It was an interesting puzzle. Still—did it really matter? The whys and wherefores of Miss Covington's life had nothing to do with me. I was here, in her room, and for that I was grateful. I was grateful to her—or her family—for their good taste, for building this charming house, for planting the wooded garden with its astonishing variety of trees. One, a sweet gum, I think it was, stood outside the window, its leafy branches giving cool, protective shade from the summer sun.

That night I fell asleep quickly and did not wake until much later, when a door slammed down below. It did not frighten me as it might have done had I been living in my city apartment. In fact I didn't feel the slightest twinge of uneasiness (I never did feel uncomfortable in that house), just a vague, sleepy annoyance. I turned over and went to sleep again.

The next morning I drove into town with a twofold purpose—to buy groceries and to thank the Bradleys again for their kindness. I had wanted to stop at Miss Covington's also to express my gratitude in person, but Dora Bradley suggested I write a note instead. "Miss Covington's not up to company," Dora said, "she's in her eighties, you know."

As to the sachets, she told me that Gladys Loeffler, the café waitress, had been responsible for those.

"You've all been so kind," I said to Gladys later, as I sat at the café counter.

" 'Twas nothing." She poured a cup of coffee from the glass server. "Cream and sugar? No? That's how you keep your slim figure, I guess."

"Maybe my figure's what Miss Covington liked about me," I said, and we both laughed. "Well, it couldn't have been my witty conversation. I hardly spoke two words to her. As a matter of fact, she practically slammed the door in my face."

"She's an old maid, you know. Not senile—or anything like that—but she has her ways."

A man wearing a dark-blue turtleneck sweater and blue slacks came into the café. He gave a quick look at the empty stools and then chose the one next to me. "Good morning, Gladys," he said. "The usual, if you please."

Gladys threw him a sour look, the same kind of I-could-kill-you look she had once given me, and, turning her back, went to the grill.

I could feel his eyes on my face.

"I haven't seen you before," he said suddenly.

Ought I to answer, or ignore him? "I just moved to Stone Mill yesterday," I said. No need to stand on ceremony in a small town.

"You related to someone here?" He had light-brown hair. His age I guessed to be about thirty-five.

"No, not that I know of, not unless there is a Rawlins family living in Stone Mill."

"There isn't," he said. "The place is full of Bradleys, Loefflers, Perrys, Davidsons—and Rylands. I'm Wade Ryland. . . ." He waited, an expectant smile on his face, and when I didn't provide my own name, said, "You're Miss Rawlins, I presume."

"No, it's Stewart. Jeanine Stewart." Was I behaving like a prig? Yet there was something about his self-assured forwardness that grated on my nerves.

"So you're a stranger, an outlander, just like me." Gladys brought a plate of sausages and eggs, dumping it down in front of him.

I said, "But I thought your name was Ryland."

"I belong to the black-sheep branch. My grandma skipped out of town years ago." Then, leaning over, whispering intimately in my ear, "I think they caught old Addie robbing the church collection plate."

"Very funny," I said.

"S'truth. And they haven't forgotten it. I came up here for a vacation, had a devil of a time getting someone to rent me a place—no one will speak to me. I get the same cold shoulder wherever I go. But *you*—moving right in. What's the password? What did you tell them?"

"Nothing," I said, suddenly wondering myself. "That's just it. Nothing."

Chapter 32

WADE Ryland, ignoring his food, went right on talking. He was a doctor, he said. He wanted to know all about me, where I was from, why I had chosen to live in Stone Mill, questions which I parried with a polite evasiveness. Nothing daunted, he continued what had now become a one-sided conversation. Talk, talk, talk.

My head began to ache.

Gladys said, "Why don't you stop pesterin' her, Dr. Ryland? Can't you see the girl's not interested?"

He looked at me with raised brows.

"I—I must leave," I said. I paid Gladys.

He followed me out to the car. "Would you have dinner with me tonight? There's this little Italian place in Novotno...."

"No," I said, annoyed, sorry I had spoken to him at all, "no, thank you."

"Tomorrow, then? Well, what about the day after?"

"No ..." My hands had begun to sweat.

"Next week?"

"I—I'm busy. *Please* ..."

I drove home with a churning stomach, nervous, upset. But the moment I stepped inside the house, the cool interior acted like balm to my nerves—the quiet, the steady tick-tock of the hall clock picking up each second, putting it down, unhurriedly, patiently. Upstairs, I lay on the bed watching the moving shadows of the gum tree on the ceiling. The wisteria-scented breeze slipped in through the curtains, ruffling the calendar pages on the wall. Was it wise to become a man-hater, a hermit? Dr. Ornstine had cautioned me against it. "Mingle with people, make friends. Don't go off on your own." I hadn't told him about Stone Mill. But then what did he really know about me? He gave the same advice to everybody. Mingle, meet people. ...

314

A door slammed, that same door. Or was it a shutter? I must remember to look.

Five minutes later, a knock on the front door startled me from a doze. I closed my eyes again, squeezing them tightly, hoping whoever it was would go away. But the knock came again, loud, shattering the silence.

When I got downstairs, the white-haired man with the large nose, the same man I had seen in the café on that first Sunday, was standing on the porch.

"I hope I haven't taken you from a nap," he said. "I am Reverend Davidson, or Preacher Davidson as the folks call me." He had very bright blue eyes.

"It's quite all right. Won't you come in?" I invited, trying not to show my surprise. We had never been much of a churchgoing family and, as far as I knew, never entertained a clergyman in our home.

"My, haven't they prettied up the place, though," he said, looking around the parlor.

"Yes, and I thought it the kindest thing the people here could have done for a stranger."

"But you aren't a stranger. You're kin to Kate Rawlins."

Was that why everyone had become so friendly? I wondered. "Kate Rawlins died before I was born," I said modestly, "I didn't really know her. And from what I understand, she only lived here a few years."

"Kate was well thought of. My pa spoke of her often. Well thought of." He looked rather solemn. I wondered if it was true or whether he was fabricating it just to be polite.

"She was a native of a place called Hickory Cove," I said. "But I can't find it on the map."

"Hickory Cove ... mmmm. Yes, I remember now. It was one of those hollows taken over by the park people. The government, you see, made up the Shenandoah Park around nineteen thirty-five, and they moved all the folk away."

"Did the Hickory Cove people come here, then?"

"No. They went to Luray or Front Royal, where the government built them houses. They couldn't fit in here. You see, they'd been out of touch for almost two hundred years. Couldn't read nor write nor speak so's you could understand. They had no way of earnin' a livin' 'cept to make moonshine, and sometimes they were too lazy to do that." His eyes twinkled. "Now Kate, she was different, from what I've been told, an up-and-comin' young lady. Went to school and all. Just fit right in with Stone Mill folks. That's why they took to her, just like we took to you."

"Thank you." I wanted to believe his flattery was sincere. And maybe it was, though I didn't see how he or the others could tell so soon that I would "fit in."

"Would you care for a cup of coffee, Reverend Davidson?"

"Preacher. Just call me preacher. Don't mind if I do."

"It will have to be instant," I apologized.

"Suits me fine."

It took me awhile to get the stove going, and another long while to get the water to boil. By the time I had the coffee poured into a Covington Wedgwood cup, the cream and sugar arranged on a tray, I thought he might have given up and gone home. But no, he was sitting in the parlor where I had left him, gazing out the window.

"Ah—that smells good," he said, rubbing his hands together. "Aren't you havin' any?"

"No—I've had quarts of coffee today. Sorry there's no cake or pie."

After a minute of silence I asked, "Is Stone Mill Hollow very old?"

"Older than these United States," he said.

"I suppose that will make the Bicentennial even more of a celebration, then."

"What?"

"The Bicentennial," I said. The two-hundredth birthday."

"Oh—oh, that. No, I can't say we have any special plans for the Bicentennial. Not that we ain't patriotic, you understand, it's just that—just that we've other business on our minds right now."

I nodded knowingly, though I wondered what sort of business he was referring to.

"I came to invite you to church services," he said. "Sunday mornins, nine o'clock. Not pressin', you understand, just invitin'. We're plain folk here, stick pretty well to the Lord's Bible, no fancy fol-de-rol. Just God's simple Word. So come join us."

"Thank you," I said. "I will."

I went the following Sunday, not because I especially wanted to but because I felt I should make an appearance. I hated this clinging to hypocritical convention, but they had all been so kind to me I didn't want to hurt their feelings by playing the snob. The men sat on one side, the women and young children on the other. A wheezing organ, but no choir. Everyone sang. Old hymns. "Washed in the Blood of the Lamb" and something that began with, "There was a man in ancient times. . . ."

The sermon was even more basic than I had expected. Preacher Davidson took his text from Isaiah. For such a little man he spoke with a dramatic eloquence that amazed me. "He will swallow up death forever!" he declaimed, each syllable a ringing bell. "And the Lord God will wipe away . . ."

He had endurance, too. When he closed the Bible, he began to harangue us about man's natural inclination toward sin, about Hell, and the Devil riding the black wind, about being humble and accepting, about homage; warming to his sermon, his voice rising as he paced back and forth, rising, growing louder and louder, echoing, rebounding from wall to wall.

I felt myself caught up in a growing fear; there was no good telling myself that Davidson was just another Fundamentalist preacher, that the sermon was a stereotyped one, no use at all. His nasal, twanging voice, those flashing, fierce blue eyes seemed to reach into the dark recesses of my soul, stirring up vague, half-remembered bogies, nightmares of outstretched clawlike hands and painted death's-heads. My hands grew clammy, the hard wooden bench under me became a bed of nails, the walls seemed to be drawing closer and closer.

And the shouting and the scolding went on and on and on.

What was happening to me? Why this fear, this terrible claustrophobia?

Finally, miraculously, we were released at noon, after the collection plate had been passed. I believe I was the first to reach the door, stepping out into the noon air like a swimmer who has been submerged underwater far too long.

"Enjoy the sermon?"

I turned. It was Dr. Wade Ryland.

"Well—yes," I answered.

"Oh, come on, now. It was terrible. Be honest." He was wearing a dark suit, complete with vest. Very conventional, very Sundayish.

"At least it wasn't boring."

"Hell, no, better than a movie. Where else could you see a performance like that? The good Preacher Davidson ranting and raging, cajoling and damning, pulling out every stop?"

"Is that why you came—to be amused?"

"There isn't much else to do in this one-horse town. And speaking of something to do . . ."

Dora Bradley tapped him on the shoulder. "Pardon, Dr. Ryland, but you really shouldn't have Jeanine all to yourself. Jeanine, dear, come home with us for a bite—just a simple meal, but we'd like to share it with you."

The preacher's sermon had exhausted me, but again I felt obliged. "I'd love to," I said.

I noticed that Dr. Ryland was not invited.

"Stone Mill," Tom Loeffler was saying, "is a mixture of the old and the new." Tom was the town lawyer. Along with his own practice, he had inherited his uncle Harry's, an old-timer who had lived to be ninety.

"What do people do here?" I asked. "I mean to earn a living. They all look so . . . so prosperous."

We were sitting in a corner of Dora's parlor, trying to digest her "simple" meal—a groaning board of chicken and dumplings, roast pork, ham, five kinds of vegetables, and three kinds of pie.

"What do we do? A little bit of this and that," Tom said. "There's the roadside stands—you'd be amazed at the profit they turn. Bradleys and Loefflers are in that together. And there's an apple-packing and -canning plant just outside of town, and we've got quite a few farmers hereabouts, some in alfalfa, cattle, too—good grazing land. And the rest of us—why, we take in each other's washing." He grinned, a nice-looking, beefy man with a high color to his cheeks.

"Do many of the young people leave?"

"Very few. One or two might try their wings down the mountain, but they come flying back. Stone Mill's got everything a body in their right sense would want, good living, no unemployment, everyone caring for everyone else."

"Sounds like Utopia," I said, meaning it.

"No—not exactly. But we earn it. Believe me, we work for whatever we get."

Our conversation lapsed after that. It was past four o'clock, but no one made a move to leave. A small pain had settled over my right eye. The room had become thick with smoke, the walls ringing with strident voices. I thought longingly of my quilt-covered bed, the window opened to the cool breeze. At last, when I felt my show of good manners had gone beyond the call of duty, I thanked my hostess and left.

I was getting into the car when a middle-aged woman came out of the house, waving. Her broad face and brown hair braided into a coronet were vaguely familiar. Her name—yes, her name was Elsie, Elsie Perry. Mrs. Webb Perry.

"I meant to speak to you before," she said through the car window. "But I've been in the kitchen helping with the dishes. You must come by to see me." She spoke rapidly. "I live out on Albemarle Road. Take Main north to Tulip, then west. You can't miss it. White brick with brown shutters."

"Elsie!" a man called from the house. "Elsie . . . I They want to know what you did with the leftover ham."

"In a minute, Webb," she said.

She bent to the car window again. She had a frank, wide-eyed look that I liked. "Come tomorrow morning," she said in an urgent voice. "It's important. You seem like a nice person, and there's something you ought to know." Then she straightened up. Webb was standing on the porch waiting for her. "Lovely day, isn't it?" she remarked to me rather loudly. "Nice to have met you."

I stared after her, trying to imagine what Elsie Perry, a woman I had never before seen until that day, had to tell me. Something important. Perhaps it was gossip, a rumor about Wade Ryland—or fact. She wanted to warn me away from him. Oh, God, I thought, the last thing I wanted was to get involved with a man. Involved with anyone.

By now, my head was a cap of throbbing pain. A tension headache, Dr. Ornstine would have called it. And I was out of aspirin. But the general store was closed, so I drove to the café down the block, only to find that it was closed, too. A car pulled in beside me. Wade Ryland sat in the driver's seat.

"Honest," he said, grinning as he rolled down his window, "I am not following you. Sometimes Gladys opens up on a Sunday afternoon. But I guess that's only on the Sundays they have their afternoon church meetings. You looking for a cup of coffee, too?"

"No—as a matter of fact, I want some aspirin."

"Aspirin. You've come to the right person, then. I've got cartons of them in my office. Samples. Hop in"—leaning over to open the passenger door—"and I'll get the sirens going."

"No . . . I . . . I'll follow."

His office—or what he called his office—was a desk, a cabinet, and an examination table in a storefront. His living quarters were in the back. "I'm not in actual practice," he said, handing me the aspirin and a paper cup of water. "Shall I level with you? You're my first patient."

"I am?"

"Well, look—I came up here a month ago from Newport News. Damn near died of pneumonia, I was so rundown. Worked my fool head off—it's a wonder I didn't have a heart attack. I thought, Well, here's a town without a doctor. Small, yes, fifteen hundred maybe, when you count the farmers all around. But no doctor. And there are Rylands all over the place. Say"—pausing—"would you like some coffee?"

"No, thanks."

"You can keep the aspirin. I've got enough to open a drugstore. You'd think I had it made, wouldn't you? No soap. These people—would you believe this? These people don't *want* a doctor. Midwives—that's their preference. Lurline Davidson and Nancy Loeffler—granny women—straight out of hillbilly heaven. 'We don't need a doctor,' Old Man Perry —he's the mayor—told me. No hospital, no doctor."

"I guess they could go into Novotno if anyone got really bad."

"I know, but they don't. I went over and asked. There are two doctors in Novotno. Neither of them has ever had a patient from Stone Mill."

"That *is* funny. Doesn't anyone here get sick?"

"Beats me." He sat on the edge of the desk, swinging his legs. "Old Man Bradley, the storekeeper, owns this building. I rented the office through the mail. Posted the letter here in Stone Mill. Tricky. He thought I was one of the Stone Mill Rylands." He grinned. "Sometimes I wonder why they haven't tarred and feathered me."

"Why do you stay?" I asked.

He thought a moment. "For some crazy reason, the place fascinates me. And besides, I like the mountain air. Never felt better in my life. If you could bottle this air, you'd make a fortune. Now—enough about me. I believe I asked this question before, but I'll ask again—why did *you* come?"

"The mountain air," I said.

"Mmmm. Do you get those headaches often?" His eyes went over me, but in a very unprofessional manner.

"Not too," getting to my feet. "But I didn't come for free medical advice. Thanks for the aspirin."

"Sure you won't go to dinner?"

"No," I said. "Thanks just the same."

* * *

The next morning, I went to call on Elsie Perry. She seemed somewhat surprised to see me, but covered it up quickly, taking me by the hand and drawing me inside. "Well, Jeanine, I do declare.'

"I hope I haven't come at the wrong time," I said. Her eyes were red-rimmed, as if she had been crying.

"Not at all. 'Course not. Glad to see you any time. Come into the kitchen and set awhile. I'm putting up the last of the cherries."

She had a beautiful kitchen, buttercup-yellow walls and curtains, brown-tile counters, a set-in oven, a dishwasher. Everything gleamed.

"I'm just at the pitting stage," she said. A large basin of cherries stood on the table. "Draw up a chair. Can I get you some coffee? A Coke, maybe?"

"Not now, thanks."

She sat down at the table and picked up a little silver cherry pitter. "Lovely day, isn't it? Though it might turn hot later."

She went on speaking of the weather, of June in Stone Mill, of the flowers which customarily bloomed at this time of the year, of how it always turned hot when she had canning to do. Her voice, I thought, was unnaturally loud, and I wondered if she were slightly deaf. But she seemed to hear me all right.

"You said you had something to tell me," I reminded her after she had paused in her flow of talk.

"I did?" And she gave a funny laugh. Scared, I thought, the woman's scared of something. "Now, what could I have meant? Oh, yes, how silly to forget. The ladies of the church are holding a rummage sale. Three weeks Saturday, and if you have anything you can give, we'd appreciate it."

For a moment I didn't know what to say. Surely she hadn't given me that urgent invitation yesterday just to tell me about a rummage sale? "I—I am sorry, but I got rid of all my old clothes and things before I moved," I told her.

"Anything at all would do fine—china, knickknacks, books . . ."

"I may have some books," I said.

"Good. We could use those." Her hands, as she worked over the cherries, had begun to shake.

I got to my feet. "I must go—and you have your canning to do."

"Don't rush off," she said, giving me a weak smile.

When we reached the door she hesitated, then, with a quick look behind, followed me out to the shaded porch. "Take care of yourself, Jeanine," she said, squeezing my hand. There were tears in her eyes.

"Mrs. Perry—Elsie . . ."

But she turned and hurried back into the house.

Strange woman, I thought, and then with a shrug dismissed her from my mind.

I spent the rest of the day doing nothing, just lolling about. I thought of writing Sally, but it seemed like such an effort. Around six I went out into the garden, a place I had grown to love. It was the sort of garden I had dreamt of as a child, wild and tangled, a vast, mysterious bower with hidden paths and mossy nooks, a garden of secrets, of fabled romance. I strolled slowly through my enchanted wood, breathing deeply of the heady, fragrant air. The setting sun cast long, dark shadows under the trees, and a cool little wind touched my cheek, rustling the leaves overhead. When I reached the creek, twilight had already set in. A white mist had begun to curl and sift, floating over the water, probing ghostlike fingers among the hanging willows and larches. Even as I watched, the fog grew more opaque, spreading into the garden, damp and tangy with the sharp smell of rich, newly turned earth.

Back at the house, I lit a fire against the evening chill, and and then sat down to eat a snack. I had hardly begun when there was a tap on the door. The preacher again? Or maybe Wade Ryland? But it was a stranger, a young man, tall and blond.

He removed the cap from his head. "Saw the smoke from your chimney." He has an engaging smile, I remember thinking, but he's dressed like a down-and-outer or like a wandering flower-child. "Didn't know old Sarah had a tenant—and such a fetching one!"

"Thank you—and who might you be?"

"Gil Clayborne," he said.

And that's how it started. As simply as that.

Chapter 33

H E had knocked at my door, he said quite frankly, out of curiosity.

I invited him in. Later, when I thought of it, I wondered that I hadn't been the least bit reluctant, the least bit wary. Clayborne was not a name I recognized as belonging to Stone Mill. But he seemed to know Sarah Covington. And there was that smile. Engaging. Disarming.

We sat on cushions in the parlor before the fire and were soon talking like old friends. It was the strangest thing. I didn't in the least resent his questions as I had Wade Ryland's. He wanted to know what I had been doing, where I had lived, why I had chosen to come to Stone Mill. I answered everything without hesitation. It was only when he asked if I had a beau that I backed away. "I did," I said. "But that's over."

He didn't press it, and I was grateful. I couldn't bring myself to talk about Vance—yet.

I offered to share my snack with Gil Clayborne, but he declined. "Some coffee, then?"

"Thanks, no. I've just had my supper," he said. He had deep-set eyes, haunting in repose. It was hard to guess his age. He might have been twenty-five or thirty-five.

"The Claybornes were among the first settlers in Stone Mill Hollow," he said when I asked if he was a native.

"My great-grandmother once lived here," I told him. "Kate Rawlins."

"Kate ..." He smiled in a bemused sort of way.

I laughed. "But that was before your time."

"What's time?"

"Oh, I guess whatever you think it is. You haven't told me where *you* are living now."

Still smiling, he watched the flames on the hearth sputter

323

and dance before he answered. "No place in particular. Just drifting . . ."

He looked like a drifter—the baggy pants, a funny, antique military jacket (the kind one picks up at a rummage sale or in the back bin of a used-clothing store), scuffed, dusty boots. But a *nice* drifter. Comfortable to be with. Easy. No need to be on guard, no need to cross swords in a perpetual man-woman duel, to be witty, or to act the clown. I could be myself, relaxed, unself-conscious.

I brought out my hand loom, and we discussed weaving. "You seem to know as much about it as I do," I said at one point.

"Do you think it unmasculine?"

"Of course not."

It was past midnight when he left. "I'd like to visit again if I may," he said.

"Please do. I'm home most evenings."

It was not until I had doused the fire, turned out the lamps, and started up to bed that I realized Gil Clayborne had not told me where he was staying; in fact, had hardly spoken of himself at all. Curious man.

I slept late the next morning, completely forgetting that Gladys had promised to come by and show me how to light the stove properly, a trick I hadn't quite mastered yet.

"I'm sorry," I apologized sleepily as I let her in. "What time is it?"

"Eleven. Have a heavy night?"

"Not really. But I did have a visitor. Maybe you know him —Gil Clayborne."

We were standing in the hall when I said that, a dim place even at that hour, but I could see her face clearly. It had gone completely white.

"Is there something wrong? You look pale," I said anxiously.

"No—no," she said. "It's the light here. Let's go to the kitchen."

She followed me through the dining room, remarking on the sturdy quality of old furniture.

"Gil seemed like a nice young man, a little spacey, but nice," I said, opening the kitchen door. "He said his family were old-time natives of Stone Mill."

"Yes. They had a house out on Burnham Road once. And

—and they moved away. Now, is this the stove that's giving you so much trouble?"

Obviously it was, and obviously she didn't care to talk about Gil Clayborne. "What's his problem?" I asked.

"Who?"

"Gil Clayborne."

"Problem? Did I give you that impression?" she asked, reaching for the matches. "I—I hardly know the man. Now, look, Jeanine, first you make sure there's enough kerosene. The main thing is patience. . . ."

We went through the process of lighting the stove several times until I finally caught the knack.

"Join me for breakfast?" I invited.

"Don't mind if I do."

Over bacon and eggs she told me that she had been married at seventeen. She had a son who had joined the army last spring. "He'll be back, though," she said. "Stone Millers always come back."

"That's what Tom Loeffler told me."

"He's right. This place is far from perfect. But what place is?" She laughed. She must have been a pretty girl at seventeen, I thought.

"How long have you been a widow?"

"Too long," she said wryly. "Fourteen years. He—he was killed in an accident." She looked down at her hands. "A hunting accident." Then she sighed. "Well, thank you kindly for the bacon and eggs. Can I help you with the dishes?"

"Heavens, no. There aren't that many."

I walked her through the garden to the front gate. "I would like very much to see Sarah Covington," I said. "I know she's old and doesn't like visitors, but I keep hoping she will make an exception of me."

"No, I don't think she would."

"But she thought enough of me to let me have her house, and . . ."

"Why don't you let it rest?" Gladys said with what seemed to me a forced smile.

I saw him again a week later. It was sundown, and I was standing under the huge oak in the garden watching the golden light tremble through the leaves, feeling unaccountably sad, the same sort of poignant sadness I had experienced on that first morning in the garden. I could not understand this sudden surge of painful memories, but the longer I stood there, the more unhappy I became. Tears crowded my eyes, spilling over, running unchecked down my cheeks.

Then I saw him coming up the path. "Jeanine!" he exclaimed. "Why are you crying?"

"I don't know," I said, feeling foolish, wiping my eyes with the back of my hand. "I'm just a sentimental fool about nothing."

"Isn't everybody a sentimental fool at heart?"

"Sometimes—sometimes I wish I didn't have a heart."

"What? Not have a heart? And such a pretty girl like you."

He gave me his arm, and we walked slowly down to the creek. "People cry for all sorts of reasons," he said. "Out of fear, out of happiness, out of loneliness."

"I don't think I'm lonely," I said. "At least, not now. Are you—are you lonely?"

"Nearly always," he said. And then he smiled. "Two by two in Noah's Ark, Preacher Davidson says. Two by two, though I never married. Have you?"

I shook my head. And then suddenly I found myself telling him about Vance. I spilled it all out, there on the creek bank, releasing all the poison that had been locked inside me these past months. And when I had finished the pain had finally vanished.

"You were betrayed," Gil said.

"It doesn't matter now," I said. "Thank God, it doesn't matter now."

"You're wrong," he said. "The only time betrayal stops mattering is when you get revenge."

I looked at him in surprise. "Revenge? And I thought you were such a gentle soul."

He laughed. "Gentle? No, I'm not all that gentle."

"And you believe in revenge? Why that's—that's barbaric."

"Maybe. My ancestors came from the Scotch Highlands. They had what you might call a chip-on-the-shoulder pride. A clan love and interclan hate. An eye for an eye, a tooth for a tooth. That's pretty hard to get out of your blood."

"Oh, Gil . . . ," I said, dismayed, touching his arm.

"Well," he said, smiling ruefully, "it's not the merriest topic, is it?"

We sat in silence, watching the creek. "Gil . . . ," I said

suddenly. "Doesn't that look like a . . ." I slid down the bank. It was wedged in between two rocks. "My God, Gil, it's a skull."

He joined me. "The jaw's nearly gone," he said.

I picked it up, and the skull crumbled in my hands. "It must be very old. An Indian's, do you think?"

He shrugged.

I gathered the pieces carefully. "I'm going to take this in to the sheriff or whoever represents the law in Stone Mill."

"Why?"

"Isn't that generally what's done with a skull? There might have been foul play."

"He or she might have fallen in and drowned. Or maybe just died of old age."

"You're probably right, but I'll have someone look at it anyway." It was growing dark. "Come up to the house?" I invited.

"Not this evening. Another time. You won't have trouble finding your way back?"

"Hardly," I laughed.

"Good night," he touched my hand briefly.

I went up the path. When I turned to look back, he was gone.

The next morning, carrying the skull in a shoe box, I called at Tom Loeffler's office, but a sign on the door said he would be out until three. On impulse, I decided to look in on Dr. Ryland.

"It's a male," he said after he had pieced the fragments together on his desk blotter. "A young Caucasian male."

"How did he die?"

"Can't say. There's nothing here to show that he met with violence. He must have died some time ago. The eye sockets and nasal cavity are pretty well eroded. May I ask what you are planning to do with this morbid object?"

"I thought I'd show it to Tom Loeffler."

"The local justice department."

"You sound sarcastic."

"Sorry about that. Have dinner with me tonight?"

"You never give up, do you?"

"You mean it's hopeless?"

I didn't want to have dinner with him, yet I couldn't bring myself to slam the door completely in his face, the way everyone in Stone Mill seemed to have done. I felt a little sorry for him. "I don't like to go out much at night," I said lamely.

"Maybe I could come over some evening and keep you company," he suggested hopefully.

"Maybe—but not just yet."

Tom Loeffler gave me a hearty handshake and pulled a chair up to his desk. "Sit," he said. "Mighty pleased to have you come by. You're looking pert."

"Thank you," I said. "How's the family?"

"Couldn't be better."

I put the box containing the skull on his desk.

"What's this—a present?"

"It's a human skull," I said, removing the lid. "I found it down by the creek."

He glanced inside. Today, in shirtsleeves, his stoutness was more noticeable. He had a considerable potbelly which hung over his belt buckle. "Dr. Ryland says it's a Caucasian male," I volunteered.

"Dr. Ryland?" he said, annoyed. "You showed this to Dr. Ryand?"

"He's a physician, and I thought . . ."

"He's a quack. A meddling quack. My wife has had medical training. She'd be able to tell you all you wanted to know."

I had forgotten that he was married to Nancy, one of the Stone Mill midwives, but I didn't feel like apologizing. Why should my speaking to Dr. Ryland be cause for apology?

"I brought it to you in case—well, in case violence was involved."

He closed the box. "There hasn't been a soul missing and unaccounted for from Stone Mill in the past twenty years. But,"—he leaned back in his chair and gave me a condescending smile—"if it would make you happy, I'll show this to the county sheriff."

"I'm sorry to have bothered you. It's just that I thought. . . ."

"You did right, Jeanine. You did right." He tapped his fingers on the box lid. "You finding things suit you up at the house?"

"Oh, yes."

"Gladys says you're doing just fine. Says you met a young man."

"Gil Clayborne—do you know him?"

"Not well. Just in passing." His eyes shifted to a fly which had found its way into the room and was buzzing at the windowpane. "Old family, the Claybornes."

"How long has Gil been in Stone Mill?" I asked.

Tom grabbed a newspaper and, leaning over the desk, swatted at the fly. "How long?" he asked, watching the fly from a corner of his eye. "All his life, except for a two-year hitch in the army."

"But Gladys said his family moved away."

"*They* did. *He* didn't."

"But Gil told me. . . ."

"Tell you the truth, Jeanine"—relinquishing his hunt for the fly—"I don't know much about him, except he's a nice young man." He gave me the kind of smile which said, "Be a darling, quit pestering me." Then he said, "You coming to the ladies' rummage?"

"I'd almost forgotten."

"Next Sunday, after church. They'd be awful disappointed if you didn't show. We generally have a barbecue in the evening. Mill Park, you know. Right by the town hall."

Sunday dawned bright and clear. The minute I pulled out of the shaded alleyway and the sun hit the windshield, I knew it was going to be a scorcher. Hot as the hinges of Hell, as Sally would say. And thinking of Sally, I suddenly remembered I hadn't answered her letter. Tomorrow, I promised myself, I'll write for sure.

On Main Street the trees were like sentinels holding up a brassy sky. Hot. My air conditioner wasn't working, worse luck. In a few moments I could feel the moisture gathering at the nape of my neck as the blistered air rose in waves from the tarred street. A nice day to sit barefoot in the shade by the creek sipping cold lemonade from a tall, frosted glass, I thought longingly.

A ray of light struck my eyes and I flipped the visor down, but the sun was still blinding. Why had I ever left the house? I could have skipped the rummage sale. Said I was sick. I didn't have to attend, no one was forcing me to. Even now I could change my mind and go home. But I kept driving, past Sarah Covington's house, past the general store and post office, the school, Clarke's Fine Clothing, the church, and then I was at the town hall, parking in the lot behind, and Gladys was waving and shouting, "Hi, Jeanine" and it was too late to turn back.

"I haven't brought anything," I told her.

"It's all right. You brung yourself. Here's Nancy."

Nancy (Stone Mill midwife, Tom the lawyer's wife, I reminded myself), big-breasted and big-hipped, in a tight, too-short, striped dress, said, "Glad you could make it. Come see Lewis's puppets."

Lewis? Oh, yes, Nancy and Tom Loeffler's son. Would I ever get all these people straight?

Lewis made puppets as a hobby. They were sitting on a card table, each with a handmade price tag pinned to its clothing—Punch and Judy, boy and girl puppets. "Mother Goose," I said, recognizing Little BoPeep, Little Boy Blue, Simple Simon's pieman. The carved figures were cleverly made, but on closer examination I noticed that each had a defect—here an eye larger than the other, there a lopsided mouth, a foreshortened arm, a neck slightly awry.

"Purty, ain't they?" said Nancy, watching me.

"Yes—I . . . ." They weren't pretty; the longer I looked at them, the more grotesque they became.

Lewis said, "This one's my best. Jack the Giant Killer." He pointed to a pole where the puppet dangled by its strings. The face was horribly distorted—bulging eyes, wide nostrils, a gashed, red mouth from which protruded a scarlet tongue. "Only five dollars," he said, giving it a twirl. It spun helplessly, a monster, an ogre mocking from its gibbet.

"Lewis sells a lot of them at the highway stand," Nancy said. She had a voice that twanged like the preacher's. I wondered if she was related to him. Probably.

"How much is this one?" I asked, pointing to Miss Muffet, not wanting it but feeling they expected me to buy.

"For you, two fifty," Lewis said, skillfully disentangling the puppet from the others, popping it into a used paper sack, and holding his hand out for the money. He'll go far in merchandising, I thought, and wondered if the Loefflers were related to the Bradleys. Everybody kin to everyone else. They all looked healthy, though. No idiots, no cripples. Except the puppets.

"Maybe you'd fancy some cherry-bark bitters," Nancy said. "Them's one of Lurline's herbs. Here. . . ." She led me across the grassy aisle to another card table. Lurline, an exact replica of Nancy (sisters, of course) was the other midwife. She gave me a big grin, her chins quivering as she said, "It's all for a good cause, Jeanine."

"Cherry-bark bitters," Nancy said. "Mix that with a little whiskey, and you'll have a spring dose can't be beat."

"Goes through the system like white lightning," Lurline said. She smelled of cheap lilac perfume. Her fingernails were not very clean.

"A dollar a jar, and you never had a better bargain," she went on. "Thank you kindly, Jeanine. You won't find anything like this over to Dr. Ryland's."

I slipped the jar in the paper sack with the puppet. My hands had begun to shake.

"Why don't you look at the clothes?" Nancy suggested. "Some mighty good bargains there."

The dresses and skirts, stained blouses, and outmoded pants hanging on racks reeked of mothballs. An airless humidity pressed down on my head, banding my forehead with sweat, while high above, the relentless sun blazed in a cloudless sky. I looked around for some shade and saw Dr. Ryland inspecting a box of paperbacks.

I slipped behind another clothes rack, not feeling up to an encounter with him. The back and collar of my blouse had gone sticky. The sun climbed another notch.

"Finding lots of bargains?" Dora Bradley asked loudly from across a row of sweaters. She was wearing a garish, purple-red lipstick applied in slapdash fashion. Some of the color had come off on her teeth.

"Yes, yes," I said hurriedly, pretending to have seen something on another rack.

Voices rose, the shrill voices of women, the booming tones of men, voices harsh and discordant, the kind one hears in a feverish dream. Why am I being so critical? I asked myself, wiping my sweaty palms on a tissue. These people have all been kind to me. And yet I felt resentful. I felt they had forced me, somehow, to come to their rummage sale against my will.

Two boys chasing a third ran helter-skelter through the clothes racks, upsetting the one next to me. It fell with a shattering crash, spilling jackets and ties and dresses to the ground.

I swallowed. But the lump in my throat would not go away.

The people of Stone Mill went on jabbering and gesticulating, showing their teeth, laughing with gaping mouths. They were all stout, well-fed, obscenely so—like porkers.

Dr. Ryland had seen me; he was coming my way.

I turned and fled, upsetting another clothes rack, but I didn't care.

The drive home took a sweating eternity, the clamor of the crowd still ringing in my ears. Not until I reached the shaded alleyway did my hands relax on the wheel. A few moments later the house came into view. Never had it looked so much like a haven.

And Gil was waiting on the porch. I ran up the stairs into his arms. "You're here," I murmured gratefully. "Thank God, you're here."

Chapter 34

WE sat under the green trees, watching the creek as it poppled over smooth black stones. "I don't know why I made such a dramatic scene," I said. "Throwing myself at you. The heat must have gone to my head."

"You're still trembling." He put his arm about my shoulders.

"Silly of me." Was I falling in love with him? I hoped not. I didn't want all that pain and agony again. And yet . . .

I turned my head to look at him. "Gil—you've never told me about yourself. Where you live, what you do . . ."

"Is it important?"

"No, I suppose not. Not very. Not when I'm with you." I smiled up at him.

"Am I making a mystery of myself? I don't mean to. I'm a hired hand. I work on Jeb Loeffler's place. He has that big apple orchard on the other side of the packing plant."

"I think I've met him somewhere—church, maybe." I wondered why Gladys or Tom hadn't known that Gil worked for Jeb.

"I may be leaving the end of September," he said.

"Oh, no!" I exclaimed in dismay. "Can't you stay?"

He laughed, but he didn't say he would.

Again he refused my invitation to supper, but he walked me to the door and kissed me good night, a kiss so tender, I wanted to cry.

"Tomorrow," he said. "Wait for me tomorrow evening."

He did not come at six, though I walked down to the creek and sat there for a long time. At nine I finally gave up and climbed the stairs to the bedroom.

I sat by the window for a long time, looking out at the gum tree, thinking of Gil, how healing I found his presence, how much I missed him when he was gone. Gil.

If I craned my neck and turned my head sideways and squinted, I could see the moon high above, a segment of pale lemon among the dark, starry leaves. I wondered if Sarah Covington had watched a similar moon from this same window. And other Covington girls before her. For this was a girl's bedroom, and the tree outside, spreading its branches, was the sort a lover would stand under at night, calling softly to his sweetheart.

Suddenly an object hit the window—*ping!*—startling me. It sounded like a stone. I waited, holding my breath; again—*ping!* I pushed the window up and leaned out.

"Jeanine . . . ? Jeanine . . ."

"Gil! Where are you, darling?" He was looking up at me through the branches. "Wait!" I cried. "Don't go away. Please don't go. . . ." And I was out of the room, running down the stairs and through the front door.

His arms went around me, drawing me into a tight circle, shutting out the world, all the ugliness, all the unpleasantness, all the terror and the pain. Safe . . .

"I love you," I murmured.

And he answered, "Jeanine . . . ," and his voice uttering my name was a caress. "Jeanine . . ." A whisper, a breath of wind, "I love you, too."

I don't remember much after that, like a drunk who's had too much liquor, only flashes of memory return. He made love to me tenderly, passionately, without Vance's urgency or naked lust, saying my name over and over. But when I awoke to the morning light pouring in through the open window, he was gone.

I didn't drive into town that day or the next, or the next, or the next. I didn't want to go. I didn't want to see Dora or Gladys, or Tom Loeffler or Mr. Bradley. I didn't want anyone except Gil. He came every evening now, always leaving just before dawn. "I've chores to do," he would say, getting into his clothes.

During the day I would drift from room to room or wander out into the garden and roam through the wilderness, listening to the birds chirping, watching the way the light changed color from hour to hour, sniffing at the late-blooming mock orange growing in abandoned profusion.

A week passed, and then Dr. Ryland drove into the yard one overcast morning.

"Where have you been keeping yourself?" he asked, after

he had invited himself in. "Not bad," looking around the parlor. "A little musty and rundown, but I suppose all old places are like that."

"Thanks," I said dryly. I resented his criticism, resented his presence.

"You're not looking too well," he said. "No color."

"I feel fine."

"Good, then. Good! Care to go to lunch?"

"No, thank you."

"I'm disappointed," he said, settling himself in one of the cushioned chairs, crossing his legs, leaning back as if he were prepared to stay all day.

"Look—Dr. Ryland . . ."

"Wade."

"Wade. I have things to do, and . . ."

"Go right ahead. I'll just read a book or a magazine. Oh, I see you have an old copy of *Vogue.* . . ."

"I suppose the only way to get rid of you is to accept your offer for lunch."

He grinned. "I think you've caught the idea."

We had left the main highway and were on the road to Novotno when he said, very casually, "Someone tried to kill me yesterday."

"Are you serious?"

He turned and looked at me. "I don't joke when it's a matter that concerns my own neck."

"But why? And who?"

"Why? Because my presence is not wanted in Stone Mill. Who? It could be any of a half-dozen people. As for how—anticipating your next question—someone tampered with the car brakes to the point where they simply didn't work at all."

"But . . ."

"I had the car checked the day before yesterday, and the brakes were in working order. Don't you see? They—whoever—*meant* for me to have an accident."

Now who's being paranoiac? I thought.

"It was obvious someone knew I drove up the mountain first thing every morning," he went on, "to see this patient of mine."

"Patient? I thought you said you didn't have any."

"I didn't until last week, when a woman came into the office and asked me to call on her father. She had been visiting from Cincinnati when the old man fell ill. To make a long story short, I happened to mention my caller at the café, showing off, I suppose, that I finally had a bona fide patient, and that I went up to see him every morning. There's a hairpin curve about a quarter of a mile from his house."

I shuddered.

"I got the car stopped on a rock, one wheel hanging over the edge. A rock. A beautiful rock."

For a moment neither of us spoke. "All right," I said. "They don't like you here in Stone Mill. But really—isn't murder kind of drastic?"

"Very. By the way, I happened to be talking to the sheriff in Novotno the other day and mentioned the skull you'd found. Seems Tom Loeffler never brought it over to him."

"Maybe Tom thought it wasn't important."

"Maybe. Maybe Tom got wind of my speaking to the sheriff about the skull and resented it."

"Dark, sinister plots," I said, trying to make light of it, yet thinking, What if someone had really tried to kill him?

We drove in silence for a few minutes, then, speaking my thoughts aloud, I said, "They're all a little strange, now that I look back. I never could figure out why the people of Stone Mill took to me so suddenly. They said it was because Sarah Covington liked my looks."

"That I can understand," he said, rolling his eyes at me, imitating Groucho Marx. He put his hand on my knee.

"It was just for lunch, remember?"

I began to think about Gil Clayborne. He was a Stone Miller, too—the strangest one of them all if you considered him objectively—the outlandish clothes, the cavalryman's boots, the funny peaked cap. And so vague about his past, evasive about the present. A hired hand, he had said. *I work for Jeb Loeffler.* Yet he spoke like an educated person. And his hands, though strong and supple, were white and smooth, not the hands of an outdoor laborer.

"Do you like Italian food, Jeanine?"

"Why . . . yes . . ."

"There's an old Italian couple—how they got up here is a long story, but they have this restaurant. . . ."

Gil had never offered to take me to a restaurant, hadn't offered to take me anywhere, not even to the café for a cup of coffee. Nor had I ever encountered him in town. It was almost as if he shied away from being seen in public.

"Here we are," Wade was saying. "Doesn't look like much from the outside, but wait till you taste their ravioli."

We had scampi and a bottle of Bordeaux. Both very good. I ate heartily, surprising myself, until I realized I had been skipping meals during the past week.

"Have you noticed the variation in dialect in Stone Mill?" Wade asked.

"What?" I said. "Oh, you mean people speaking differently. I suppose it's because some of them have had more education than others."

"Exactly. Now take the preacher—don't let all that fire and brimstone fool you, nor his folksy, put-on talk. He's a clever man, very clever. He runs the town."

"I thought it was Bradley who had his finger in every pie."

"He does, but I'm willing to bet the preacher has the last say. Besides, he's married to a Bradley."

On the ride home, Wade tried to put his arm around me, but again I managed to brush him off. When we reached the house I said, "Thank you for the lunch," and, getting out of the car quickly, ran up the stairs.

I stood for a few moments leaning my head against the closed door, and when I heard Wade's car start up, I turned away, sighing with relief. I climbed the stairs slowly, sliding my hand along the smooth bannister. Why was it that I felt happiest here, in this house, with the clock ticking solemnly away and the muted light falling softly through the curtained windows? It was a curious thing, but always when I left it—and the garden—I began to feel irritable, began to feel a dislike, a repugnance toward others. I became suspicious, questioning people's motives, critical of everyone, even Gil. His clothes. My God, when I compared him to the "casually" but ultra-expensively dressed Vance, I had to laugh. And Gil not taking me anywhere? How petty could I get!

One sullen, humid afternoon on a whim I got in the car and went for a drive, taking the road which led back into the hills. It was rural country, apples mostly, and a few open fields where cattle grazed. The orchards were well tended, old fruit-bearing trees interspersed with young saplings.

As I drove, the dark clouds began to pile up overhead into frowning battlements. I passed a white mailbox leaning a little on its wooden post. JEB LOEFFLER, it said. I slowed the car, then put it in reverse.

A dirt driveway led past the mailbox, losing itself under the white-girded apple trees. Should I? I debated, biting my thumbnail. Gil might not like my coming to see him in the middle of a working day. On the other hand, it wasn't as if he might be tied up in a board of directors meeting.

Distant thunder rumbled as the car moved slowly, bumping gently over the ruts left by the last rain. I'll tell him the truth, I rehearsed; I'll say I was just passing and happened to see the name, and thought I'd drop in to say hello. It was a long driveway, darkened by trees and gray sky, a tunnel which came out into a circle at the foot of a large clapboard house, two stories, painted a dazzling white with blue trim. A farmhouse that spoke of good crops and ample profits.

Forked lightning split the lowering sky. The place looked deserted. Beyond the house I could see a long, low building, also painted white, which must have been a barn. From it came the busy cackle of chickens.

I got out of the car and pressed the bell at the door. I couldn't very well wander about aimlessly, looking for Gil. No one answered, so I took the little walk which skirted the house, going around to the back. A small garden was planted here, rows of herbs neatly labeled with empty seed packets—thyme, rosemary, basil, marjoram.

I knocked at the screen door, peering through it to a large kitchen. "Anybody home?" My voice was lost in a peal of thunder. "Anybody home?"

A woman appeared in the kitchen. "Oh," she said, "I thought I heard someone." She was in her mid-thirties, plump with that rosy shine to her face so characteristic of Stone Millers.

"I'm Jeanine Stewart," I said.

"Of course, I remember," she said. "Do come in. We've met at Dora Bradley's. But I expect it's hard for you to keep all our names and faces in mind. I'm Lydia. Please have a chair, I'll fix us some coffee."

"I—I can only stay a minute."

"Make it fifteen—unless there's a special hurry?"

"No...I...all right."

Her kitchen was as neat and clean as a pin. All sterile electric. And plastic flowers. Vases of them on the window-sills, on the table, on the refrigerator, and a cascading, rubbery vine hanging from the ceiling.

"How's the weaving?" Lydia asked. "I heard from Dora that you brought a loom."

The weaving. "Not very well, I'm afraid." I hadn't touched my loom since I had shown it to Gil, hadn't touched much of anything these last two months, not my books or my mending or the seeds I had planned to plant.

"The Knit and Purl carries wool," she said, bringing cups and saucers to the table. "It's just off Main, cattycorner to the bank."

"I'll give it a try," I said.

Lightning flashed, illuminating the kitchen with blinding light. "You'll have to stay till the storm's over," she said. Then she went into a long story of how her grandmother had handwoven all her linens. "I still have a tablecloth. Embroidered in cross stitch."

I wondered why she didn't say anything about Gil. Surely he must have told her about me? She brought the coffeepot to the table and began to pour.

"I've been seeing a lot of Gil Clayborne lately," I said.

Her hand jerked, and the coffee splashed onto the table. All the color had drained from her face. "Oh, dear!" she exclaimed. "Look what I've done." She got a dishcloth and began to mop up the spill.

I kept silent for fear of upsetting her further. What was there about Gil that made women turn pale with fright at the mention of his name?

"I'm extra clumsy today," she said, going to the sink and turning on the tap.

A clap of thunder bounced off the roof. Rain spattered briefly against the window. Breaking a long silence, I said, "Gil tells me he works for your husband."

"Oh . . . ," she said, without turning. "Oh—yes, of course."

"Would you mind if I had a few words with him? Gil, I mean."

She faced me then, rubbing her hands on the sides of her skirt. "He—he's not here now. He's gone to town on an errand. And, speaking of errands, Jeanine, I'm so sorry, but I just remembered I . . . I promised my mother I'd pick up her laundry."

The sudden recollection of her mother's laundry was so obvious I felt embarrassed for her. She was asking me to leave in the politest way she knew. "I was just going."

She walked me through the house to the front door. "Come again," she said. "And stay longer."

But her invitation lacked warmth. She didn't want me, especially if I was going to ask for Gil Clayborne.

Chapter 35

DRIVING home through the rain, I pondered why Lydia
—and before her, Gladys and Tom—had seemed so reluctant to discuss Gil. The only logical answer I could come
up with was that Gil was a fugitive from the law, and the
people of Stone Mill, loyal to their own, had been hiding
him. Since I could not imagine Gil committing a violent or
heinous crime, I decided that he had been operating one of
those much-rumored illegal whiskey stills tucked away in the
mountains. It had been discovered, and now the revenuers
were searching for him. Under the circumstances I could see
why friends would be evasive or fearful.

I reached home just as the rain had tapered off, only to
find Wade Ryland sitting in his car reading a newspaper.
Nervy, I thought. I had never fully believed that story about
his brakes being tampered with, someone trying to kill him.

I got out of the car, frowning. "I've got this awful headache," I said to him through the car window. "Do you
mind . . . ?"

"Look, Jeanine. Don't put on an act. I'd rather you'd say
go away."

"Go away," I said.

"All right." He started the car. "I just wanted to talk to
someone. The old man died."

"Your patient up the mountain?"

"Yes. This morning. I feel terrible. I thought I had him
coming along fine. And then—well, those things happen, I
suppose. All the time, in fact. But I liked the old guy."

"Look," I said, feeling ashamed of my earlier curtness,
"come on in, and we can talk."

"Feeling sorry for me? Is that it?"

"Maybe."

"Okay, I'll buy that." Tucking a paper sack under his arm,

he got out of the car. "I brought a bottle of Mondavi Zinfandel."

We sat in the parlor, sipping wine from Sarah Covington's cut-glass goblets. "It's a California wine, but superb, don't you think? The original vines were supposed to have been brought over by a Hungarian count. Well, here's to whoever . . . !"

I wondered if he'd had a few nips earlier. "Wade—what do you know about moonshine?"

His eyebrows went up. "White lightning? What prompts that question?"

"Just curious."

"They're still making booze up here. All through Appalachia. Have made it for over two hundred years—and, I guess, will for the next two hundred."

"Don't they ever get caught?

"Certainly. Pay fines, go to jail, serve their sentence, and most of them go right back to brewing again. Only they might be a little sharper the second or third time around." He sipped at his wine, an amused look coming into his eyes. "The old man knew a lot about moonshine. Never made it himself but could if he had to. There's one point in the process where a fire is built under the pot, and the smoke rising out of the trees can be a tip-off to revenuers. So the moonshiners devise all sorts of ways to hide the smoke, building elaborate Rube Goldberg contraptions of stovepipe chimneys and extensions carrying the smoke away to an underground hole or cave. Foxy, I call that. More wine?"

"No, thanks."

"A lot of people have been killed over moonshine." He twirled the wine in his glass. "The old man believed that Stone Mill folk have been operating a big still for years."

"Who?"

"He didn't know for sure. Just guessed the storekeeper, the banker, maybe even the preacher might be the ringleaders."

"Isn't that a farfetched conclusion without proof?" Yet I couldn't help wondering about Gil. It was possible he was involved, too—very possible.

"That's what I thought. But he told me that the people of Stone Mill have always been secretive. Playing their cards close to the chest. And he couldn't figure any other reason except moonshine."

"What did the old man die of?"

"Heart. But then he was ninety-one."

"Ninety-one!"

"Incredible, isn't it? Did I tell you he was a doctor in Novotno in the twenties? Dr. Willoughby. *He* tried to get up a side practice in Stone Mill and was told his services weren't needed. He claimed his predecessor, a Dr. Caldwell, was murdered because he knew too much."

"Murdered! That skull I found. . . ."

"Could be."

There was a small silence while Wade poured himself another glass of wine. "Still," I said, "your Dr. Willoughby might have invented the whole story. A lonely old man, probably senile."

"He seemed to have had all his marbles. Did I mention he knew my grandmother Addie? Well, he did. Said she left Stone Mill because she was scared."

"I thought you said she stole money from the church collection. . . ."

He grinned. "Maybe that's why she was scared. No, the old man figured she had come onto something. You see, my grandma midwifed here in Stone Mill and in a place called Hickory Cove."

"Hickory Cove!" I exclaimed. "That's where my great-grandmother was born."

"Small world, isn't it? Well, Addie must have stumbled onto a still while traveling through the woods. At least that's what the old man believed, though he said Addie never came right out and admitted as much. Instead, she gave him some kind of cock-and-bull story. Come on, Jeanine"—holding the wine bottle up to the light—"there's plenty left."

"No, thanks, I'm still working on this one."

"Dr. Willoughby gave up his practice when his wife died thirty years ago. And he had that little house built on the mountain. Nice, cozy place. He and I had some long talks about Stone Mill. Did you know that people here are not all that fond of one another? According to Dr. Willoughby, they stick together because they're *afraid*."

"Afraid of what?"

"Afraid of going to jail. Afraid that one of them will rat."

It was growing dark outside, and I began to light the lamps. "They don't seem the least bit afraid," I said. "They look hearty, healthy, happy. . . ."

"How would *you* know how anyone looked? If I've ever seen a chick walking in her sleep . . ."

"Listen, Wade. . . ."

"Dopey. Beautiful but dopey."

He was getting drunk. God, what a nuisance. And Gil might be walking up the path at any moment. "I think you'd better go," I said.

He stared at me with glazed eyes. "All right"—staggering to his feet—"but what I really came for was . . . was to invite you to the funeral."

"Funeral?"

"The old man *died,* damn you, don't you listen to anything I say? The old man. Dr. Willoughby. His daughter didn't want the expense of hauling his body back to Cincinnati—a bitch if I've ever met one—and so she asked the good mayor of Stone Mill, Jim Perry, if her father could be buried here. Well—let me tell you—she hassled with that man for hours. She's a real virago, and Jim finally had to say yes. So the funeral's tomorrow. And there won't be anyone except . . ."

"I'll be there."

"That's a good girl," he said, taking an unsteady step toward me. And before I could push him away, he grabbed me, but he was too drunk to do more than give me a boozy kiss on the ear.

"G'night," he said.

"Are you sure you're all right to drive?" I asked.

"No," he said. "But I . . . I'll walk."

"I'll take you," I offered halfheartedly.

"I said I could walk. Here, give me another kiss."

I managed to get him to the door without the kiss. "See you in church," he said.

Fifteen minutes later when I looked out, the car was still there, with Wade fast asleep, his head slumped over the steering wheel. It wasn't until two in the morning that I heard the car start up and drive off.

And, for the first time in a week, Gil failed to come by.

Preacher Davidson spoke a few perfunctory words at Dr. Willoughby's grave. "Ashes to ashes, dust to dust . . ."

There was only myself, a sobered Wade Ryland, and the old man's daughter, a fiftyish woman with a nervous tic in one eye.

"Thank you for coming," she said, shaking Wade's hand,

then mine. She had left her car at her father's house, and Wade was to drive her back to get it.

After they had gone, I took a leisurely stroll through the churchyard cemetery, intrigued by the antiquity of some of the tombstones. "Hezka Loeffler—died 1761—a good man with a rifel [*sic*]." "Betsy Dawson, aged eighty-seven, died 1803—kind to the pore and ailin'." All the graves, even the old ones, were clipped, trimmed, neat as the front lawns on Main Street.

Then out of the jumble of tombstones the name Clayborne caught my eye. I went closer. ASA CLAYBORNE 1809–1864. And next to it, MARY CLAYBORNE 1813–1849, wife of Asa, mother of seven sons. The sons were buried in adjacent graves. Reading the inscriptions I was shocked to find that they had all died young. Baby Chris's death in infancy I could understand, infant mortality being what it was in the last century. But the other deaths puzzled me—Gilman (obviously, Gil's ancestral namesake) at age twenty-six, Lonnie, twenty-four, Patrick, twenty, Philip, seventeen, Tommy and Harley (apparently twins) at fifteen. And then my shock was compounded when I realized that they had all passed away in the same month and year as their father—September 1864.

I stared at the graves. Though the noonday sun blazed down in full summer heat, I felt cold. There was a mystery here, some dark tragedy which had occured over one hundred years ago.

Eighteen sixty-four was the last year that marked a death for that family—at least in Stone Mill, unless there were other Clayborne graves scattered throughout the cemetery that I had missed.

I touched the stone cherub angel sitting atop Mary Clayborne's tombstone, a stone memorial larger and more elaborate than the others. The angel's nose had been worn away, but the plump winged figure still kept its vacant stare, the hollowed, almond-shaped eyes gazing steadfastly into eternity.

"You find the cemetery interestin'?" Preacher Davidson smiling, hat in hand, was standing a few feet from me.

"Yes," I said.

He mopped his forehead with a large white handkerchief. "Old family, the Claybornes."

It was like a litany, a song, a mantra. *Old family, the*

Claybornes. "How is it that so many of them died in the same year?"

"Fire," he said. "The house burned down."

The preacher, though he was a short man, still looked imposing, even when standing in a cemetery in the midday heat. Imposing, but not real. He was more like the caricature of a country preacher. A cartoon. But they were all that way—Gladys the waitress, tough with a heart of gold, Bradley the storekeeper, portly and genial, Nancy the midwife, fat and comfortable. Cardboard creatures, puppets playing roles.

"All the Claybornes?"

"Them that didn't die moved away."

"But it seems to me the whole family . . ."

"My, but you're curious, aren't you? Lonnie had a wife, and there was a child, a son." He smiled with his teeth.

"I—I'm not asking because I'm morbid. Or—nosy. It's"—I lowered my voice—"I'm interested in Gil."

" 'Course you are," he said, patting me on the arm. " 'Course."

We fell silent, and I pretended to read the inscriptions again. I had the feeling he was waiting for me to leave.

"Would you"—I began, turning back to him—"would you mind if I took a stroll through the churchyard?"

"It's not much of a place for a body to walk. Besides, it's a right hot day."

"I promise not to litter or to step on any of the graves"—this with my most engaging (I hoped) smile.

"I guess, puttin' it that way, I can't refuse. We don't 'specially like people to make a public park of the cemetery."

He walked away then. I suppose he considered the cemetery his private little domain. Or was there something here he did not want me to see? Like what? Well—like a cache of bottled moonshine, perhaps, if I were to believe the dead Dr. Willoughby's story.

I walked along a flagged path under the shade of silver-green acacias and came to the low stone wall which bounded the churchyard. On the other side was another walled plot and a little gate which led through to it. The overflow, I thought.

A beech tree grew in one corner, an old tree with a thick, short trunk and spreading branches. Under it I found a simple marker with the words barely discernible. FRANCINE

COVINGTON, it read. DIED 1864 AT THE AGE OF TWENTY. MAY GOD FORGIVE HER.

What a strange inscription! What had this twenty-year-old girl done so long ago to be forgiven for? Had she been a thief, an adulteress, a murderess?

"I see you're still here." I looked up to find the preacher watching me from the other side of the wall.

"Yes. I was wondering about this grave—Francine Covington...."

"I don't know every soul in this churchyard, child"—giving me the toothy, meaningless smile.

I had a strong feeling that he was lying, that he knew all about the dead Francine and probably a good deal about all of the Stone Millers buried here.

"I'll walk you back to the gate," he said, giving me his arm. "It's time to lock up."

Chapter 36

THE next afternoon, driving along Main Street, I caught a glimpse of Miss Covington on her hands and knees, working in her tiny flower bed. Parking at the curb, I got out and went up the narrow walk.

She did not hear me until I called her name.

"Oh!" she said, turning her head to look up.

"I'm sorry I startled you." She was wearing a wide-brimmed straw hat, and her eyes in the shadow of the brim were large with fright.

"I don't usually have callers," she said.

"Please forgive me. I simply wanted to thank you in person for renting your lovely home to me. I enjoy everything, the house, the garden. . . ."

"I don't have callers," she repeated, her eyes darting nervously from side to side.

"I'll leave, then," I said. "But I do thank you."

I had taken two or three steps when she called, "Miss . . . ! Miss . . . !"

Turning quickly, I said, "It's Jeanine," and smiled.

"I don't mean to be rude, but it's best for me to be alone." With the aid of a cane, she got painfully to her feet and slowly shuffled up the stairs to the porch.

"Yes, I understand." I stood on the walk, not knowing whether to stay or go. I had the strong feeling she was lonely, that she would welcome a visitor.

"What did you say your name was?" she asked.

"Jeanine," I told her, coming closer.

She nodded. "Miss, I suppose. Well, I'm a 'miss,' too. It happened that I didn't . . ." A painful spasm crossed her face.

"There's a picture in the bedroom inscribed to you," I said, leaning against the stair rail. "A man with black whiskers."

"Grandfather Judd," she said musingly. "Is he still there?"

"If you'd like to have it . . ."

"That's mighty kind of you. But you had best be going now. They don't like for me to talk with strangers."

"They? Who?"

"Everybody," she said with a flutter of a clawlike hand. "They . . . they take care of me. You see, I'm very old. And it taxes my strength."

"You seem remarkably chipper to me."

She smiled, and for a moment I imagined her as she must have been when she was young, the webbed wrinkles replaced by smooth skin, the faded eyes by dancing blue ones, the heart-shaped face looking up at the light.

"Are you the last Covington?" I asked.

"The last," she answered. A large tabby cat jumped into her lap. She began to stroke it, her hand sliding over the cat's head and down its striped back.

"I noticed there's a Francine Covington buried in the cemetery," I said. "Is she by chance your grandmother?"

There was a long silence. Sarah Covington sat with bowed head, her hand tangled in the cat's fur. "I don't know who she is," she said at last. "I don't know."

She got up on creaking limbs, the cat jumping from her lap. Her lips were white and quivering.

"Can I help you?" I asked anxiously.

"Go away," she said. "Please, go away."

All the way home I puzzled over Sarah Covington's abrupt dismissal of me the moment I mentioned Francine's name. Who was she—the girl God had been asked to forgive? Why did the preacher and Sarah Covington deny knowing anything about her? Did Francine's death in 1864 have something to do with the deaths of the Claybornes? Perhaps it was she who had set the fire. Perhaps she had been a witch, a devil worshiper, although mountain people, as far as I knew, had never gone in for witch-hunting like their Salem cousins. Perhaps—but then, she could have committed any number of transgressions.

Even after Gil came that night, the enigma of Francine continued to haunt me. We sat on the porch steps, I with my head on his shoulder, enjoying the cool of the evening. A few faint wisps of fog had crept up from the creek, but overhead the sky was clear, the stars diamond-bright. I told him about Dr. Willoughby's funeral.

"Are you one of those women who make a practice of going to funerals?" he asked.

"No. But the poor old man didn't have anyone except his daughter, and she didn't seem to care all that much."

"Hmmm."

"Interesting place, the cemetery. I saw scads of Claybornes."

"No doubt," he said. "But must we dwell on this morbid subject?"

"Sorry. Oh, look, a falling star. Make a wish, make a wish!" I grasped his hand and squeezed my eyes shut.

"What did you wish?" he asked after a long moment.

"Happiness. When you wish for happiness, that takes care of everything."

"How do you mean?"

"Well—for instance, the fairy stories of the three wishes or 'The Monkey's Paw.' There's always a zinger on the third wish. If you wished for health, you would get it, but then you'd lose all your money. If you were granted riches, you'd suddenly get ill. If you wished for love, it turned out you were doomed to die."

"And happiness covers every contingency?"

"Can you think of one it doesn't?"

We fell silent again. A lightning bug glowed momentarily, winking off, then on. The night throbbed with myriad sounds —katydids and crickets and the deep call of the bullfrog.

"Gil," I said, "something puzzles me."

"Mmmm."

"Now, I'm not being morbid again, but I saw this grave. Francine Covington, who died . . ."

"You *are* being morbid," he said coldly.

"Why?" I wanted to know, suddenly annoyed. "Why are people in Stone Mill so slippery?"

"Am I being slippery when I don't want to chitchat about funerals and graves?" he said, drawing away angrily.

"Nobody, but nobody ever gives me a straight answer."

"Straight answers!" he shouted. "Do you have to have everything tied up neatly?"

"Never mind the neatly bit." I had never seen Gil lose his temper, never knew he had one until then. And I sensed that he could also be passionately violent if he chose. Yet I went stubbornly on, demanding, "What do you know about Francine Covington?"

There was a stunned silence. "I was madly in love with her," he said sarcastically.

"I didn't mean that, I meant. . . ." And then suddenly I laughed. A slow smile curled his lips, and he began to laugh, too.

"Sweetheart," he said, taking me in his arms, kissing my hair, my eyes, my mouth. "Sweetheart, let's forget Francine, shall we?"

And I did. For ten days.

I fell into the old routine of doing nothing, of going nowhere. Again I drifted from room to room, and in the cool of the evening trailed out into the garden where I would wait for Gil. I moved unhurriedly, not in lassitude but in a strange state between waking and sleeping, acutely aware of color, of form, of sound and smell. I remember composing a whole poem in my head one afternoon while I watched the moving shadows of the green leaves across my bedroom floor. I didn't read, I hardly cooked, I didn't weave. Like a lily of the field, I simply existed. And yet it wasn't unpleasant or boring or tedious, those long hours until Gil came.

I believe I could have gone on forever that way. But one afternoon I had a visitor who jolted me out of my lovely cocoon. Not Wade Ryland, but Sally.

"I had one helluva time finding you," she said, sinking down on the sofa and kicking her shoes off. "Nobody would tell me a damn thing. Could I have a drink? Something cold that tingles, please."

I gave her a glass of sherry with a lump of ice I had chipped from the shrunken block in the box.

"How *did* you find me?" I asked. Sally was homely in an attractive way—wide, large cheekbones, short, flattened nose, kinky hair. And she wore her far-out clothes with marvelous flair.

"I saw this kid kicking a can down Main Street," she said. "Isn't that what lads do in small towns to while away the summer hours? Anyway, I said, 'Where is the Covington house?' very authoritatively, and he said, 'You mean the haunted place?'"

"Haunted?" I laughed.

"Isn't it?" she said, looking around, stenciled brows arched. "My God, this house must have been built at least a thousand years ago."

"The early eighteen hundreds, I think."

"Fairly new, then, huh?" She sipped at the sherry. "Don't you mix with the locals?"

"Certainly," I said. "I've made lots of friends in town."

"Then how is it people said they didn't know you?" Her fingernails were painted lavender, and she kept snapping her thumbnail on the rim of the glass as she spoke.

"Who did you ask?"

"I went into that general store—and if *that* isn't a holdover! Men sitting on the porch chewing and spitting tobacco as if they'd never moved out of their seats since Harding was President. Anyway, I went into the store and questioned the clerk, who referred me to the proprietor, a Mr. Bradley. . . ."

"I know Mr. Bradley."

"He said, 'Sorry, but I haven't had the pleasure of the young lady's acquaintance.' "

For a moment I didn't know what to say. I couldn't guess why Mr. Bradley had made such a statement. "I think he might be trying to protect my privacy," I said at last. "He understands the whole idea of my coming up here is to get away from everything."

"Privacy? Okay. Okay." She clinked the ice in her glass. "I wouldn't have come, Jeanine, except you didn't write and I got worried. . . ."

"I feel terrible about that. I kept meaning to write. And of all the friends, you've been the closest. No, really. You helped me when I needed it the most. You saved my life."

"Oh—come on."

"You did. If it hadn't been for you, I would have been stashed away at the funny farm."

"Rats. No such thing." She sipped again. "How are you? You're looking awfully thin and pale."

"It's been too hot to lay out in the sun, so I haven't my usual summer tan. But I feel fine. Never better."

"And you've gotten over Vance?"

"Vance?" It surprised me how completely he had passed from my mind. "Oh, yes, yes. I . . ." On the verge of telling her about Gil, I suddenly decided against it. She would want a full biography—age, occupation, description, tastes, education—and might even insist on meeting him. And afterward she would be sure to make some well-meant comment about his hippie appearance, about my having "taken up" with a farmhand.

"Met anyone interesting?" she asked, just as I expected she would.

"Not really. There's a young doctor here—Wade Ryland— I've had lunch with. But he's rather pushy. Not very popular in town."

"Yeah. I know the type."

She shook the glass; the ice had melted.

"More sherry, Sally? No. Well, how's about some lunch?"

"Here?"

I laughed. "I do have a kitchen. And I can still fix a mean tuna sandwich."

"Let's go out."

"You don't like my house."

"No. If I have to be honest, no." Her eyes traveled the parlor again. "I suppose one old house is much like another, the same peculiar, musty smell, the same creaks and groans. But *this* place gives me the creeps. I think that kid was right."

"Oh—Sally!"

"Listen—isn't there someplace nice we can have lunch in Stone Mill? My treat."

"No—you're my guest. But there's only one café."

"What about Novotno?"

We went to the Italian place. Over minestrone, Sally said, "Seriously, Jeanie, do you like it up here?"

"Seriously, I do."

"I wish—I wish you'd come back."

"Why?" I laughed.

"Because I miss you." She ran her lavender thumbnail along the tablecoth. "I miss you, but I also know you have to do your own thing. It's mainly . . . I don't like the town. I don't like Stone Mill. And I don't like that house. There's something spooky there. . . ."

"Sally! From you? Spooky? Just because it doesn't have Formica counters in the kitchen and a sunken tub in the bathroom. . . ."

"Lord knows, I'm not psychic. I don't believe in that crap, but, Jeanie, so help me, I've got the strangest feeling that something terrible happened there."

"People live and die," I said. "It's an old house, as you say, and things happened. Sure. So what?"

"Leave it." She leaned across the table and squeezed my arm. "Leave it."

I drew my arm away, suddenly resenting her, my old, my

loyal friend. Resenting, almost hating her.

"Shall we go?" I said coldly, getting to my feet.

On the drive back to Stone Hill, Sally didn't mention the house again but kept up a gossipy patter about people we both knew. I exclaimed, "Is that so?" or, "Really?" at intervals without actually listening. My mind, perhaps because of Sally's allusion to past tragedy, had turned to Francine Covington again. Francine hadn't entered my thoughts for ten days, not since Gil and I had quarreled and made up. But now I suddenly remembered her gravestone and its cryptic message.

The mysterious Francine might once have lived at the house, perhaps sat in the parlor, heard the clock, climbed the stairs, even slept in the same bed as I did now. I tried to visualize what she must have looked like. Dark hair? Or light? Light, probably. Most Stone Mill folk were light-haired and blue-eyed. She would have worn her hair tied back in a bow, the way unmarried girls did in those days. She would . . .

"I have to get back to Washington," Sally was saying.

We had reached the house. "Won't you stay the night?" I asked. But she refused my polite, rather stilted invitation, and I did not insist.

A half hour later I was standing at Francine Covington's grave. I don't know what had brought me there, a compelling force or maybe just simple curiosity. I had come surreptitiously, the back way, climbing over the low wall so that the preacher or his wife could not see me from their house across the way.

The first thing that struck me were the other graves hidden in the tall grass, graves I had missed on my first visit. The one next to Francine's was that of a young girl, too, Alene Perry, aged twenty, who had died in 1878. Strangely, her stone marker bore the same inscription, MAY GOD FORGIVE HER.

And then, as I walked slowly around that walled plot, a growing horror seized me.

MARY DAVIDSON AGED TWENTY DIED 1885 MAY GOD FORGIVE HER. ELLEN LOEFFLER AGED TWENTY-ONE DIED 1892 MAY GOD FORGIVE HER. ANNE PERRY AGED EIGHTEEN DIED 1906 MAY GOD FORGIVE HER. ELLIE-MAE RYLAND AGED NINETEEN DIED 1913. . . .

And so it went. Fifteen graves, fifteen girls, the last buried in 1969.

The wind whispered in the beech tree, and a leaf fluttered down, a single leaf dying before its time.

I went from stone marker to stone marker once more. And again—1864, 1878, 1885, 1892, 1899, 1906 . . .

I stood very still. Except for the year 1871, a girl had died in Stone Hill every seven years, a girl for whom it was necessary to commemorate in stone by the inscription MAY GOD FORGIVE HER.

Seven years. And the last in 1969. Which would make 1976. . . . *Now*, the wind whispered, *now*!

Chapter 37

"THE preacher isn't to home," Mrs. Davidson said when I knocked at her door.

"May I come in?"

I declined her offer of coffee, of cake, of lemonade, of a Coke. I sat on the edge of a straight ladder-back chair in the stuffy Victorian parlor and came right to the point—or tried to come to the point. "Please don't think me morbidly curious, Mrs. Davidson, but . . . ," I began.

She was looking at me, her head slightly cocked to one side, her blue eyes expectant behind steel-rimmed glasses. I was sure she had seen me crossing the street from the cemetery. I cleared my throat. "Mrs. Davidson, I don't make a habit of inspecting tombstones, but I've just seen something very upsetting." I told her then about the walled plot.

When I had finished she said, "I know naught about the churchyard. You'll have to ask the preacher."

"It's useless to ask him," I said.

"I can't help that." I had the feeling she was angry at me, and for some reason afraid to show just how angry. "I can't help that," she repeated in a tight voice.

"He didn't want me walking around in the churchyard."

"It's a sanctified place," said Mrs. Davidson.

"He doesn't like me asking questions, is that it?"

"What's the good of questions?" she said.

No good at all if they weren't answered. And I had the feeling no one in town would oblige me. The graves frightened me—all those girls dying, some my age. Perhaps I was foolish to be frightened. Perhaps the explanation was quite simple. And yet I couldn't let it rest.

The only person I could think of who might be able to throw some light on the matter was Wade Ryland.

He was looking out through the curtains of his plate-glass window when I parked in front of his office.

"And to what do I owe the honor of this visit?" he said, swiping imaginary dust from the extra chair with a clean towel.

"I thought you might be able to help me," I said.

"At your service. Aspirin? Birth-control pills? Or maybe an appendectomy?" he asked in mock hopefulness.

"No, sorry, nothing medical. It's a puzzle, a puzzle that bothers me."

"I love puzzles. Where have you been keeping yourself?"

"I've been staying pretty close to home."

"I came by one night," he said, seating himself on the edge of the desk. "But your lights were out, so I figured you'd gone to bed early."

"I usually do."

"Alone?" He gave me a long, meaningful look.

I forced myself to meet his eyes. "I can see where you got your reputation for being a Nosy Parker."

"Ha! Ha!" he said in mock grimness. "What's the puzzle?"

I repeated my story, and when I had finished, added, "The preacher didn't want me to see those graves, I'm sure of it."

He thought for a few moments, chin in hand. "All right, I have it. It's obvious. They must have been suicides, and they were buried separately from the others in unconsecrated ground."

"But *fifteen?*"

He grinned. "What's so strange about that? Life being what it is in a place like Stone Mill, I can hardly blame them. The wonder is there aren't more."

"You would have a flip answer."

"But logical, very logical." He tapped my knee. "See here, Jeanine, suppose you and I go for a moonlight stroll tonight."

"No, thanks."

"Do you find it pays? I mean, playing hard to get?"

"I'm not playing," I said, getting to my feet.

He pulled me into his arms and tried to kiss me. I pushed him away. "You try that again, and I'll chop your head off!"

"Now, come on," he said, grinning, "don't tell me you're spoken for." And he made another lunge at me, his mouth closing on mine, hard and insistent.

I smacked him, and he let me go. "Just for your information, I *am* spoken for," I said, outraged. "His name is Gil

Clayborne, if you must know, and I advise you to stay away from the house, stay away from me!"

He began to laugh. When I slammed the door behind me and got into the car, I could still hear him laughing.

I said nothing to Gil that night about the graves. It was obvious that he had this thing about death and I didn't want to risk another quarrel such as the one we'd had over the long-gone Francine. And, in truth, five minutes after I had met him under the big oak tree and he had put his arm about my waist and kissed me, I had shoved the mystery of the churchyard to the back of my mind.

But the next morning, driving into town for groceries, I thought of the graves again. Somewhere, I told myself, there's got to be an answer. There's *got* to be.

I didn't stop at the general store but drove past it, past Dr. Ryland's office and down the street to an older, brick-faced, glass-windowed building. Here the *Stone Miller*, a breezy little weekly was published. DEL DAVIDSON, the lettered sign read, EDITOR IN CHIEF AND BUSINESS MANAGER.

I couldn't recall having met him, but apparently I had. "Howdy, Jeanine!" he exclaimed in greeting. "How's yourself?"

"And you?"

"Never better."

We discussed the weather, the prospect of rain, the satisfying success of the rummage sale. Finally Del asked, "What can I do for you?"

"I'm interested in looking through your back files." I gave him a bright smile.

"Any particular reason?"

I hadn't expected that, but I said, "Yes. I want to look up some obituaries. You see, I saw these . . ."

"We don't keep the papers but one year."

"But I thought all newspapers kept files."

"No room for them," he said, waving his hand vaguely.

I got back in the car, telling myself that it was all in the past, anyway. Those graves had nothing to do with my life. So why worry myself silly over them?

A week went by, two weeks, and then it was September. It amused me to see that the month at last coincided with the yellowed calendar on the wall. Seventy years ago to the day, Sarah Covington must have folded the *August* page back, stared at the new month and thought, Autumn will soon be here. And then suddenly she had left, gone away, leaving the calendar, this delightful room, and the portrait of her grandfather on the marble-topped dresser.

I tried to give her the photograph.

Wrapping it in tissue, I carried it to her house one sunny morning. She would not open the door, though I knocked and knocked. Finally I heard her say, "Go away, please, go. . . ."

"I have the picture of your grandfather, Miss Covington. Shall I leave it on the porch?"

A momentary silence, then her quavering voice, "Please go away." And so I brought the portrait back with me.

It was two days later that I overheard the conversation between Lurline and Nancy. I hadn't meant to eavesdrop, but I happened to be in Bradley's looking through some shirts with the thought of buying one for Gil (his had become so seedy) when I recognized Nancy's whining twang on the other side of the merchandise-stacked counter.

"She's goin' 'round askin' questions about Francine," Nancy said.

She could only be me.

And then I heard Lurline say, "How'd she know?"

"She saw the grave, Preacher Davidson said. And then she come back a couple of days later and saw the others. She went over to Mrs. Davidson and started askin' questions."

"Well, let her ask. There's nothin' to fret over."

"But supposin'. . ."

"Nancy, you always was a worrier. She can't find out. There's no way she can find out."

I stood there for a long time after they'd gone, the shirt I had been inspecting dangling limply from my icy hand.

Early the next morning I drove to Novotno. The *Novotno Register*, I was relieved to find, was one of the few small-town Virginia neswpapers which had survived the War Between the States as well as the subsequent Reconstruction. And yes, they had all their back files, the papers until 1900 on microfilm. A modern little city, Novotno, and that morning I liked it for all its pizza parlors and fried-chicken stands and noxious automobile fumes.

I started with the year 1864. The reproductions of what must have been faded print in the first place were not very clear. But my diligence was soon rewarded by a curious item. "Gilman Clayborne of Stone Mill Hollow was hanged yesterday, September 24, by order of Lieutenant Beau Hodges of the Confederate Army. Clayborne, a traitor to the Virginian cause, was found hiding near the house of his fiancée, Francine Covington." The next three lines were blurred beyond recognition, and then the article went on to say, ". . . the execution took place in the Covington garden . . . for the Claybornes (one of the first families in Stone Mill) . . . suffered another tragedy, a fire which demolished their house." A few unintelligible words, then, ". . . all perished."

All.

All of the Claybornes had died.

I shut the machine off and went to the front desk, where an adenoidal young woman sat, the file clerk. "How did your people get the news from Stone Mill in the old days?" I inquired.

"I have no idea," she said. "Now we receive news by mail or phone from the editor of the *Stone Miller,* which saves somebody the job of going over there or us hiring a stringer on the one hand, but on the other, we can't vouch for accuracy."

"How accurate do you think reports were, say, during the Civil War?"

"Mmmm. If my history is any good, I do remember that there was a lot of fighting in the Shenandoah Valley, a few skirmishes at Front Royal, but nothing up here or at Stone Mill."

I returned to the microfilm, and there found the item I had been looking for. "We regret to report the passing of Francine Covington, age twenty, daughter of Eli and Margaret Covington of Stone Mill. She died on September 28 by her own hand. Remorse was given as the motive. May God forgive her."

Remorse. What a strange word to use. Remorse for what? Had she betrayed her lover?

But then, what of the fourteen other young women? Why had *they* committed suicide?

It took me hours, but I went through the film and, after the 1900s, the newspapers, searching obituaries for the names of the dead girls. I found them—the names, all right, the names, the ages, and the dates of death. Nothing else.

Waiting under the great oak that night for Gil, I could not

get those newspaper items out of my head. Usually the house, the garden, the quiet twitter of birds at dusk had a peaceful, calming effect, but not tonight. When Gil finally came walking up from the creek, I overcame my reluctance to speak to him of the past and told him that I had read of his ancestor, a Great-great-someone-or-other Gilman, who had been hanged because he had been a traitor.

To my relief he didn't become angry.

"So you've been reading local history," he said, putting his arm about my waist. "Gilman fought for the Yankees. Do you think he did wrong? Do you think he was a traitor?"

"Heavens, no. But why should they hang him?"

"I suppose they thought he was a spy. But he wasn't."

"And they killed him without a trial or anything? How terrible!"

"Yes—terrible."

We strolled up to the house without speaking.

"There's something else which troubles me," I said as I lit the lamps in the parlor. "In that same plot where Francine is buried. . . ." As soon as I mentioned her name, his face became pale and wooden. Still, I went on, ". . . I found fourteen other graves, all of young women. I can't get them out of my head, all those young women committing suicide, because that's what they must have done."

He didn't say anything, he didn't look at me.

"And then there was this fire. . . ." But I knew he wasn't listening.

I've gone and done it, I thought. Graves and cemeteries. "I'm sorry, Gil," I said. He sat as if carved of stone. "Gil . . . ?"

He roused himself. And then he turned his head and smiled. Ah, that smile! I truly believe it could have enchanted a stone. "Jeanine . . ." He got to his feet and came to me, drawing me close. "Jeanine, such a foolish girl to be troubled. . . ." He kissed me, a long, ardent kiss, and everything fell away but the moment.

"What have they got to do with us?" he murmured, caressing my face. "Old bones crumbling to dust. . . ."

"Nothing," I said. "Nothing." The lamplight glowed like a nimbus in his hair. Nothing was wrong, nothing ever could go wrong. Only good, wonderful things could happen.

"I love you," he whispered, kissing my cheek, my throat. "I want to marry you."

"What?" I said, drawing back, wondering if I had heard right.

"I want to marry you. Do you find that shocking?"

"I . . . yes, yes, I do." I had never thought of marriage. How could I, when I had never even thought of tomorrow as long as Gil was with me?

"Why?" he asked, a dimple appearing at the corner of his mouth as he smiled down at me.

"It's so . . . so *practical*."

"And you don't think I am?"

"No. What will we live on?" I teased.

"Love and kisses, honey and dew." And he kissed me again.

Absurd, utterly absurd, and yet I was filled with such euphoria, such overwhelming love and happiness, I could think of nothing but our being together always.

"I'll arrange for the preacher," Gil was saying. "We can have the wedding here in the garden. Next Saturday. Does that suit you?"

"Suit me?" I laughed. "Oh, Gil—yes—yes."

Chapter 38

GIL, wanting a simple wedding, had vetoed extending an invitation to my Washington friends.

"Not even Sally?" I asked. I didn't care about the others, but Sally was my best friend and I had treated her rather shabbily when she had come up to see me.

"If we make one exception, then we'll have to ask others," he said.

"And my folks?"

"Do you really want them?"

"No—I don't think they'd come, anyway, on such short notice." Besides, I thought, Mother would turn her nose up at Gil. A farmhand!

Gil said, "I know it sounds selfish, but let's make it as private as possible."

Private. Somehow, perversely, the word stuck. Did he want it private because he was reluctant to show himself? "Gil . . . ," I began and couldn't go on.

"What is it, Jeanine?"

We were sitting on the sofa, his arm about my waist. "Gil— is there—is there something you ought to tell me? What I mean . . . is . . . is there something about you I should know?" I finished awkwardly.

He stiffened. Even though he did not withdraw his arm, I felt his defenses go up, windows and doors slammed shut, bolted, locked.

After a long, terrible silence, he said, "I don't get your meaning."

"I—I thought maybe, since you"—floundering, making vague motions with my hand—"since we didn't go out . . . you might have done something . . . something against the law. Like running moonshine. . . ." I gave him a silly, tittering laugh.

"Running moonshine?" he asked, surprised. "Whatever

gave you such an idea? I've never broken the law. Never. I've killed several men. . . ."

And when I gasped, he smiled. "But that was in war."

The Vietnam War, of course, that bloody, futile, tragic war in Southeast Asia. Funny, it had never occurred to me that Gil might have been there. Already the war had faded into limbo, but then most of us, most of my friends, anyway, had been on the sidelines, either marching in protest or watching the battle on television. But Gil apparently had seen combat, and that fact opened a whole new vista, an insight into why he found it hard to speak of death and churchyard graves. Poor Gil, I thought, nestling closer.

"My father," he was saying, "brought us up very strict. He was an old-fashioned man, I suppose. Honest and foursquare. Did I ever tell you about him? He had a terrible, white-hot temper—like mine—but he could be kind and generous, too. And understanding. He respected my principles, even though they might differ from his. I loved that man."

"He's dead?"

"Yes," he said. I could feel his sadness then, his unspoken grief, sharp and painful. It was like standing under the oak that first time and listening to the bird trill his one lonely note.

"Oh, Gil . . . I'm sorry." But the words seemed empty, my apology meaningless.

"I died when he did," he said.

"Oh, no, Gil! Please, don't say that."

"Sometimes I get so tired, so tired of the whole thing. . . ."

"No, Gil!" I cried in terror, flinging my arms about his neck, straining him to me, kissing his mouth, his cheeks.

"Please . . . You love me, remember? You *did* mean it?— my breath catching—"I couldn't bear it if . . . if . . ."

"If . . ." His finger trembled as it traced the curve of my lips. "I forgot myself. Of course I love you. Jeanine, you're not crying? Oh, my darling, I do get morbid. See what happens? I love you. I swear it."

The wedding, it turned out, would not be strictly private after all. "A few of the townsfolk," Gil said, "might be nice. And—though I don't especially care for old Preacher Davidson, I'm willing to overlook his faults, since he's the only one who can marry us."

"Tom Loeffler is a justice of the peace," I pointed out.

"I still prefer the preacher. And we'll leave it up to him to send out the invitations."

"Leave it up to him?"

"Do you mind?"

"No—not really." Because suddenly they all—the Bradleys, the Davidsons, the Perrys, the Loefflers, the Rylands—seemed like dears. In love, I loved everyone.

"I don't want you to do anything but look pretty," he said.

Dora Bradley was the first to congratulate me. The preacher had given her the news. "Jeanine, dear," she said, "Leave all the arrangements to me."

"I'd like champagne," I said.

"Champagne, it will be. And Mrs. Davidson has this very beautiful old wedding dress I'm sure she'll let you borrow."

"But I thought . . ."

"If it doesn't fit, a little needlework will alter it."

"That's very kind."

"You're the bride. And since your own mother won't be able to be here, why, we older women will try to substitute. My dear, it will pleasure us no end."

The preacher's wife came the next day with her sewing basket to take my measurements. I wondered why she did not bring the dress itself and have me try it on, until she explained that the gown reeked of mothballs and that she had left it airing on the sun porch.

"I don't reckon it will take much redoing," she said, her bony fingers slipping the tape measure around my waist.

"You are all so good to me," I said with an impulsive rush of warmth. I wondered why I had ever found fault with these good people of Stone Mill. They had gone out of their way to prepare the house for me when I first arrived, and now they were taking the burden of the wedding from my shoulders. Perhaps I had been too much influenced by Wade Ryland's carping. *He* certainly would not receive an invitation; in fact, I would make a point of asking the others to keep my upcoming marriage a secret from him.

"May I use your bathroom?" Mrs. Davidson asked after she had finished.

"Certainly. Upstairs, first door to your right. Would you like some coffee?"

"Thanks, no, Jeanine."

When she left, I noticed she had dropped a thimble from

her sewing basket on the seat cushion. I opened the basket to replace the thimble and saw a yellowed photograph of a girl. Her hair was done up in ringlets and curls, and she wore a long dress inset with lace, high-collared, wasp-waisted, and bustled. A few scrawled words at the bottom of the picture read, "Alene Perry's wedding dress."

I closed the basket quickly, not wanting Mrs. Davidson to catch me prying. The thought came to me that the old wedding dress might have been destroyed by moths or simply fallen apart from age, and that Mrs. Davidson, not wishing to admit it, was making a replica. But the name Alene Perry struck a familiar chord in my memory. After Mrs. Davidson had said good-bye, promising to bring the dress itself in a few days, I suddenly remembered.

Alene Perry was one of the girls in the walled-off plot.

I sat down by the window, clasping my hands tightly together. It has nothing to do with me, I kept thinking, repeating the phrase over and over in my mind. Nothing to do with me. Hadn't Gil said, "Old bones crumbling to dust"?

The wedding dress Alene Perry had worn had never been used for her wedding. She had died at age twenty, unmarried, a suicide.

Would I be wearing *her* dress or one like it?

I remained there at the window for a long time, listening to the clock in the hall, to the birds calling one to another in the gum tree. And gradually the quiet house restored my tranquillity, and I began to see how foolish it was to dwell on such morose fancies. Really! A wedding dress. So many dresses were copies of others, older ones. Alene Perry hadn't been the only woman in Virginia who had worn a high-collared, bustled gown. It was the man I was marrying, not the dress.

That little worry over the bridal gown was the last doubt I had. Even when Mrs. Davidson brought the dress and I saw that it was newly made, an exact copy of the photograph's, I felt no curiosity, no need to comment on it.

So I went blithely ahead, enjoying the fuss generated by the coming festivities. Dora, Mrs. Davidson, Gladys, and Nancy bustled about, cleaning from parlor to attic, dusting, sweeping, polishing, excited as if they themselves were to be brides. Refusing my help, they banished me from the house, and I went walking through the garden to sit by the creek, daydreaming, content to be alone. Gil had said he would not see me again until the wedding. He gave no reason, and I did not ask.

It was strange how few questions I had asked of him, how little I knew about his past, his plans for the future, and, for that matter, the present. I assumed that we would live in the Covington house, that he would go on working for Jeb Loeffler. Content together, we would take each day as it came. What more could I ask?

I had never been happier. I felt as if my entire life had been one long preparation for Gil. Even Vance. How could I possibly have appreciated Gil, his gentleness, his passion, unless I had known someone to compare him to? Gil's personality might be—and I remember searching for a word—ephemeral, but what I felt for him was solid. Loving him had made me whole again.

We were to be married on Saturday night under the oak tree. The ladies and I had decided on colorful Japanese lanterns as the most romantic type of outdoor illumination. Dora's husband had ordered them from a firm in Richmond, and I went into town on Thursday morning to pick them up. As bad luck would have it, I bumped into Wade Ryland on the threshold of Bradley's. There followed an awkward tussle —he wanting to assist me with the boxes, I clinging to them, murmuring between my teeth, "I don't mind, it's really nothing."

He won out in the end.

"What have we got here?" he asked, shaking a box.

"Yarn for my loom," I said, opening the trunk of my car. Taking the packages and stowing them away, I said, "Thank you, Wade," in what I hoped was a tone of dismissal.

"Why haven't I seen you lately? Busy, I know"—following me, opening the car door, leaning on the window. "What about dinner tonight? Lunch tomorrow? No? Why don't I come out and visit with you while you do your weaving?"

"No, Wade. I hate to be rude, but there's no use in pretending. I'm not interested. You'd just be wasting your time."

As I drove off, I caught a glimpse of him in my rearview mirror, watching me with a quizzical expression on his face. I felt sorry for him, I really did. I could afford to feel sorry for him, for all the poor souls who didn't have someone to love.

Saturday dawned with cloudless blue skies. No rain had

been forecast. "Fair weather will continue throughout the weekend," the paper had said. It couldn't rain, I told myself, twirling before the clouded mirror, it wouldn't. It was my wedding day.

The women came at noon, sending me out of the kitchen and upstairs to nap. Afterward, Gladys drew me a fragrant, foaming bath, and I lolled in it while she did my nails, fingers and toes, a lovely shell pink.

Nancy brought me a sandwich and coffee, but I was too excited to eat. When I asked her what they were cooking in the kitchen below, she said it was to be a surprise. From the bathroom window I saw Tom Loeffler drive up to the rear door and unload the champagne and several casks which I assumed to be hard liquor or beer. Moonshine, maybe. Stone Mill moonshine. How funny! Some things seemed absurdly amusing; others, like Lurline presenting me with a bouquet of autumn roses and baby's breath, made me want to cry.

At six, Gladys helped me fix my hair, curling it with an old-fashioned, stove-heated curling iron, and piling it into a pompadour on top of my head. The veil was to be held in place with a tiara of seed pearls. Nancy helped me into the dress, and Gladys buttoned it down the back.

"You certainly don't need one of them corsets they used to wear," Gladys said.

"I think I've lost some weight,"—observing myself in the mirror, cheeks flushed to a high color, eyes dancing with excitement.

"The fiddlers have come," said Gladys. "Listen!"

Through the window I could hear the squeak of fiddles tuning up, and one scraping away at the first bar of Mendelssohn, *Here comes the bride.* . . .

"Has Gil arrived?" I asked nervously, going to the window for the dozenth time.

"Not yet," Gladys said. "But Donald Bradley has." Mr. Bradley was to give me away.

More cars drove in and parked at the foot of the drive. Three sets of Loefflers, the Dawsons, the Perrys, the Rylands—all those who had befriended me.

"Hasn't Sarah Covington been invited?" I asked.

"She was, but didn't feel up to it," Gladys said. "Too old, you know. But she sends her best."

The veil was adjusted carefully so as not to muss my hair.

"Have some champagne," said Dora. She had brought a glass of it up on a tray.

"Not before," I said. "After, but not before."

I thought I would suffocate with excitement.

A few minutes later Nancy, puffing up the stairs, announced, "They're ready!" And I came slowly down to the hall, Gladys carrying my train. Mr. Bradley gave me his arm.

We went out of the house, descending the wooden steps carefully so I wouldn't trip over the hem of my gown, walking along the stone path toward the sounds of the "Wedding March" now floating up to us in full voice on the chill September air.

I felt as if I were moving down the aisle of a lofty, darkened cathedral, and suddenly wished that it was my father's arm I was leaning on.

But there was no time for sentimental regret, for we had arrived. The lanterns had been strung from the lower branches of the old oak, and they cast a fairyland rainbow of lights, swaying and shimmering in the breeze. Preacher Davidson, a white rose in his buttonhole, was waiting, Bible in hand. Gil, I saw with a sinking heart, had not yet arrived.

We took our places, and the fiddles fell silent. For a full minute there was complete quiet. Those sixty seconds were the longest I had ever spent in my life, sixty seconds during which I hoped and despaired alternately. I was just beginning to feel that I had been jilted and to wish fervently that I was dead, when I heard a twig snap behind me, and turned.

Gil!

He came through the trees wearing those disreputable clothes of his, hat in hand, and smiling apologetically.

He took his place beside me, and I glowed up at him through my veil. A sigh went through the watching crowd of guests, and Preacher Davidson began to read the wedding service.

He had got to "And do you, Jeanine Ruth Stewart," when someone came crashing through the shrubbery. Wade Ryland shouted, "Stop! Damn you all, stop this atrocity!"

Wade! I thought, angry, disgusted. Wouldn't you know he would do something like this!

Above the shocked murmur of voices the preacher said sternly, "This is a private affair, Dr. Ryland. You have not been invited, and I must ask you leave at once."

"I'll do nothing of the kind." His face was very red, and

he stood with feet apart, fists clenched belligerently.

"Please go," I said, tears burning my eyes. "Please don't spoil it for me."

"You fool!" he shouted at me. "Don't you see what is happening? There's no one at your side! Your bridegroom does not exist. Look!"

I turned to Gil, and for one shocking moment he seemed to have disappeared. But then, as Mr. Bradley and Tom Loeffler began hustling Wade from the scene, I blinked and Gil was there again.

It was my eyes, that was all, a sudden blurring of my eyes.

"It's revenge!" I heard Wade shouting in the distance. "Your lover is a ghost!"

"Pay him no mind," the preacher said. "The man is as crazy as a bull bat." And he opened his Bible, his finger searching for the place.

The guests smiled—the fiddlers, the Dawsons, the Loefflers, the Perrys (though I noticed Elsie Perry's forehead was beaded with sweat), all smiling in encouragement.

"Lord, help us," someone sighed.

"Gil," I said, turning to him. He did not speak; his eyes were deep hollows of pain. And suddenly his image began to waver.

Dear God—what was happening? I blinked again and again. But his face continued to pulsate in a terrifying way.

Was I going mad?

Or was it a dream? A nightmare?

And all at once I knew that the dress I wore was exactly like the one each of the fifteen girls had been laid to rest in, their once-young bodies disintegrating under the same kind of lace and shot silk.

"I can't," I heard myself say, "I can't."

"Of course you can, my dear," the preacher soothed. "It's been too much for you. Bring a chair, Tom."

I sat down, bewildered and afraid, terribly afraid. Gil was still there, standing in the shadows, far, so far away.

"That Wade fellow has upset you," the preacher said. "Tom, give Jeanine some of that. . . ." He motioned with his chin. Tom brought a glass of colorless liquid, and I sipped on it. White fire, burning a hole in my chest, bringing tears to my eyes. Moonshine, I thought. Then why doesn't it burn away this cold feeling in the pit of my stomach?

I leaned back and looked up. A rope, knotted into a noose, dangled from the limb of the tree.

"Why . . . ?" I asked, horror-struck, suddenly shaken completely from my dreamlike trance. "Why . . . ?"

Gil had vanished.

"Why?" I looked from one to another—a ring of white, silent faces, all hostile, all gross. "Why . . . ?"

The preacher cleared his throat. A female voice shouted shrilly, "Git it over with!"

"No!" I screamed, bewildered, close to tears, to rage, to hysterics. "I must know!"

"I see no need," the preacher said.

Elsie Perry, her face white as wax, stepped forward. "Tell her," she said. "You owe her that much. Tell her."

The preacher cleared his throat again. "Gilman Clayborne was betrayed by Francine Covington. . . ."

"But *that*"—my mind reeling—"that was over a hundred years ago!"

"September twenty-fourth, eighteen sixty-four," he said. "And he was hanged from this tree."

The sadness, the unbearable feeling of sadness, and the bird whistling that one lonely note.

". . . before he died he condemned the town for the murder of his family . . ."

Revenge, Gil had said, everyone needs to have their revenge. And the uniform, the shabby blue jacket with its brass buttons. "I was in the war. . . ."

". . . he said that he would marry Francine in Hell for her betrayal. And that he would come back every seven years to claim another bride. If we do not give him one, he damns us as he did in eighteen seventy-one. No one prospers. Misfortune, disease, death—all the misery you could find a name for will be our lot unless he has his way."

"But it's murder! Not suicide, murder!"

". . . he chooses. We don't. The girl who sees him is the chosen one."

And what of the kisses, the arm about my shoulders, the man in my bed? Not real. A fantasy. A wish-fulfillment or Gilman Clayborne's ghost? The Stone Millers believed, though they could not see him. *They* believed. And all those girls—Alene and Ellie-Mae and Mary—*they* had seen him. He had wooed and married them, and they had been hanged, and he had carried them off to Hell.

"No," I said. "No."

But Tom Loeffler and the preacher were lifting me to my feet. The noose was lowered and fitted about my throat.

No ... !

He almost always came at twilight, when the mist was rising from the creek.

No!

I felt the rope tighten. "Gilman ... !" And everything went black.

He was standing in the green shadow of the gum tree, looking up at me through the leaves. "Come down, my love, come down."

"You're a ghost," I said. "A phantom. You're not real— poor, sad, tired Gilman, you're not real. Why did you say you loved me?"

"I did love you. For that moment in time I loved you."

I was lying on the bed, and the lamp made a circle of light on the ceiling. My throat felt raw.

"You're all right. You're going to be all right."

Wade.

I stared at him, and suddenly memory came rushing back with a suffocating jolt. I opened my mouth and screamed. And screamed. And went on screaming.

He hit me. Not a gentle slap, but a bone-shaking smack across the face. I went limp and a moment later felt the sharp prick of a needle in my arm.

It was morning, and the lamp had gone out. Wade was sitting there on a chair beside me. There were deep circles under his eyes.

"May I"—my voice was a croak—"may I have some water?"

He raised my head gently. "You'll be all right," he said again as he brought the glass to my lips.

"Will I?" I whispered hoarsely. "Will I?"

He gripped my hands tightly and nodded.

"It wasn't a dream, was it?"

He looked away, a different Wade, older, subdued.

"Tell me," I begged, though it hurt to talk. "Tell me I imagined it all. That I'm a nut, ready to be certified."

He said, "You didn't imagine it, Jeanine."

And somehow that was worse. I grew cold. I began to shiver.

"Here," he said, tucking the coverlet around my shoulders. "Don't go to pieces on me again."

"Where ... where are the others?"

"Gone. When they saw the sheriff pull in, they took off like scalded rabbits."

"The sheriff? But how ... ?"

"I'm a Nosy Parker, remember? I found out by happenstance that your boxes the other day contained Japanese lanterns, not yarn. That set me to thinking. I had a gut feeling that something was planned out here, and when the stores closed early yesterday afternoon, I guessed it would be that night. Fortunately, before I left the office I gave the sheriff a jingle. Strange thing, but it was staring me in the face all the time."

"Not moonshine?" I managed to smile feebly.

"No—not moonshine." He took a deep breath. "I always thought Grandma Addie's stories were pure lunacy. You know, she claimed she tried to stop a wedding similar to yours—and barely escaped with her life. If it hadn't been for that letter, they'd probably have given me the ax a long time ago."

"What letter?"

"Didn't I tell you? After that business with my brakes, I wrote to the sheriff in Novotno—one of those 'in-case-of-my-death' letters—and I also sent copies to Preacher Davidson, Tom Loeffler, and Mr. Bradley. They didn't dare try anything."

I wet my lips. "Your grandmother ... did she ... did she see the ... ?" I couldn't say it.

"No. But she guessed a good part of their bloody ritual. Appeasing the gods, the spirits ..."

"But supposing ... supposing the ... he ... Gil really damns them, and they suffer?"

"Who doesn't suffer? Who doesn't have misfortune and illness? You do the best you can. So—it's a ghost, an evil, malevolent. ..."

"No. He's not the one who is evil. They are. He's tired. They won't let him rest."

"You're still hypnotized," he said incredulously.

I shook my head. "Strange how I feel no bitterness toward him. You see. ..." I looked up at the ceiling for a moment.

"In a funny, twisted way, he gave me the will to live. Or maybe it was myself—but I found I still had feelings, I still could love."

"What a weird girl you are," Wade said, looking at me with admiration.

"I never believed in ghosts," I said. "But now . . . Some strong personalities, some who feel wronged, who have suffered a great deal, perhaps, live on. Gil's revenge is terrible, it's ugly, but there was a gentler, loving side to him."

"I wonder if those fifteen girls in the graveyard feel the same," he said wryly. "Maybe they did. He must have been some charmer."

"Or maybe they charmed themselves."

I couldn't bring myself to file charges against the people of Stone Mill, though Wade urged me to. "I'm not being altruistic," I argued with him. "Can you see me up there on the witness stand trying to prove past murders, trying to answer questions about a ghost? Why, the case would be dismissed in five minutes flat."

(And I was later proved correct in my assumption, for when the sheriff went around questioning Stone Millers he found nothing amiss. "A suicide once every long while isn't strange," he was told. Notes were even produced, purportedly written by the more recent suicides, to prove the girls had taken their own lives for a variety of the usual reasons. As for me, it was brought out by someone—Mr. Bradley, I believe—that I had suffered a breakdown and had been depressed and was given to morbid "fancies.")

Wade pointed out, "What's to prevent Stone Millers—the Dawsons, Perrys, and Davidsons—from going through the same ritual in another seven years?"

"We'll find a way to stop them," I said.

And that's why we went to Sarah Covington's little house on Main Street again, determined to see her. I had the feeling that she knew a good deal about Gil Clayborne and what had happened so many years ago. Wade, who came along for moral support, agreed with me.

It wasn't easy getting her to let us in, but we camped on her doorstep until she finally opened the door. Feeling every inch the bully, I followed her into a tiny parlor, Wade close on my heels. We sat on an uncomfortable, slippery sofa, not quite knowing what to do with our hands and our feet.

There was a long silence. Then I said, "No one will die this year."

There was another silence. "I don't want to talk about it," Sarah Covington said at last. "It has nothing to do with me."

"It *has*," I said, trying to control a rising irritation. "All those young girls dying. . . ."

Tears rose to her blue eyes, and her lips trembled. *Browbeater, inquisitor,* I called myself, and yet there was no other way.

"I thought you—and we," I said, nodding toward Wade, "could find a solution."

A tear found its way to the brink of her eyelid and slowly coursed down her cheek. "It's been so long, so many years," she said, taking a handkerchief from her pocket, "so many years, but it's pinned to my memory like a picture. God help me. I was engaged to a fine young man, and then one day I saw Gilman. But I didn't love the young man, you see, and here was Gilman reminding me of the man I once really loved." She dabbed at her eyes. "And when I told my grandfather, he sat me down. . . . It was in the parlor, I remember, and he took a drink of whiskey, his own corn whiskey. Bradley makes it now, but it isn't half as good as they tell me Grandfather Judd's used to be. He drank his whiskey neat, and he said, 'It wasn't Francine who betrayed Gilman Clayborne or caused his house to be set afire and everyone in it burned to ash. It was Eli—my own father—Eli Covington.' The Rebs promised Eli money and transport for his logs —he owned the sawmill then—if he'd turn in Union spies. And so he gave them Gilman, who wasn't a spy, but just a Yankee soldier. Eli even murdered another man because he had somehow found out the truth. Tyson McAlpin was his name, a boy from Hickory Cove, and Eli buried him in the garden."

"*That* must have been the skull!" I exclaimed.

"McAlpin had come to fetch his girl home. She'd been staying at our—the Covington house. Her name . . . let me think. . . ."

"Kate Rawlins?"

"Yes," she nodded. "I remember. That was it."

I asked, "Why didn't you tell Gilman it was Eli, not Francine, who had informed on him?" How natural it seemed to speak of the dead man as if he existed.

Sarah's thin white brows rose. "A ghost? Argue with a ghost?" Her head trembled. "And how could I have said anything when Granfather hurried me away?"

Wade shifted uncomfortably on the sofa beside me. He said, "I think you're going about it the wrong way. The townspeople here are a venal lot. Let them learn to live without their bloody sacrifices."

"No, Wade," I protested. "No, it's hard for me to make you see, but I want Gilman Clayborne to find peace. I want him to know he wasn't betrayed by the girl he loved." I looked at Sarah. "If we can convince him . . ."

"I can't," she said. "I don't want to."

"He will listen to you. Francine was a Covington. She was your. . . ."

"My great-aunt. She committed suicide after Gilman was hanged. But I can't."

"Think of all the lives you will save." I went on arguing, cajoling, pleading. "The suffering you will ease." It took me over an hour, but in the end she agreed to help.

Evenings fell earlier now, the days getting shorter. Sarah Covington and I sat under the oak as the chill mist trailed up from the creek. I had helped her dress warmly, and Wade had brought her a comfortable chair. (I wouldn't let him stay with us as I thought his presence might keep Gilman from appearing.) We didn't speak; our eyes were turned toward the creek.

We waited an hour, two hours. Sarah began to cough.

"You aren't catching cold?" I asked anxiously.

"I don't think so."

"Let me go up to the house and fetch you something hot to drink," I offered.

"That will be nice."

I must have been gone twenty minutes, a half hour at the most. When I got back, she looked as if she had fallen fast asleep in her chair.

"Miss Covington . . . ? Sarah?"

Her head was resting on the cushions, her lips curved in a lovely, sweet smile. She was dead.

We came back to Stone Mill Hollow, Wade and I, in September, just as the leaves were beginning to fall, seven years later. For five of those years we had been married—happily, strangely enough, despite our little differences, or maybe because of them.

We spoke to no one, but went directly to the Covington house. I was sorry to see it had fallen into such appalling disrepair, but we made ourselves as comfortable as possible, for I was determined to speak to Gilman Clayborne if I could.

He never came.

I'm sure now he and Sarah Covington met before she died, and Gilman has finally gone to his rest.

Last month I engaged a stone carver. And now if you should stroll through the churchyard of Stone Mill Hollow, you will see an old, hoary tombstone dated 1864 with the fresh inscription, GILMAN CLAYBORNE—REQUIESCAT IN PACE.

Rest in peace.

The magnificent staircases
were overgrown with ivy.
Her hostess was gone without warning.
Her host was grown sullen and coarse.
And David Field, a tall, broad-shouldered stranger,
seemed to know her at once,
though they had never met.

What had befallen the castle?
What part was Mary to play?

A fear surged within her
such as she had never known
—and something stronger, a rapturous love,
that called to her very soul.

She knew now that she belonged there—
to share the tortuous destiny of

CASTLE CLOUD

ELIZABETH NORMAN

Avon/31583/$1.95

CLOUD 6-77